RESURRECTION

By David Gilman

The Englishman series
THE ENGLISHMAN
BETRAYAL
RESURRECTION

Master of War series
MASTER OF WAR
DEFIANT UNTO DEATH
GATE OF THE DEAD
VIPER'S BLOOD
SCOURGE OF WOLVES
CROSS OF FIRE
SHADOW OF THE HAWK

Standalone novels
THE LAST HORSEMAN
NIGHT FLIGHT TO PARIS

Dangerzone series
THE DEVIL'S BREATH
ICE CLAW
BLOOD SUN

———

MONKEY AND ME

RESURRECTION
DAVID GILMAN

An Aries Book

FSC
www.fsc.org

MIX
Paper | Supporting
responsible forestry
FSC® C013604

Head of Zeus Ltd
First Floor East
5–8 Hardwick Street
London EC1R 4RG

WWW.HEADOFZEUS.COM

For Suzy

Human blood is heavy; the man that
has shed it cannot run away.

African proverb

PROLOGUE

The full moon sat low on the desert horizon; its light dressed the corrugated sand dunes in veils of shadows. A night breeze scudding across the sand broke the stillness, eroding and reshaping dunes into another landscape.

The man's skeleton stared upwards into the moon's glow. His head hinged back into the nape of his neck as his mouth, the jawbones cracked, seemed to scream silently at the night sky. The flying jacket was well preserved but bore no insignia, no identification, nothing to link him to any deeds committed in the often squandered name of justice and truth. The dead pilot sat immobile, his shoulder holster split and worn by the ravages of the desert heat, but the service-issued Colt .45 still nestled snugly against his ribs. The obligatory round held in the chamber. Always ready. That had been part of his life – always knowing the back door in any building, ever the professional. His sweatshirt and cotton trousers were tattered, exposing the taut, age-blackened skin, like oiled canvas stretched across his bones. The aviator glasses that once shielded blue eyes from the altitude's glare as he soared across the African sky had been knocked from his face by the impact. The bubble canopy had been lost at three thousand feet and his helter-skelter ride down to earth had ripped free his cap. He'd cursed when he felt gravity pulling it free. Bitched and screamed. Because of all things he didn't want to lose the best damned baseball cap ever to come out of his team's winning season. He'd fought blurring vision – pulling himself back to consciousness against the G force of the falling plane... the plane... Sweet Jesus, she was more than a machine... she was his... he trusted her with his life, and she'd always done as he'd asked.

She screamed with him as they plunged in a vertical dive towards the desert below.

His hands still gripped the control stick from his final determined effort to bring up the nose of the plane. And he'd done it. In the last moments, yelling in triumph, he'd levelled off, then settled down on to the arid ground of a land waiting for victims. His shattered legs at the rudder controls and splintered fingers were evidence of the force of that landing. Had the impact not snapped his neck, death from the shock of his injuries would have claimed him before that nightfall thirty years ago.

The dune rose forty feet above the floor of the desert. At its base, the breeze had brushed aside sand and exposed the fuselage and its long-range tanks. The aircraft's glistening metal reflected a dreamer's moon. The wind increased, shifting more sand from the cockpit, open to the elements. The P51 Mustang still embraced the man, cradling him, human and machine fused in spirit. The pilot and his mission were now alive only in other men's memories. Men who feared what lay hidden in that wasteland. The worn leather attaché case was manacled around his left wrist, tucked next to his crushed legs. It held a document men would die for. Information about two names. One a spy and traitor. The other the vital link to him.

Raglan.

1

Edwardes Square in the Royal Borough of Kensington and Chelsea lies just off Kensington High Street. It is a wealthy area, even by London standards. The Georgian houses, four storeys including a basement, sell for eye-watering amounts.

A man gazed down into the dimly lit square from a top-floor apartment. He was half-naked, a towel wrapped around his midriff. At sixty-seven, his hair was still thick enough to be slicked back from the shower he'd taken after making love to the woman who lay sprawled asleep on the bed behind him. He liked to watch the streets, especially at night when shadows might reveal a concealed watcher. John Barton's senses, honed over years of intelligence work, would alert him to anything untoward. He wasn't on his home turf, but he liked the neighbourhood. Wealth always encouraged a far more attentive patrolling by the police and that helped keep unfriendlies away. God knew there were enough of them still around. He lit a cigarette as he watched a police tow truck lifting a Porsche. To park in these car-choked streets, you needed a resident's parking permit. No permit – no park. The flashing blue lights illuminated a form, barely visible to the untrained eye. Beyond the iron railings securing the private park in the square, a man was standing back in the latticed moon shadow under the trees. Unmoving.

The old spy glanced across the far side of the square as the tow truck finally manoeuvred the offending Porsche down the narrow street. The watcher remained in darkness. Barton looked up with an unromantic eye at the full moon as the woman in the bed turned over, felt for him and then restlessly belly-flopped into a new sleeping position. They had spent the evening together at a book publishing launch. Over the years, his name had found its way on to many such invitation lists. The London Game. See and be seen. He did not play it often, but at times it was a distraction and could be a helpful cover when the former MI6 officer wanted to meet people others thought long dead, but who lived in exile under witness protection. The woman was a wealthy widow who had inherited her husband's publishing company. Old friends, they would meet occasionally, have sex and lie in what he ruefully referred to as past-their-prime splendour – soft flesh warm from mutual exertion, happy to be enfolded in the luxury of her lavish apartment and the tenderness their ages afforded them. He envied her untroubled slumber. He was sleeping less these days. Too many memories forcing their way into his consciousness, distorting his dreams. And the insistent voice in his unconscious demanding he get the explosive new information into the right hands. Now. The information that was typed and pressed into the envelope in his suit's breast pocket, hanging neatly on the back of the bedroom door. How far would he get with his subterfuge? Much depended on him leading his enemy astray.

The book launch had been the perfect place for the envelope to be passed to him. But if the watcher below was following him, and knew what he carried, then he must have seen the handover from Barton's old contact the night before. Barton's contact, a Russian friend in exile here, had warned him the old enemy was closing in. And since then, his friend had not answered his phone.

His lover half raised her head, muttered something and turned over again. He stubbed out his cigarette and sighed. The approaching dawn did not herald a bright new day for him; all it promised was a dull glow as befitted a tired man. Barton was very tired. He'd served his country thirty years and more. A double first at Cambridge meant politics had beckoned, but the Service had been more seductive. Had remained so for all these years. First an active field officer and then the inevitable slow decline to sitting behind a desk with an occasional lecture to bright young things keen to join the Service. Old foes often shared the same fate. Some came over to his side. Some became friends. His had been a solitary life – a woman married to a spy needed exceptional qualities; sadly his wife did not have them, and after three childless years she had divorced him. The final papers had arrived when he was neck-deep in trying to calm the slaughter during another small war in Africa. A long time ago. No regrets. He had lost touch with his wife, but he had maintained contact with his old networks and now, unexpectedly, they had yielded treasure. Pure gold. And, he admitted to himself, a frisson of panic at what could be exposed. His memories flared with a passion he had all but forgotten how to feel: in recent years he had buried his emotions as deeply as the secret consumed by the desert. A secret now resurrected.

He glanced at the sleeping woman. Now he had a chance to serve his country again. One last roll of the dice. Others wanted what he had, and they would kill him to retrieve the envelope in his suit pocket and the information it contained. His journey was coming to an end, but at least he would go out with dignity, and in a worthwhile cause. The new day would probably be his last. There was no better death than to sacrifice oneself for love. And he loved his country.

2

Barton decided to lead his followers towards the Secret Intelligence Service building at Vauxhall Cross. Time was short. The book launch and the lovemaking had been a safety barrier for a few hours. He could walk to Vauxhall Cross and the MI6 HQ – it was only a brisk hour – but that route would give his pursuers opportunities to pull him into side streets. He wanted them to be identified, if possible, and while street cameras were plentiful, those in the London Underground would suit his purpose better.

It took him fifteen minutes to reach High Street Kensington Tube station. He did not try to give whoever followed him the slip, but used the crowds as cover, though he knew full well how easy it was to be killed by lethal injection, particularly in a busy thoroughfare. It was still his best chance of getting as close as he could to his friends in the Service. And the closer he got, the more urgent those following him would become. If they were experienced agents, they would wonder at his naivety, perhaps thinking that he did not know he had been compromised, which was why he had not used his fieldcraft to avoid them. If they were simple-minded thugs like so many in Russian military intelligence, which these men would be, they would not question his actions. Barton needed to lead them astray.

Four stops later, he alighted and walked to the Victoria line platform. One more train connection and he would be within sight of what many MI6 officers referred to as Babylon-on-Thames: his old office, MI6 HQ. He'd barely got his seat warm in the new building back in '95 before he was put out to pasture.

Doubt crept in. Would those following him let him get so close to his destination? The answer came moments later as he approached the platform and saw there were a few people left standing there as a train pulled away. There would be another in two minutes. Long minutes. Three men boxed him in. One at either end of the platform, another ambling towards him. They looked no different from many other tourists. Jeans, a rainproof jacket, a small daypack. A map folded in a hand. Nothing out of place. Except for their concentrated look of intent. They would expect him to make a run for it. The man approaching him was in his thirties and bearded; he was four metres away.

'I'm too damned old to run back up those steps,' said Barton.

The man faltered, surprised perhaps he had been identified. He stepped closer. He nodded. 'All right,' he said, without fuss or threat. 'You know what we want.'

Barton nodded and unbuttoned his overcoat, his hand reaching for the inside suit pocket. 'Your accent. Chechnya or Georgia? I'm not sure.'

The man extended his hand, wanting the envelope. 'Does it matter?'

'No,' said the old spy, 'but I like to keep my ear in.'

The man grunted, uncertainty niggling him at Barton's behaviour. The older man stood fearlessly in front of him. 'Georgia,' he said.

'Good to know,' said Barton, who had not yet tugged free the envelope. The longer he delayed, the sooner the next train would arrive and with it the usual throng of people.

The Russian frowned. 'When we have what we want, you can go.'

The former MI6 officer had faced desperate men before. This one was getting agitated. Enough to kill him there on the platform? Perhaps not with anything as brutal as a knife or gun: more likely a poison. That was the Russian method of choice for killing in a crowded place. Yet there was no sign of anything in the man's hands. Barton's chances were improving every minute. He had chosen his position carefully. When he first arrived on the platform, he'd looked up into the security camera to identify himself and then turned his back so that the man would face the lens. His hand came free from his pocket but did not hold the envelope.

'You were careless. There were a dozen places you could have taken me. I'm a few minutes away from my people. You won't stop me now. Not here. New at this, are you? My old KGB chums would turn in their grave.'

The sound of an approaching train and a sudden influx of passengers on to the platform gave him a flicker of hope. It was important that these men believed that what he had was worth fighting for. If he had been running these agents, he would have the three men on the platform and a fourth unseen. The ghost. Barton had to make them work for it. He waited as a throng of passengers surged on to the carriage. He shoved the man aside and shouldered his way on to the train.

Platform man tried to barge his way forward, but the crowds blocked him, and the doors closed. Barton edged his way into the centre aisle, gripping the overhead bar. A minute later, as the train rolled along the curved tracks, he felt the scratch on his hand. He turned, saw a face close to his shoulder. The stranger's eyes met his. Expressionless. Barton tried to push through the passengers, but moments later he fell. A heart attack. He looked up as the stranger waved a hand at the alarmed passengers. Heard the words I'm a doctor. Felt his coat being pulled open, hands on his chest, knew that they would retrieve the envelope. Barton smiled. Job done.

The train bore him into his own dark tunnel.

3

Three days later a slim, fit-looking man in his fifties, with close-cropped greying hair, stood in front of the French Foreign Legion's Quartier Capitaine Danjou basic training camp just over three kilometres from the medieval town of Castelnaudary in the south of France. The town lay at the foot of the Pyrenees, had one main street and a couple of budget hotels. Maguire looked no different than any other passing tourist who had been driving on the Route de Pexiora and pulled over in the sunshine to watch the immaculately dressed legionnaires on their parade square. He wore jeans, a thin-knit dark lambswool sweater and padded jacket and had a satchel bag over his shoulder. The taxi driver who'd brought him from Toulouse Airport joked that the cut-off age for the Legion was thirty-eight in case he was thinking of signing up. With a glance in the rearview mirror, he saw what he took to be a flicker of amusement in the man's eyes, but his face remained impassive. Maybe he had spoken out of turn and the man had a son who served. During the hour's drive, he spoke warmly of the legionnaires just in case he had caused offence. On reflection, the cab driver reasoned that the man looked as if he could have spent thirty years in the Legion himself. Best to shut up and drive.

Maguire had been told to wait at the camp gates at a certain time by the man who was the only means of reaching the ex-legionnaire Raglan, Maguire's off-the-books asset. Much valued, yet there was nothing on any official document regarding his past work for the intelligence service. He was unaccountable, which gave Maguire a free hand. Maguire was ex-British Army, a Special Air Service commander who'd then been drawn into the intelligence world. He watched the legionnaires marching at their distinctive slow pace of eighty-eight steps a minute, singing the Legion's 'Le Boudin'. Their hypnotic rolling gait and raised voices, extolling the Legion's past deeds, would touch any observer's heart. They might have been rehearsing for a passing-out parade, so immaculate were their pressed almond-green uniforms, white kepis and red epaulettes and so precise their movements. He had come across legionnaires when he fought in far-flung conflicts and had the greatest respect for their fighting skills and *esprit de corps*.

A tall, hawk-faced civilian stepped past the guardroom. He wore a black roll neck under his jacket but the tattooed raptor on his neck still peeked clear, like a hungry bird of prey raising its head from a nest. Maguire noticed that the young legionnaire sentry squared his shoulders as the veteran former legionnaire stepped past him. Respect where it was due.

Serge Sokol, known as 'Bird' to those who had served with him in the Legion's elite 2nd Parachute Regiment, studied Maguire for a moment without extending his hand in greeting. Then he gave a satisfied nod.

'My car's over there,' he said.

Maguire followed him to a battered-looking Peugeot 205. He guessed the car was at least twenty years old and looked barely big enough to accommodate the man's height. Maguire wrenched the stiff passenger door open and sat on the torn seat.

Sokol turned the key but hesitated before engaging gear. 'This is unusual,' he said to Maguire.

'How so?'

'You wanting to meet Raglan on his home ground.'

'Yes,' said Maguire.

'Last time, you sent a young woman. One of your people. Not this time?'

'No. She died.'

Sokol nodded. He already knew that.

'Still, you come instead of anyone else.'

'Yes.'

Sokol nodded again and turned the car towards the mountains. If the man from MI6 was here in person, then it was important. More than usual.

Maguire's urgency getting to Raglan was part of the pressure that came with the job. He knew how to deal with it. Patience was the key – and the ability to bring in the right people for any mission. Especially true if the job demanded someone special. He had known hard physical and mental challenges himself during his youth. Nothing as difficult as Raglan's, and perhaps that's what made the Englishman dependable and resolute. He'd read Raglan's file when he stepped into MI6. His background held all the clues an observer needed to gauge the measure of the man.

The death of Raglan's mother when he was eleven had meant he was sent to a hard-arsed boarding school, while his father, a British Army defence attaché, was posted abroad. Raglan excelled there: hardship drove the boy through his grief. He became a damned good fighter and boxed and played rugby for his school. Academically bright as well, he was on track to attend a good university. Maguire never knew whether Raglan had been motivated by his father and determined to follow in his footsteps – the University of Oxford and then the military – or if there was an inner demon that made him shine at everything he attempted. He didn't need to know. The seeds of Raglan's service to the Crown were sown as that teenager. The tragedy of his father's death in a car crash a few years later hit the boy hard. After that, he began to show a killer instinct when he fought in the ring. Outside it, he went out of his way to find trouble, and the police had him flagged as a potential nuisance in the town. He was saved by his housemaster and his wife, who acted as foster parents, which gave Raglan the closest thing he had to family, and Raglan and their teenage daughter were soon like brother and sister. Still were.

Maguire looked out at the rolling countryside. Wide-open spaces, something a boy like Raglan might have yearned for. A place to escape. Returning home from a training session at the boxing club one night, he saved a black kid from being knifed by a gang and, in the tussle, one attacker had died. The gang framed Raglan for his death and he ran. Six months later, he walked into the Foreign Legion recruitment office at Aubagne not knowing that CCTV footage and the black teenager's testimony had proved his innocence. But by then Raglan had vanished and found another new family. The Legion.

★

Serge Sokol swung the Peugeot off the A61 towards the Montagne Noire on to a small unmarked gravelled road. He slowed the car and looked in his rearview mirror. When he'd left the Legion's gates, he'd checked both sides of the road. A nondescript dark blue Renault had been parked several hundred metres on the town's side of the road. Lost tourists or something else? When he drove off with Maguire, the car had waited until he would have been almost out of sight and then peeled into the near-empty road. Now, as he turned on to the unmarked road, he slowed right down. The Renault also slowed as it passed the turn-off, checked its progress and then moved off again. Maybe nothing. Maybe.

Despite the lack of signposts, Maguire knew where they were heading: a place whose remote location suited tribal men whose loyalty was first and foremost to each other. He glanced at his guide, but the hawk-nosed man kept his eyes straight ahead as they entered the foothills. Minutes later, around one of the twisting bends, they met a couple of rough-looking men, standing smoking next to a pickup truck. One had a rifle, the other a shotgun. Good weapons for an ambush, Maguire thought. Short- and long-range: stop any immediate threat with the shotgun; pick off anyone making a run for it with the rifle. Two alert hunting dogs sat obediently beside them, staring intently at the approaching car. When Maguire had served with Special Forces he'd lived with brigands, and these bearded men looked no different. One of them stepped forward, Sokol slowed, the man recognized the car and its driver and waved it on. Maguire glanced at Sokol, who changed up a gear.

'Security,' he said. 'They like to know who's visiting.'

Maguire understood why the hamlet had become a refuge for former members of the Legion, especially the former paratroopers: comrades who had served together, many of whom now hired themselves out as assets, wanted to keep themselves and their wives and family under the radar. It had been Raglan's idea to buy the abandoned village and bring in others like him. The village had been empty for twenty years before the tall Englishman had walked into the district mayor's office and pledged to regenerate it with men like himself and their families. Le Maire embraced him, and damned near wept for joy. Local authorities in rural communities were desperate to keep French country life intact, and who else would have been crazy enough to buy a derelict village and rebuild it? Mad men was who. Trained killers, yes, but men whose legend was deeply respected. The Devil's own, some said. Not the mayor. They were his angels.

After fifteen years of hard-fought service, Raglan had been recruited by the French counter-intelligence service, la Direction Générale de la Sécurité Extérieure. And after that, his language skills and network of contacts of all nationalities from his time in the Legion also made him a valuable freelance asset to the British and American intelligence services.

Raglan was an expert hunter of men. And that's why Maguire used him. The MI6 officer would soon have to share the secret of the operation codenamed Malaika. There was no guarantee that Raglan would accept the mission. He was under no obligation. But Maguire was going to dangle bait that would open a door in Raglan's memory. A shadow from time past. A death.

4

Fifteen minutes later, the road led into a broader street with dwellings scattered either side. It was quiet. A builder was repairing a roof; a woman walked by carrying a basket of bread; a handful of men and women were hovering at the doorway of what was obviously the village cafe. A side alley revealed a stone outhouse. Two wild boars hung upside down, throats slit, a large bucket beneath each collecting their blood. Sokol pulled up outside the cafe's entrance and wound down the window. Maguire saw a dozen scattered tables covered with chequered tablecloths inside. Sokol greeted one man in a wheelchair. 'Sammy?'

The man – younger, with an unruly mop of hair – smiled. 'Bird!' he called, wheeling himself closer to the open window.

Maguire realized there were boardwalks and ramps connecting the houses, the village bar and the cafe. Unfettered access. The former legionnaires looked after their own.

'Where is he?' said Sokol.

'With the kids. You staying?' He looked through to the stranger next to Sokol.

Sokol shrugged and nodded towards the hulking man who had stepped into the cafe's doorway with a carving knife gripped in his fist. His stained apron denoted he was the village cook. His shaven head, the repository for tattoos climbing up his arms and neck, denoted a lifetime of not giving a damn.

Sokol greeted the fearsome-looking man whose beard hung like barbed wire. 'Willem. What's the *plat du jour*?' said Sokol.

'Your balls if you don't come and eat,' the man bawled in a guttural South African accent.

Sokol nodded, pushed the gearstick into first. 'You don't have a pot big enough,' he shouted back.

Maguire smiled. He missed the rough and tumble of soldiering. Working for the government in this day and age meant watching what you said. Giving a subordinate a verbal kick up the arse could soon have anyone in a senior role up before an inquiry. 'The man in the wheelchair, did he serve with Raglan?'

Sokol nodded. 'Mali.'

He said nothing more. There was no need. Maguire knew how intense the fighting had been a decade ago when legionnaires fought Salafist insurgents in North Africa. British troops had recently been sent out there as part of a multinational force.

Sokol drove to where the houses petered out and a school playing field stretched out across the plateau. Two teams of youngsters, probably no more than ten years old, were being coached on the rugby field. Everything Maguire had seen told him this self-contained village had all it needed. The elementary school would care for the younger kids up to the age of eleven; the older children would be bussed to a high school beyond the village.

Sokol pulled up.

'Here,' he said, and got out of the car.

Maguire followed him. The mountain air was keener here. Winter snow had already fallen on the north-facing hillsides; the sun was weak but warm enough to fool those who didn't know that temperatures could plummet – evidenced by the stacked woodpiles outside most houses. Maguire felt a stab of envy. The silence was broken only by cheerful cries from a bunch of kids, a buzzard's screech and a breeze that whispered across the tree- and gorse-covered hills. Why the hell would anyone want to leave here, let alone put themselves in danger in a hostile place far from home?

As he followed Sokol into the schoolyard, he found himself hoping Raglan had not succumbed to the bucolic lifestyle. The stone schoolhouse looked large enough to accommodate however many young children there were in the small village. A dark-haired woman in her thirties waited in the yard, her cardigan buttoned tightly up around her neck, watching a stubble-faced, lean-muscled man sitting on a school chair reading to a rapt audience of a dozen seven-year-olds on cushions. She smiled at Sokol, but then frowned at Maguire's presence, while he nodded politely in her direction. Sokol waited, and it was only then that Maguire realized that the man reading to the children was Raglan.

It was incongruous, knowing what Maguire knew about him. Raglan closed the book, glanced to where Maguire waited, and then told the children to go to Madame Didiannet and have their lunch. The children duly got to their feet. Looked towards the woman, questioning. She nodded. One by one, they approached Raglan and offered him a gift. Confectionery, a book, small trinkets. Raglan looked surprised.

'It's your birthday tomorrow,' Madame Didiannet explained. 'And you said you were going into town early so the children wanted to give you their presents today.'

His look told her he'd forgotten. She glanced at Sokol in disbelief. 'Did you remember?'

Sokol winced.

'I didn't think so,' she said.

Raglan stooped to receive each child's present and whispered his thanks. One girl extended her hands, holding a length of cord with a dangling medallion. 'This was Papa's,' she said. 'And Mama said you were his friend and you should have it because it will be lucky for you.' The dangling medallion was a winged hand holding a sword, the Foreign Legion's 2nd Parachute Regiment beret's badge. Raglan towered over the little girl. He bent lower so she could put it over his head.

'Will you please look after it, M'sieur Raglan? And can I have it back please when it has brought you good luck?'

'Of course, Dominique. I promise.'

The gift-giving ended and the teacher stepped forward and herded the youngsters into the schoolhouse.

The Englishman turned. He acknowledged Sokol – 'Bird' – but didn't take his eyes off Maguire.

'Good book?' said Maguire.

'It's about an ogre who comes into the magic forest and creates havoc,' he said.

'I'll try not to trample on the fairies,' said Maguire.

Sokol turned away; he knew this was Maguire's meeting. 'I'll check out Willem's offering. I saw a couple of boars hanging up. With luck he's made blood pudding.'

They waited until Sokol was out of earshot. 'Too important for a phone call?' said Raglan. A whistle blew down on the playing field. He walked towards the rugby pitch where the coach ushered the kids off the field to get their lunch.

'Pigs' blood in a bucket will look like a spring salad if this operation goes pear-shaped,' said Maguire.

'*Bonjour*, M'sieur Raglan,' rang out as the muddy boys passed by. Raglan ruffled one of the boys' hair.

'Henri, don't tell your mother we let you play in the scrum.'

The boy grinned.

'Kids look happy,' said Maguire.

'Not for much longer. They get to play the girls' team next week. They just don't know it yet.'

A cold breeze picked up from the valley. Both men ignored it.

'Maguire, I'm not sure I can help you. I've promised the kids here a training programme, and there's work to be done on some of the houses. I have two men who could take my place. It might be a long winter this year.' Raglan picked up one of the rugby balls, turning it in his hands. 'Some of the men... well...' He shrugged. 'They need to get out of the village. Security work's thin on the ground these days.'

'This isn't a job for which I'd want anyone else,' said Maguire. He cast a shrewd glance at Raglan. '*Cafard?* Don't you feel it as well?'

Raglan smiled. Trust Maguire to know of the malaise so prevalent among legionnaires – a malady of the soul that stemmed from a sense of not belonging, adrift other than with their own kind.

'Legionnaires leave whatever life they had behind them, Maguire. What we have now came to us in training and combat.'

'That's why I'm here. You fought in Africa. I want you

to go back and retrieve some information for us. French intelligence is leading a mission and I want you with them.'

'French intelligence? Really? The DGSE is involved? I worked for them once when I left the Legion and that was once too often. Half-arsed idiots with hare-brained schemes. So now you're wanting me to work with them again?'

Maguire nodded.

After a moment's consideration, Raglan responded with a shake of his head. 'Not back there. We've all done enough damage to Africa over the years. We've never let a scab form on Africa's wound. We pick at it and it keeps bleeding.'

'Your father was there, did you know that?'

Raglan was surprised. 'On the ground? Fighting?'

'No, nothing like that. When you were sent to boarding school after your mother died, he was defence attaché in our embassy in Nairobi. But he took himself out of the safety of Kenya and into the Congo's hot zone when all hell broke loose. No one in the West wanted the Russians getting a foothold again. And what he did back then has been of invaluable help to Britain and the West ever since.'

'What did he do?'

'He went after a KGB agent.'

'To kill him?'

'No, to save him.'

5

The mention of his father, of a part of the man's life that he knew nothing about, was as good as being caught by a sucker punch. The devotion the boy had felt for his beloved father, who was killed before his son had the chance to grow into manhood and come to know him, had remained undimmed by his absence, and Maguire's words took Raglan back to being a teenager. The void left by his father's death after that of his mother had been unfathomable. Lost in bereavement and running from the law, the wound it had caused was only seared closed by the hardship and demands of the Legion.

Raglan ushered Maguire back into one of the empty classrooms. Plastic chairs and easy-wipe desks faced a teacher's desk and wall-mounted whiteboard.

Raglan dragged aside a couple of chairs and motioned Maguire to sit. The MI6 controller glanced around, checking the closed door. Children's voices echoed in the distance.

'Kids are eating. We won't be disturbed. No one can hear us. So, what exactly did my father do?'

Maguire was cagey. 'You were at boarding school. Did your father ever tell you where he was posted?'

'He wasn't the greatest letter writer. The Balkans, then

Vienna, I think. Being a defence attaché left little room for bringing up a son.'

Maguire hesitated. Raglan was irritated. 'You come out here personally. You tell me my father was in Africa and that he saved the life of a KGB agent. What is this? Are you telling me he was working for the Russians?'

Maguire raised a hand to calm Raglan's impatience. 'Absolutely not. Let's take a step back in time. Central Africa, Somalia, Sudan, Ethiopia and the rest – well, a lot of it is still in a mess. Militia and warlords wreak havoc as we speak, but when your father was with the British embassy in Nairobi, it was the old Soviet empire clawing its way into Africa. Angolan forces with Russian weapons. The Chinese were too weak back then, not like now, though they also made their attempts. But you know the key race was between the West and the Soviets.'

'And my father had a connection? With the KGB?'

'Yes. Before Africa, when your father served – as you said – in the Balkans and Vienna, so too did a certain KGB officer. Over the years they'd met officially and socially. The KGB man tried to turn your father when he was in Vienna. Imagine having a defence attaché ready to expose British government policy from the heart of the embassy. Almost as good as having the Foreign Secretary in your pocket.'

'And my father reported back to whom? The embassy's MI6 station chief?'

'Which was long before my time,' said Maguire.'

'Then the KGB officer and my father's careers shadowed each other and he was told by your lot to do what?'

'Turn the Russian instead.'

'That wouldn't be my father's role. He would have handed

it over to MI6.' Maguire's half-explanation teased Raglan's imagination. Two professionals on opposing sides spending years in close proximity. 'So?'

'So,' Maguire said, 'our Russian refused.'

'End of story,' said Raglan. 'Then how does that bring us back to Africa?'

'You've missed a vital step, Raglan. The Russian and your father apparently shared many interests—'

'My father had no interests but his work,' Raglan interrupted, a note of unbidden regret creeping into his voice. For a moment Raglan was surprised at the sense of loss that still overcame him.

'—but I don't know what those interests were,' said Maguire.

An image presented itself to Raglan. Himself as a boy, his father showing him how to cast a fly in a trout stream. Perhaps that was what had been between his father and the Russian. But it was a small treasure he didn't want to share with Maguire.

'Well, whatever it was, it was their way of learning to understand each other. What we had thought was an attempt to turn your father was in fact the Russian reaching out to come to us. He refused to speak to MI6 and would only speak to your father. But the time wasn't right. He couldn't take the big jump. And being based in Europe was too dangerous for him. KGB officers were watched all the time. A year later he was posted to Africa, where the Soviets were training militia and supplying weapons. The war in neighbouring Rwanda spilled over the border into the Congo. There were massacres on both sides, so when the shit hit the fan, your father was sent to try and reel him in. He went out on a limb and saved his life. At enormous risk to himself. The time, the place and your father's courage brought him to us.'

'Then where is this double agent now? Still in Africa?'

'No, step by step over time he went up the ranks from the defunct KGB into the Russian intelligence service. He now holds high rank and has the ear of the Kremlin. He's been feeding us information for thirty years.'

6

Maguire had related one of the most stunning secrets of British intelligence. He let its importance sink in.

Raglan shook his head. 'My God, that's gold dust.'

'And all thanks to your father's courage.'

'OK, so you've resurrected my past, filled in a blank about my father and shared a state secret. Where and how do I fit into this? What's so damned important in Africa that connects these three things?'

Maguire walked over and locked the classroom door. Raglan watched as he fiddled with the class teacher's computer. 'Drop that blind, will you?' he asked, nodding towards the window and the shaft of winter sun streaming into the room. Like a good pupil, Raglan complied. Maguire had swivelled around the laptop and focused the projector for a PowerPoint presentation on to the whiteboard. He slotted in a USB stick. An image appeared of a man in his thirties standing on a London Underground platform speaking to what appeared to be an older man whose back was to the lens. Maguire left it on screen.

'Five days ago a retired MI6 officer was murdered. The man whose back to us is that officer – his name was Barton. A very brave man. The man facing him is a Russian GRU intelligence

agent named Major Yuri Gelyov. Using the underground
security cameras we identified two more GRU agents. They
and Gelyov are members of a black ops section of the GRU's
Unit 29155. The same unit that attempted to murder Skripal
in Salisbury in 2018. The Russians are clumsy but brutal, and
finding any of theirs who defected drives them as mad as a cat
with fleas. And the night before Barton died they killed such
a man. We now know it was he who had passed some vital
information to Barton. Barton positioned himself so we could
make that first identification.' Maguire ran the next images.
A video clip showed the man, who looked to be in his sixties,
barging past the Russian and on to a train moments before
the doors closed. 'He was leading them astray. Heading for my
office with that information. A fourth unidentified Russian
administered a quick-acting drug that mimics a heart attack.
Our former colleague died within two minutes of getting on
the train. We haven't been able to identify who killed him, but
whoever it was took the information from his coat pocket.
Barton suspected he was going to be killed.'

'How do you know that?'

'He spent the night before he died at a lover's apartment.
The following morning the concierge from that building
hand-delivered an envelope to me at my home address. In it
Barton told me what he planned to do in order to protect the
information and that all the evidence suggested he would not
survive long enough to reach my office.'

Maguire waited as Raglan took it all in.

'Then if he knew he was being followed he will have
swapped or altered the intelligence he carried. Kept the altered
documents on him and had the original given to you by an

unsuspecting third party he trusted and who the Russians did not suspect.'

'Correct,' said Maguire.

'And how did he get hold of this information?'

Maguire sighed. 'By the grace of God, I would say. Barton was an old Africa hand. In the envelope he sent to my house Barton told me he had kept in touch with a long-time Russian exile—'

'Is this the man who was also killed?'

'Yes. He in turn was friends with a German geologist, a neighbour, a man who spent time in Africa. The Russians have exploration teams out there checking the feasibility for a natural gas pipeline – the German was a field consultant for them. A month ago he came back to London and showed the Russian photos of the tail fin of a plane he had found in the desert. He thought it very exciting. His friend asked who else had seen the photos and was told only the exploration team. The exiled Russian broke cover and gave Barton what he had. Barton knew that if *he* remembered the story of what happened with your father and the KGB agent, then so might anyone serving in Russian intelligence from those days. We know there was a strong rumour at the time of one of theirs being turned. And, more than that, how that information was sent out of a war zone to reach western intelligence. One lone aircraft making a dangerous run. And when your father returned, that rumour became fact. It would be a real coup if any of their lot found evidence that there really was a mole in Russian intelligence. If anyone connected were to see these photos they would know their importance.'

'And the geologist?' said Raglan.

'Found gassed in his car in his lock-up garage. They obviously
got to him as well. We know that the man whose company
is doing the exploration is one of the Russian President's
siloviki, so-called strong men – former intelligence officers,
businessmen and politicians who compete for his approval.
And the Wagner Group, the Russian mercenary army, are
spread far and wide in Africa, shoring up Africa's strong men
and getting mineral and exploration rights in return. There's
a connection between the gas pipeline and them. Killers at
large, well equipped with armoured vehicles, fighter planes
and ground troops, and all under his protection – but whose
actions don't reflect back on him.' Maguire shook his head.
'And after the Afghanistan debacle they bought up swathes of
American arms and equipment from the Taliban. They've got
more weaponry than our own troops.'

'When are you going to get to the point, Maguire?'

Maguire raised a hand. 'Hang on, Raglan, you have to
know as much as I can tell you.' Maguire moved to the next
image: a Second World War P51 Mustang fighter. It had a red
star of China on its tail fin. 'Ever see one of these when you
were in Africa?'

Raglan's look was as much as if to say *are you crazy?* 'No.'

'Don't look so incredulous, Raglan. There were a few
there in the late fifties and sixties when all that crazy stuff
was going on in Angola and anywhere else where unsavoury
characters were scrambling for power and influence. South
African mercenaries and the CIA were in the mix. The Chinese
bought a bunch of P51s from the Americans after the Second
World War. Then they tried to get a foothold in Africa but
the Soviets beat them to the draw. All those old planes ended
up as scrap or sold or left until they fell apart. One, though,

remained in private hands. And...' Maguire brought up an image of a near-buried aircraft, nose-down by the look of it, the tail fin just visible above a sand drift showing the same emblem of a Chinese star. '... here it is.'

Raglan looked from the photo to Maguire who appeared to be as perplexed as he felt. 'Dammit, Maguire, I don't have a clue what all this is about.'

'Neither did I until we scoured archives and retrieved your father's reports from the nineties. When he was in Africa, when he saved that KGB agent's neck.' He took an envelope from his satchel and handed it to Raglan. 'This is the report your father wrote when he returned – see his signature on the bottom. You can read it – it's succinct – but I have to take it back with me. The name of the former KGB officer has been redacted for national security. Not even the PM knows who the source is. Only the Service. We can't let this information be known even to those who hold high office of state.'

Raglan pulled out a thin buff-coloured folder with a single sheet of paper stapled inside headed *Codename Malaika*, and the admonishment that the document was *Top Secret* and *For UK Eyes Only*. A strange sense of uncertainty touched Raglan, holding a report from his father.

A report that immediately gave Raglan a picture in his mind's eye of his father racing towards danger while others retreated. Had his father sat at an old manual typewriter and pecked out the report? Hunched over with that same fierce concentration Raglan remembered so well? The precise way to tie a fly. His father's hand on his own showing him how to cast. Pictures of a distant man who barely showed any emotion towards his son. He never saw his father cry, not even when Raglan's mother died. Stoic. Dispassionate. Just like the precise no-nonsense report he now held in his hand. All of which was an obvious necessity for the work he did. As Maguire had said, the report was simple and concise. And there in the final paragraph was the explanation about the old fighter plane. Raglan raised his eyes.

'My father got the agent out. But he had no means of telling the embassy or MI6 in case he himself was killed. So he used the Americans. He gave the message to a young hot-shot CIA pilot to get it out.'

Maguire reached out for the document. Raglan's reluctance to surrender it was understandable but he allowed Maguire to ease it from his fingertips. 'Yes. What you've just read is the official report your father made when he reached safety. The pilot flew a fixed-wing aircraft for the CIA, but it developed engine problems so somehow he found the Mustang. Your father asked him to get out a hastily handwritten letter that confirmed the KGB officer was willing to work for us. Desperate times require desperate measures. Your father had no access to a radio set. Towns were burning. People were being massacred. The pilot took off, but was never heard of again. In the end he was reported missing in action, believed killed. The CIA gave him a star of remembrance on their memorial wall at Langley for giving his life for his country. And ours, I might add.'

Raglan thought of his father alone in a hot zone. Impossible to imagine what his thoughts would have been other than to keep the vital secret intact. Maguire was right. If he'd thought he was facing imminent death, he'd have done anything to get the information out. 'And "missing in action, believed killed" meant everyone in British Intelligence thought the plane had gone down and this information with it.'

'Yes. Until the German geologist found it. We cannot risk this plane being found again by anyone but us. That's why I'm asking you to accompany the French mission. If three men are already dead because of its discovery then we believe there must be a link to someone who knows the rumour of your father turning our man. That person has to be someone in Russian intelligence who was stationed in Africa at that time. Why else mount an operation to retrieve the information?' Maguire tucked the document back into his satchel case. 'Obviously once your father reached safety and we began getting intelligence from the Russian, we all thought we were in the clear. And the Service has been thinking that for nigh on thirty years.'

'That document will be buried. Is the KGB officer named on it?'

'His identity is concealed in the letter. Your father told us there are enough clues for anyone from the other side to put the pieces together. There was barely a handful of KGB men posted out there. A process of elimination means just that. Thankfully, the message from your father was encoded. But if the other side unscramble that, then our Russian might soon find himself with a bullet in the back of his neck and we'll be fed false information from their counter-intelligence.'

Raglan gazed at the picture of the downed aircraft. 'If there's anything left of that document the dry desert air would make it so brittle it would crumble at the slightest touch – like the Dead Sea Scrolls.'

'I agree.'

'Then why the panic?'

Maguire pointed to shelves holding children's books. He tugged free a plastic storage box holding lesson sheets.

35

'We think of plastic as the curse of the modern age. They didn't back then. Your father folded the message inside a plastic medical syringe box no bigger than the palm of my hand.' He clicked on to the next picture. It showed a satellite image of desert fringed on one side with scrub. 'Given what information Barton received from his contact and the geologist, we think we know where the crash site is. The sands come and go. Right now the plane's buried.'

'But if it isn't?' said Raglan.

'Whether it resurfaces or not, the Russians are already hot on the trail of this missing aircraft. They had a head start trying to figure out where it's located once the German innocently showed his Russian colleagues those photographs. Barton doctored the map and that will throw them for a while.' Maguire shut down the computer lid and retrieved the memory stick. 'Whoever finds that aircraft will find information that could reveal the most valuable spy our country has ever known. Then, as Custer said at Little Big Horn: I think we're fucked.'

7

Raglan had remained silent. Maguire knew anyone tasked with a mission as dangerous as the one he proposed would already be calculating the odds on exfiltrating from a hostile environment.

'They're bound to have a team already out there. Even with the false trail that Barton left them,' said Raglan.

'No doubt. But Barton bought us time. Trouble is, our ambassador in Moscow is reporting heightened activity around the embassy. Surveillance has been increased, and if this goes to the wire, I don't see how we can even get our man out and into the West. Russia is playing hard and fast. It wasn't just Ukraine where they'd set their sights. Russia is clawing its way back into Africa. Their warships are docked in Port Sudan where they've bought a twenty-five-year lease. Red flag, big time, but after thirty African countries turned to Russia for the Covid vaccine, the West was already way behind the curve. Simple truth is that we can't fail with this. Over the past couple of years we've shut down Russian-linked interference in several countries' elections, including America. We knew about their President's intentions in Ukraine even before the politicians did their fan dance in front of him. They thought they could bring Putin around with diplomacy. We even knew they were planting Ukrainian nationals who were Russian sympathizers in key positions. Two were politicians in their government. And we found out because our man with his ear to the door at the Kremlin told us. That and a hell of a lot more. So... now you have the facts and the people in play,' he finished, 'what do you say?'

'Let's eat,' said Raglan.

Maguire's look of incredulity was enough to make Raglan smile. 'You're in France, Maguire. We eat by the clock here.'

They left the relative warmth of the classroom and walked back up towards the village. Maguire turned his face into the stiffening breeze from the north-east. All the way from Russia. And it could get a damned sight colder if the operation fell apart. 'I need you on this, Raglan. I don't trust the French not to pull a fast one over the operation.'

'Do they know what the information is?' said Raglan.

'Only that it's vital to the security of western intelligence. I've whetted their appetite and that's as much as they'll know until I tell them differently.'

Raglan grunted. 'They already know too much. Why not send in an SAS team?'

Maguire shook his head. 'I'd like nothing better, but this location is borderline Central African Republic, which since day one has been under French influence. The language, the military, the civil and government systems. Our government had no choice but to go to them to set up the mission with the promise that we would share future intelligence – well, more than we do now, shall we say. So you'll do it?'

'If I go in on my own.'

'Not this time,' said Maguire.

'How many men?'

'Twelve. All French Intelligence Action Division.'

Raglan stopped. 'The Action Service? The knuckle-dragging brigade? They've blundered into more military operations and caused more problems than a bull in a china shop. I work best alone, Maguire, you know that. And I would never choose to work with them.'

'I have no choice but to ask you to work with them.'

Raglan swept his arm across the village. 'I can pick a dozen men from here. All veteran legionnaires, all fit, all ready to go.'

'This is a French intelligence operation, but you're my man, and only you will know the location where we think that old plane is buried and what it is you're looking for. They have to keep you alive.'

'Who's in charge?'

'You. Their commander is a Serb. Name of Dragonović. An old Legion sweat. Not your mob. Never served with the paras. But this is your mission. That's my line in the sand.'

'No commander likes an outsider being brought in. That's trouble from the start. You trust them to get me in and bring me out?'

'No. I don't know how far they'll go when you get your hands on that document. It's gold dust. And it's ours.'

'Then we'd better hope you're not digging my grave in the sand. Don't you think this Dragonović hasn't already been briefed to make sure I stay out there?'

Maguire knew there was a good chance Raglan was correct. Once the secret was in his hands his life would be worthless should the French play the high-stakes game of trying to keep the information – and the only way they could do that was if Raglan did not return. Not only would Raglan be dead but the French would eventually break the coded letter and have access to the mole at the heart of Russia's intelligence service.

'If that happens then everything could unravel, and fast,' said Maguire. 'France wants to be top dog in Europe. Russia is on a military and economic offensive on every front.'

'I'm still better off with my own people.'

'No, you're not.' Maguire hesitated. 'You care for these people, don't you? This whole community here? How many of these ex-legionnaires are married with families? Half, seventy-five per cent? More?'

'Most are,' Raglan agreed.

'Then see this operation for what is. It's hostile territory. Warlords there create terror. Factions fight within their clans. Terrorist groups vie for power. If I'm honest I don't think many of the Action Division men are going to get back alive. And if you do and they were your men, are you prepared to face their widows and their children? Let the French supply men who are expendable.'

They reached the cafe. Maguire looked at the two dead boar hanging. 'We could end up like that. Our lifeblood draining away. Raglan, I don't care what you have to do to bring home the bacon.'

After a moment Raglan nodded. His father had started something years before and now fate had handed the responsibility of finishing it to his son.

Maguire turned down Raglan's offer of staying in the village overnight. He needed to return to London now that Raglan had agreed to lead the mission. Sokol and Raglan squeezed into the Peugeot and drove him back to Toulouse; Raglan walked him into the departure hall.

'Tomorrow, fifteen hundred hours at Istres air base. It's a forty-minute drive this side of Marseille.'

'I know where it is,' Raglan said, and shook Maguire's extended hand.

'I'm asking a lot, I know,' said Maguire. 'But there's no one else.'

'Dumb enough to take it on, you mean? Like you said: expendable.'

Maguire didn't crack a smile. 'Check out those coordinates I gave you on the crash site. I'll fly into Istres tomorrow for the briefing.'

Raglan and Sokol stayed at the airport until Maguire's flight time, long enough to have a coffee. They watched the dwindling crowd, scanning for anyone who looked as though they shouldn't be there. If Maguire had been compromised like his man in London, then all it would take was for one or two surveillance teams from the other side to track and kill him. Sokol nodded towards two men who were approaching each other from different sides of the departure area. They wore jeans and leather jackets. They looked like cops but they weren't; they were something else.

'I was followed from the camp,' said Sokol. 'My guess is Maguire was followed from here. I lost them at the turn-off to the village when I brought him through.'

They shadowed the two men across the car park. 'Blue Renault,' said Sokol when he saw them head towards the car. He peeled away, letting Raglan follow the men as he flanked them. The driver and the passenger went to their respective doors and both were half in the car when Raglan and Sokol slammed the doors closed on the men's legs. The shock of the sudden attack gave Raglan and Sokol the advantage. The two men went down under rapid, well-placed blows from the two former legionnaires. Raglan had the driver face down, arm bent behind him, wrist in a swan-neck hold.

'Who are you working for?' Raglan demanded.

The man grunted. Raglan tightened the wrist hold; the man yelped in pain. 'You're up shit street,' he gasped.

Raglan pulled free the man's holstered semi-automatic from his belt and pressed it into the nape of his neck. 'You should think about that.'

'They're official,' Sokol called, 'French Intelligence.' He tossed an identity wallet across.

Raglan flipped it open. 'Let him go, Bird.'

Raglan stepped back as the man rolled to his feet, clutching a useless arm. Sokol released the man on the passenger side. The two hapless men stood facing their attackers. Bird must have caught his man with a hefty blow to the face because he stood cradling a bloodied jaw with both hands, whimpering in agony.

'You were following someone. Why?' said Raglan.

'You'd better back off now because you're dealing with an official surveillance operation,' the driver threatened. 'You're in over your head.'

Raglan tossed the identity wallet to him. He snatched at it with his one good hand. 'You can't drive with your arm like that and your friend needs a hospital. Shall I call your regional headquarters and tell them that two of their intelligence officers got jumped in broad daylight?' He saw the look of defeat on the man's face. They would have to make up a story to cover themselves. 'So, why were you following the man who arrived from London?'

'You know nothing about him,' said the driver.

'I know a lot about him,' Raglan answered. 'You're going to have a hard time explaining yourself to your boss, but an even harder time after I put a bullet in your leg.' Raglan cocked the pistol and levelled it. The man half crouched.

'Christ! All right! We had to know who he was seeing here. That's all.'

'Why? You don't know what's going on.'

'What? No, we don't – how could we?'

'Precisely. It's on a need-to-know basis. And I needed to know. That's why he came to see me.'

The man swore.

Raglan kept the pistol levelled, reached into the car and pulled the keys from the ignition. He threw them among the parked cars and then stripped the pistol and tossed the pieces in different directions. Sokol followed suit.

'Tell your people that if they pull another stunt like this, they will never find what they're looking for.'

The man's brow furrowed.

'You don't have to understand more than that. It's above your pay grade. Need to know.'

Raglan and Sokol left the stranded men, the driver clumsily trying to use his phone in a call for help.

'Whatever it is, you've already got the government's attention,' Sokol said as they walked back towards the car.

'French intelligence want to get their hands on something before I do. They're obviously being kept in the dark by their Action Service. It's dirty tricks time. I'm leaving from Istres air base tomorrow afternoon for the border between the Central

African Republic and Sudan. An Action Service team is going to babysit me.'

Sokol pulled a face. 'You have a reason for doing this crazy thing?'

Raglan smiled. 'Just following in my father's footsteps.'

8

They left early next morning after Raglan had spent a long night going over the French satellite images Maguire had left him. It was obvious that the Americans had not been informed, otherwise the British could have asked for a pass over the suspected crash site. This was one piece of information MI6 did not wish to share. The Russian traitor and his intelligence value was being kept under wraps.

The images showed a no man's land and even Maguire was uncertain if the sliver of metal visible in the satellite image was the downed aircraft despite the intensive magnification available. By the time the next orbit came over the area there was no sign at all. In hours, the desert winds could cover a small object, or reveal it. Raglan checked the weather reports. It was already 39 degrees Celsius there and would get hotter. And the risk of sandstorms was always present, which posed a serious threat for men in the open. The winds were light, no more than fifteen kilometres an hour from the north-west. Visibility on the ground should be good. Trouble was that if Raglan and the others had a clear sight of the horizon, then they too could easily be seen. Tribal warlords were spread from central Africa east across Sudan, into Ethiopia and Somalia. Like scrapyard dogs each warlord was chained to their territory, their violence extending only so far before encroaching into another's region. The trick would be to stay out of their reach. And in the middle of this inhospitable desolation were the shifting sands of time, ready to expose the most important spy the UK intelligence service had.

Sokol turned the battered Peugeot on to the A61 towards Marseille. Raglan wore jeans, T-shirt and dark blue crew-necked knitted sweater under a waxed jacket. There was no need for extra clothing. This wasn't a vacation to see the sights. He would change into issued combat fatigues at the airfield.

Once they reached Saint-Martin-de-Crau, Sokol ignored the turn south for Istres air base and carried on straight for Salon de Provence. An hour and a half later he drove through the buttressed pillars signposted *Institution des invalides de la Légion étrangère*. The retirement home for former members of the Legion was built, maintained and financed by different Legion units. The stone-built buildings gave way to a delicate honey-coloured Gallo-Roman main building. The complex cared for more than a hundred senior wounded or sick veterans. Those who were physically able worked in the vineyard, olive groves and workshops. Men from different nationalities shared their final years with each other as they had done when they served together. The Legion was family.

Raglan glanced around him. The mountains of Provence rose in the distance.

'I came here once to see an old friend before he died of his wounds,' said Raglan. 'What's the idea? Booking me a room?'

'There's someone you should meet before we get to the

base. He's an old sweat who might help keep you alive out there,' Sokol answered and pulled a supermarket bag from behind the seat.

Raglan heard the clink of bottles. He followed Sokol into reception where Sokol asked for Ulrich Becker. They were directed to the vineyards and after twenty minutes Sokol saw the man he wanted. A wiry older man in his seventies with a slight stoop was pruning the vines alongside others. He wore an old forage cap; his long white beard reached his chest; his equally long white hair was tied in a ponytail. He saw the two visitors standing at the end of the row of trimmed vines. Wiping a sleeve across his runny nose he told the others to continue without him. His limp did not impede him over the uneven ground.

He looked from Sokol to Raglan. There was no smile of greeting. 'Serge, you come to bother an old soldier again?'

'It's only been eight years, Ulrich. Sorry to be a nuisance.'

'Man comes here for a bit of peace and quiet, and all he gets is intruded on. Eight years, is it?' He grunted. 'Time flies. Especially when you get to my age.' He nodded towards the carrier bag. 'Been shopping?'

'No, I'm homeless and these are my possessions.'

'That's not funny to those of us who don't have a home, Sokol, you hard-nosed bastard.'

'And you're living in the lap of luxury. I wouldn't be surprised if they don't wipe your arse for you.'

'I'm working on that.' He looked at Raglan. 'You know this streak of piss?'

'We served together.'

'And you're still alive? Sweet Jesus, Sokol was always neck-deep in shit and bullets.'

Sokol made the introductions. 'Raglan, this German outcast spent a lifetime trying to stay in the fight until the fight spat him out. Now he's a limping old goat who can still get up to the top of Sainte-Victoire on a bad day.'

'Bullshit. I can barely get out of bed in the morning. Arthritis and old wounds.' He looked at Raglan. 'Comes to us all. You too one day.' His gaze didn't falter. 'Were you in the Second?'

'Yes,' said Raglan.

'And then he went into special forces,' said Sokol.

'That's all right then,' said the elderly German. 'If those bottles you're carrying aren't schnapps you can piss off. So, what's it to be? Drink or talk? I don't have all day.'

Becker's room was at odds with his scruffy appearance. The single bed was as neatly made as a new recruit's. The room was small but spacious enough for one man – a toilet and shower off to one side, a small desk overlooking a view of the hills. There was space enough for a guest chair tucked in the corner next to a slim but extensive bookshelf. The room was functional, but with half a dozen small flowering pot plants on the windowsill. As homely a touch as a man like Becker could hope for after his long service.

Raglan's eyes scanned the books. There were titles in four languages. A glass picture frame on the wall showed Becker's commendations and medals. As Sokol and Becker found glasses for the schnapps, Raglan studied the man's medals. Next to the Legion's parachutist's beret badge a silvered and gilt bronze Military Medal took pride of place. Below were a dozen more awards for valour and Foreign Legion clasps for service in overseas conflicts. A medal with the Republic of Congo clasp, then those of Zaire, Senegal, Somalia and, settled beneath them all, as if it had the least significance to its owner, was the Bronze Cross for war wounded. Quite the service record.

Sokol handed Raglan a shot of schnapps. Raglan accepted it. Becker had downed two already.

'You were at Kolwezi in '78,' said Raglan.

'I was. We jumped in and did the business. Our colonel was first out the door.' Becker pointed to a group photograph from the 1978 conflict in the Congo when Katangan rebels based in Angola launched two invasions. 'That's him. Him and me. He was the bravest man I knew.' Becker poured another for himself. 'Died the next year while jogging. Heart attack. There's no telling.' Becker sat on the desk chair, nodded for Sokol to sit on his bed. Raglan sat in the corner chair.

'We saved hundreds and killed more.' He shrugged. 'Maybe not more, but our body was count was close to three hundred. We did a good job and stopped the slaughter.' Becker coughed, cleared the heavy phlegm and banged a fist against his chest. 'Should never have quit smoking. Felt like shit ever since. Imagine feeling shit for ten years. But they said I had to, so being a good legionnaire, I did as I was told.' He drank. 'So, here you are, two retired legionnaires out for a nice drive on a sunny winter's day, saying to themselves: let's drop in and see old Ulrich Becker. See if he's still kicking.' He stared at them. 'My arse.'

Sokol gave Raglan a nod.

'Bird said you might help. I'm going close to the Central African Republic on the border between Sudan and Chad with a small Action Service team. It's a covert mission. We can get in and there'll be a plan to exfil us but I want to keep the odds on my side.'

Becker sat unmoving, hunched, eyes gazing at Raglan. Not seeing him. Watching, instead, his own past when he was young, fit and brave, fighting France's wars in Africa. The three men remained silent. And then Becker scratched his beard, finished his drink and nodded.

'Son, a few thoughts come to mind. Thirty-odd years back, President Mitterrand fell out with his generals, and he put the covert Action Service agents under civilian command. They're drawn from French armed forces but they're out of the army's control. They're all right up to a point but most aren't legionnaires. There'll be the odd one gets recruited, the rest are from regular army, so you don't have the right people watching your back. Then you're going where it's a hell hole to be exfiltrated from.' He sighed and folded his arms. 'Years ago, thirty of us were in Sudan on reconnaissance on that border.' He nodded towards Sokol. 'That's why Bird brought you to me. Only four of us got out. No one ever reported the cock-up. France's pride was already taking a knock from the old colonies telling us to piss off. I'm the only one left now – the other three died a couple of years ago. But what happened to us out there was the one thing we survivors talked about all the damned time afterwards.' He shook his head. 'I fought some hard wars, son, but none like that. The rebels thrashed us. We were cut off and we ran out of ammunition, food and water. We killed as many as we could, hand to hand, and then we ran into the desert. We left our dead comrades behind and they mutilated their bodies. I swore I would go back one day and avenge them. I never did of course.'

He bent down, reached beneath the bed and pulled out a

small suitcase. 'Bird, sit here, why don't you?' he said, giving his desk chair to Sokol as he hefted the case on to the bed.

He flipped open the lid. It was full of old folded operational maps, dog-eared and stained. He rifled through them, tossing the ones he didn't want on the bed. 'You still use a map and compass, Raglan?'

'Sure,' he said.

Becker kept his head down, rummaging. 'Good. Never trusted GPS. You can turn a satellite off; a map, you have in your hand. Map, compass, eyes and brain.'

He found what he was looking for, piled the extraneous maps back into the case, pushed it aside and spread out the map on the bed.

'Here,' he said, nodding to Raglan and Sokol to peer over his shoulder.

It was a waxed map of the area that lay along the Central African Republic's border with Chad and Sudan. Faded marks showed the old reconnaissance waypoints and RVs.

Becker traced his finger towards a small mark on the map. 'This village, there was an abandoned airstrip. Old World War Two strip. Long gone now. We were interested in it. Thought it could be a good place to use if we were committed in force. Which never happened anyway. When we first went in, militants were threatening the Masalit villagers. We saved them. Killed every last one of the murdering bastards and buried them and their vehicles in gulleys and covered them over. Then no one could blame the villagers. These Masalit tribesmen have honour. On our way out we stumbled back there and they helped us. They hid us and got word out. That's where we were rescued.'

He folded the map and handed it to Raglan. 'It's a long

shot, son, but if you are caught out there, you make sure they know you are Legion. Beyond that there's nothing I can tell you. You have Legion tattoos?'

'No, nothing like that,' said Raglan.

Becker sighed and nodded. 'Well, I can see how in your line of work you wouldn't want to be identified.' He shrugged. 'If you get there, tell them the story I told you. Some of the elders might remember. The clan leader who saved us was an old man whose name was Saleh. Long dead by now, but stories are how those people pass down their history. We were part of that history.'

'Thank you,' said Raglan. He held the folded map in one hand and extended the other. The old man's rough-skinned handshake was firm.

'You're welcome. Now get to where you're going and stop drinking my schnapps. Bird, give me a cigarette, will you?'

9

Sokol drove west and then turned south to the air base at Istres-Le Tubé, a military airfield neither had been to before. Operationally, the Legion's 2nd Foreign Parachute Regiment would fly from their base at Calvi on Corsica. Istres was better known for having the longest runway in western Europe, capable of accommodating an emergency landing site for the American space shuttle programme. Sokol brought the Peugeot up short of the guarded entrance. Both men sat without speaking for a minute as they took in the base sprawling before them.

'You know where I am if there is anything I can do,' said the veteran.

'I know where you are, Bird – it'll be a damned miracle if I know where I'll be.'

Raglan got out of the car and walked towards the guards. Sokol waited a moment longer while his friend was identified and ushered through the gates. Raglan never looked back. Never did. No point. Sokol knew where Raglan's mind was focused. The thought occurred to him that one day, sooner or later, no matter how efficient and skilled in survival, Raglan's luck was bound to run out.

*

Raglan was escorted into the side door of a hangar vast enough to house the space shuttle. Instead, a camouflage-painted C130J Super Hercules stood menacingly in the shadows. The Herc always struck Raglan as a belligerent beast. Its sturdiness was legend, its reliability second to none. The protruding nose cone stood out like the face of a pugilist looking for a fight. Two stripped-down militarized five-door Masstech T4 Toyota Land Cruisers, older models built to take punishment and standard vehicles for the French Army fighting a desert war, were being loaded through the tailgate of the C130. His guard pointed to a door and told him it was where he had to go. The huge cave echoed with the squeal of the Land Cruiser's tyres crossing the polished concrete surface.

Raglan pushed open the door into a side room. It was a storage facility. Racks of aircraft spares and tools hung along one side while on the wall nearest to him stood a row of trestle tables with army equipment laid out neatly so that the dozen men in the room could each pack their own rucksack with the ammunition and supplies. Most of the men were still in their civilian clothes – jeans and T-shirts – as they sorted through the disruptive-patterned camouflaged uniforms. The overhead lamps cast shadows across the men's faces. Once Raglan closed the door behind him, they stopped what they were doing and faced him. Raglan surveyed the room. The men were lithe and tanned; none were overtly muscled, but looked to have the strength to give them stamina in arduous conditions.

At the far end of the room a projector screen rose beyond

a dozen metal folding chairs. The black man nearest the door stepped forward and extended his hand. His face broke into a grin. Raglan guessed he was Senegalese: a soldier who served with the French army and had been brought into the Action Division.

'You're the Englishman, eh? Raglan? I'm Malik Bayo.'

'Malik,' said Raglan, greeting him, then looking past the man to the others, some of whom raised a hand and called out their names – Algerian, Central African, European. The uniforms – standard camouflage – weren't the usual Action Division issue and bore no name tags, rank or insignia of any kind. They were recycled. Washed out. Easy to wear. No brand-new hard materials to chafe in the desert heat.

Malik pointed to an older man. 'He's Jarnac. Been with the unit the longest. You want to know anything about anyone, who's the best sniper, who does demolition, comms, medic. He'll break it down. He's the boss's right-hand man. Has been before any of us signed up.'

As if on cue, Jarnac saw Raglan and came forward to greet him. 'Raglan, I'm Jarnac.' They shook hands. 'You've already pissed off my boss – better you know this before we get on the ground. He can be a man of disagreeable temperament.'

'It's understandable,' said Raglan. 'No team leader wants an outsider calling the shots.'

Jarnac studied him for a moment. 'You think that's what you're going to do? Dream on, Raglan. You're a passenger, that's all. The boss will get us wherever it is we have to be and then bring you back. This is little more than an Action Division taxi service.'

'Then why is he pissed off?'

'Because our lives are on the line for you.' He called across the room to a man half obscured by the shadows. 'Boss! The Englishman is here.'

Raglan moved further into the room, greeting each man as he passed; some were cool towards him, a couple more agreeable in their welcome. He made his way towards the older man whose features gradually became clear. Dragonović appeared to be edging towards his mid-forties. With rugged, etched features and close-cropped hair, he looked every inch the tough field operative he was. His combat shirtsleeves were rolled and squared away neatly on tanned, thickset biceps; a hint of grey hair peeped below his khaki T-shirt. Like the other men he was bareheaded. Also like the other men, except for the African, Malik Bayo, he bore fading tattoos on his muscled forearms.

The burly Serbian did not extend his hand in greeting.

'Your kit is there,' he said, pointing to a place on the long table. The Serbian spoke flawless French. The language of the Legion. Raglan had served with Serbians, Russians and Eastern Europeans. They were the prevalent nationalities. Every man had his own reason to join, and he had come across a handful of Serbs escaping their part in the Kosovo conflict. Was that Dragonović's background? he wondered. No outsider, not even a government minister, is privy to the real identity of those who serve in the Legion and spill their blood for France. No questions asked and no answers given. The contract is holy. Some say written in blood. Dragonović turned his back and attended to loading his assault rifle's magazine.

Raglan's measurements and boot size had been relayed to the French operational HQ. Raglan unzipped the small valise he carried and took out a pair of his own broken-in combat boots. Going into an operational area with new boots was asking for trouble. His feet would be blistered in hours. Raglan noticed the men had their own well-worn boots next to the neatly folded uniforms. Experience showed.

The men peeled off their clothes and dressed. Raglan checked the assault rifle and the magazines tucked into the pockets of the personal body webbing, its yoke looped for convenience around the upright backpack. He pulled out the magazines for the F1 Special Operations Combat Assault Rifle next to the kit. It could be chambered for either the 7.62-mm round or the more usual 5.56 mm. It wouldn't be the first time a clerk in the quartermaster stores had issued a magazine with the wrong ammunition, but here they had issued the correct thirty-round version rather than the twenty held in the 7.62 mag. Killing power and range was one thing but when engaged in close-quarter contact the extra rounds gave its shooter an advantage.

Everything was familiar, pretty much regular issue. The PAMAS G1 semi-automatic 9-mm pistol was standard, so too the GPS, medical pack, personal radio, water camel and rations. It would be the usual beast-of-burden slog in the desert. He settled the load-carrying webbing's yoke on his shoulders. It fitted and was ready for when it was needed. Men sidled up, making themselves known. Only first or last names were given, and Raglan memorized the faces and names. He was the outsider coming into a team, but did not sense any animosity from them towards the stranger in their midst, although they weren't exactly offering manly hugs of welcome. Nothing new there. Just your usual bunch of emotionally disabled soldiers. And they would want to get the measure of who they were babysitting. He noticed some of the men gravitated to certain others: friendships forged over time. Men in the field worked closely with those of their own choice. The team depended on each other, no question about that, but close partnerships were the glue that bound them.

When the men were changed and ready to be briefed, Dragonović told them to be seated. Raglan took a chair at the back as Maguire and another civilian, a man in his forties, came into the room. The man's tailored suit contrasted with Maguire's still casual attire. Perhaps, Raglan thought, Maguire did not want to be thought of as one of the 'suits'. Well-cut-suit man nodded to the female aide who accompanied him to make her way to the back of the room where the projector stand was set up. The men craned their necks appreciatively. She was attractive, and a smartly dressed woman in high heels – a woman in authority, had its appeal. Dragonović called them back to order. The unsmiling civilian introduced himself.

'As you men will know, I am Claude Delmar. I am from the Directorate of Operations in Paris, which makes me responsible for the covert operations of the Action Division. My presence here today should impress upon you the urgency and seriousness of this operation. This incursion is critical. My colleague from the British Secret Intelligence Service'— he gestured to Maguire—'has brought this mission to our government and they have chosen the Action Division to undertake it. You are honoured, gentlemen. It could have gone to Military Special Operations, but we know how to conduct this business.' He looked beyond the seated men and raised a hand. 'Thank you.'

The lights dimmed and a map of central and north Africa

appeared, showing a flight route from Istres. 'Gentlemen, your flight is listed as a relief flight taking supplies of food and medicine to our base at Djibouti and then on to N'Djamena in Chad for distribution throughout the region. It is the extended range Hercules with a light payload flown by special ops pilots. Once you cross the Red Sea, your aircraft will cross into Chadian airspace, fly south along the Chad–Sudan border and continue onwards at a low-combat-level height into Sudanese airspace below their radar until you reach the Central African Republic and South Sudan border where...' He nodded to the woman handling the projector. '... it will land on a plateau, here.' A red triangle appeared on the map from his pointer. 'You will disembark tactically; the aircraft will keep its engines running and then take off for Bangui, Central African Republic, the closest and friendliest refuelling airfield.'

The next slide appeared. It was an enhanced image of the satellite photo Maguire had given Raglan. An overlay had been used to show the approximate site of the crashed aircraft and then beyond it a road running east to west, Sudan to Chad. 'We believe the information to be recovered is inside a buried aircraft. We do not know in what form.'

Raglan saw Maguire look his way. So, Raglan realized, the French still didn't know just what was thought to be there. Claude Delmar checked his watch. Maybe, Raglan thought, he was late for a dinner date back in Paris.

'The British government and intelligence service have come to us for our cooperation and once the information is recovered, it will benefit both our countries. You will see the line marked on the map. That is your exfiltration point out of Sudan and into Chad. Once across the border it is several hundred kilometres to our base in N'Djamena. Once we receive your signal, we will send a helicopter to airlift you out. You will destroy your land vehicles. The man chosen by MI6 is an Englishman who has worked for French and British intelligence; he is a former legionnaire and special operations commando. He is the mission leader.'

Delmar's comment caused a few heads to turn. Not Dragonović. He remained apparently unconcerned.

Delmar looked across the room. 'Questions?'

Jarnac spoke up. He showed no sign of anxiety either, but every avenue needed to be explored when they were effectively going into unknown territory. 'If we need the vehicles then a high-altitude parachute drop is impossible, but why not do a low-level jump? Do the heavy drop first and then we follow. That way we don't risk the aircraft on the ground.'

Some of the other men murmured agreement but Delmar replied, 'We dare not risk anything happening to the vehicles. They are your lifeline.'

'Heavy-drop malfunctions are rare,' said another of the men. 'Safer for us to jump low at a hundred and fifty metres. We'd be on the ground in half a minute.'

'Landing a Herc in the desert is risky,' said Jarnac. 'One mistake and we're screwed. All of us. And that's the end of the mission.'

Delmar shook his head. 'Your pilots are special forces, low-level trained, experienced in what we are asking them to do.'

Dragonović pointed at the projected map. 'Unfriendlies?'

Delmar gave a Gallic shrug. 'Other than your own men, commander?' The comment raised laughter. Then he answered the question. 'Who can say?' He turned to face the map and pointed left and right of the border. 'Boko Haram are active in southern Chad and Al Shabab in Sudan. Your biggest problem might be Janjaweed militia but we believe they're raiding further north of your intended target at the moment.'

Raglan raised a hand. Delmar nodded. 'What about the Russian Wagner Group?' said Raglan. 'They're well equipped, heavily armed and doing good business in the region. You think they won't be a problem?'

'We have no sign of their involvement,' said Delmar. 'And if you see them avoid making contact.'

Raglan glanced at an expressionless Maguire.

Delmar looked around the room once again. 'No more questions? Very well. Good luck, gentlemen.'

The screen went blank. Delmar went out the way he came in. Maguire gave a nod to Raglan. As the men pushed aside the metal chairs and returned to checking their kit, Raglan followed Maguire outside the hangar. A twin-engine private jet with its passenger steps down was preparing for take-off. Claude Delmar, flanked by two assistants, bent into the wind as he made his way to the aircraft.

'He's pissed off,' Maguire said.

'Seems to be a common problem around here,' said Raglan.

Maguire watched Delmar's retreat to the aircraft. 'He wanted it to be a full-on French operation. You're already a thorn in their side. I'm linked in to your satcom phone. Try and give us a sitrep twice a day if you can. There won't be any more satellite overflights. The Americans have an interest in the region and we don't want to flag this. So what we have is what we've got. We have no resources out there. It's up to them to get you in and out. I have to return to London once I've soothed a few more ruffled feathers in Paris.' He pressed a small mobile phone into Raglan's hand. 'Here and there among those villages and towns there are mobile masts. If this goes pear-shaped you use this.'

'To do what? Check the cricket score?'

'It's one of our Service phones. Double press the hash key and that comes to me. It's encrypted. If there's a Russian team already on the ground and you're compromised there's nothing in there for the Russians to see if they search you except a few dozen non-existent names and numbers. It's camouflage. You're going into bandit country and if there's one thing that might save your life it's paying off the bad guys. I have contingency money. I want you out alive.' He shook Raglan's hand. 'Good luck.'

10

By nightfall arc lamps' yellow light cast a hazy veil over the hangars. A brief and unexpected rain shower slicked the black tarmac. The C130J with its lowered rear-loading ramp remained concealed in the hangar. Even with the hangar doors open ready for the aircraft to be towed on to the runway, no one beyond the perimeter would see what was happening inside. Nor would any Russian satellite, should it be on an overflight, be able to detect anything unusual at the French air force base. The Land Cruisers were loaded. The men had stacked their gear inside each of their designated vehicles. Raglan would command the lead vehicle, Dragonović the second. Nothing would be needed until they touched down at first light. They carried their personal weapons and their webbing. Once they landed and the 4x4s were rolled clear of the tailgate, it was to be a fast dash to reach and secure the objective and then get to the exfiltration point. A straightforward plan. Every man in the hangar knew no such plan ever existed.

Raglan stood a short distance apart from the other men and watched as they double-checked and loaded their weapons. Then he turned and stared into the gloom. Trying to see beyond the perimeter of light. The bulk of the C130 hemmed in the men. In the distance a man emerged from the darkness, moving through the shadows, totally at ease. The certainty of Dragonović's movements was of a predator completely at one with its surroundings, confident of its own power and stature. Raglan saw him more clearly now. Still distant but a threatening presence. There would be no time to avoid this man if he decided to kill. Unsmiling and seemingly unaware of his status among his men, he moved slowly. A word, a gesture. A comment about a piece of equipment. Thirty metres. Twenty. He reached the end of the stick of men. Ten metres. Close enough to see the eyes. Unyielding. And then Dragonović stopped and gazed directly at him. The Englishman answered with an unblinking stare.

Dragonović had been briefed less than twenty-four hours before. He was to lead a strike team into the heart of Africa. His mission: to secure certain information known only to the man in charge of the mission – Raglan – a specialist used by British intelligence. The commander's task was to keep the Englishman alive. And Dragonović would not like risking his men for a mystery passenger. 'You follow my orders, Raglan. I know my team: I don't know you.'

'You do your job and I'll do mine,' Raglan answered.

Dragonović ignored him and checked his watch. 'Time to go.'

A ground crew's tractor eased the lumbering aircraft into the open. Raglan could see the two special forces pilots in the cockpit, faces caught in the glow of their instrument panels. The heads-up displays were sophisticated electronics whose computers had already been fed the exact position of their proposed landing strip. Raglan had enormous respect for these pilots: if anything went wrong it was their flying skills that had to get them out of trouble.

The two Land Cruisers were strapped securely by their running gear, held by their restraints on their axles which stopped them rolling, effectively tying them to the aircraft itself. The twelve men who were to keep Raglan alive settled back into the netted webbing that served as body support behind the canvas seats that ran along each side of the aircraft. As the engines rotated, the smell of Avgas permeated the bare metal interior, triggering Raglan's memories of past descents. He would have preferred to have jumped rather than risk a landing in hostile territory.

Raglan thought Jarnac had been right to question landing this brute of an aircraft in the desert. Better to get the men on the ground rather than risk anything unforeseen on the LZ. Did any of those who'd planned this happy excursion know that it's impossible to spot a concrete-hard termite mound from the air? Even from cockpit-level height they'd be hard to see. Hit one or put a wheel in a pot hole, and one Super Hercules and its cargo would be cartwheeling from the desert to the coast. Raglan would have taken either option of a low-level parachute drop or a HALO descent on to the target. To hell with the vehicles – they would buy or steal what they needed from villagers. But then he settled back. It was no good worrying about decisions already made.

The tailgate closed. The outside world shunned. Raglan couldn't help but feel the long arm of his father's mission reach out to him from all those years before. Not just his mission. His father had unknowingly left him a legacy. Now Raglan was travelling into the past to retrieve it.

The C130 surged into the sky, the deafening noise of its

four Rolls Royce turboprop engines making normal speech inside impossible.

Once the aircraft reached its cruising altitude, four of the men clambered to the Land Cruisers, one in each of the front seats, the third and fourth men squeezing into the rear amid the stored rucksacks. There was a tussle for the best seat: riding out the journey in a Land Cruiser was a damned sight more comfortable than the standard-issue bone-aching seats. The dim overhead lights threw shadows across the remaining men's bowed faces as they rested, determined to grab sleep. Raglan stayed close to the cockpit where he could check with the pilots cocooned in their own green glow from the instrument panels.

From the belly of the aircraft Dragonović sized up the Englishman. No clues yet as to how good he was, but Dragonović never underestimated anyone, and certainly no one with a man like Raglan's background.

Raglan looked over his shoulder as a shadow cast across him. He knew Dragonović had been watching him; now the Serb turned to move along the men and equipment. Jarnac accompanied him and glanced briefly at Raglan with a bemused smile, because he sensed there could be bad blood between the man he followed and the Englishman. A mission commander and a team leader. Who would prevail when the shit hit the fan? He had no desire to get caught in the middle when that blood came to be spilt.

Raglan watched the solid-boned team leader move away. Dragonović was the toughest-looking bastard he had seen in a long time.

A thoroughbred killer.

11

The black snub-nosed Hercules pushed through the night sky, the four turboprops driving the aircraft at a buffeting speed close to 650 kilometres per hour. In the French-supported, mid-African state of Chad, a mobile communications centre sat in the exposed desert. Camouflaged and protected by three sandbagged machine-gun positions, it was designed to be moved quickly. Inside, the green glow from the tracking screens seeped into the corners of the cramped control centre. A lieutenant, a career legionnaire, chain-smoked and paced. The tattoos needled into his arms years before were now fading, subjugated by age and the weathering effect that desert soldiering has on the skin. He was waiting. His orders: to get from the Legion's base in Chad to this position on the Sudanese border and transmit the arrival of the attack team as they swept low across the horizon flying an evasive course between the mountain valleys. The signal would be transmitted directly back to British GCHQ in Cheltenham, England, and Action Division HQ north of Paris. It was early yet. But they would be in range soon. He smoked, and waited, fingering one of the tattoos and trying to remember in what sweat hole of the world he'd had it done.

South of the mobile unit's position, between Chad, the

Central African Republic and Sudan, is a once-disputed strip of land fought over and won, with French help, from one warlord after another. And this was where the mission was heading. Politics and money chose the strong-arm men of the region. The passage of time produced warlords ever more brutal than their predecessors in this blistering country of concrete-hard desert, towering sand dunes, and swamp, the natural seepage of the Kotto River. The mountainous region is an immense rolling plateau along a crest south-west to north-east. A vast central plain rises 1,330 metres near the border with South Sudan where the river separates the Tondou Massif from the higher Bongos chain to the north. Savanna vegetation covers treeless hills, scorched by hot desert winds. A region practically devoid of people and resources. An unforgiving place where men die and secrets lie buried with them.

'*C'est eux?*' asked the tattooed lieutenant as a blip appeared briefly on the console. Was that them?

'Yes. Now they've gone below the radar,' replied the radar operator.

The officer nodded. That was their job. 'Anything else?'

The operator shook his head.

The officer chain-smoked another cigarette. He knew that Sudanese radar might pick up the skirmishing aircraft before too long. Djibouti and his own unit had tried to block their radar as best they could but the attempt was a calculated risk. He paced behind the operators, their six screens reflecting the aircraft's intermittent blips. It was getting close now, he thought, knowing the aircraft would have to rise above their operational height to clear the low hills. It would be as clear to an enemy as it was to the control centre.

*

The sun probed a laser of light through the crags still shrouded by an early morning blue haze. Into that mountain pass flew the Hercules, skimming below the sunbeam. Engines thundered and reverberated across the mountains. The men had been entombed for hours and as the pilot hauled the aircraft over low peaks and plunged back down to the desert floor again, they cursed and grabbed whatever stanchion was near enough to stop them losing their balance.

One of the men he hadn't been introduced to almost fell into the seat next to Raglan. 'Better to have jumped than this, eh?' he shouted over the aircraft's racket, bending his head close to Raglan's ear defenders so he could be heard.

Raglan nodded. 'You a Brit?' he shouted back.

The man nodded and extended his hand. 'Jordain. I joined the Legion five years ago. Infantry. Rest of this lot are French regular army. Except Dragonović. Same as me. Infantry. But everyone in our lot do their jumps. None of them were with your crew though.'

The man's approach had been friendly enough and Raglan knew he might need someone on his side by the end of the mission. It was worth a few minutes' conversation.

'British Army beforehand?'

Jordain shook his head. 'Marines. I was drunk one night and slugged a major. Didn't fancy going inside so I went AWOL. Wasn't a police matter, so I got in the Legion without much bother. Changed my name to Jordain so the other Brits called me Geordie.'

Raglan realized the ex-legionnaire had a Newcastle accent. The name he had taken made sense.

'I'm with you in your vehicle,' he said. He pointed to one of the men in his designated Land Cruiser who stretched out asleep. 'Me and Rico. He's my mate. Two of us been together for a while. We watch each other's back.'

'Best way,' said Raglan.

Jordain pulled a wallet free and showed Raglan a picture of a woman and three young children. Raglan held it closer in the dim light and saw that Dragonović was watching.

'Nice kids,' said Raglan.

Jordain leant closer and pointed. 'Not mine. I'm not married. This is my mate's wife and kids back home. I carry it with me in case I get nabbed so I can plead that I'm a family man.' He pushed his face closer to Raglan's ear. 'Thought you should know, I overheard that French intelligence bloke telling Dragonović that he wants whatever is in the plane. So watch your back. Yeah, lovely kids.' He smiled and took back the wallet.

Jordain went back to his place. Dragonović showed no sign of interest.

Now Raglan knew there was a chance he might not survive the mission, but whether Jordain would be prepared to help him against his team leader was another question.

Raglan climbed up into the cockpit, pulled on a headset and plugged the jack into the plane's communications system. 'How long?' he asked, bending forward to view what the pilots saw through their narrow cockpit windscreen. The pilot was skimming the desert floor along the breadth of the valley. The co-pilot, a young woman whose slight frame suggested she was little more than a teenager, though Raglan guessed she was early twenties, held up her hand and spread her fingers. Five minutes. Raglan took off the headset and microphone and turned back to where the men watched and waited. He showed the palm of his hand with outspread fingers. He sat down and strapped himself in. The men who had been sleeping in the Land Cruisers turned the ignition keys and checked that everything that was supposed to light up on their dashboards did so with no warning lights. Dragonović's men made last-minute adjustments to their webbing, an extra cinch, a tighter helmet strap and a final assurance that their assault rifles were ready. The loadmaster checked the Land Cruisers' straps. No one knew how hard the aircraft might hit and a 4x4 breaking free would act like a blade in a blending machine.

In the unforgiving wilderness an old man was lifting his water sacks from the well he used to survive, as had his father before him. It was sheltered in the lee of the shadowed mountains. He did not know what lay beyond those mountains, nor how far the valley extended. The needs of his goats defined his territory. He stopped as he heard the distant echoes of a low, rolling thunderstorm. He waited, unmoving, as a man learns to do in the desert in order to conserve energy, gazing towards the distant horizon that was still a deeper blue from the night's darkness. Behind him, and to his left, glowed the first touches of the sun's rays.

Thunder. Louder now. An invisible storm. A dark bird of prey cut towards him from the horizon. He had never seen anything like this. The raptor was closer now. Shimmering. The hovering wingtips clearer. He gazed in uncomprehending wonderment as the hunched silhouette of the Hercules bore down on him at ground level. He threw himself flat, spilling the water from the hessian sacks as the thunder enveloped him. He rolled, his arms covering his head, air shuddering as the aircraft swept past him. Despite his terror he leapt to his feet and watched as the low-flying machine bore away from him, wallowing with power and intent, the black smoke burn-off from the engines corkscrewing behind it.

Inside the aircraft the loadmaster braced himself against the rolling aircraft and listened to the pilot's instructions through his headset. He raised an arm in warning to the men. The secured Land Cruisers would go out as quickly as possible after Dragonović's team formed a protective cordon for the aircraft on the ground. Two of the men clambered into their respective driving seats. The loadmaster nodded as the pilots gave him the two-minute 'ready' into his headphones. He indicated to the men. There was tension now, but they were smiling, some laughing: it was all part bravado, except for their commander – this was one of the few times he was smiling and clearly meant it. Raglan had served with men like that before. They enjoyed it. Dragonović belonged to the same tribe.

The younger man next to Raglan folded back his girly magazine to a page showing a full-frontal nude of a girl lying back on her elbows, her legs spread apart. He showed the picture to Raglan, seeking camaraderie; Raglan looked and smiled at the youngster's enthusiasm. Dragonović shouted from across the aisle as he notched in his webbing: '*Regarde bien – ça sera la dernière fois!*' The young man cupped his hand to his ear. Dragonović's words had been lost under the roar of the engines.

Raglan leant in closer to him and yelled, 'He told you to take a good look – it's the last you might see.'

He smiled in acknowledgement and kissed the girl between her legs then reverently folded the magazine and pushed it into his smock.

Dragonović strapped in. Raglan steadied himself as the aircraft lurched, gaining height as it rose above an escarpment before dropping to begin its landing approach. The pitch of the engines altered. The loadmaster, one hand pressing the headset closer to his ear, gestured for the men that there was one minute to landing.

12

In the no-man's-land mobile tracking unit the Foreign Legion lieutenant flexed the faded dragon on his arm. Its jaws stretched wider. He stubbed out the cigarette.

'Fighter!' cried one of the controllers. 'Sudanese. Their radar must have pinged them. Looks like it came out of Nyala!'

The lieutenant stepped quickly to the console and followed the man's indication on the screen.

'How soon?'

'High and fast – two minutes.'

He shouted commands to various controllers. 'Break radio silence! Alert the plane! Tell them they've got less than a minute and a half!'

Inside the C130 the loadmaster covered his microphone and yelled into Raglan's ear, 'Evasive action!'

The aircraft lurched, climbed and banked, throwing those men not yet strapped in across the space. Raglan realized the mission might be over before it had started but he prayed to God not to let them be caught in the air because there was only one reason the aircraft was now flying an evasive course.

Adrenaline coursed through the men as they gripped the webbed seats, planting their feet to balance against the bucking aircraft. Sweat glistened on their faces. Another engine-howling lurch and Raglan steadied the young soldier next to him. Raglan looked across at Dragonović, who was staring out of one of the small windows. Raglan forced himself against gravity to reach the cockpit. He pulled on the headphones.

'MiG-21!' the co-pilot yelled once she saw Raglan hanging on, as the pilot scanned sky and instruments, searching for the fighter. He didn't want to die no matter how vital the mission. He banked around a rocky outcrop – no mean feat given the weight of the Hercules. Damned if he was going to be caught like this: a sitting target. He glanced at the co-pilot, whose face was as fearful. But it was their job to make sure the aircraft and the mission survived. Evasive action and then bank and turn back for the landing strip.

'Incoming!'

The co-pilot hit the controls to release the infrared counter-measures. How long could that fighter stay in the air? And how damned old were its air-to-air missiles?

Two missiles swerved, struck the flares trailing behind the aircraft, the blast tilting the big beast almost on her nose. The two pilots were shouting information to each other, technical stuff Raglan did not understand. What he did understand was that they needed to be as manoeuvrable as possible.

'Drop the ramp!' Raglan shouted into his mic. The co-pilot turned and looked at him.

'You need to dump the vehicles. Give you less weight.'

There was no argument. Raglan saw the pilot nod his understanding. Hands flicked levers. The ramp began to lower.

Raglan pulled off the headset and staggered back towards the buffeting slipstream and glaringly bright light assaulting the men from the ramp's gaping maw as they held on, knuckles white against the bucking of the plane. Dragonović glared at Raglan. It took only a second for Raglan to point at the two Land Cruisers and cut his palm across his throat. It was a vital decision if they had any chance of survival. The terrain below was a death trap if they crash-landed. Dragonović nodded and steadied himself, ready to help undo the restraints. The two drivers clambered free of the vehicles. The loadmaster held on to his safety strap as he reached for the release mechanism on the first vehicle but fell against the bulkhead as the pilot banked. Raglan slammed hard into a steel rib. Pain shot through his shoulder. He wished they had the chance to parachute, to throw themselves into the light and noise. If he was going to die, he at least wanted a chance against the enemy who was trying to kill him.

A missile wavered two hundred metres ahead of the Hercules, detonating against the craggy outcrops. The pilot threw the plane into a stomach-churning banking manoeuvre, skimming the valley floor, the wingtips dangerously close to the outcrops. Men tumbled again, fell, swore as flesh came in contact with metal.

Years ago Raglan had sat in the cockpit of an old MiG in Mali after a Libyan pilot had crash-landed. A French air force pilot attached to the Legion showed Raglan the myriad of instruments. It wasn't easy shooting down a plane, no matter where it was in the sky. It took skill. The MiG carried air-to-air and air-to-ground missiles, any of which would blow this C130 out of the sky if the pilot had the experience. If they were lucky, this MiG would be so damned old that it would have no modern ordnance. The first missiles fired would have been heat-seeking and the C130's counter-measures had taken care of those. The missile that had just smashed into the rocks ahead was not heat-seeking. It must have been a cockpit-guided missile which meant it relied on the expertise of the pilot trying to hit a moving target.

The explosion rocked the Hercules, throwing it dangerously close to the mountainside. Pilot and co-pilot sweated at the controls; kicking right rudder they banked, the engines roaring at full throttle. They thanked God, through their fear, they were flying a Hercules, a forgiving aircraft that could take whatever was asked of it. The MiG pilot had fired just one further rocket so he might have only his guns left. If the C130 crew kept their aircraft low there was a good chance the MiG's radar would be upset by ground interference. Aircraft and terrain would become indistinguishable to the MiG-21 pilot. Now the C130 cockpit crew did what was counter-intuitive – they slowed the aircraft. Low and slow. That was what they had been trained to do if attacked by a high-performance plane. The MiG would be forced to fly behind them, and would be nose-high and unable to train his gun sights on his target. And if he lowered his sights he would fly into the ground. The manoeuvre took cold courage by the Hercules's pilots.

Raglan hauled the injured loadmaster to his feet. The men edged forward on all fours, grabbed what support they could, began releasing the restraints, then fell back quickly as the first Land Cruiser tumbled, cartwheeling into space.

Raglan clung to the loadmaster's safety strap, eyes scanning the open sky behind them. Where was the damned fighter?

*

The raptor hunting its prey transfixed the radar operators in the mobile communication centre. One of the controllers yelled: 'The MiG's broken off! He's picked us up. Heading this way.'

The old legionnaire leant in across the console. He pushed the operator aside and shouted, 'Everyone out! Now!' And sat down in front of the screen, hands outstretched on the keyboard. 'La mission est sacrée': the Legion's mantra was tattooed on one of his forearms. He still had vital seconds to send a message to Paris and England. He held a cigarette between his lips, his Zippo lighter lying to hand on the console. Keying in words, he glanced at the radar screen showing the approaching MiG bearing down on him. Rapidly his fingers moved across the terminal's keyboard as he watched the words appear on-screen: 'ACKNOWLEDGE – PRIORITY'. Another desperate glance at the radar screen and he saw the missile surging away from the MiG.

'*Merde,*' he muttered to himself and waited for the stupid Brit on the other end of the invisible lifeline to acknowledge the emergency call he was still tapping out. As much information in as cryptic a means as possible. The channel was still not open. He could not send until they gave clearance. *Come on, COME ON!*

The screen laid a message across the top half of his text: 'CLEARANCE VALID – TRANSMIT'.

He hit the send key and faced the radar screen. The blip from the MiG's air-to-ground missile was now on his location. He narrowed his eyes in anticipation, fired the Zippo and, as he lit his final cigarette, said to no one in particular, 'Fuck you too.'

The MiG-21 Mach 2 interceptor screamed away. Old technology compared to the latest interceptors but still plenty of firepower, range and destructive capability; third-world countries like Sudan bought such surplus aircraft from the Chinese. Below the plane the mobile control centre disintegrated.

The Hercules flew down the barrel of a valley and the pilot watched as the rock face loomed towards him. He had a chance if he could stay low and dance between the rock faces, using every evasive tactic he knew. He prayed that when he yanked the control column back and pushed the engines to their maximum effort, he would clear the moonscape ridge of the mountain. And he hoped that on the other side of the ridge lay a desert floor so that the men behind him could get out.

Raglan felt the strain of the aircraft plunging and climbing. The crazy see-saw showed first sky and then jagged rock through the open ramp. He braced his legs to ease the strain from his arm that kept him balanced. The pain in his shoulder pierced deep below the scapula; the muscle was in spasm and the tendons in the top of his arm burnt as the fire crept down into his bicep. He helped the soldier in front of him, closest to the door, hauling him upright. There was blood on the rescued man's face from his fall. They were all soaked in sweat now. He saw Dragonović bellowing at the men to get the restraints loosened on the final Land Cruiser. It fell, tumbling into space. Shattered as it hit the ground. The aircraft lifted as its burden was released. The noise was deafening. The engines howled; the searing light and noise from the outside had men clinging grimly, feet off the floor, the gravity lifting them as the pilots sought sudden height.

The co-pilot clamped her hand over the fist of the man in the seat to her left. Together they pushed the throttle controls full forward. The C130 shuddered with effort. They were too low, too fast and too fucking close! The plane's response was too slow! Sweat ran into the pilot's aching hands.

'Come on... come on...' he muttered. Slowly, the bottle-nosed Hercules lifted itself, painfully, bravely, over the rim of the looming high ground.

Almost clear.

Three hundred feet more. That's all!

Now! NOW! COME ON!

With a bellow from the turbos that echoed the length of the valley, the Hercules defied gravity and kicked dust on the lip of the ridge.

'Yes!' the pilot yelled.

That surge of victory gave them hope and the pilot levelled the aircraft. He snapped on the red standby light for the men hanging on grimly behind him. He was going to put them down. Behind him the red and green lights nestled next to each other above the open ramp's door. The red light glowed. Once the pilot had landed and reverse-thrust the engines, he would switch to the green light for the men to take their chances. That was the best he could do for them.

The men grabbed whatever handhold they could find. Weapons slung, they would go into this hostile environment with only what they had in their webbing pouches. The wide-eyed loadmaster saw the ground rushing up to them. They were at their most vulnerable now. The pilot would have to throttle back soon to land.

The pilot trimmed the aircraft; another kilometre was all he needed and they would be beyond the ravines and jagged rocks that scarred the ground beneath them. *There!* He could see the flat pan of desert. That was the best he could do. They had made it.

'Starboard! The bastard's coming in low!' cried the co-pilot.

The brief flash of sunlight glinting on the horizon was the delta-winged MiG-21, cannons blazing, flying low and level on an intercept course. Now he was at the same height as the C130 his manual gyro sights would frame the laterally moving plane.

The shells smashed into the Hercules, raking one side of the cockpit and punching explosive holes into the fuselage.

It was a slaughterhouse.

Men were blown into bloodied pieces.

The aircraft shuddered as the force of the cannon halted its progress through the air.

Raglan wiped blood from his face, uncertain where he had been hit and realized it was the man next to him. Frothy blood that was once a man's torso lay pooling across the woman from the magazine.

The screams rose above the deafening sound of howling wind and punished engines. Acrid smoke failed to conceal gore splattered across the bulkheads. The ragged holes in the fuselage screamed an eerie howl. Swirling shrapnel had downed the loadmaster but Dragonović was unscathed. Hydraulic pipes were spewing oil. The plane was bleeding to death. Metal screeched. The aircraft spiralled forty degrees, tearing through sharpened rocks.

★

The flight deck was devastated, the co-pilot dead from cannon fire. The wind roared through the shattered windscreen. Two engines were out and the pilot was rapidly losing what was left of any back-up hydraulics. He wrapped his arms around the control column yoke, hugging it to him, using the last few minutes of strength left to him. The altimeter was gone, like the other instruments, but he could see he was almost on the ground. The pilot strained to see anything through the blood that washed into his eyes; every couple of seconds he loosened his grip and wiped them clear but then almost as quickly more blood flowed from the deep cut in his head to obscure his vision. The pain from the wounds ground into his nervous system. He was crying. And it was his tears that kept most of his vision clear. He was crying because he was twenty-eight years old, because he wanted to live and he knew he was going to die in less than a minute. He cried because he was frightened.

Another piece of windscreen broke free and he ducked to avoid the flying shards. The wind smeared the tears and blood away from his eyes and in that moment, through the jagged windscreen, he saw the ground below. The attack had forced them off course and the desert pan now lay far to starboard and he could not turn the aircraft. He saw a narrow strip of desert directly ahead beyond saw-tooth rocks. He clung desperately to the control column, his body shuddering as the plane vibrated, trying to stay in the air.

He held the dying aircraft in his arms.

The desert strip ahead was the best there was. He noticed that the fingers of his left hand had been shot away. He braced his legs and pulled the control column tighter to his chest but the blood was seeping from his body as fast as the hydraulics from the doomed aircraft. It was defeating him and the tons of pressure required to keep the aircraft flying were beyond his efforts. He could hold her no longer.

Smoke billowed from the aircraft, the fire probing backwards towards Raglan and the men clinging to life for the vital few seconds remaining. Dragonović was throwing out abandoned backpacks. Raglan admired him for being cool-headed enough to know they would need whatever equipment they could get their hands on if any of them survived. Raglan bent and hurled a backpack at his feet through the aircraft's gaping wound.

Metal ripped from the low rocks but slowed the plane's momentum, and then it hit hard. The pilot had got them down, yet they were still travelling with sixty- or seventy-kilometres-an-hour forward motion – too fast to survive a jump. The rear ramp acted like an anchor and helped decelerate the stricken aircraft. Raglan held on to a rear stanchion. How many had survived so far? He counted six apart from Dragonović who stood opposite him, knees bent against the bouncing ride. Raglan waited that last nerve-racking moment. The aircraft was still slowing. Forty, thirty. Propeller blades twisted and tore free. The cockpit was an inferno. Fuel spilled from fractured pipes. Flames reached for them.

Raglan leapt.

13

Colonel General Alexei Verskiy had lived in one of the older, less prestigious districts of Moscow for twenty-three years. The apartment had been small but in the beginning, when he had first started in his career, it was considered a privilege: he'd been doing well compared to most junior intelligence officers. That was thanks to his devout Stalinist father, who he suspected wore his KGB uniform to bed. In the whole of Verskiy's life he had never seen him wear anything else. But when Alexei's wife Mila died nine years ago, he began to find the old apartment too dismal. Besides, the traffic had become appalling, like just about everywhere in Moscow these days. Back in Soviet times the streets had been empty by comparison – because only high-ranking officials warranted a car. The time it took him to get to work, even with the official unmarked car's blue light flashing, was profoundly irritating, so he decided to move on. His new apartment had been modernized; it was spacious and light and near the river in the Khamovniki District, close to the prestigious Prechistenka Street. It reflected his status as deputy head of the GRU. And it had the benefit of being close, also, to the Russian Federation's Ministry of Defence where his monthly meetings with superiors were held. Other than those times he was left to carry out his operations as he saw fit.

The ghost of Verskiy's father was raised every day as they drove to his office past Vagan'kovskoye cemetery. His father had taken him there regularly when he was a child and shown him where thousands were buried in mass graves during the Great Purge of the thirties when Stalin slaughtered Bolsheviks and the intelligentsia. His father had taken part in the killings when he was in the NKVD, and had numerous photographs of the executions. When history moved on and the KGB was formed, he had become one of its most honoured officers. There could be no other path for Alexei Verskiy to follow other than to serve his beloved Russia as an intelligence officer, but his father had insisted he join the GRU rather than the KGB. That way the KGB had someone inside military intelligence.

Verskiy's father was a monster, of that his son had no doubt: he'd witnessed the way his mother was treated. His father's perverted obsession with the Motherland meant he relished showing filmed recordings of KGB atrocities, and eventually the horrors became too much for his wife. One evening she asked him not to show another in their apartment. She was left on the floor unconscious, her cheekbone and shoulder broken from a savage beating while her husband demanded his only son watch in her stead, insisting that Alexei understand what should always happen to those who betrayed the Soviet Union (a term he insisted using even after it crumbled). No one was to be trusted, his father always asserted. Verskiy often replayed in his mind a scene from one particular film: the death of Major Piotr Popov. Popov had been a GRU officer arrested for passing information to the CIA in the 1950s. No clean execution by firing squad:

instead, KGB and GRU officers had gathered in a boiler room to witness the major being thrown alive into a furnace. Just as often, Verskiy's thoughts harked back to the blackest moment of his childhood: the death of his beloved mother from one beating too many.

Verskiy's father bemoaned the loss of the KGB when the then President Yeltsin disbanded it and created the Federal Security Service. Despite the FSB under Putin's directorship re-engaging many KGB officers, Verskiy's father insisted that what Yeltsin had done meant the end of Communist Russia. The KGB had reported solely to the Communist Party, but the FSB was totally under Vladimir Putin's control. Communism was finished. Despite the old agent's despair at the direction the Motherland was taking, his son enjoyed a steady climb to power. As he rose in rank, he gained and wielded ever greater influence. No one ever doubted Verskiy's loyalty or ruthlessness. He knew a great many secrets and that power protected him. Fear was the key to his success.

This morning, ensconced in the back of his official Mercedes E-Class, Alexei Verskiy unlocked his briefcase. He took out the information he'd received from his agents in London and reflected on the chain of events that had triggered the operation in London and ended in a retired MI6 officer's death. A gifted engineer's photographs shown to his Russian colleagues, some of whom were keen to make money by passing on information to their employer: an oligarch whose mining company had been granted favours by the Kremlin. That oligarch had secrets of his own which needed erasing and had approached Verskiy with the information, knowing that Alexei had enough influence to help him. Over the years Verskiy had given him one simple edict: wherever his business took him in the world, whatever looked unusual, out of place, did not fit, no matter how seemingly unimportant – take that information to Verskiy. The veteran GRU man knew intelligence-gathering could depend on such trivial matters. There had been no doubt in Verskiy's mind that the past had resurfaced just as the half-buried aircraft had emerged from the sand. There appeared to have been no communication alerts coming out of London, so was it possible they did not know about the photographs and the information showing the likely location of the downed aircraft? Verskiy had wasted no time in despatching agents to Africa. A small team that would not arouse suspicion from anyone in Britain, or for that matter, Moscow.

As his driver left Vagan'kovskoye cemetery behind them and pointed the Merc towards the glass-fronted five-storey building at Number 3 Grizodubovoy Street, the GRU headquarters, Verskiy smiled. Despite the freezing weather, there was a warmth within him, less from the prospect of another day in military intelligence, more from the memory of the last time he had accompanied his father to the burial ground, many years ago, where his ageing parent had relived the slaughter of the past and Alexei Verskiy had shot him dead.

14

Verskiy sat at his uncluttered desk reading the desert report once more. Always the professional, he knew how eyes and mind could skip a word, miss an inflection in the writing, a subtle change of tone that could take the reader in a different direction. His phone rang. He pressed the receiver to his ear. Half a minute later he hung up and ordered his car. Instinct told him his confidence that only he knew about the buried aircraft had been misplaced.

He travelled out of the city. Snow had fallen and the city's bleakness yielded to an equally Spartan landscape. As the driver headed north-west towards Volokolamsk, hills rose to greet them and Verskiy's boyhood memories of the Georgia steppes flitted through his mind. The green, rolling hills and the thatched villages. On a day like this, windless and cold, he thought, the smoke from the chimneys would barely rise. A shout could carry across a valley as if it were no distance at all. And the geese would honk their way across the torn sky, tatters of blue causing disharmony on the surface of unbroken cloud. Surely there used to be far more laughter from the children in those days? Quickly he dismissed the thoughts. Nostalgia was not a word in his dictionary.

The driver swung through the tall gates of the complex

and stopped next to the sentry post. The guard peered into the back of the car and hesitated for a moment before recognizing Verskiy. He recovered quickly and snapped out a hand for the general's identification. Verskiy handed it over. He never played games involving his ego. It was clearly understood that if ever Verskiy were to come past your sentry position without being challenged, the far corners of the Russian–Chinese border beckoned as your next posting. The sentry was careful not to be too cursory in his examination of Verskiy's identification. Be suspicious of every living soul: that had been part of his indoctrination and he abided by it.

Verskiy left the window down as the car moved further along the two miles of twisting single-track roadway. The trees gave some cover to the blind-domed complex, but it was the iceberg principle that was its real strength. Beneath the ground lay the massive technological resources known only to a few in the West. The snow fluttered through the window, but Verskiy didn't feel it. He was watching the patrolling guards and their dogs on the killing strip, with its anti-personnel mines and the standing operational order to shoot to kill anyone within two hundred metres of the outside wall and wire. One hundred metres below the surface was the protected concrete labyrinth of the Volokolamsk ELINT (Electronic Intelligence) Centre. The driver guided the car down into the yellow-lit subterranean cavern where guards again vetted visitors.

Like the Master of Darkness he was, Verskiy descended to join his disciples.

★

When a man is perceived as being fearless he creates fear in lesser men. As Alexei Verskiy strode down the corridor of the underground ELINT centre, anyone stepping into the connecting corridor moved quickly aside. He was accompanied by a younger man, a junior officer, a SIGINT (Signals Intelligence) captain, who ushered him into a dimly lit communications room. Men and women sat bathed in their consoles' glow. The main area of the room was dominated by a tracking and plotting screen on which the captain indicated two markers.

'Here and... here, general,' he said, more nervously than he wished.

Verskiy looked at the hieroglyphics suspended on the screen. Without expression he turned on his heel and left the room. The officer hesitated, uncertain whether to go with him. Discretion had already been abandoned; now was the time for courage. He followed.

A few moments later he stood in a simply furnished but comfortable room with a colonel and the GRU general as Verskiy accepted a glass of tea from an orderly. The underground complex was a small city, able to function for months without recourse to the outside world. The kitchen fare was splendid, a perk to compensate for the long hours without daylight, the ventilation and heating systems efficient, based on plans borrowed in the 'old days' from the Americans. Verskiy faced a large wall screen, synchronized to that of the main room. When the orderly closed the door behind him as he left the room, Verskiy spoke.

'This is highly irregular.' He turned to the men, wanting to watch their faces. He addressed the young captain. 'You were the duty officer?'

The colonel cut in. 'General, I—'

Verskiy killed the sentence with a look and returned his gaze to the younger man.

'Yes, sir.'

Verskiy sipped the tea. 'Why did you consider it important enough to contact me?' He watched the men's eyes. There it was. The fear. But different in both men. One seemed to feel threatened; the other was taking a chance.

The junior officer hesitated. He had no rational explanation. What had he got himself into? 'Just something about it, sir. A feeling. I apologize, general.'

The colonel stepped forward, and Verskiy nodded, allowing the coward to speak. 'I ordered the captain to file the signal in the usual manner, general. He exceeded his orders.'

Verskiy paused, and then quietly agreed. 'Yes, he did.' He redirected his gaze to the now stricken captain while still talking to the senior officer. 'Colonel Shevenko, I would like to deal with this matter... would you leave us?'

The man stiffened, uncertain, but then nodded and left the room. Verskiy waited. Always claim the advantage was one of his doctrines; and if you already have it then you can take even more time. Finally he spoke; sweat was now beading the young man's forehead. 'All right, what do you make of it?'

There was no hesitation now. 'The French were flying an evasive tactical course,' said the junior officer.

'It could have been an exercise against insurgents in Chad,' responded Verskiy.

'Yes, sir.' Meek obedience.

'But you thought not.' Gently now, drawing out the ambition.

'No, sir.'

'Why not?'

The captain stepped to the wall screen monitor. 'Sir, this aircraft, a C130J Super Hercules—'

'How do you know this?' Verskiy interrupted.

'Its infrared heat signature, sir.'

'Very well.' Verskiy sipped his tea. He could see the young man growing more confident. 'They use such aircraft for their legionnaire paratroopers.'

'Yes, sir. Well, if it had been Foreign Legion paratroopers who are fighting in Chad and Mali as you suggested then they would have taken off from their base in Calvi, in Corsica.'

'I know where Calvi is,' said Verskiy.

The man nodded, moving swiftly on. 'They filed a flight plan to Djibouti to refuel and then onwards to N'Djamena in Chad. The manifest listed medical and food supplies for refugee camps.' He turned his eyes away from the arced route showing the proposed path of the aircraft to explain. 'We monitor all movements of French forces going into Chad and listen in to their control centres.'

Verskiy sighed and placed the cup and saucer down. The captain saw his frustration. 'Apologies, general, I thought it better to explain my reasoning.'

Verskiy pulled out a chair and sat, crossing his legs. 'I'm a patient man, captain. Take your time. But this had better start making some sense.' He lit a cigarette despite the strict non-smoking rules within the complex.

'So, logistic and transport bases for the French air force are...' The captain pressed buttons on the remote, which brought up a larger-scale map of France. '... here, at Criel, north of Paris, but they're jet transports, and for C130 aircraft from here at Vélizy, thirteen kilometres south-west of Paris. This aircraft took off from Istres-Le Tubé Air Base all the way down here north of Marseille. Istres, general, is part of the French Space Force as well as special ammunition storage for France's mid-range nuclear missiles for their strategic Mirage 2000 squadron based there. There's also a helicopter squadron, and repair hangars. Occasionally it is used for the American air force refuelling stratotankers. It's unusual for a C130 supply transport to fly from this airfield.'

'So?' said Verskiy. There was still nothing proved. Perhaps the boy was nothing more than a chancer. Wanting to make himself known to the hierarchy.

The captain changed the screen again. 'They descended on their flight path to Djibouti, and we did not pick them up again...'

'For God's sake! They landed, what more is there to say?'

The captain's calmness surprised even himself. 'They did not land, sir. They did not refuel. They have long-range tanks. The aircraft went below radar when they flew south into Sudanese airspace. We picked up a French mobile tracking unit right here, on the border between Chad and Sudan – in fact, sir, they were over the border by a kilometre. They were operating in Sudanese territory. That same aircraft had to gain some height, then it dropped down again. And again rose, briefly, seconds only, here and here.'

Verskiy was already at least one step ahead. The projected curved route south-west from Djibouti put the aircraft directly on course towards the coordinates that Verskiy's men had recovered in London. Was it possible that the French knew about the buried aircraft? How they might know didn't matter. The question was: were others chasing the same prize? He nodded for the captain to continue.

'It was enough for us to see it. And I believe so did the Sudanese air force. They sent up a MiG-21 to intercept.'

A flutter beat in Verskiy's chest. 'They shot it down?'

'The aircraft was under the radar, sir. Impossible to be certain.' With lips dry and his tongue sticking to the roof of his mouth, the young officer struggled against the mounting fear that none of this might mean anything to the man who could wreak havoc on his career.

'An old MiG-21 has only forty-five minutes in the air. The French transport pilot made no distress call. I thought that unusual. If Sudan scrambled a fighter plane from its base in Nyala, it wouldn't be for a sightseeing trip.' He paused because his final hunch was about to be played. 'And then the mobile French communications ground unit was destroyed. They must have seen the attack coming in but they stayed at their post. They sent an encrypted message directly to London – to the Cheltenham communication intelligence headquarters. That same message was also transmitted simultaneously to French Intelligence Action Division HQ north of Paris.'

'If, and it would seem to be a big if, that aircraft was shot down, was there any intercepted radio contact that indicated any survivors?' Verskiy said.

'No, sir.'

Now he's given it all, Verskiy thought. There's nothing else. But he's right. Why would the French be communicating with the British? 'It is possible that the Sudanese fighter was scrambled to strike against rebel ground forces in the south. 'There's an ongoing conflict in Sudan. You do know that, captain?'

'I do, sir.'

'And you went over your senior officer's head because of this guesswork?' Verskiy's voice had an edge to it.

'I... thought it unusual.'

'So you keep saying. For God's sake, communications traffic often goes between French and other western forces.'

'But, sir, the French mobile tracking station operator must have known an attack was being directed against him. It would have been like looking down the barrel of a gun... and yet he stayed at his post and sent his coded message.' The captain emphasized his words with a pleading gesture. 'That made me think this was an essential mission...'

He's right, thought Verskiy again. The boy is right.

'... and that his message was crucial,' the captain continued. And then, receiving no response from Verskiy, he faltered. 'As I said, a feeling, sir. I apologize again, sir.'

Verskiy turned away, as if bored. Why in hell would a man sit and sacrifice himself and his men like that? A gutsy bastard who knew his message was vital. *Vital.*

'Nothing else, captain?'

The young officer shook his head.

'How did you know I attend to matters such as this? Why did you not contact the head of the Signals Intelligence Directorate, or those responsible for Africa? Why the GRU and not Foreign Intelligence?'

The captain stared as bravely as he could at the most powerful man in military intelligence. 'I knew you were once head of the Fourth Directorate that covered Africa and the Middle East, and I thought you to be the more appropriate person to contact because I believe you have the ultimate authority.'

Verskiy dumped his cigarette into the remains of the tea. 'To do what?'

'Whatever is necessary to protect our country. I overheard Colonel Tamarkin one day, he was handing over to Colonel Schevenko and they were talking about past events, and he said you had given the order to shoot down the Malaysian civilian aircraft over the Ukraine back in 2014 when we first went in.'

'You understand, captain, that even senior officers may not be privileged to that information?'

The captain nodded and averted his eyes. He needed Verskiy to acknowledge his course of action was correct. He had already circumvented procedure by ignoring his senior officer. My God, if the old GRU bastard walked from the room without giving him the nod, he was sunk. He'd be thrown to the wolves. But he had no desire to stay a lowly paid captain. He believed a brighter future beckoned for daring and free-thinking young men like himself. He waited.

'Who else knows about the signal sent to the British and French?' asked Verskiy.

'Only the colonel, sir.' He did his best not to let the surge of hope he felt reflect in his answer.

Verskiy moved to the telephone and dialled. He never took his eyes from the captain. 'So, you want to climb, do you, boy? Want to cling to that slippery pole of ambition. And to do that you betray your immediate superiors.' He saw the captain's eyes flare. Aspiration mingled with anxiety. Or downright fear.

Verskiy spoke into the handset. 'I want Colonels Tamarkin and Schevenko arrested immediately.' He watched with satisfaction as trepidation registered on the captain's face. 'What was your name?' he asked.

The effect was instantaneous. The voice that answered had lost any hint of bravado. The confidence shattered. Verskiy controlled him now. 'Lipetsk, general, Captain Lipetsk.' He barely managed his own name.

Verskiy pondered without moving his gaze. And then finished speaking into the receiver. 'You will liaise with Major Lipetsk.'

He replaced the handset and for the first time blessed the boy with a conspiratorial smile. 'Well, you have stepped into the lion's cage now. Be prepared to be damned scared for your life from here on. It starts now. Success in this matter is essential. You will report everything directly to me. Understand, major?'

The sweat down Lipetsk's back chilled, and he could only nod in agreement, relief mingled with dread of what lay behind the door his actions had opened.

Verskiy retrieved his hat. 'When did this event take place?'

'One hour and forty-three minutes before I phoned you, sir. Djibouti and Moscow share the same time zone.'

Verskiy nodded. 'The message that was sent from the mobile communications unit – I want the code broken. Do not disappoint me.'

15

Gasping for air after the impact, Raglan raised his face from the dirt to watch the approaching strafing run of the MiG.

'Too bloody bare-arsed this place. Come on, boss!' said Jordain as he spotted a more effective shoulder of rocks to lie behind. Raglan was on his feet and running as he heard the first short burst of cannon fire. Adrenaline overcame fear and any pain from the impact of their jump. Rocks exploded as the cannon shells raked their position and the howling roar of the MiG scalded their senses as it completed its run. The survivors belly-hugged the dirt wherever they were, scattered over a hundred metres. Raglan heard Dragonović shout from somewhere behind him.

'Stay down! No one move!' And the men remained motionless. They waited. The MiG must be low on fuel now.

Raglan understood the command. The MiG pilot might see only the stationary soldiers and presume no one had survived the crash or his strafing run.

The men surreptitiously scanned the sky. Raglan knew the MiG would have barely four or five seconds of cannon fire available but all it would take was one short burst of what ammunition he had left to tear them apart. The sun burnt down and as he lay watching a dead soldier's eyes, he realized just how much of a miracle it was that anyone had survived the attack on the aircraft. The MiG banked, silhouetting the delta wings.

Jordain was crouched next to Raglan. 'Here comes the evil bastard again – hold on to your balls, boss, this bugger'll try and separate you from them.'

The terrifying firestorm overtook them again. Cannon fire tore across the ground around them. Boulders shattered. The men remained unmoving in the lee of rocks. They waited for another pass but the pilot had turned for home, either out of fuel or ammunition. Jordain pressed his back against the rock face and rubbed his palm across his head and face. He had a gash on his leg. It wasn't deep. 'All right then?' He grinned.

Considering the recent carnage the man's casual comment seemed ludicrous and before Raglan could respond the man was already second-guessing his team leader.

'Uh-uh, there's the boss on his feet.' He pushed past Raglan and limped to where Dragonović stood. Those who had jumped clear of the doomed aircraft were scattered around him; the charred remains of the aircraft lay four hundred metres away. Raglan counted six men as well as the Serbian and himself. Five dead. One man raised himself painfully and held his arm as though it was broken. Raglan saw the black soldier, Malik Bayo, covered in dust, a cut on his head, dry blood encrusted with dirt, standing next to Dragonović.

'Weapons and packs. We kicked them out. Find them,' Raglan told the men. He pointed to Dragonović's right-hand man, Jarnac. 'Check the injured. Get that man's arm sorted.'

Jarnac looked to the Serbian who nodded. It was the right call.

Dragonović pointed to a couple of men and they tracked

their way back as Jarnac fashioned a support for the man's broken arm. Jordain took a field dressing from his webbing and covered the gash on his leg. Their weapons were the last thing that went out of the door with them. They were the first to be found and checked. This was hostile territory. The black pall of smoke from the downed Hercules might attract the wrong kind of search party.

Within the hour the men had put together whatever they could find. Two packs had split, but one was fairly intact from the impact. No others were discovered. Dragonović showed Raglan the readout on the GPS. It gave them their location. At least one bit of useful kit had survived. Raglan studied his map as Dragonović had the men share out the food and ammunition. There was not much but added to what they carried in their personal webbing it would have to be enough. A satcom radio had survived, although it was probably useless without its antenna, which lay in pieces somewhere.

'We always carried spares,' said Raglan. 'A radio is useless without its antenna.'

'You think we're stupid?' said the soldier Raglan had challenged. He pointed to the burnt-out aircraft. 'There's a full pack of everything we need in there.'

Nothing would have survived the twisted, scorched hulk. Raglan scoured the ground, found a piece of torn metal the size of a dinner plate. He rammed his heel into it. It gave slightly. He tossed it to the soldier. 'Try and rig up a parabolic reflector aerial. It's worth a try.' Miracles were always on any soldier's equipment list. The French telecoms satellite might still pick them up.

★

Jarnac took Dragonović aside. Another survivor had been found thirty metres away in the rocks. The impact from jumping had shattered his lower spine and broken his legs. The men were uneasy – the rules for this kind of operation were simple: no badly wounded could be carried. Nor could they be left to die a protracted death at the hands of marauding tribesmen or wild animals.

Dragonović took out his 9-mm pistol and stalked over to where the man lay. Jordain called after him, 'That's my mate, Rico.'

Dragonović turned. 'We can't take him with us, you know that.'

'Yeah, but... shit, boss, that's... a crap way to die out here. He's one of us. There must be a better way.'

Raglan watched the Serb move towards Rico. His distaste was not only for the ruthless efficiency of this man at that moment but for Maguire and the whole stinking, murderous business of what went on in Africa.

Raglan blocked his way. He tried to dismiss his emotions. He ought to leave it. Get the job done first. But the feeling in his belly overrode the warnings from his mind as he faced the Serb. Dragonović waited a moment, and then spoke.

'Whatever is out here, Raglan, it's so important that the Secret Intelligence Service and the French DGSE are crapping themselves. If it's that big it means we are all expendable. And my orders are to keep you alive. But you get in my way or stop me from doing what I have to do and I'll put a bullet in your head without a second thought. Then it's mission over and we find our way home.'

Raglan remained in his way. Dragonović was right. He and his men could scrub the mission and walk out of the desert.

No one would know what had happened to him. Killed in action. Problem solved. Except Raglan's presence meant that what they sought could be worth a lot to Dragonović's masters and the Serb would reap the benefit of the success.

'I'll deal with it,' said Raglan, dipping his head towards the badly injured Rico.

Dragonović looked surprised.

'Not your way,' Raglan told him.

He called to Jordain. 'Geordie?'

The soldier knew he was being invited to be in at the death of his friend. He nodded and joined Raglan while, behind them, Jarnac bullied the men. 'All right, check what we have, be ready to move. Picot,' he said to one man, 'you'll take point.'

As they approached the stricken soldier, Raglan asked Jordain the one question few were ready to answer.

'If you had a choice, would you want to know you're going to die? One of your own pointing a gun at your head?'

Jordain shook his head. 'Best to give me a bit of hope and then put one in me when I'm not looking.' He glanced over to his friend. 'Yeah, that's what I'd want. Him as well.'

'Me too,' said Raglan.

Raglan and Jordain went to the injured man, who was lying behind some boulders. His lower body looked twisted; bones protruded from his legs.

'Rico, we'll help you.'

The man managed to turn his head. 'Back's gone. Can't feel a thing, Geordie.' He raised his head and looked at his shattered limbs. 'Can't even feel that. I'm fucked, Jesus, I'm fucked.' Tears welled in his eyes. Jordain gripped his friend's hand.

'Give him water,' said Raglan as he took out a small medical pack from his webbing pouch. Jordain eased his friend's head forward and dribbled water from his bottle into his lips.

'Shit place to die,' said Rico.

'Everywhere's a shit place to die,' said his friend. 'It's what we signed up for, remember?'

Raglan held a lozenge-sized tablet in his fingers. 'You know what this is?'

The injured man nodded. 'Fentanyl, yeah?'

'Yes,' said Raglan. 'I'm going to check out those legs, see if we can splint them. So you take that just in case.'

'You think my back's not broken, Raglan?'

'Let's take a look, shall we?'

Rico nodded. 'All right, then. Yeah. All right.' He stared wide-eyed at Jordain, who knew as well as Raglan that his friend's back was broken and he would feel nothing in his legs.

Raglan put one lozenge into the injured man's mouth, and then slipped in another. They would suppress his breathing, easing anxiety and fear.

Rico lay back; he nodded. 'Thanks,' he said to Raglan. A tear trickled down Rico's dirt-encrusted cheek.

Jordain clasped Rico's hand. 'I'm here, my friend. I'm here.' He watched as Raglan held his razor-sharp combat knife close to the injured man's leg.

'Christ, don't cut my balls off, Raglan.'

'Just your trouser leg.'

Rico grinned at Jordain. 'Bad enough having my legs and back gone – don't want to lose them as well.'

'Shit, Rico, they've never been any use to you. All the women you shagged told me that.'

'Uh-huh. Your sister didn't complain.'

'Don't have one.'

'If you had she wouldn't have complained.'

'Probably not.'

'Odds are she'd be as ugly as you. That could put a man off.'

Jordain kept the banter going, holding his friend's hand, keeping him face to face. What Rico couldn't see was the slow almost surgical incision Raglan made in his groin, cutting the femoral artery. He would bleed out and slip into death quietly.

'I'm going to see if we can get some kind of stretcher for you,' said Raglan. He stood, gave a nod to the dying man and walked away, leaving Jordain to stay for the final minutes of his friend's life.

When Jordain eventually walked back, Raglan addressed the men. 'Strip his webbing, share what he had. Bury him. Cover him with stones then rocks. Jackals will have him otherwise.'

'He's dead meat,' said Dragonović. 'Better the wild things eat him.'

'Hey! That's my friend. We bury him,' said Jordain.

'This is bandit country,' said Raglan. 'You want parts of him dragged around? The less seen the better. Let anyone who finds the aircraft think it was a transport on a supply flight. It means nothing. But finding a man in uniform will have them looking harder for us.'

Dragonović considered Raglan's reasoning. 'All right. Do it.'

The men turned away, and the Serb continued. 'This is my team, Raglan.'

'This is my mission,' said Raglan. 'You do as I tell you.'

16

There was no shade.

No thorn bush or rock outcrop tall enough to block out the searing heat. The direct rays were bad enough but the heat reflected off the ground as well, burning skin already toughened and weathered by hardship. The survivors moved past the Hercules's twisted burning frame. Even if there had been no pall of smoke the remains of the pilot and the bodies of their friends would not have been visible. The funeral pyre had consumed them.

They marched for three hours; Picot, a wiry Frenchman who had taken point position, was guided by Raglan working off dead-reckoning compass fixes, the elevation of the sun and instinct. After the Hercules pilot had thrown them over the sky with his evasive tactics, they were way off course. Raglan orientated his map to the distant mountains. It seemed likely that where the mountains contoured down into the valleys, there would be water. The escarpment ahead rose two hundred metres and it was this raised area Raglan headed for. Climbing to the summit would give him a better idea of what lay ahead.

Dragonović called a halt. He watched as the men sipped their meagre water ration. That was going to be the biggest problem. In these conditions a man could lose more than four litres of water a day. They would do everything they could to ease the danger – no smoking allowed; the men would breathe through their noses, helping to keep the dry air directly out of their throats; and there'd be no unnecessary conversation. But the exertion would take its toll. They posted sentries while they rested, alert but already tired from the energy-sapping violence they had endured. Men helped each other dress wounds sustained in the Hercules as the Serb watched Raglan study the map. This Englishman, why the hell was he so important anyway? They could have found what was needed without him. How many operations had Dragonović been on that had gone sour? Enough. But he had always done what was asked of him. And he always got his men home. Those that could make it. Still, over the years he had left too many behind. And he was the one who had to make the tough decisions. Not the Englishman. Him.

'Anything?' Dragonović asked the man with the satcom handset who had managed to fashion a small parabolic aerial from the piece of metal Raglan had given him.

The man shook his head.

Dragonović shrugged. 'Well, if it was easy it'd be no fun, eh?'

The Serb approached Raglan and waited for him to look up from the map. He wanted the Englishman to squint into the sun. To be at a disadvantage. Raglan ignored him.

One man called out to his commander. 'Where we goin' then?'

Dragonović smiled down at Raglan and poked the map with his gun's barrel. 'Well?'

Raglan swilled water around his mouth, spat some into

his hand and rubbed the moisture into his neck. He retied his sweat rag, the water cool beneath the cloth. He folded the map and tucked it away beneath his sweat-soaked cotton shirt. He gestured to the wasteland with his assault rifle. 'I think the GPS is out. I'm looking at that mountain range and it doesn't add up.'

Dragonović grunted, squinting into the heat haze. 'Wouldn't be the first time. Crap atmospherics. So? Where to?'

Raglan gestured. 'Out there – fifty Ks.'

Fifty kilometres in that arid anvil after what they had been through? Silence. The men waiting. It was so hot it seemed they could hear the earth crack.

'I've got six survivors in my team. We've already paid a high price, Raglan.'

'It's that kind of job. We're lucky we have what we have.'

Dragonović hunkered down next to him. 'What is it? What's so damned important out here?'

Raglan looked directly at him. 'You just follow the orders you were given.'

'Western intelligence need whatever it is pretty badly, eh?'

Raglan moved away from him but Dragonović hooked his arm and the grip sent a raw nerve pain cutting into his shoulder from when he was slammed into the fuselage during the aircraft's rollercoaster ride. He hid his reaction by twisting his body free but Dragonović was insistent. Quietly now, coaxing the answer. 'What is it we're looking for?'

Raglan hesitated. No matter how many missions Dragonović had done for French intelligence, he knew men like the Serb had their eye on the prize for their own self-interest. If Dragonović discovered what they were seeking and where it was located Raglan knew he'd be dead within moments. But he also realized that these men needed more than blind orders to follow, especially after the bloodbath they had endured.

The men were watching them. He could give a hint, enough to keep Dragonović interested. In the last moments, when both men knew the target, then the matter between them could be finalized. Dragonović squinted in the glare; Raglan had moved carefully so that it was Dragonović who now faced the sun. The Serb pulled the peak of his forage cap lower. 'Come on. Give. What is it?'

'A dead man – with a living secret.'

Dragonović looked at the men. He had no doubts about them but their morale was a direct reflection of his leadership and he needed to ensure they stayed positive no matter how bad their situation. He smiled. 'So we're looking for a corpse.' He waved an arm. 'Not too difficult out here. Bound to be plenty lying around. So now you know. And don't ask what secret,' he said, pausing momentarily. 'Remember our briefing: our orders are to keep the Englishman alive.'

As he turned away, he muttered under his breath, 'For the time being.'

They set off again into the shimmering curtain of heat.

Beyond the mountains harsher terrain awaited. Windswept sands more arduous than the arid broken land where the men now walked doggedly onwards. There the desert started as if from a designated plan. The Great Architect of the Universe had said that was where the line of sand would start. And it did. The desolate powdered waves changed with the wind that continually reshaped the desert. The Mustang was almost free from the weight of the concave sand dune facing the horizon. The desert breeze gave momentum to a snake zigzagging its way downwards to the sandblasted wreck. The snake detected another heat form at the base of the sand slide, perhaps a place of shelter away from the sky shadows that struck so unerringly, bringing rapid, painful death to this inhospitable place. One such shadow hovered now. The brown harrier eagle had used the mountain thermals to reach the area, and occasionally took a snake or lizard, manipulating the writhing body through its talons to seize and sever the head. The snake slithered across the moving sand and found sanctuary in the dark heat offered by the pilot's seat. The breeze had eroded the edge of the sand mountain and now only one wing remained buried. Even the sand from the cockpit had been lifted and brushed back across unseeing eyes. The breeze touched the skeletal claw that still held the control column, and a broken, bony finger tapped out an unrecognizable and unheard Morse code.

Still manacled to his wrist, the pilot's secret waited to be discovered.

17

Maguire was frustrated. At MI6 he had access to many official and unofficial resources but the satellite he needed to locate the downed aircraft and men had a pre-set orbit with a list of pre-qualified targets. The officials who gave the go-ahead for each request to pinpoint an area were a bureaucracy within a bureaucracy. Like a grocery list, the desired objects were picked up, ticked off and placed in the basket in strict rotational order. Maguire wanted his requirements on the list so he could identify the wrecked Hercules and locate any survivors. The high-resolution images were transmitted electronically in real time. So right now, if he wanted to, he would be able to see a vulture on the ground scratch itself. The biggest problem was that the UK Skynet satellites were an open source for the Five Eyes intelligence agencies in the West, and in this instance, secrecy was, for MI6, imperative. Whichever intelligence division he chose, be it Far East or Africa, a national intelligence overseer controlled each analyst from those divisions. A request for overflight information had to be cleared by that officer. Maguire, like any good intelligence man, had favours owed and was certain he could pull them in, but the stumbling block came at the next stage up the hierarchal ladder. The reconnaissance committee was composed of representatives from various intelligence agencies. These were the people who gave the go-ahead for the satellite reconnaissance shopping list. Even if he took the chance of drawing attention to the shoot-down, it would be several orbits later before the satellite could comply with the ground request. And that took too much time. All of which left the French.

Maguire had already been in touch with Claude Delmar. Delmar would do what he could to use the French low-orbit satellite to locate the crash site and any survivors.

'What about the locator beacon on the Hercules?'

'Turned off. We didn't want any aircraft identification available. A ground radar unit knew their route.'

'These aircraft are equipped with a GPS that automatically kicks in if they crash.'

'There's nothing. It must have been destroyed. And we are not picking up any personal locator signals from the vehicles or the men. I'm told there's high sunspot activity. It's regional. Central Africa is affected.'

Maguire had experienced the same thing when on special operations. Irregular magnetic fields from sunspots impact the Earth's ionosphere, causing GPS equipment to compute an incorrect position. Or distort the signal so badly it is completely lost. It can take minutes or days to clear. 'Then we're blind. And that might explain why the Hercules flew into Sudanese airspace too soon. They were off course.'

'Does France have electronic surveillance aircraft in the region?'

'Nothing. Ground radar was our best hope of tracking them.'

Delmar reaffirmed what Maguire knew already: they

would have to find another means of reaching the target if they heard nothing from Raglan or Dragonović within the next few hours. Maguire hung up, suppressing the anxiety that began to gnaw at him. Once that rat of uncertainty got into your brain it would devour all hope. The situation was now critically unstable. A buried secret that, if discovered by the enemy, could blow the lid off British intelligence. And a personally chosen asset, Dan Raglan, who might already be dead. And if he wasn't, he might be injured and fall victim to the unforgiving land or die at the hands of a ruthless combat leader who had no reason to bring an injured Raglan home. It had all gone pear-shaped. Very quickly.

Maguire scribbled on a pad as he cradled the receiver in his shoulder. Over and over again he doodled the word 'TIME'. There was not enough of it and no one could spare any. But it was important not to panic. If there was to be a Plan B, it was preferable that it come from the British side of the operation. MI6 was answerable to the Foreign Office, and to reach them, Maguire had first sought an urgent meeting with 'C', the SIS Chief, Michael Welland. The situation was serious enough for the two of them to then approach the minister responsible, the Secretary of State for Foreign and Commonwealth Affairs. The JIC, the Joint Intelligence Committee who tasked all MI6 operations, had given their tacit approval for Maguire to send in a SAS team from where they were stationed in Kenya – provided, that is, the Secretary of State and the PM agreed. The Prime Minister had already expressed his reservations prior to leaving for an American conference that morning. He would withhold his decision until the Foreign Secretary had been approached. No one wanted the covert incursion to escalate into an international incident. And no one wanted to flag the operation to other foreign intelligence agencies, be they friendly or otherwise.

Margaret Stoneham's authority was hard-earned. The Foreign Secretary was a former high-powered lawyer who had entered politics a decade earlier, and over the years had cut a swathe through her contemporaries. Pragmatic and impersonal, she showed favour to no one. But she had a feral instinct for political survival. Intelligence services could be wrong. National security was paramount and it was stating the obvious that losing their source in Russia would seriously damage UK intelligence, but the evidence supposedly lying buried in the desert that might identify that source, whose name even she did not know, was slim. She did not invite the two men to sit.

'The French are panicking,' she said, letting a communique slip through her fingers on to her desk. 'Their Minister of the Armed Forces confirms that a covert aircraft has been shot down over Sudan. The Sudanese government has accused them of arming insurgents in West Darfur. And now you want permission to send in our own special forces? Do I look as though I want to be boxed into a corner and lie my way out of it – because that's what will happen if the press get wind of this.'

'Foreign Secretary, I briefed you previously on the operation and its importance to us. There are no British personnel on that aircraft. We were obliged to turn to the French because you would not sanction a covert operation of our own, even knowing how vital the information is that we are attempting to secure,' said Welland.

'And the facts bear out my decision. Even the PM has exercised caution.'

'The PM did so prior to his visit to America, Foreign Secretary. Matters have since worsened. No matter how cautious we are we cannot risk this latest development leaking by speaking directly with him. As Secretary of State and Deputy Prime Minister we need your approval for us to do what we can to get this operation back on track.'

'Don't think you can shift the blame on to me for your own lack of competence. There is an Englishman involved. Yes?' She looked sharply at Maguire. 'If that's not British personnel then what is?'

'He's a former legionnaire. He is resident in France. He helped us before when Jeremy Carter was abducted and murdered.'

'Maguire, I don't deal in murder. It's not my concern. Avoiding a diplomatic incident is.'

He curtailed his impatience. 'Foreign Secretary, you know the Russians are in Africa in their thousands. Libya, Somalia, Central Africa, the Sudan: they are establishing military bases everywhere. They are running rings around us! We have to move quickly now to get our own people to where that information can be retrieved in case the Russians alert their men on the ground.'

Stoneham fingered the documents on her desk. 'The Russians in Africa are not legitimate forces; they are Russian mercenaries, that's a well-known fact.'

Maguire saw they were losing the minister's interest. 'The Wagner Group is backed by the Kremlin. Mercenaries who are so well organized they have formed international companies that receive mining concessions for gold and diamonds because they keep despots in power. They are vicious and highly trained and effective. America has put sanctions on the companies they control. You know all this. We don't know if there were any survivors in that plane crash because we have no feedback from the location finder beacon. GPS is degraded in that area so we must assume the worst and get our people on the ground. We have a SAS unit training Kenya's armed forces in northern Kenya; we have an army logistic training company in Uganda. Between them I can have a unit in south-west Sudan in hours. The Defence Secretary has agreed. He believes, as do we, that the Kremlin's proxy army must not be given a clear run at this.'

'MI6's story of evidence buried in the desert is already incredible. A wild goose chase, men already dead, a major political row brewing. It's not feasible,' Stoneham said.

Welland pressed home their case. 'Foreign Secretary, you must appreciate that for years intelligence coming out of Russia has been invaluable.'

'And you must appreciate that if we send special forces into such a volatile area and they are killed or captured, then we will have an almighty mess to explain.' It was a rebuke. She took a breath and adopted a more conciliatory tone. 'Have there been any Russian intercepts picked up to show they knew about the C130 crash or its possible destination?'

'Not that we are aware of.'

'Then surely you can see that if we send in our own people, the Russians might learn of it. That alone could raise alarm bells and tell them we are panicking. That the information is genuinely vital.'

'Which it is,' stressed Maguire, unable to restrain his impatience at the minister's lack of ambition.

'Might I remind you,' said Welland, 'that a retired MI6 officer gave his life to get the information to us? That he bought us time by doing so? He altered the location of where the information lies hidden to throw the GRU off, but it's only a matter of time before the Russians begin a wider search.'

'If Russian military intelligence sent a team into the area—'

'Which they surely will have done,' Welland interrupted. 'From the start. As soon as they got their hands on the doctored information, it would have raised an alarm bell for any of those who had served in Africa all those years ago. The old guard is still entrenched. They have long memories. If you had agreed from the beginning to make this a British mission, we would not be having this conversation.'

'I will not be lectured!'

'Then you should bloody well listen, Foreign Secretary!' Welland's irritation spilled over. 'We are on the back foot here. We risk losing the best double agent this country has ever had. And all because you are afraid of making a mistake in judgement. This is the time to make that judgement now.' Welland's frankness would no doubt earn him a reprimand from the Prime Minister and most likely cost him his knighthood on retirement.

Margaret Stoneham looked furious but bottled her anger. For a moment it seemed the two men had convinced her. Boxed her into a corner. But it was a fleeting hope. She sat behind her desk, palms flat on its inlaid top, and faced them. 'The Russians are poor at keeping their signal intelligence quiet. We would know if they were running around like scalded cats. The operation will stand as put together by the British and the French. Secrecy is the key word. No British ground troops are to be involved. If the French team are dead or captured, then there is no association between the UK and the mission. That there is an Englishman involved means nothing. If captured and interrogated, he would respond as a French-speaking former legionnaire.' She sighed, content that she had quelled what to her was a risky and unnecessary operation in pursuit of rumour.

Maguire knew they had lost the argument. The old military adage, that a non-nuclear war will eventually be won by one soldier and his rifle being in the right place at the right time, still held good. Raglan would have to be that man.

Big Ben towered behind Maguire and Welland as they turned south on their way back to Vauxhall Cross. The half-hour walk from the Foreign and Commonwealth Office through the gardens and then along the Thames to Vauxhall Bridge and SIS HQ gave each man time to think through their best line of defence against an obstructive government cabinet minister, a woman who was prepared to risk nigh on thirty years of vital intelligence coming out of the Kremlin.

'She won't be Foreign Secretary for long – not after the next cabinet reshuffle. Damned if I know why the PM chose her in the first place,' said Welland. 'I suspect it's because she gave him a close run in the leadership contest. Keep your enemies close and all that.'

'Be too late for us all by then,' said Maguire. 'We have to sort this mess out. I can speak to some of my old friends. "L" Detachment could get out there.'

Welland shook his head. 'We can't. The moment we involve anyone associated with special forces, even their reservists, and it goes pear-shaped, we simply worsen the problem. We have assets of our own, of course, but sending anyone else out there, after Raglan and the French have gone missing, is pitting our people against unknown forces.'

'I'd like to get Raglan out if I can,' said Maguire.

Welland nodded. 'Of course, but we have a more pressing issue. We need an exfiltration operation in place to get our source out of Moscow.'

'That's a consideration we've had for some time,' Maguire told him, 'but it needs people on the ground there. We have no direct contact with him. He uses his own conduit to get information to us. And since this mission fell into the hands of the GRU, there's been increased surveillance on the embassy. Our people are being more closely watched than usual.'

Maguire ignored the chill breeze from the Thames. Welland tugged his coat's collar.

'Still, we need a firm plan now. Whatever we thought we could do before now needs to be reassessed. Get on to it.'

'There's one added problem,' Maguire said. 'A while ago, when there was the reshuffle in the Russian intelligence services, we offered to get him out then. He gave us a determined *nyet*. It's his homeland. He'll die there. If we want to exfil him and save his skin, we'll have to kidnap him to do it.'

'Well, even that's better than what might happen if he's exposed. They could be feeding us false intelligence for years and we wouldn't know it. We have Russian oligarchs here with no love for their President's mob: shall we turn to them? See who can find a way if we do that?'

'Too risky,' said Maguire.

Welland nodded. Of course it was.

Street lights came on as they crossed Vauxhall Bridge. The Thames was as busy as ever with sightseeing craft.

Pedestrians and traffic flowed across the bridge. Time to go home for many: a day's work done. But not for everyone on this side of the Thames. The beating heart of the nation did not lie upriver where politicians formulated policy; it lay in the MI6 edifice buttressing the river where men and women dedicated themselves to keeping the nation safe – at times in defiance of the politicians' best efforts to avoid risk and save their own careers for the history books. The silent war often went on without them knowing of the subterfuge demanded by the very nature of the Secret Intelligence Service. And that was why so few were privy to the identity of the Russian informer. He was of such incalculable value to MI6 that ECI, the Exceptionally Controlled Information blanket orders, kept his anonymity intact.

Maguire turned his face to the north wind whose bite was a constant reminder of where it came from. Given the three-hour time difference it would be dark in Moscow. Probably snowing and far colder than London. By far.

A double agent's life was on the line. And ruthless men would seek him out.

'If your asset is still alive, then right now that's all we can hope for,' said Welland. 'Meanwhile, firm up a plan to get our man out of Moscow. That one we keep to ourselves. And don't tell the ambassador. He'll bleat. Our Moscow station chief must put something together. Airtight, should we need it. Bugger the Foreign Secretary.'

18

Alexei Verskiy had served in Angola back in the old days, earning his spurs by supplying the communist MPLA guerrilla movement with weapons and military expertise. He and five others, men from the KGB, worried men who hurried home when the Soviet Union fell and the Russian Federation was born. Men who had to prove themselves in the eyes of their new masters. Verskiy was one of the safest because military intelligence was the only agency to survive untouched by the reforms. Even so, in a time of such turmoil, men like him looked over their shoulder. Back then there had been a rumour that one of them was speaking to the British. The rumour died when they left the rigour and heat of Africa and returned to Russia to find their place in the new regime. Now, Verskiy told himself, the rumour had been resurrected. One of them might have gone over to the other side after all. The tantalizing story of an old aircraft being used to get out vital information, a story long disbelieved, might be reality.

Verskiy put two lumps of sugar in the glass of black tea on his desk. Where were the men from those days? He had never met them when he was in Africa, but he knew for certain there had been five others spread from Angola to Kenya, causing chaos by arming and financing insurgents to help bring down

Western-backed governments. Verskiy sipped the sweet tea. He would wait for the agents he had sent into Sudan to report, but in the meantime he would try and identify those men who had once served in Africa and then narrow down the possibility of a double agent. But how? Their names would be buried in the archives of the FSB Internal Security Directorate. And they were held in the place once renowned for terror inflicted behind its walls.

Lubyanka.

A few blocks from the Kremlin, a short stroll up Teatral'nyy Proyezd past the Ferrari and other high-end car showrooms, is a six-storey Gothic-style building in Dzerzhinsky Square. It is neither of architectural interest nor truly Gothic in style – only in nightmarish reputation. The unyielding stone facade has narrow arched windows cut into the thick walls. They permit little light into the fortress-like chambers. The doors, heavy with grief, have closed on thousands of victims.

Once home to the KGB headquarters and its notorious prison, it had been where the torture and execution of dissidents, suspects, innocent and guilty took place. The usual method of death, often a thankful release from unimaginable horrors, was a heavy-calibre pistol shot at the nape of the neck. Salted or disinfected water was sluiced across the floors every couple of hours. Walls were mopped, leaving tell-tale smears and an irremovable odour of blood and excrement. The cheap alcohol the interrogators and executioners drugged themselves with added further nausea-inducing fumes to sicken the newly arrived victim.

Today the building, with additional storeys built on, shows

little of what happened in the Death House. The torture chambers and underground cells which saw unspeakable atrocities now serve as offices, a cafeteria and, once, when the new Russian Federation feebly attempted to be more transparent, a KGB museum. Yet the drab government-issue green paint and the old-style metal furniture did little to erase the spectre of fear. It was soon closed. Repainted and refurbished, the offices in Lubyanka now serve the day-to-day machinery of the Russian intelligence service, the FSB.

Verskiy made his way inside. A great deal had been inherited from the old secret police infrastructure – agents, names, places, missions – and also what Verskiy needed: archives held from the sixties when the Soviet Union had strengthened its influence in Africa under Yuri Andropov's cold and calculating leadership of the KGB. A master of deceit and subterfuge, he had inflicted terrorism on the world, ordered Jews to be hounded and dissidents destroyed. His firm hand was also felt almost immediately by long-serving officers of high rank who were there by way of the Russian bureaucratic system's 'jobs for the boys'. He rid the service of such privileged leeches and encouraged promotion based on potential, ability and results. One such officer was Vladimir Putin, who served in East Berlin and, after the fall of the Soviet Union, headed the newly formed FSB before becoming prime minister and then president. Now, the FSB control the government, the media, swathes of the economy and the military and security forces.

Alexei Verskiy might have been stationed in Africa when the Soviet Union collapsed, but even from afar, the trick had been to see where the future power lay and to back the right horse. His position now gave him access to the Kremlin security council, a means of playing off one directorate against another. His credentials were impeccable. A devoted KGB officer for a father and a string of successes across the world within his own GRU. He was favoured by the President, who valued the military intelligence machine because they could do the dirty work the FSB preferred not to and could be 'smoke stacked' if they ever embarrassed him by failing. Verskiy stepped into the building. 'Smoke stacked' meant being disappeared. It referred to the burning alive of the traitor Popov.

The office he sought was in the basement along the corridor from the cafeteria. The room was cramped, tables laden with files. Paper files still dominated Russia's bureaucracy as they were still being slowly digitized. He knocked on the door out of feigned politeness. Six people – four women and two men – looked up from their desks.

'Andrei,' Verskiy said genially to the harrowed-looking man whose desk was in the far corner, a clear position of authority.

Andrei Golyev's look of bafflement quickly gave way to a tight-lipped smile. 'General Verskiy. This is an honour and a surprise,' he responded formally in front of the junior personnel.

'Of course it is. How often does anyone visit the basement unless they want a coffee and *medovik*?' He laughed, making a joke of the truth. 'I was in the building and thought I should say hello to my old friend. Besides, the honey cake here is some of the best in the city so I followed my nose.' He smiled again. 'And thought of you.'

It was a cruel jest. Golyev had been demoted years before, having fallen foul of powerful men in the FSB. Golyev would know this was more than a casual visit.

'Anyway, I hope you and your family are well. Your son is doing an excellent job, by the way. I won't keep you – I can see you are all extremely busy.' Verskiy closed the door and headed back out into the snow-cleared pavements. Golyev knew where he would be. A ten-minute walk would reward him with the *medovik* in a favoured coffee shop that made the one in the Lubyanka taste like cardboard and shaving foam. In half an hour Golyev would arrive.

Poor old Golyev. He had once had authority and power but the existence of someone with such responsibility in the FSB can often be measured in months. Existence not as a career term but in life expectancy if they stepped on the wrong toes. Golyev had been lucky. Yet he was not a born survivor. He was too intelligent. Insufficiently feral. Not like Verskiy, the longest-serving and -surviving deputy head of the GRU, who had caused more trouble for the world than any of his predecessors. Rumour and legend about his power and influence had turned into fact. It seemed he could ask for anything and get it. Unlike the other intelligence services, the GRU did not report directly to the President. Verskiy was responsible to the Minister of Defence and the Chief of the General Staff. Not exactly arm's length from the President and the FSB, more of a hand's width, but it gave him space to manoeuvre. What he could not do was get into the old KGB files that might help him discover whether that rumour from another time was true. His pulse quickened. If it *was*, then he would unmask a traitor and reap his rewards.

By the time he had sipped his second cup of coffee and was halfway through the honey cake, Golyev found his booth. He slid on to the green leather bench seat.

'You must try this, Andrei. It's delicious.'

'I don't have long,' said Golyev, casting a wary look over his shoulder. The coffee shop was a favourite with Muscovites and tourists alike. Verskiy had pre-ordered Golyev's cappuccino. He signalled to the waitress.

'Safety in numbers, Andrei. Relax. They're tourists.' He swallowed a mouthful. 'You have become more nervous these past years.'

'Can you blame me? If someone sees me talking to you, I'll have some explaining to do.'

'Now, now, Andrei. You are still a serving FSB officer, not with the rank you once had, I grant you, but you are still sufficiently senior to be believed that you came across here and bumped into me. They know your son is one of us at GRU. What could be more natural than you asking me how he's doing?'

'I haven't heard from Yuri for months. Is he all right?'

'Yes. I sent him to London on a job. He pulled it off admirably.'

'Good, good. Is he still there? Does he still work with Galina?'

'You know I can't tell you that.'

'Of course. Stupid of me. Thank you, Alexei.' The coffee arrived. He sipped it nervously.

'You see, Andrei, it's asking the wrong questions that got you into trouble. The mistake you made was you thought that the President really wanted you to do your job when he put you in charge of the Internal Security Directorate. I know it was an independent body for five years but you investigated senior FSB officials on the take – and *had them arrested*. Friends of *his*. My God, what were you thinking? You were the best, I grant you that. When you went after someone you

brought them down.' Verskiy wiped his lips with his cloth
napkin and sipped the cappuccino. 'And that is why I come to
you asking for your help because you were – no, you still are
our best investigator.' Verskiy's tone altered. Crisp, concise.
'Six KGB officers in Africa. Mid-eighties into '91. I need to
know who they were.' He gazed at Golyev. 'And of course I
shall see to it that your son receives a benefit in kind. He's a
good agent. One of my best. Get me what I want and I shall
promote him.'

'KGB days?' said Golyev. 'Alexei, it will take time.'

'Which is something I do not have a great deal of.'

Golyev nodded. 'Leave it with me.' He slid out of the booth.

Verskiy dabbed his mouth and smiled. 'One more thing,
Andrei.'

'Yes?'

'You have chocolate on your mouth.'

19

The man had watched them for an hour.

The soldiers came through the heat haze like holy men from the wilderness. The dust had risen and covered them. Their eyes, irritated by heat and dirt, watered, streaking the caked mask on their faces. The watcher could not understand who they were or why they were on foot with no equipment. Were they French? He had fought Frenchmen before, but they were always well armed; their vehicles made them fast, mobile and fearless. He thought about the local warlord Faraj Hamad's indiscriminate torture and killing: did he now have an alliance with the French? Were these the vicious dogs of a sadistic master? But why so few of them in this wilderness?

He waited, unmoving despite the flies around his eyes. Movement was the way to die in the wilderness. At least the loose-fitting Arab-style dress afforded some protection from the heat.

He lowered the binoculars; they were close enough now for him to watch with his own eyes. The desert soldiers stopped to rest. He pulled the cowl further around his face. He had been careful to make sure the lens of the binoculars did not reflect the sun by wrapping a piece of cotton camouflage netting around them. He had learnt that when he fought the French. He had seen enough. He moved back slowly, never taking his eyes from the invaders and keeping a firm grip on his Kalashnikov assault rifle.

It was hard going. Although Dragonović's men needed to conserve energy they would not reach their objective if they moved at a snail's pace. The Serb led and they followed. Three hours since the last stop and now they were at the foot of the escarpment. He called a halt. He noticed the Englishman hadn't faltered.

Raglan stabbed a finger at the map. 'Al-Kadique's the nearest settlement, I reckon.'

'Do you know that place?' said Dragonović.

Raglan shook his head.

'If he's still around, there's a warlord, Faraj Hamad, who had a place somewhere near there. The French government helped him years ago. His base is built like an old legion fort with adobe walls and reeds. He thinks he's some kind of prince of the desert. It's next to a lake. The only good thing about it is that it's cooler there.' Dragonović did not hide his distaste for the warlord.

'He's still pro-French, do you think?'

'These bastards change their mind every day. He's not to be trusted, I know that. He plays one side against the other. Six years ago we helped him boot out the Janjaweed militia. Then he made an alliance with local Al-Qaeda fighters to control a bigger area and France gave the thumbs down. The last thing they wanted was to support anyone associated with a terrorist group. Rather than risk the terrorists turning against him he invited the local commander for dinner and slaughtered him and thirty of his men. He became more powerful. And when he burnt out their villagers' reed huts with the women and kids inside, Paris gave a definite *non!* No, Raglan, he's definitely not pro-French.'

'We need supplies and vehicles.'

Dragonović squatted on his haunches. 'Not from him. I don't want to get cornered there.' He scratched a crude map in the sand. 'If Hamad's between us and the objective we should skirt his stronghold. There's a plateau runs up to a thousand metres, here. We climb it. Then the nearest tribe are the Masalit. They're busy killing Arab nomads.' He shrugged. 'Choose your poison. They might supply us. What about your people and ours? We haven't checked in; they'll know we're in trouble. Do you think they'll send people in for us?'

'Not unless we can make contact. We might be on our own for a while.'

Dragonović was about to drag out the exact location they sought when a gunshot felled one of the men and all hell broke loose.

They were caught unprepared and off guard. The volley of gunfire that followed was from semi-automatic and automatic weapons. That knowledge penetrated the men's consciousness as they saw Dragonović moving to one flank of the escarpment and the Englishman to the other. It was obvious he knew what to do and Jordain peeled off to join him. Jarnac commanded two men to lay down covering fire as Raglan and Dragonović attacked on opposite flanks. Adrenaline banished exhaustion.

Dragonović skirmished with two men, while Raglan and Jordain moved rapidly across the broken ground. The enemy firing was wild, undisciplined and mostly badly aimed. That did not stop another man being killed before the first rocky protection could be gained.

Jarnac and the two men with him chased after Dragonović when Raglan threw a smoke grenade and gave the men cover. They fell on to the enemy's position. Some turned and ran, terrified at the unexpected response to their ambush. Raglan and the survivors were quickly among the rest. Close-quarter killing.

Jordain took refuge behind a rocky outcrop to get a better firing position. He did not see the tribesman aiming his AK-47 in his blind spot. Raglan slowed and fired. The man tumbled. Then Raglan pursued those who had broken from the contact. Lungs burning, he crested the rise to find two tribesmen turning towards him. He fired a quick burst. The rounds shattered rock face but caught one of the gunmen. A third loomed up from cover and aimed directly at him. Raglan was moving fast, his vision blurred, but a voice was yelling in his brain that he stood no chance against the two men's crossfire. The cowled figure rose higher to take a clearer aim but was punched backwards as Jordain, who had followed Raglan, shot him.

Raglan ran hard, trying to get a clear shot at the surviving gunman, who turned and ran for one of two abandoned pickup trucks in the dry wadi below. Raglan wanted to stop, to gulp air; his injured arm pulled his back muscles into a knife-cut of pain. The others stormed through the gunmen's position. Eight bodies lay in the sand at the ambush site, three more where Raglan had gone in pursuit. It was likely a patrol of six men in each of the two vehicles. Raglan's quarry was the last tribesman. His foot caught a low rock; he stumbled, fell, rolled, felt the searing pain in his back and lungs as his fall winded him. Ignoring the pain he clambered to his feet again but saw the man had escaped in a trail of dust.

They buried their dead comrades and left the other corpses for the raptors. They stripped the bodies of their weapons and ammunition. There was no telling how much firepower they might need before reaching their objective. Cold hessian sacks of water slung on the pickup's bonnet revived them. They did a weapons check, dressed what cuts and wounds they had and clambered on to the remaining pickup.

Jordain grinned. 'Not too many of those bastards around, I hope, boss.'

'I wouldn't bet on it,' said Raglan.

Jordain shielded his eyes and looked across the landscape. 'Just hope they haven't got any women with them. They're harder than the men – they'll cut your balls off before breakfast. Especially white men's balls.'

'I'll do my best to keep a tan going,' said Raglan.

Dragonović took the wheel with Raglan next to him. The surviving tribesman would obviously head for his base. Once there another force would be assembled to come after them. Their only course of action was to drive as hard and fast as they could away from the enemy. Whoever they were. They were in an internecine war zone. The men looked done for. One man next to Jordain couldn't stop his body trembling. There was nothing anyone could do. He had to fight that one on his own.

Raglan had spent years in the wasteland in his legion days. It offered sculptured beauty and a timeless silence. It was also a lousy place to die.

20

Dragonović did not ease off the accelerator until they were twenty kilometres from the ambush site. The sun was lower, almost setting, and the orange light softened the harsh, shrub-covered terrain.

They rounded a bend in the track and their way was blocked by a long-wheelbase 4x4 with a heavy-calibre machine gun straddling its load bed, the long barrel aimed directly at them. Dragonović braked sharply as two more camouflaged 4x4s burst through the undergrowth and well-armed militia levelled their weapons at the pickup. The Serb stalled the engine. In the silence they heard the water gurgling through the engine block.

After a moment of no one doing or saying anything, Jordain spoke quietly. 'Well, I could always be a eunuch in a bloody harem.'

They had no choice but to follow the order given by the militants' leader to follow his lead vehicle, their own boxed in by the other two behind them. The convoy moved through the African night. The time between daylight and darkness was brief, the twilight barely existent. They drove through a reed-and-mud-hut village, swollen with refugees who had constructed lean-tos of corrugated iron sheets nailed together for shelter. Animal skins hung stretched across drying frames; bleached animal skulls caught the moonlight. Torches burnt, casting shadows into the urine-soaked alleyways. Here and there a figure could be discerned in the shadows, cautiously staying back from the attention of the armed militia.

Raglan glanced at Dragonović. On the plus side, they were still alive; on the negative, they were angling away from the direction they needed.

'Faraj Hamad's people, you reckon?' said Jordain from the back.

'Could be,' said Dragonović. 'Not Janjaweed. If they were, we'd be dead.'

'That's a Utyos gun. Russian-made,' said Jordain, pointing at the malevolent-looking weapon aimed at them. 'I didn't think the Russians were in this neck of the woods.'

'You can buy them online from Libya. Once Gaddafi was killed, it was a buyer's market. Did you see the assault rifles they were carrying? American. The US equipped the African Union UN peacekeeping forces in Somalia, who sold them on to Al-Shabab. Arm the so-called good guys, then fight the bad guys with the weapons you gave the good guys in the first place. The Pentagon procurement budget is as healthy as ever,' said Raglan.

The vehicles kicked up dust on the winding road until an hour later they reached a lake; reflected moonlight shimmered on its surface. A boathouse nestled into the bank. The horizon was darker on one side of the water. It was the walls of a compound.

'That's one of Hamad's bases that I told you about,' said Dragonović.

Arc lamps hummed with power as they surged on. Four of them, each one at a strategic corner of the compound, now illuminating Dragonović's unarmed men. High metal gates strung with razor wire opened, letting the vehicles into what could have been a parade square. They climbed down from the 4x4 and waited. Militia patrolled the wooden ramparts and they, along with the men on the ground, casually levelled their weapons at Raglan and the others. Raglan took the place in. A side yard had several pickup trucks parked with machine-gun mountings in place. That meant there were probably forty men in the place.

'I bet he didn't bring us all the way here to shoot us on his front doorstep,' said Jordain. 'Very messy. Take a while to clean up afterwards.'

Faraj Hamad's summer base was, as Dragonović had described, built like an old Foreign Legion fort, with clay-covered wattle-and-timber walls. Cool breezes from the lake eased the suffocating heat. There was the fragrant scent of neem trees close to the lake's bank. Raglan looked up to a double-storey building from where a balcony jutted beyond the regular catwalk. A black, round-faced man appeared; he wore a strikingly white cotton kaftan-like garment. Another man accompanied him. Open-necked white shirt and slacks. Taller, fitter and harder. Faraj was powerful and wealthy and the easy living showed.

'Man in the white shirt is Hamad's right-hand man,' said Dragonović. 'If Hamad says stop the world I want to get off, White Shirt is the one who puts the brake on. Look the wrong way at these people and he'll have your head.' Dragonović called up to the man looking down at them. 'Faraj Hamad, sir, we've stumbled into your territory. No offence was meant.'

Hamad stayed where he was, surveying the sweat-stained, bloodied men. 'You look in need of rest. We are always pleased to offer hospitality to our French friends. I welcome you.' He offered a benign, slow-moving gesture.

Like a sluggish snake, thought Raglan, still to be treated with caution.

Faraj Hamad watched as his men unloaded the AK-47s taken from the ambush site. 'You have cleared out a nest of Janjaweed vipers who are our enemy. We are grateful. Avail yourself of our humble surroundings. There is food. We will speak to you in the morning.'

Hamad turned back; his henchman gestured to the men in the courtyard. Their weapons raised waist-high, the men stepped forward, indicating their captives should drop their webbing, which was scooped up and taken to a room across the yard. Now that the men were disarmed Raglan hoped Maguire's phone, which he'd hidden in one of the pouches, would not be discovered. The soldiers ushered Raglan and the men towards one of the buildings. Raglan saw the radio antenna above a room on the far side of the courtyard. Dragonović nodded. 'Basic comms, but that's all we need.'

The disarmed men were billeted in a barrack room. Straw mattress cots would serve their purpose and like all soldiers Raglan and the others could sleep wherever and whenever the opportunity presented itself. They sat elbow to elbow at a long wooden table finishing the hot food that Hamad's men had provided. Goat stew with plateloads of the corn porridge common in Africa. They ate with their hands, soaking the meat of the stew into the malleable *putu*. The men ate their fill in a continent where food is a privilege.

Jarnac plucked a bone from the liquid on his plate. 'You have to watch old Faraj Hamad, I've heard he's partial to a bit of cannibalism once in a while,' he said through a mouthful of food.

Raglan swilled the food down with the water provided. 'Then whoever it was must have tasted good enough to eat.'

Jarnac laughed, and the men grinned their approval.

Dragonović sat opposite Raglan, and his voice was meant only for him. 'Hamad could turn at any time. I've no idea why his men didn't kill us on the road.'

'Maybe he's getting lonely out here in the middle of nowhere,' said Raglan.

Dragonović grunted. 'Neurotic as hell. We won't get our weapons back until we leave, or he lets us go – there is a difference.'

'We need to get into that radio room.'

Dragonović shrugged, wiped his hand and tapped a cigarette free from the cellophane packet. 'You'd need his personal authority, and you won't get that until tomorrow.'

'That shows our hand. I need to make contact tonight.'

'You get caught and we'll get hurt,' said Jarnac. 'It's a spit away from the guardhouse.'

'You've been here before?' said Raglan.

Dragonović glanced at Jarnac, who turned away after a look that said they had. 'Once,' replied Dragonović. 'I told you we uprooted the Janjaweed for him. And what Hamad did to anyone we captured alive was bad juju. I never wanted to come back in case we were on the wrong side. Like now.'

He swung his legs over the bench and walked towards the door.

Raglan followed as Dragonović checked outside. The Serb tugged a packet of cigarettes out, broke off the filter tip and put the other end between his lips. Raglan was at his shoulder.

'We've got a babysitter,' said Dragonović, nodding towards a lone soldier perched on the edge of the boardwalk fifteen metres away. The soldier suddenly looked up when he saw them and brought his rifle to waist-height. Dragonović gestured with his cigarette. 'We smoke. OK?'

The soldier nodded; then he looked left and right, and made a gesture for Dragonović to give him a cigarette. The Serb stepped forward and tossed the packet to him, then pointed to the bench outside the billet. 'OK?' he asked.

The guard nodded and went back to his post. Dragonović settled down on one end of the bench.

Raglan sat. 'I saw them put our weapons and kit in that room over there,' he said. 'Time comes we'll have to get across the open space.' He glanced up. 'They'll have us in a crossfire.'

Dragonović ignored him. 'Why you? Here. On this job. What's the connection? Because you were in the Legion?'

Raglan didn't answer.

Dragonović exhaled a plume of smoke. And rubbed a hand across his face. 'We get the shit end of the latrine-cleaning stick and no thanks for it. But we do it because it's our job. You volunteered. Or you're being paid.'

Perhaps, Raglan thought, there was a chance of mellowing the man's antagonism towards him if they shared some common ground. A man's reason for joining a fighting unit usually gave an insight into his motivation and character. 'I still have strong connections to the Legion, and I've worked for French intelligence. The Brits needed someone on the mission. They came to me.' He shrugged. 'Work is hard to come by these days.' It was an easy lie to draw out the Serb.

'You get a bonus for finding whatever we're looking for?'

Raglan shook his head. 'Better than being at home.' He waited and let the man at the other end of the bench smoke his cigarette. Then he said, 'Why are you here? The Legion and then Action Service? Like you said, you get the shit end of the stick. You ever have a life before any of this or were you as screwed up as the rest of us?'

Dragonović remained silent, his eyes following a sentry's walk across the wall's parapet. 'I was born in Yugoslavia. Which is what it was back then. The Albanians ran everything. They were anti anything Yugoslav. My family were poor. One day my father came home and said he couldn't get any credit at the store which the Albanians ran. We were starving. He was a proud man. All Serbs are. But he begged. They laughed and threw him out of their shop. He went back that night and broke in, but they caught him and beat him to death. I was five years old. Then they came to the house and really taught my family a lesson. I was hiding in the cellar. My mother, my sister, they suffered.'

Dragonović reflected on the memory. Then, without showing any pain, slowly pressed the glowing tip of his cigarette between finger and thumb. 'The Albanians chased us out of the village.' He shrugged. 'When I was old enough I joined the militia. And after a couple of years I found the bastards who had hurt my family. The Albanian shopkeepers had moved to Pristina. After what I did to them I had no problem finding work.'

Dragonović got to his feet. 'Get some sleep. It won't

seem unreasonable to ask Hamad for the radio tomorrow.'
Dragonović's suggestion sounded like a direct order from a
team commander to one of his men.

Raglan stood and looked across to where the radio room
was situated. He needed to press home his own authority.
'No, we do it before first light. That's our best bet. A quiet
night ahead with no trouble from us lowers their guard. It's
my mission.'

The soldiers slept, boots and sweat-soaked shirts crumpled
by their beds. The stench of their previous twenty-four hours
mingled with that particular smell that Africa exudes. It comes
from the ground and the breeze carries it: a smell of age from
where man first walked upright and realized his power over
the lesser creatures. It is a smell that never changes. There
were fighting men cynical enough to say that Africa simply
smells of death.

Raglan slept, having mentally recorded he wanted to be
awake by 3 a.m. He slept deeply, confident that his in-built
alarm would, as always, rouse him. He woke later than
expected. It was three fifteen. The men's deep breathing and
snores announced their deathbed-like exhaustion. For a
moment he lay still, before quietly swinging his legs free. He
tapped out his boots checking for scorpions and then, rolling
his foot on to the side of the boot, moved to the door: an
old trick from working in dense undergrowth that allowed
minimum contact with the ground when closing silently on
an enemy.

He checked for signs of wakefulness from the men but saw
none. Easing through the door, opening it only a few inches,

he confirmed that the outside guard was also sound asleep and then quietly pulled the door shut.

Dragonović, feigning sleep, watched him go.

21

Built to protect from the mud in the rainy season, the boardwalk hugged the sides of the buildings, while above, a split-pole, rush-matted pergola gave protection from the glaring sun. Raglan moved cautiously, using moon shadows. He had already taken a mental photograph of his surroundings when standing beneath the arc lamps at Hamad's reception. Security was plentiful but most of Hamad's men were sleeping. The sentry who guarded the barracks was six metres away at the end of the reed-roofed walkway, his chair tilted back, head on his chest. Sleeping on guard duty was a serious offence in anyone's army; here under Hamad's cruel regime it would surely be fatal. The sentry cradled a French-supplied F1 rifle in his lap: a weapon that in the right hands was effective and deadly at either close or long range. It was wasted on most of Hamad's men. The sleeping man's weapon could slip and clatter to the ground at any moment. Raglan reached for it, trying to take the weight in his hand. There was virtually no light in this corner.

A guard commander moved around the corner and gazed out across the complex. Those few seconds allowed Raglan to grasp a beam above him and, ignoring his shoulder's protest, swing up into the reed-matted roof. The commander turned and in a few steps kicked the sleeping soldier, hard, sending him sprawling. The soldier cowered from the threats and returned to his foot patrol.

The guard commander lingered. Had he looked upwards and to the right when he struck a match to light his cigarette, Raglan would have been caught cold. The pungent smell wafted upwards. The man's boredom saved Raglan's life. He strolled away and after a cautious few seconds Raglan dropped, ignoring the deep stab of pain from his shoulder. There was no time for it; fear was a more crippling force to contend with, far more than an injured arm if he gave in to it for even a moment.

The radio room, like the rest of the fortress, was basic and unsophisticated. A forty-foot antenna loomed into the night sky and the soft drone of a transistor radio helped the duty operator while away the hours. Wireless traffic was likely to be scarce and odds were that Hamad would use a satellite phone to run his personal fiefdom and there was little chance of getting access to that. Satellite phones were illegal in Sudan but Hamad was a politically connected warlord: the question was whether he would risk using a satellite phone when he was on the move between his bases. If the West decided it was time to track him, they could use that to find him.

Raglan sought the darkness, the impenetrable areas where a man could stand and not be seen. There was still some distance to go and he did not have the luxury of time. He had swung almost 180 degrees following the flow of the buildings. An old-fashioned but functional water trough and pump were across and to his left. A dash over there and he would be within five metres of the radio room. The guardhouse was only fifty metres further on, tucked into the same line of buildings as the radio room. The risk now was being caught in the open.

He looked around. The moonlit silhouette of a sentry on each rampart showed they were looking beyond the walls. He walked brazenly across the open space. Slow, nerve-racking strides were the least likely to catch anyone's peripheral vision. Once across the yard he stepped back into the shadows. He peered through the radio room's window but the operator was not at his station; all he could see was a cigarette butt burning in a tin-lid ashtray and a sports magazine folded back at the page the operator had been reading. There was movement and sound through the beaded curtain where there was obviously another room. Raglan stepped through the open door and went silently to the curtain where he saw a soldier making coffee. An old primus stove was wedged among spare parts for the transmitter and a small open window above a work bench allowed any cooking and brewing smells to escape.

The man suddenly glanced nervously over his shoulder directly at Raglan, who froze. The beaded curtain and broken shadows obscured him. The man had not been alerted by Raglan's presence; it must have been guilt that made him unconsciously check behind him. The radio operator reached into the shell of an old transmitter, cannibalized for parts, and hauled out a bottle of liquor; he poured a liberal quantity into a mug, took a belt directly from the neck of the bottle and then replaced it in the hideaway, returning to watch and wait for the water to boil. Raglan knew the smell of *araki*, the potent alcoholic brew. Between that and bangu, smoked regularly by these desert fighters, it was a miracle any of them could shoot straight at any time.

Raglan moved to the transmitter, noted the frequency

and then reset the dial. He winced as the Morse key clicked beneath his middle finger, deafening to his own ear. The coded message went out fast and he concentrated on the precision needed to be as cryptic as possible. The hissing kerosene stove dulled any sound he made but less than a minute had passed before he heard the beaded curtain pushed aside. He turned, facing the startled radio operator who held a mug of coffee in one hand. His mouth opened in bewildered amazement as Raglan smiled. 'Just letting my mother know I'm all right,' he said.

The words gave him enough time to step towards the man and hit him hard and fast in the solar plexus then finish him with a precise blow to the neck. The man had not uttered a word. Not even as he died. Raglan stepped over him, retrieved the bottle from its hiding place and sprinkled the contents liberally on the floor. Then he carefully tipped the chair on its side and dragged the dead man across it. A cursory look would show a drunken man had fallen and broken his neck across the arm of the chair. Raglan placed the empty bottle just out of reach of the dead man's hand.

He keyed in more information for another thirty seconds and then flipped the receiver back to its original frequency when he heard guards approaching. Raglan dropped the still burning cigarette into the waste paper bin, igniting the paper with the man's lighter, which he then pocketed. He needed a distraction to get back to the barrack room. As flames threatened to flare he checked the doorway, looked outside and saw two guards walking away fifty metres past the radio room with their backs to him. He reached the water trough in full view of anyone moving into the outside area. Part of the buildings jutted into the area with no catwalk parapet, and he guessed, correctly, that they were Hamad's accommodation. Raglan was about to take his chance and set off but a figure moved in the upstairs room. A woman, backlit by the soft light, raised a hand, palm forward, warning him, telling him to stop. Raglan stopped. Watched her. It was obvious she had a better vantage point. Her neck craned as she followed the men's position below. Her face was in shadow but Raglan kept his eyes on her. She made a rapid gesture showing him when to move.

He sidestepped along the side of the building. The woman disappeared. He pressed his back against a door which creaked. Diagonally across the compound a door opened, spilling yellow light into the moonlit yard. Two soldiers moved out of the room and Raglan guessed they were the guard relief. If they turned left, they would be facing him. He pushed back against the door. There were no shadows to cloak him. He watched the men's body movements, willing them to turn to their right. They laughed, talking with the men in the room and then turned directly towards him.

Raglan pushed his back against the rough-hewn door. The risk was greater outside than in. He eased into the darkened room and closed the door behind him. It was cold inside, the thick walls keeping out the heat. He flicked the cigarette lighter and soon realized that the hessian-covered shapes alongside each wall were blocks of ice. Hamad must have them brought in from somewhere. Haunches of meat hung on meat hooks.

A warning voice outside raised the alarm. Raglan had a choice. Stay where he was and hope no one did a head count in the barrack room or use the flurry of men outside to slip back. As he turned back to the door the lighter's flame revealed the figure of a sleeping man. Raglan's first instinct was to kill the flame, but he kept it held high. Something about the sleeping man wasn't right. He was naked, and his arm hung down. He wasn't breathing. Raglan stepped closer. The lacerations to the man's face and torso were from being tortured. The fingernails on the visible hand were missing. Raglan eased a finger beneath a slender cord around the man's throat, hoping the unseen weight he felt might prove to be identification tags. He pulled out a small, thumbnail-sized medallion that had slipped behind the man's neck. Raglan lowered the flame. The medallion was an engraving of the winged Archangel Michael, sword and shield in hand. A religious token. Raglan eased the cord over the dead man's head, turned it over and saw the neat dedication. A Russian inscription. *For Yuri*. Raglan held the light across the man's face. It was familiar. Where had he seen him before?

And then he remembered. It was in a photograph of a GRU officer taken from a London Underground security camera.

It was Yuri Gelyov.

22

Shouts of alarm echoed around the compound. Men ran to the radio room to help quell the small fire. It took less than a minute for Raglan to make the sixty metres back to the barrack room. He stayed outside in the shadows, watching the chaos. A figure reached out of the darkness and Raglan wheeled, already preparing for the blow he felt was coming.

Dragonović smiled, showing he had no intention of fighting, and stepped back into the darkness. 'The radio room?' he asked. His casualness was deceptive. 'Did you make contact?'

'I don't know.'

'You weren't seen by the operator?'

'Yes, but it won't do him any good.'

Dragonović understood. 'What else?'

More men ran past. Lights flared in the upper rooms.

'They'll check on us,' said Raglan. They stepped into the doorway, pulling the door ajar as if they had just stepped outside. A moment later a soldier arrived, brandishing his weapon.

Dragonović raised his hands. 'We just wanted to see what happened,' he said.

The soldier's intention was clear, forcing them back inside.

The men were awake, alert in case the soldiers outside

turned on them. Raglan saw their determination not to go down without a fight.

Dragonović raised a hand to calm them. 'There's a fire. There's no danger. Get back to bed, men, we need all the rest we can get. For all we know we'll have a fight on our hands tomorrow.'

Then Dragonović lit a cigarette. 'What else, Raglan? You were gone too long.'

'There's a woman here.'

'One of his town whores?'

'Doubtful. She's white.'

'Mistress then.'

'Maybe.' Raglan decided to share what he had discovered. 'Something else. There are other players after the same thing. There's a room with a dead Russian GRU agent in it. He was tortured before he died.'

Dragonović winced. 'No wonder Hamad's playing games – maybe he got information from him. Is it possible there's a team out here somewhere? The Wagner Group perhaps? Maybe they've already found what we're looking for.'

Raglan shook his head, watching through the window for any guards not pulled to the scene of commotion. 'Do you think we'd still be alive if they had? Hamad's suspicious, that's all. One dead Russian, and then we arrive. That's got to give the bastard more reason to make sure we don't leave without finding out what it is we're after. And the Russian was way off course.'

'Off course?' said Dragonović.

'It's a long story,' said Raglan.

'Then give me the short version,' Dragonović insisted. 'I need to know. If the GRU had an agent in the field then they are after the same thing. So why was he looking in the wrong place?'

Raglan knew there was no choice but to tell him. 'Because the Russians got fed false information,' he said. 'Question is: how did he get here?'

'I'll brief the men to recce the place. Sentry positions, fuel dump. Vehicles. If we make a big enough noise, we might have a chance. But we need wheels,' said Dragonović.

'Or a boat. The lake could be our way out,' said Raglan. 'I saw a twin-engine Zodiac in the boathouse on the way in.'

Dragonović lit a fresh cigarette. 'All right, tell me, what is it we're after?' He paused, knowing he had to get closer to the answer. He wanted to reel Raglan in, so as not to have the Englishman in control. 'One of us has to reach the objective. Obviously it's too damned important not to.'

Raglan knew Dragonović was better with him than against him for as long as possible and he knew both how tantalizing a secret can be and how powerful a motivation greed is. Drip-feeding a man waiting to kill you kept him at bay a day at a time.

'The men mustn't be told,' Raglan said.

'All right, just you and me.' Impatience held back from his voice.

'There's a plane down. There's something in it I need.'

Dragonović paused. 'What kind of plane, what kind of cargo? A transporter?'

'A Mustang.'

Dragonović wore the same look of disbelief as Raglan when Maguire had told him. 'A P51?'

That was all Raglan was prepared to give. He turned away and Dragonović grabbed his arm, felt the bicep tense and released it. 'Raglan. The Mustang.' There it was: the taste of excitement. The booty almost in sight. 'Gold? Is that it? Is it gold, Raglan? Was the bastard flying out a payroll? A mining payroll? Big money for an arms deal?' No, as soon as he said the words he realized it wouldn't be money. But gold was a possibility. The currency of all ages.

Raglan let Dragonović think what he wanted. If it was a prize worth having, then the Serb would stay determined and focused. 'It's been buried by the desert for almost thirty years. Now it's not. We have to find it.' He could see Dragonović weighing the odds.

'It's not gold. No covert mission is sent out to retrieve gold. A downed transporter might carry that but not a Mustang. Barely enough room for the pilot. No, it's not gold. So what is it?' It was a rhetorical question, Dragonović working through the options of the missing cargo. ·

Raglan gave no answer.

'OK – but it's valuable. Yes? The cargo – it's worth a lot,' Dragonović insisted.

Raglan would not give him any more, but he had a better chance of surviving now. 'Just remember it's worthless to you without me. I'm the only one who knows where it is and, more importantly, what it is.' He turned away, leaving his future in Dragonović's hands.

The Serb whispered, 'The Russian knew – now maybe Hamad knows?' No – confusion had fogged his reasoning. Raglan was right – if that were the case they would have been slaughtered in the desert.

Raglan was drained. He needed a couple of hours' sleep. He knew Dragonović could trade him to Hamad and save his own neck if it came to it, but he hoped that the desire for the prize and the possible pleasure of killing Raglan himself would work in his favour. He reached his bed, pulled over the blanket and, after wondering for a moment who the mystery woman might be, fell asleep.

23

The pestilence of war, famine and flood over the previous year in the border land that was West Darfur had been as relentless as the desert storm now growling from the north would be. Sometime in the next two or three days it would become impossible for man and beast to do anything other than seek shelter. The deceptive blue sky and scorching heat offered no clue as to what would soon be inflicted on the blighted land. Only men used to surviving in such harsh conditions knew instinctively when such a storm would arrive.

The field commander of the Wagner Group gazed at the circling vultures. The Russian mercenaries had left a charred path of destruction behind them. He tugged down the howli covering the lower half of his face and inhaled deeply on a cigarette. He and his men had killed over three hundred Masalit tribesmen and Sudanese miners in the past month alone. The Sudanese government sends tonnes of gold from its mines to Russia in exchange for arms and protection by the Wagner Group. The Masalit tribesmen had given shelter to artisanal gold miners. These freelance peasant miners were stripping wealth from the Wagner Group's coffers. They and those who sheltered them needed to be stopped. But his unit had done no killing in this area. Who were the vultures feasting on?

He and his thirty men had not taken long to discover the remains of the militia at the ambush site. The survivor from the attack had made it back to the militia camp only to die of his wounds. And the Russian mercenaries who had been tracking them finished the killing that Raglan and Dragonović had started. Then the commander's men had backtracked to the downed C130 Hercules and discovered the body of a man dressed in French battle fatigues buried beneath stones. It looked to the field commander as though the warlord Faraj Hamad had enlisted help from France despite the ill will between them. There must have been enough survivors from the crashed aircraft to kill the militia who had lain in ambush.

The French and the Janjaweed militia had fought before, but the Janjaweed Buffalo Brigade was better armed now thanks to UN soldiers selling their weapons and the Libyan arms market offering heavy firepower at bargain-basement prices. Increased firepower for the militia meant the Russian mercenaries shot first and asked questions later. And now the Russian commander had received a message that gave him a new mission other than controlling vast areas of tribal lands. He exhaled the last of the smoke and pulled the howli's cloth across his mouth. His new orders were to destroy Faraj Hamad.

24

The red and purple bracts of the bougainvillea splashed against the gleaming walls of Hamad's residence. The veranda, glistening in the morning light, smelled clean in the dew. Several metres below and eighty metres beyond, the lake shimmered, ruffled by a cooling breeze. Some of the bigger trees on the landward side had been cut back for security but the fragrance from the others still carried. Thorn bushes melded into low scrubland, and brightly coloured birds flitted through tree branches. Further along the lake's shallow edges hundreds of storks waded. Raglan saw the road that had brought them to this oasis and the open-sided boat shed where a six-man Zodiac and outboard was moored. It was far enough from the road to limit access but a path from what looked like a door in the fortress wall led directly to it. The boat would be Hamad's way out if he needed to escape the confines of the walls in a hurry or if he was sufficiently bored to seek excitement in a high-speed powerboat. An additional thrill would be added by the need to avoid capsizing the boat. Doing so would make the dark shapes basking on the scattered sandbanks slide into the water. The lake, Raglan realized, afforded adequate defence against any waterborne attack – the crocodiles were man-eaters. They had no natural enemy.

The bougainvillea intertwined with indigenous vines curling across the overhead walkway. As always, protection from the sun was a prime consideration. Hamad was breakfasting with the woman Raglan had seen at the window. She was slim, wearing a khaki shirt and trousers, their hems tucked into desert boots. Her layered fair hair was shaped into the nape of her neck.

The starched coat of the servant would not have looked out of place in a five-star hotel, unlike the disruptive-patterned camouflage of the three tough-looking soldiers carrying Armalites, standing at a discreet distance. The man who had been at Hamad's side the previous night when the legionnaires were brought to the palace now escorted Dragonović and Raglan on to the veranda.

Hamad raised his head, dabbed his lips with a crisp white linen napkin and studied his captives. 'Gentlemen, how good of you to join us.' The affability gained from an English public-school education belied their lack of choice in the matter.

'Merci, M'sieur Hamad...' Dragonović began answering in French.

Hamad raised a hand. 'One moment, if you please, my guest speaks only English. The lingua franca that binds the world together.' He indicated the woman. The bruise on her cheekbone was visible, unhidden by makeup. 'Dr Liisa Karvonen works for Médecins Sans Frontières. As you can see she is bruised from an accident she and her guide were involved in. They were heading for a remote village when their vehicle crashed and sadly her guide was killed.'

Raglan studied her. She looked directly at him and then

turned away to gaze beyond Faraj Hamad, her look of disdain at the warlord's proprietary hand covering her own obvious to both men. Her bush shirt and trousers were unstained. Her desert boots were new, barely scuffed. Pale skin – not long in Africa then.

Dragonović nodded in acknowledgement, ignoring the woman. 'Sir, I am Colonel Dragonović and this is my second-in-command, Major Raglan,' he lied. Rank had its privileges. Best to use it. 'I have served here before, sir. Some years back. The Janjaweed operation?'

'Oh yes.' Hamad was obviously in good humour.

Raglan searched the eyes for the man behind the mask. Dragonović had told him of Hamad's addictions, which made an already dangerous man more lethal. He noticed the wide pupils and surmised that Hamad had already had his first fix of the day. One of the uppers, Raglan thought, anything from amphetamines to cocaine. 'Mr Faraj.'

'Ah, an Englishman. My second favourite country – after my own of course,' Hamad answered. 'The French are old masters of Equatorial Africa – thankfully it was the English who plundered Sudan in their colonial days.' He smiled at Dragonović. 'No offence. Your government has always been most generous.'

The mottled skin and moist, pulpy centre of the yellow pawpaw fruit yielded easily to Hamad's knife. 'So, you are legionnaires, of course you are – who else ventures into the wilderness so far from home?'

Hamad's aide, the quiet man, hovered by Faraj's shoulder. Raglan looked at the woman who had saved his life. She was in her thirties, athletic-looking. He nodded at her. She ignored him.

'My first occasion to speak with an Englishman as a member of the Legion, major. They are usually Germanic and other Europeans. And your French?' The last sentence tinged with mockery. If Raglan was an educated Englishman he would have a decent enough command of the language, but probably with the unmistakable accent an Englishman always fails to lose when speaking a foreign language. If Raglan was a legionnaire, he would have a sound enough command of French and express himself in a different manner.

'*Le français est la langue de ma famille adoptive. La Légion attire beaucoup de nationalités,*' Raglan said.

Hamad nodded approval at Raglan's fluency.

He skewered a piece of pawpaw and let the sweet fruit settle on his tongue as he gestured to the points of the compass. 'There, West Darfur, Sudan; there, Chad; turn south and we are bordered by the Central African Republic. Where we are has been fought over for decades. Whoever takes it controls the borders and its mineral wealth. You came here for a reason.' He mulched the yellow flesh in his mouth, grinning, letting its pulp squeeze between white teeth. Then he shrugged, eyes wide with his own sense of power. 'You come to my desert castle. I am the Prince and the Pawpaw!' He laughed. And as suddenly as he cracked the joke, his expression twisted into a scowl. 'I know why you are here!'

'Our aircraft was brought down by a Sudanese fighter,' said Dragonović. 'Only a handful of us survived, as you can see. We were flying through Sudanese airspace on our way to N'Djamena.'

'Liar,' said Hamad without effort. A signal for the soldier standing behind to slam his rifle butt between Dragonović's shoulders. It was a hard enough blow to put most men down.

The woman flinched. Raglan suddenly had a pistol pressed into his neck by Hamad's aide in case he tried to react. Dragonović's knees sagged but he drew himself upright.

'As I said, we were flying to N'Djamena.'

Faraj Hamad wagged his knife. 'No, no. You came here to rescue her. That's why you came. Because the French government who embrace her organization as their own have not yet paid me the fee I asked for rescuing her. *That* is why you are here.' He studied Dragonović and Raglan. 'And yet... and yet you wear no insignia. Ah, perhaps you are not legionnaires. Perhaps you are a different kind of mercenary. South African? American? Russian? All three?'

'We were shot down. We were ambushed. We made our way towards here because you are known as a friend to France,' said Raglan.

Hamad shook his head and continued eating. 'That was yesterday. Every African dawn differs from the one before. It makes life more interesting. The French and I are like lovers.' He looked at the woman and then the two men. 'You understand? A man and his mistress? France is my mistress. She can be troublesome. When a man has a troublesome woman in his life, he dispenses with her.'

Dragonović took a half-pace forward. 'If you would give us a vehicle, we can head for our base in Chad and leave here without impinging further on your hospitality. France would be grateful.'

Faraj Hamad dabbed his lips and pushed back from the table as the servant held the back of his chair. 'No, you must stay. At least until payment is made for her. Besides, there is a storm coming. Another day and we will not have the pleasure of being out here in the morning sun admiring the view.' He smiled. 'And as legionnaires you will know how deadly a desert *haboob* can be.'

'It's not the season for sandstorms,' said Raglan.

Hamad smiled. 'And yet we have them. It must be because of climate change.' He beckoned them and his reluctant guest to join him at the wall. 'We must all learn to tolerate each other's company, at least until the storm passes. And the poor doctor here needs time to recover from her ordeal.' Hamad reached out and squeezed her arm. Raglan noticed her flinch again. 'But,' Hamad continued, 'your health is improving, is it not, my dear?'

'Yes,' she answered, quietly submissive.

Dragonović said, 'My superiors will be concerned about us. We must take our leave. And we will convey to the French government that the good doctor here is alive and unharmed. Our report will speed up payment. We have no concern in the matter.'

'And where is there to go? Even in a vehicle a day's drive will put you in the teeth of the storm. No, I insist you and your men rest. Your government will soon pay me for rescuing Dr Karvonen. Then you can all leave together.'

'Then let us at least use your radio to contact our base and let them know what happened to us,' said Raglan, probing to see how imprisoned they were.

Hamad acknowledged the request with a small, helpless gesture of the hand. 'I am sorry but there were was an accident last night. A drunken soldier damaged our transmitter. It needs repair, major. We are without any form of communication.'

The final sentence was spoken with an apologetic smile that clearly said he was not ready to let them go. They stood at the veranda's wall as the aide gestured to the approaching soldiers below. Two of them carried the body of the dead radio operator Raglan had killed and a struggling man was frogmarched behind them.

Half a dozen soldiers went forward into the low scrub, weapons at the ready. They formed a defensive half-circle beyond a clump of trees. The men carrying the body reached the tree, tied the dead man's hands with rope and hauled him up. The prisoner, despite calling out to Faraj Hamad for mercy, was kicked to his knees, and his wrists tied in a similar manner.

'The soldier was drunk; he fell and broke his neck,' said Hamad. 'One cannot keep a body in this climate so we have our own methods of disposal.'

Raglan had a fair idea of what to expect, and he imagined Dragonović did too, but the woman was uncertain and tried to back away from the wall. Two paces behind her the aide stood blocking her path. Raglan protectively held her elbow and brought her a step closer to him.

'The other man?' asked Dragonović.

Who was now being controlled like a beast. Sweat coursed off him and his muscles and sinews bulged. But the grip and expertise of the slaughtermen held their sacrifice.

'The guard commander,' answered Hamad. 'He must be punished.'

The dead man was disembowelled, his intestines spilling out on to the ground. Liisa Karvonen turned away. Hamad's aide grabbed her face and made her watch.

'Come, doctor, do not be squeamish,' said Hamad. 'He is already dead. You must have seen worse things than that? Besides, the dead serve a purpose, do they not? You, doctor, would perform autopsies to teach other aspiring medical professionals; I use the dead to teach the living that I do not tolerate mistakes.'

The two men returned from tying the guard commander to the tree. The soldiers made a hasty retreat back inside the walls. Raglan felt Liisa stiffen next to him. The guard commander began screaming. Dun-coloured movement pushed aside the low shrub. A pride of lions emerged into the open area around the trees, drawn by the scent of blood. The lead lioness lunged at the disembowelled man. A second lioness loped towards the guard commander bound to the next tree.

Liisa tried to turn and push past Hamad's aide, who twisted her arm and slammed her against the wall, his open palm drawn back ready to strike her.

Raglan moved so fast no one could stop him. Slamming his elbow into the soldier next to him, he punched the aide hard in the nape of his neck. Before the aide slumped to the floor a soldier had clubbed Raglan to the ground.

Dragonović could do nothing. Raglan lay unconscious. More of the warlord's men appeared on the balcony, levelling their weapons.'

'Take him back!' Hamad yelled.

Soldiers grabbed Raglan's arms and dragged him away.

Hamad tried to recover his composure. A gesture was enough for the remaining soldiers to hustle Dragonović back to the barracks. Liisa Karvonen ran from the balcony to the safety of her room.

Below the walls the lions gorged.

25

Raglan was thrown unceremoniously into the barrack room. Soldiers covered the men inside and then backed away. Dragonović followed with a sub-machine gun pressed into his back. The door was slammed. The oppressive heat in the room was taking its toll. Jordain and Malik Bayo and the two other men lifted Raglan on to the bed. The gash across the back of his skull was still bleeding.

'He needs stitches,' said Jordain.

'Do what you can, said Dragonović. 'You're the team's medic.'

'With what?'

'Christ knows!'

'Then get that woman doctor in here, boss. We have to keep the Englishman on his feet,' said Bayo.

The survivors looked at Dragonović. 'The sooner we get out of here the sooner this mission is done with,' said Jarnac. 'We need a breakout.'

Dragonović pulled open the door. Two guards levelled their weapons. 'Tell Faraj Hamad that we need the doctor. If this man dies at his hands, then the French will side against him.' He slammed the door closed and nodded to Jordain. 'OK, clean him up as best you can. We're getting out of this place tonight, one way or another, before that storm hits us.'

Liisa Karvonen was ushered into the room carrying a medical bag. She faced the men, who stared at her the way a lion gazes at its prey.

'Ignore them,' said Dragonović. 'They're soldiers. They like women. What do you expect?' He pointed at Raglan lying face down on the bed. Jordain had cleaned the wound as best he could. She sat on the edge of the bed and opened the medical pack. Jordain and Dragonović waited. She was hesitant.

'He needs stitches,' said Jordain. 'You've got sutures in that bag?'

She nodded.

'What do you think? Am I right? It needs stitching, yeah?'

She reached forward towards the wound. Her hands were trembling. Jordain grabbed her wrist. 'We need to sterilize the wound. You've got iodine?'

She looked blankly at him. Dragonović saw her hesitation. 'Geordie, she's in shock. You do it.' He took her arm and guided her away from Raglan, pulled out the bench seat with his boot and sat her down. As Jordain pulled on surgical gloves, swabbed the wound and found the sutures and needle driver he needed in the pack, Dragonović turned to Picot. 'Get her water.'

Dragonović extended the tin cup. She nodded her thanks and sipped the water. Dragonović offered her a cigarette. She shook her head. He broke the filter off, lit up and sat opposite her as Jordain and Bayo attended to Raglan.

'We need to get out of this place. How did you get here?

She held his gaze. 'Take me with you,' she said.

'It's too dangerous. You're better off here. The French will pay what he wants for you. It's not a terrorist situation. They'll pay and then he'll have to deliver. It's a game. Both sides know that.'

'I know how to get out of here. No one will pay for me.'

The men were as interested as Dragonović. 'There'll be shooting,' he said.

'I can manage.'

'Yeah? You didn't look as though you were managing up there on the balcony.'

'Hamad's barbaric. You blame me?'

Dragonović drew on his cigarette. 'There's a dead man on ice across the way. Was he with you?'

She nodded. 'He got me here. I was supposed to go to one of the refugee camps but my medical flight never got to me.'

Dragonović was testing her. 'Where were you? Where's the Médecins Sans Frontières base out here?'

'Rokero in West Darfur and Pieri in the south.'

'That's a long way from here, doctor. How did he die?'

'Farad told me he had a heart attack.'

'You knew him?'

She shook her head. 'Can I have one of those now?'

He tapped out a cigarette. Was she buying time before she answered? She drew the smoke in and exhaled. Her hands were steady now.

'He's Russian. There's a pipeline they're putting through. He said he was their surveyor. He offered to take me.'

'You drove here? Through these badlands?'

She paused and looked at the men who were listening as intently as Dragonović. 'There's a plane. We flew here.'

That got everyone's interest.

'All right, where?'

'Take me with you.'

'If you go down in the crossfire, you're dead meat and no good to me. Tell me where.'

She looked across to where Jordain had finished stitching Raglan's wound.

'He's coming round, boss.'

'I'll tell him,' she said, looking to Raglan. 'He owes me.'

By the time she'd finished her cigarette Raglan was upright. His head was pounding but the wound was stitched and if he had concussion he'd soon know. Malik Bayo handed him a glass of sweet, milk-free tea.

'The doctor was too shook up to patch you. Geordie did it. You'll probably look like Frankenstein's monster for the rest of your life. Geordie can't stitch for shit.'

Raglan thanked Jordain as Dragonović scowled at the woman who faced Raglan.

'Everyone's got fucking secrets around here,' said Dragonović. 'She's got a dammed plane hidden somewhere.' He put his hand in her back and urged her forward. 'Hurry, they'll be back soon enough.'

Liisa went to Raglan and lowered her head. 'I was flown in here. It's a small plane. Maybe big enough for four or five. After Hamad's men found us they covered it with camouflage netting.'

Raglan sipped the tea, making sure she faced only him so

that no one else in the room could pick up what she said. 'Where?'

'You will take me with you.'

He nodded.

'You promise?'

'I'll take you.'

'When?'

'First thing.'

'He sends for me about five in the morning. He likes to watch me dress.' She showed no sign of embarrassment.

Raglan remained silent.

'That's all he does. So far,' she added.

Raglan saw the briefest flicker in her eyes. Was it shame? She was lying. To tell the truth would destroy what was left of her dignity.

'All right, I'll be there just before then. Where is the plane?"

'Half a day by road. The lake will take us close but then it is high up, on a plateau. We had to make our way down to the road. It took hours.'

'Is the plane damaged?'

'I don't think so, but there was something wrong with the engine. My pilot was really worried, which is why he landed.'

'What kind of problem?'

She shrugged. 'I don't know. It was spluttering.'

'Could be a fuel blockage,' said Jarnac.

'And might be easy to clear,' said Dragonović.

'Maybe,' said Raglan. 'Worth a chance.'

'Ask her about the dead Russian,' the Serb said. 'The pilot. Says he was a surveyor for a pipeline.'

Raglan remembered the story Maguire had related about the German geologist who showed pipeline workers the Mustang photos. The story gelled neatly enough – unless you knew for sure, as he did, that the dead man was Yuri Gelyov, a GRU officer. And it was likely he was searching for the Mustang's crash site when his plane had got into trouble. And that was a direct link from the death in the London Underground. The woman wouldn't have known any of that, of course, and if a pilot offered a freebie instead of a dangerous overland route, then it would have made sense to take up his offer. If luck was on their side – and there had been little of late – then the fact that the former MI6 man had given the Russians a bogus location meant they had not yet found the prize. It was a long shot but if Raglan and the survivors could reach Liisa's plane then it was the quickest way to get what he needed.

'Do you know about Hamad's boat?'

'Yes. I've seen him and his aide use it.'

'You know where the keys are?'

'He leaves them in the boat as far as I know. Who'd dare steal it?'

Raglan smiled. 'Us.'

26

The men were briefed. The plan was simple. The immediate guards would be dealt with, their weapons taken. Jarnac and Dragonović would then cover Jordain and the two others who would use knives and bayonets taken from the dead men. And they would be dead, of that there was no doubt. And that meant there was no turning back. The objective was the armoury next to the guardroom where their confiscated weapons and webbing were held. The guard routine had been logged. Bored and weary men returning after their watch were likely to want their rest. The same would apply to those kicked out of their bunks to replace them. First light was when men were at their most vulnerable. But Raglan warned the men not to think of them as easy targets. They would be fearful of making mistakes after the guard commander incident. Once Raglan appeared with Liisa, they would use the shadows along the outer wall and make for the door in the wall that led down to the boathouse. Sunrise would be beyond the lake, so if the alarm was raised, those in the compound would have the searing low light in their eyes. Any potential to suppress accurate gunfire had to be taken.

Raglan slipped from his bed in the barrack room. It was time to fetch Liisa. He noticed Dragonović's bed was empty.

He smelled the pungent French cigarette smoke before he could make out the man in the shadows.

, He waited.

Dragonović stepped closer, keeping his voice low.

'The guards' routines are the same. Nothing's changed. Me, I'd have altered their rota. Had them switched from here to there,' he said, pointing, the glow from his cigarette's stub covered by his curled fist. He took one more drag, exhaled and squeezed its ember between finger and thumb. 'Hamad's careless. Thinks he can't be touched. The guard on each end of the walkway here, they've gone off towards the guardroom. No relief has come out. They're taking a break. Dumb bastards. We're in a blind spot now. For a few minutes at least.'

Raglan glanced around. Sure enough, the guards had moved away.

'Is he giving us an opportunity to make a break?' said Raglan.

'It would be the perfect excuse to feed us to the lions. No, I think they've lowered their guard. Maybe Hamad's underestimated us. What trouble could so few men cause him?'

'He'll soon find out.'

Everyone knew what they had to do. Jordain had slipped a pair of scissors and a scalpel out of the medical kit to use as weapons before the guards had taken Liisa back to her quarters. By dawn they needed to be in Hamad's boat racing for the target. He watched the dust in the compound swirl. The wind was increasing; they might soon be able to use it to their advantage.

'I'll be back in an hour.'

'You go out there and get caught in her rooms and you could blow the whole damned thing. Forget the woman, Raglan. We can find that plane now. Jesus, she's dumb enough to have a Russian agent fly her down here, she's dumb enough to get us all killed.'

'I'm going over the roof – there's a blind spot.'

'We don't even drag our own wounded along!' he hissed. 'Leave her.'

'She stays and she'll trade her life for us. Hamad will get to the damned plane before we do.'

Dragonović snatched at Raglan's shirt front and pushed him back against the wall. Dragonović's weight gave him the advantage. In that instant Raglan felt the power and strength of the man whose authority had been diminished by his presence.

'I don't give a damn who you want to fuck, Raglan, but I'm not dying for some whore!' he said, spitting the words.

Dragonović knew Raglan could not fight back. Both men's training for close-quarter combat was probably evenly matched but a savage and deadly fight now would draw the attention of the guards. Dragonović had made his point and had also felt the strength and resistance of his enemy. Like a shark nudging a victim before turning in for the strike. He was confident the Englishman offered no serious threat. He released his hold. Raglan pushed a hand against Dragonović and the Serb stepped back a pace.

'We get to her plane and we get to the target and then we have a fast ride to the pickup point. We reach the target – we get home,' Raglan emphasized.

He slid past Dragonović and within seconds had merged into the shadows.

The Serb watched Raglan slip through the shadows. In a day of uncertainty that lay ahead, one thing was definite: Dragonović had to keep Raglan alive until the secret was his. He stood at a vantage point that allowed him to watch the main area of the yard. The men were ready. When an attack dog is confined, the pent-up power becomes a force of nature. He and his men would wait in the shadows, and then he would unleash them and let the killing begin.

Liisa stepped from the shower, leaving wet footprints on the cool stone floor, then towelled herself in front of the full-length mirror. The shadow that passed beyond the shuttered window told her Raglan was there. Was he watching her? Was she in danger from the very man who had saved her? Whatever happened in the next few hours, she needed an ally. With one eye on the window, she dried herself quickly. She heard the faintest of movements behind her.

'How did you get in here?' she said, wrapping the towel around her.

'Over the roof. Through the bathroom window. Get dressed. We have to make a run for it sooner than we'd planned.'

She shook her head. 'I don't know. On the lake in darkness? If the storm veers this way, I'll lose what bearings I have.'

'I won't. An escarpment large and flat enough to land a small plane won't be hard to find.'

'Then if you know that, why did you come for me? You didn't have to.'

'Sooner or later that madman'll kill us all. You don't deserve to die here. It's a chance we have to take. If I don't get you out of here now and you end up in his quarters, I'll never get to you. He'll be too well protected.'

She looked uncertain. Fearful. She grabbed her clothes and went back into the bathroom. Raglan felt a nagging uncertainty. Could she hold it together if their situation became desperate? A running gun battle could unnerve even an inexperienced soldier. Yet she hadn't been afraid on the balcony when they were forced to watch the soldier being disembowelled. Sickened, yes. That was natural. And she was courageous enough to travel through war zones to help others.

'You'll be OK, you'll see,' he said.

His survival instinct nagged him. Just how badly was the plane damaged or had it been the pilot that had succumbed rather than the engine? 'Did the pilot die on the plane? Is that where he had the heart attack?'

She came out of the bathroom dressed, buttoning her shirt. 'We had engine trouble. Went off course. He panicked. He got us down but the strain of it and the exertion of getting down to the road… I suppose that helped kill him. Hamad separated us. They questioned us both.' She touched the bruise on her face. 'Hamad's man likes to slap people around. They told me he had died of a heart attack when they were interrogating him.' She bit her lip. 'Poor man. I think they must have hurt him too much and his heart gave out. Bastards.'

Raglan studied her. The story seemed to add up. She'd been lucky. Being a doctor attached to a French medical charity meant she was worth something. Hamad wouldn't want to return damaged goods.

She gave Raglan a reassuring smile. 'I'll be all right, I

promise. Don't worry about me. I won't let you down. But what am I caught up in?'

'I can't tell you that.'

'You can trust me.'

'Not a matter of trust – if Hamad thinks you know he'll get it from you.'

She took a slow deep breath, easing out the tension. Raglan decided it was not the time to pursue his doubts about her. 'Who comes for you? Guards?'

She shook her head. 'No, his aide. He's a soulless bastard. I don't know who's worse, him or Hamad.'

'OK, we wait him out.'

'And then what?'

'Play it as it comes.'

He moved to the window and watched the radio room in the distance. The wind was freshening yet more as he watched the compound area below, waiting to take Liisa over the roof before they attacked Hamad's men.

Faraj Hamad's aide's footsteps echoed outside. Raglan checked his watch. The man had come earlier than expected.

'Unbutton your shirt,' Raglan said.

The aide walked into the room without knocking. Liisa stood, her shirt unbuttoned, the cleft of her breasts partially exposed. She looked up in a moment of surprise as if caught dressing. The aide was distracted long enough for Raglan to step from behind the door and drive a blow deep into his kidneys. As the aide slumped Raglan punched hard beneath the man's ear. It was a killing blow. Liisa stared as if Raglan were a stranger. Raglan pulled the dead man away from the door.

Raglan tucked the dead man's pistol into his waistband

and then checked the window, waiting for the guards on the far boardwalk to turn away. Liisa stood close to him, concentrating on making the run across the rooftop before dropping into the darkness.

'One thing you'd better know. Dragonović will probably try and kill me once I get us to where we need to be. He won't want any witnesses, so you're in danger. Better you understand that.'

She took it in. Nodded.

'You understand what I'm saying?' he said, given her lack of reaction. Dragonović was supposed to be on their side and he had just told her otherwise.

'Will you kill him?' she asked.

'If it comes to it.'

'All right. I understand. I'll be careful.'

'Don't question anything I tell you to do.'

She nodded. She grabbed her small daypack and followed him out of the window.

27

It was seven minutes past midnight. Maguire was nursing a small Scotch and gazing out across the River Thames from his office. The city lights emblazoned the streets and buildings. His phone rang. 'You're working as late as I am,' said the Frenchman, a note of weariness in his voice.

'Delmar. Any news?'

'I think so. When we lost the aircraft, it was about a hundred kilometres from the target.'

'Satellite imagery?'

'No. Not yet. I am trying to get authorization for an overflight – without, that is, having to explain too much.'

Maguire found the transcript that the Government Communications Headquarters in Cheltenham had passed to him once they had found someone who remembered their Morse code. 'You saw Raglan's message I sent to you?'

'Yes. I am comforted that a handful of men survived but, Maguire, if he is in Faraj Hamad's stronghold, they are in a precarious situation. There is renewed fighting in West Dafur between the Arab Rizeigat and the Masalit tribes. If the Arabs reach out for Janjaweed reinforcements and they move further south to bolster their strength, then there will be more massacres now that the UN has pulled out. And our people will have no chance of breaking through to the target.'

'If anyone can get there, our men can.'

Maguire could hear Delmar drawing deeply on a cigarette and then exhaling. 'Ralph, it is time for you tell me just what it is we are trying to secure. My men are dead and my political bosses are kicking down my door. If I cannot give them something more concrete than a missing document that identifies an intelligence source then I doubt I will be head of Action Division by morning. Is there a name on that document?'

Maguire could no longer hold back what scant information there was to add. The history of the document had been shared with Delmar, its importance emphasized at the highest level from the UK intelligence service. Maguire mentally cursed the Foreign Office's timidity. For once he was thankful the French had agreed to get involved. They obviously had their own ulterior motive – gaining the information for themselves – but at least they had committed to the operation.

'There is no one named in the document – except for the codename Malaika. It's in a field agent's encryption. But by a process of elimination the Russians could identify our agent.'

'If the Russians find the document before we do, how long until they break the code?'

Maguire hesitated. Even he couldn't answer that objectively. 'Claude, it will depend who's still alive after all these years and which ex-KGB men served in Africa. If the GRU get the information, my guess is that they will focus on these men. And identifying them might only be a matter of a week. Maybe more. I don't know.'

Claude Delmar was silent for a moment. He sighed. 'Very

well. For what it's worth I am trying to organize a rescue party out of Chad. There are legionnaires stationed there but if we commit them, and the Sudanese find out, then there's a big problem.'

'I've tried here as well. Look, your people are closer, so, if you can, at least get them to the border in readiness.'

Maguire knew Delmar was shaking his head. 'We cannot expect any further commitment from my government so I am trying to use back channels, but we must be realistic. I am doubtful of success in my efforts. Oh, and there is another development. I don't understand it but there is a connection. It is puzzling. Our foreign affairs department passed on information to me only hours ago. A few days earlier they had a demand from Faraj Hamad. He is holding a medical doctor from Médecins Sans Frontières. Are you at your desk?'

'Yes.'

'Here's her picture. She's a doctor from Finland. Been working with the organization for four years, according to Hamad. Her name is Liisa Karvonen. Thirty-four years old.'

Maguire's screen flickered into life. It showed a picture of a woman: a close-up mug shot with her holding a Médecins Sans Frontières identity badge. She had a bruise on her cheekbone, another on her forehead. Her fair hair was unkempt. Her blue eyes looked puffy and tired.

'She's being held by Hamad? In the same place as our men?' said Maguire.

'Coincidences like that make me nervous. I don't know where she is. He's not saying. He's *requesting* payment for her safe return and because Doctors Without Borders is an integral part of who we are here in France, he made the demand to my government not the organization itself. Of course he would. They don't have ransom money, for God's sake.'

'How did Hamad get her?'

'Bad luck, as far as she's concerned. No idea. There was another man with her apparently, but he had a heart attack. Hamad says he's *caring* for her.'

'What are your people going to do?'

'Us? Nothing. The government can deal with it. Here's the strange thing. Médecins Sans Frontières have no such doctor working for them. We checked.'

Maguire looked at the woman's image. 'Then she must be attached to the Central Committee of Sudanese Doctors.'

'That was our next call. They have no record of her either. I thought she might have been a journalist playing fast and loose by using medical identification. Reuters and AP don't have her on the books, so unless she's a stringer we don't know. And given the mess we are in I don't care. Let's keep trying to help our people. Let me know if you get another signal from your man.'

Maguire ended the call. The woman stared back at him. Her expression wasn't fearful. Her gaze challenged anyone to try to hurt her. Despite her obvious beauty there was a look of coldness – tough, unyielding. Maguire did not know what prompted him to bring up the image of the security cameras on the London Underground. It was pure instinct. Triggered perhaps by the knowledge that the woman's companion had died of a heart attack. After two hours of moving frame-by-frame in the carriage where the former MI6 officer was killed, he found her.

She was the fourth member of the GRU assassination team.

28

Several guards lay dead. Shadows concealed their bodies. Once Dragonović's men were rearmed, they pressed their backs against the walls and edged towards the boathouse gate. Raglan arrived with the woman he knew only as Liisa Karvonen. He retrieved his webbing, checked there were still rounds in the assault rifle's magazine and led the way in the dim pre-dawn light. The purple shadow lying across the land beyond the walls would soon glow in burnt orange sunlight. The plan had been executed with deadly efficiency. No alarms had been raised. No weapons had been discharged.

They moved at pace, backs against the wall. Jarnac led, Dragonović behind him. Jordain followed with Raglan and Liisa, with the remaining two men at the rear. They were still beneath the wooden ramparts as they reached the steel gates. Jarnac stopped, checked the far end of the wall beyond them where the door led on to the path. Once there, they were free. Their stride quickened as they reached the obscured doorway and then huddled into the building's shadow. Jarnac lifted the gate's steel bar. Metal on metal, a wincing caution as he lifted it again. Jarnac was about to step through when Raglan went forward, grabbed his arm and whispered, 'Wait!'

He saw Dragonović question his action. Raglan raised a hand. He pointed to his ear. They listened. There it was. The unmistakable sound of approaching vehicles.

'We should go,' hissed Jarnac.

'We're on the far side of the road in,' said Dragonović. 'Whoever it is will wake the place.'

Raglan nodded. 'Run for the reed beds. Use them as cover.'

Jarnac hauled open the metal door, ignoring the screech of the rusting metal in its frame.

Their escape plan had been simple. And then it got complicated. The double steel gates imploded. The booming of cannon fire shattered the dawn. Birds squawked. Men screamed.

Dust, debris and shrapnel swirled through the compound. Raglan and the men threw themselves down. Beyond the lake's nearside bank, where the road led to the trees and main gate, two Russian armoured personnel carriers were parked side by side. Both had a turret-mounted, dual-fed 30-mm cannon firing High Explosive Fragmentation and Armor-Piercing Tracer rounds that could punch through a couple of inches of steel. Within a minute the compound's steel doors were demolished, the front-facing outer wall rubble.

'Fuck,' said Jordain. 'Bloody Russians.'

Without a second thought Raglan had half covered Liisa's body with his own. She pressed against him, hands cupped over her ears against the pounding staccato of cannon fire and the additional chatter of heavy machine guns. Faraj Hamad's inner sanctum was being raked with gunfire now that the wall had been demolished. Hamad's men ran, sought cover, were cut down. Here and there survivors fought back with little success. Bullets bounced off the Russian APCs.

'Stay down!' Raglan ordered, loud enough to be heard over the gunfire. 'They'll move in when the firing stops, then we run for it.'

The attack lasted seven minutes, by which time the return gunfire had almost stopped. The balcony area was a scene of carnage. Bodies lay, mutilated by cannon fire and shrapnel. Blood speckled the remains of the walls alongside the bougainvillea bracts. Farad Hamaj had not lacked courage: that or a delusional sense of immortality from psychoactive substances had led him on to the balcony with his personal guards. It was their remains that decorated the walls.

Raglan and the others stayed huddled out of sight, but Jarnac had caught some shrapnel from the first volley. Dragonović was helping him sit upright: Jarnac was close to death, probably only a few minutes left to him.

Raglan squatted next to the Serb. 'Hamad's dead,' he said. 'Before the Russians get inside, we have to make a break.' He glanced at Jarnac. They couldn't take him with them even if he had a chance of survival. Which he didn't. Dragonović nodded.

Raglan dragged Liisa after him, crouched at the doorway, told the three surviving men the order of their escape. They too knew Jarnac wouldn't be going with them. Bayo and Picot would cover the rearguard; Jordain was to run hard for the boathouse and the Zodiac. Raglan, Liisa and Dragonović would be right behind him.

*

Jarnac gripped Dragonović's hand. The numbness was creeping up now. This was death. It was coming for him. This was how it took you. It stole over you like a cloud of ice and it froze you into unconsciousness. No pain now. That was good. He couldn't see. Dragonović was there. He sensed that. Someone touched his face. Couldn't be the Serb. Not the thing he'd do.

Dragonović removed his hand. Jarnac was whispering now. Dragonović leant forward to listen.

The final whisper of air escaped his lungs. Dragonović hesitated for only a moment; he did not enjoy the feeling he was experiencing. Jarnac had been at his side and covered his back since the early days. He pushed the memory away.

Raglan stooped and grabbed the extra magazines of ammunition and the desert goggles from the dead man's webbing. As the Wagner Group motorized unit roared inside the walls Dragonović followed Raglan and ran for the boathouse.

Jordain kept the Zodiac's engine revs low. The thumping roar of the Russian APC engines disguised the sound of the boat's powerful outboards but they could push out a bow wave that might be seen from the compound. Raglan and Dragonović squatted like the others, each covering the boat's flanks. For fifty metres the high reeds between the lake and the buildings might obscure them, after that they would be in open water. They had escaped unnoticed. The Russians had concentrated on those inside. Luck had been on Raglan's side.

'Open her up, Geordie,' he said.

Jordain pushed the throttle lever gently forward. The bow

rose, the twin outboards churned water, and the men shared their satisfaction with jaw-aching grins. Liisa remained squatting between the row of seats. Raglan handed her the spare set of goggles. She nodded and mouthed her thanks to him as distant explosions, muted by deafened eardrums, were heard. Fuel dumps, trucks and the generator house erupted, adding a scene of total devastation to the charred and burning compound. Her last report to Moscow had been sent vital moments before she had lost the connection on one of Hamad's satellite phones stolen when he was disoriented from his drug use. Help had been sent but now her life and the success of her mission were in the Englishman's hands. She did not know what had caused the signal to break up but now it was clear again. The satellite phone in her small daypack was already sending out a GPS signal.

29

The radar stations on the far eastern shores of Russia had relayed everything to Volokolamsk ELINT station in the Moscow Military District. So vast was the distance between them that when the sun rose there, it was sunset in Moscow. Verskiy trudged through the empty building towards his office. The outer rooms were empty. Cones of light from empty desk lamps formed a flight path to his inner sanctum. It was late. Closing the door to his office, he chose to keep his overcoat on – the weather was bitter – pulled free his scarf and loosened the tie on his collar. He poured himself a large whisky and put his feet on the desk. City lights were the only other illumination. Leaning back in his chair he savoured the drink's warmth and the comfort of the shadows.

Major Galina Menshikova and her companion Yuri Gelyov had made good progress. Their covert mission had been close to success. But when they were forced to land their small plane they had been captured by a warlord. There had been silence for two days and then she had got hold of a satellite phone. Her report in hushed tones, fearful of being discovered, had been urgent.

Was there any other order Verskiy could have given? The decision he had made was a hard one, but it caused him no personal grief other than losing a man in the field and possibly lessening the chances of success. He sipped the whisky, stared out at the fairy-tale snow falling and laid his mobile phone on the desk. He pressed the play button. Galina's voice reached out to him from their recorded conversation days before.

'General, there is a problem here.'

'Are you hurt, Gala? We lost your signal from the aircraft.'

'We had to land. I think there was magneto or fuel trouble. Maybe the signal was lost then. Yuri was going to try and fix the plane. Can you hear me all right?'

'I can hear you. Are you in danger?'

'Yes.'

'As you speak?'

'Yes.'

'Where are you?'

'I'm not sure. We were captured by a man called Faraj Hamad. He is a Sudanese warlord. We are in his southern base, near the border. I think. I can't be sure. We were on track for the target when we had the engine trouble and his men captured us. General, the map is in the plane.'

'Concealed?'

'Beneath the pilot's seat. We did not wish to have it on us after we landed and abandoned the plane.'

'Gala, where is the plane, can you tell me?'

She sighed. 'We are being held on the southern tip of a lake. The plane is on a plateau a three-hour drive north of here. If you can locate where we are you will find it.'

'Yes, yes. I can do that. Your cover story held?'

'Yes, they believed it. But, general, they took Yuri away. I heard screams. They are torturing him.'

He heard uncertainty catch her voice. Was it fear? That

she too would be tortured? Verskiy remained silent. She had a good cover; Yuri's was the more questionable. They would inflict pain on him first if they believed the two GRU agents were not known to each other. 'Yuri is a tough man, Gala—'

A sudden muffled sound interrupted him. She fell silent. Verskiy waited, trying to picture her in his mind's eye. Far from home in a violent land. Alone. Her voice came back on the speaker.

'I thought I heard someone coming. This is one of Hamad's phones.'

'You are close to him?'

Again she hesitated. 'His bedroom.'

Verskiy sighed. 'I understand. Can you kill him?'

'Yes, but I would never escape.'

'Gala, listen to me. You know I value you both, but no one can withstand brutal torture for long. He will break. There is no shame. Have you seen him?'

'No.'

'Then you must. Find a way. Offer to take him food. Any excuse at all. Can you do that?'

'Yes, I'll try.'

He knew she was already one step ahead but he prompted her, anyway. 'You know what has to be done.'

'Yes.' She paused. 'General... I can't... It's Yuri.'

'Gala, listen to me,' he repeated. 'Don't underestimate the importance of this mission. I'm not asking this of you lightly. It would be better for him as well. A heart attack. A kindness.'

There was a pause. Her breathing sounded laboured. Was she holding back her emotions? This was no time to fall prey to them. There was a firmness to his voice. 'Do you have the means?'

Again a pause. And then: 'I have what I need. They didn't find it.'

'Gala, listen to me. I will get you out. There are people I can use. Do what is necessary to stay alive until then. And if you get out before they arrive steal the damned phone. And I will find you.'

But she had not answered. The line had gone dead.

Verskiy lit a cigarette. He had wanted a small covert unit of agents to retrieve what lay hidden in the desert. That had failed. So there had been no option but to reach out to those who were armed and on the ground. A shooting war was the last thing Verskiy wanted, but he knew a Wagner Group commander in the Central African Republic who could travel fast and strike hard. The danger lay in whether the treasure he sought would remain in Major Menshikova's hands. Loyalty among the Russian mercenaries was divided between GRU personnel and FSB officers. And if the legend of the desert proved to be a reality, then he dared not allow the KGB's bastard offspring the FSB to get wind of it. This was his mission. His key to an even brighter future. If ground units could locate Galina's plane then he was back in business. If Major Galina Menshikova did not survive the rescue attempt on Hamad's stronghold she would have to be left where she was. In this game everyone was expendable.

30

The wind moaned through the twisted propeller blades of the exposed Mustang, gently rocking the aircraft like a soothing hand comforting a troubled child in its crib. The pilot's skeleton moved slowly with the motion, head flung back, a blind man swaying to the lullaby. The sand scurried across the face of the dune, chastised by the increasing wind. Within a few hours the desert would reclaim the man and his secret: he would be swallowed back into the reshaped desert to await another chance to complete his mission.

They were caked in dirt and sweat. Black streaks from the firefight and blazing buildings smudged arms and chests; minor cuts and wounds, dried now in bloodied crusts, bore testimony to the day's struggle. The escarpment swept upwards like a rock glacier, ending in a sheer drop to the valley floor below. They had moved at pace once they had run the Zodiac aground near the base of the hill leading to the plateau and Yuri Gelyov's aircraft. A Russian attack following the discovery that the dead pilot was a Russian GRU officer had confirmed Raglan's distrust in the Médecins Sans Frontières doctor. Was it likely a Russian attack had been random? Were they trying to rescue Yuri? He kept Liisa with him and, like a training sergeant with a recruit, urged, cajoled and threatened her almost beyond the limits of her endurance as they clambered upwards.

Raglan checked his watch. If anyone in the assault force at Hamad's compound had seen them escape, they would hunt them down. Raglan needed to reach the objective and the only way that was now possible would be to get the dead Russian's plane in the air.

Dragonović called a halt. Picot, on point, went another fifty metres ahead and then stopped, looking around.

'Picot?' Dragonović queried.

The soldier turned and shook his head.

'Where the hell is it?' demanded Dragonović. He pointed a threatening finger at Liisa. 'You said it was on a high escarpment. This is the only one!'

Malik Bayo had clambered up a craggy outcrop, deeper into the cool shadow of an overhang. 'I see it!'

They moved over to him, following his angled hand, gesturing towards the high-rise plateau mostly obscured from below by the rock formations and boulders. Three tent-like military camouflage nets covered what looked to be a small, strut-braced, high-wing monoplane. Dragonović led the way, the final steep approach testing everyone's strength. Raglan hauled Liisa up behind him. Once they reached the summit, they drew breath as the wind kicked up swirling dust. Raglan pulled aside a corner of the main netting. The tailplane faced him. The Russian had done a good job of landing the small aircraft given the short length of what was his runway. Another sixty feet and he would have hit the boulders at the end of the flat escarpment.

Dragonović began cutting the nets free. 'Malik, Jordain. Get the other two nets down. Picot, keep watch on the lake.'

The nets were down and discarded in minutes.

'Turn the plane,' said Raglan, heaving aside the rocks placed beneath its wheels.

Liisa joined the four men and lent her weight. Once the plane was turned and the wheel chocks replaced, Raglan checked there was free movement on the elevators. 'Turn the control column,' Raglan ordered. Liisa got into the cockpit and did as he instructed. The elevators worked. He called to Jordain and pointed at the engine cowling. 'Open the oil-inspection hatch and check the level. It's a small, press-button hatch. See it?

'Got it.'

Liisa moved into the back seats and reached below the pilot's seat to retrieve the map she had hidden. Tracking the man into the London Underground had been the perfect plan, and his dash for freedom on to the train had been expected. She had been the key to the operation. Once inside the crowded carriage it had been easy to administer the drug. As the man lay dying on the floor, it was she who had called out she was a doctor and who took the folded map from his pocket. Now, she was in the hands of the Englishman and he and these men were seeking something hidden in the desert. It was obvious they were after the same thing. How she would retrieve the document General Verskiy needed so badly and then evade her guardians she had no idea. The unknown could not be planned. When the time came she would act.

★

Raglan saw her reaching beneath the seats. 'Have you found the flight manual or checklist?'

'I'm looking,' she lied.

Raglan opened the small luggage compartment, hoping what he wanted would still be aboard. He found the six-inch plastic tube resembling a hydrometer and clambered out and gave it to Bayo.

'Take this, push the needle into these fuel sump nipples. That's where the fuel is. Check every one. Five around the aircraft and three underneath. The Avgas should be blue. If there's water in the tanks it'll settle on the bottom of the bottle.'

Dragonović went around the aircraft, testing the flaps and rudder, and seeing there was no damage to their leading edge. Stones had sprayed up from the landing and the paint was pitted. Beyond that the plane appeared to be mechanically sound. Raglan called to Picot, who was keeping watch across the distant landscape.

'Anything?'

'Dust trails. They might come this way, and so is that storm,' he said, pointing to the horizon.

Raglan watched the smudged skyline. A tidal wave of sand would be on them within hours.

Malik Bayo held the fuel bottle aloft. The Avgas had only a small amount of water at the bottom of the blue liquid. 'Raglan! It's all OK.'

Jordain kicked the tyres and grinned. 'Good to go then.'

Raglan threw his rifle into the cockpit and climbed in. The aircraft had been stripped of flight manuals and checklist reminder. He scanned the instruments. Pre-flight routine checks were standard. All he had to do was remember them. He pressed the master switch, let the whining noise continue as it started up the electronics, then reached for the fuel-mixture plunger and pushed it all the way in. His hands moved through the pre-flight procedures with a faltering memory. It had been a while since he had gone through the checks but there was a rhythm to his actions. Fuel mix, plunger, throttle in, fuel pump on – the gauge needle jumped; he switched the pump off. The plane had been standing for days so it would be a cold start. He opened the throttle a quarter of an inch and pushed the mixture in all the way. The avionics switch kick-started the instrument panel.

He called to Liisa. 'Do you have the ignition key?'

Her expression and the shake of her head was enough of an answer. The man who had the key was dead.

Liisa struggled to hide the stricken look on her face. The memory of Yuri Gelyov struggling to land the aircraft, her cries of alarm as they raced towards the rockface, wheels bouncing, and then the relief as his skill brought them to safety. He had saved her life and she had killed him.

31

Jordain slung his rifle and looked at the small cabin. 'Are we going to fit in this box? What about weight? Shouldn't we know about the load this thing can carry?'

Raglan glanced at the men: their bulk and weight wouldn't exceed the aircraft's load capacity. That was the least of his worries.

'Did you have breakfast?' he asked.

'Not a chance.'

'Then we'll be fine,' he said, leaning out of the cockpit. 'Dragonović, we need a key of some description or a small screwdriver blade.'

The ignition key would complete the magneto circuit, necessary for starting the aircraft's engine. Push came to shove he could try to break the starter wire to the magneto, which would make it live, disconnect the ground wire on the ignition switch and swing the propeller.

Dragonović handed Raglan a small flat-bladed screwdriver. 'There's a tool box in the locker. How about this?'

Raglan took it. He'd started a small plane once when he'd lost his key by using the key to his briefcase. He jiggled the blade. The instruments came alive. But the engine failed to start.

'We need to swing the prop,' yelled Raglan.

'Wait!' shouted Dragonović, as he stepped up to the propeller. 'Brakes on!' he called as he stood a few inches back from the deadly blades. Raglan answered with the same response. If the engine fired and the plane lurched, the Serb could be mincemeat.

'Set throttle!' Raglan called. The main controls on the console sat in a line to the right of the push-pull control column. The carburettor heater lever, throttle control, the red-topped mixture control and the primer lever nestled in a row. He eased the throttle lever with his right hand. Dragonović took hold of the prop. It was a bitch of a job, thought Raglan, and no pilot ever liked doing it. If any loose clothing was caught, the effect of the rotating propeller was like a blender with a tomato.

'Mixture full-rich!' Raglan called out, a warning that the aircraft was ready if the engine could be started.

Dragonović swung the propeller and stepped back quickly in case it spun. There was no response. Again the sequence and again failure. After the fourth attempt they knew it was hopeless. They had to get into the engine.

He shouted to Dragonović, 'Open the engine cowl. See there's no oil leaking.'

Dragonović did as Raglan instructed.

Raglan could fly a plane but the mechanical servicing was a specialist job. He was scraping his memory cells trying to locate the problem. There were two magnetos on the aircraft and if one 'dropped' – malfunctioned – the other could still keep the aircraft flying. Whatever the problem, it had to be found now. And time was not on their side.

Raglan warned the men: 'Stay clear of the propeller. If this thing starts up, you'll be dead.' Raglan climbed down from the cockpit as Dragonović wrenched back the engine cover and instructed one man to find the plane's tool kit. 'Damned thing's probably clogged with sand – I doubt if it'll stay in the air,' he muttered.

It had been too long a road and both men needed the end to be in sight. Raglan turned on his heel and began pacing off the distance from the lame aircraft to the edge of the precipice. He was worried. The high-density altitude was a major headache. It could reduce lift and impair propeller efficiency, which could result in reduced thrust. And if that wasn't enough, it could decrease the engine's power output. The weather was oppressively hot and they were carrying a lot of weight. Even without the aircraft's manual, which had obviously been taken by Hamad's men, he could make enough of a calculation that worried him.

Liisa hurried after him. 'After everything that's happened you want to fly us off the top of a mountain? Can't we get up without going to the edge?'

'I doubt it. The wind's blowing from that direction, I have to get the thing airborne – and if it comes to it, going over the edge is the only way I know how to do it. You don't like it? Stay here.'

'It's my life!'

'You're already in credit.'

She grabbed his arm but he quickly turned her so that her back was towards the men, so he could watch them over her shoulder. He pulled her to him. She resisted. 'Go with it,' he whispered.

She looked at him and let him kiss her. Her eyes stayed open and so did Raglan's. He was watching the men watching him. They leered enviously. Malik Bayo said something, and Jordain laughed.

Raglan slipped the pistol he had taken from the dead aide at the compound beneath her shirt under the waistband. He needed a hidden weapon – and perhaps a final test of her. She was the best place to hide it. 'You keep this and when we get to where we're going you stay with me, understand?'

She nodded.

'You might have to help me out. You just flick the safety catch on the side, aim and shoot. Can you do that?'

She nodded.

'Good, then let's see if we can at least get there.'

Raglan finished the walk back to the aircraft alone as Liisa gazed at the terrifying drop that lay beyond. Assuming they would survive this, now was the time to contact Verskiy. Once he tracked the stolen satellite phone's GPS he would find her. And if he knew a French team led by an Englishman was out here looking for a downed aircraft, then it would spur him on.

'I need to pee,' she called.

Raglan turned. Glanced around and nodded. 'Go behind there,' he said, indicating boulders away from the men.

The moment Raglan was out of sight she pulled free the satellite phone.

Dragonović's arms were daubed with engine oil and the stained sweatband could absorb no more moisture. African dust clung across his broad back – he was a man with the power and resilience of a water buffalo. 'There was an oil-feed pipe loose. Maybe that was it.'

He closed the cowling. The men stood by. Raglan tried to start the aircraft. And failed.

The men cursed.

'Can we push start the bloody thing?' Picot joked.

Raglan gazed at the instrument panel, trying to put himself in the pilot's position. A stuttering engine. That meant fuel problems. He was missing something fundamental. A small placard on the panel gave instructions for fuel fluctuation or power surges. There were two settings for the auxiliary fuel pump to be ON in either HI and LO. The switch was in the LO position. Memory kicked in. The pilot must have thought that he would flood the engine by using the HI setting so he had put the pump to LO. But by doing that, he'd stopped the engine being able to purge the air from the fuel lines. The spring-loaded switch needed to be kept on HI.

Raglan clambered out of the cockpit and opened the small luggage compartment. There was a medical pack, a folded tarpaulin, guy lines and a length of rope. He wrapped the first three metres of rope around the propeller shaft and laid out the remaining seven. 'Load your weapons and gear inside, then grab that rope, take up the slack over your shoulder and when I tell you to haul it you break sweat and run hard. We might just kick-start this damned thing after all.'

The men's look of incredulity gave way to shouts of determination. The Serb wrapped the rope around the propellor's cone, then they all picked up the slack. Liisa joined them. Jordain said something to her with a grin on his face and she smiled back and took her place in the line. Raglan primed the engine, pressed his feet on the brake pedals and shouted out of the window.

'Now!' He tweaked the auxiliary fuel pump's switch.

The four hefty men and the lithe woman heaved, their efforts creating a spurt of pace. The rope came free, the propeller turned, faltered and then spun. The men hooted and ran for the plane. Dragonović climbed into the co-pilot's seat, the others into the rear seats. It was a tight fit. Liisa squeezed against the bulkhead with Picot pressed tightly next to her as Jordain and Bayo heaved their bulk into the cramped space. They gripped whatever handhold was available as Raglan rolled the aircraft forward. If the immediate threat of flying off the edge of a mountain had not been foremost in their minds, they would have appreciated the proximity of the woman, who turned and glanced at their anxious faces, her own creased with uncertainty.

'No one lives forever,' said Jordain.

'Shut the fuck up,' said Malik Bayo.

Raglan had already opened the cowl flaps, allowing cooler air into the engine when the men had prop-swung the plane. Raglan watched the rev counter, willing it to climb to the 1,500-rpm green sector on the dial. He held the aircraft by the brakes. The oil pressure was not high enough – and at this stage it should be at its best. There was no choice, 'close' would have to be good enough. All he could hope for was enough power to get them airborne. The engine was still running too erratically; he eased the mixture control, the throttle already at maximum, and listened to the engine shudder with power.

Raglan went through the mental checklist again – neither he nor Dragonović knew for certain what was wrong with the engine. It could still be vapour in the fuel pipes. The

Avgas reading had proved to be OK. Maybe there was sand in the fuel pump. They had cleared that but maybe there was still some in there. Maybe. He did not know the weight and density altitude for the aircraft. Too many 'maybes' and not enough information. Kicking the tyres and checking the fuel tank wasn't enough.

Still holding the aircraft with his feet on the brakes, he reached down and, using the notched trim wheel, set the elevators at twenty degrees for take-off. He applied full power against the brakes, remembered to check the circuit breakers and nursed the mixture until the engine ran smoothly – for a moment. Then it spluttered and lost power again. He quickly snatched the mixture control back a fraction; the engine steadied, the power restored. The rev needle was in the green. Good, he thought, we're getting there. Where, though, he wasn't sure. He released the brakes. If ever there was a time for prayer, this was it. Raglan didn't have the time or the inclination.

They surged forward, bouncing across the uneven terrain.

From some corner of his mind he remembered his flying instructor, a laconic Scotsman, tapping him on a knee as they taxied for his first take-off, telling him that the engine-failure rate on take-off accounted for 28 per cent of fatalities in flying.

A wee too high for my liking, sonny Jim. Let's help bring the percentage down, shall we? Right, off ye go then.

And going they were. Faster now, the airspeed indicator showing thirty knots – the engine stuttered, almost died, and Raglan grabbed for the mixture lever and nursed it. Dragonović watched him, but remained silent; they and the aircraft were in Raglan's hands now. At fifty-five knots the plane would lift into the air – whether they had enough power to climb would be another matter.

Now forty-five knots and the rev-counter needle swayed. Raglan prayed that below the edge there was no wind sheer, shifting direction across or up the face of the mountain. Fifty knots and they lost power again. This was no time to stall, the end of the improvised runaway drew closer every second: again the mixture. Flaps were down; the rugged ground conditions shook the small aircraft.

They could all see the edge now; even if Raglan aborted they would tumble into space. Raglan pulled back the control column and they climbed painfully, slowly, into the air. The engine pitch droned as it lost revs; they bounced down again, jarred as the wheels slammed back into the ground.

'Come on, come on...' Raglan urged quietly, 'this time... this time...'

Again he pulled back and they were up five, ten feet. The engine labouring. The edge forty feet away now, the chasm plainly visible; the power faltered and Raglan did the opposite of what they expected – he pushed the control column forward, forcing the plane to drop but giving it more speed. They skidded across the surface and he lessened the richness of the mixture control. Then, only as they were about to nose over the edge into the void, gave it full mixture, eased up the nose of the aircraft and hurtled into space.

They dropped like a stone.

32

Maguire was working blind. There was no means of contacting Raglan, and since the C130 had been shot down and the brief communication from Raglan, nothing more had been heard. Most would assume the worst, but Maguire's time as a professional soldier told him that Raglan and the others were MIA. And Missing in Action did not mean they were all dead. Air-crash survivors could stay alive for days and these were resilient men better trained than most. Maguire sipped his cup of tea. When the situation was uncertain and clear thinking was needed, even in the middle of a war, a brew helped concentrate the mind. Wind sluiced along the River Thames, hurling rain against the large glass panes.

Jennifer Armstrong, his SIS–CIA liaison officer, knocked and entered. She carried two slim A4 beige folders. She glanced down at the yellow legal pad on Maguire's desk. It had a page of notations. Maguire had a bigger problem than a missing covert team in the desert. If the Russians had somehow retrieved the information, he needed to forward-plan an exfiltration scheme for his intelligence source in Moscow. Trouble was, the means of communication were difficult. His source used tradecraft. Nothing electronic. No phone. No personal contact. He was deep and he was not likely to surface. Would he know there was a risk of him being exposed? He would be in the intelligence loop but that meant nothing when there were so many agencies and directorates in Russia, all fighting to keep their own secrets.

'Jennifer?'

'Sir, there's something I thought you should see.' She smiled. 'Hot off the press.'

She offered the folder. Maguire opened it and laid out a series of large monochrome photographs.

'There are local elections across Sudan and in particular West Darfur. There has been increasing violence. The Americans were monitoring the elections, given the delicate balance of power there. They have an interest, as you know, in trying to get democratically elected locals where they might do some good to help combat local government-backed insurgents. They had an overflight several hours ago. They didn't share these with anyone else. Clearly they wanted only their own people to see.'

'Should I ask how these reached my desk? We haven't shared information about this operation with them.'

'No, sir. Best not. Favours owed and all of that. And the individual concerned does not know why I wanted them.'

'All right. You've had them analysed?'

'Yes, there's a typed sheet clipped to the back of the folder. If I may?' She moved next to Maguire and the spread of photographs and, using her pen as a pointer, touched a dark shape. 'Given the length and wingspan of that image it's thought to be the charred remains of a Hercules aircraft.'

The photographs were in timed sequence as the satellite's orbit had been altered by the Americans to pass over the

Chad border area searching for insurgent strikes during the elections: a narrow focus on a volatile area. Maguire knew enough about aerial photo reconnaissance to recognize the next image: a plume of what appeared to be smoke. 'That's a dust trail from vehicles.'

'Correct, sir. Some villages not shown here were destroyed – we have intel on that – so those vehicles are thought to be from the Wagner Group. We've identified them as all-terrain Russian BPM-97s. They're the ones travelling towards...' She pointed to the next image. '... this area here, a compound at the mouth of a lake.'

The dust plumes showed two vehicles scorching the desert.

'An hour and a half later these images here... and here... show the same vehicles lined up to attack that compound. And here'—she indicated the next photograph showing clouds of smoke and the result from what had obviously been an attack—'the result.'

'Raglan.'

'Sir?'

'Go on.'

'I'm not sure why it was attacked, but that compound had nothing to do with the elections. It's a stronghold for a local warlord—'

'Faraj Hamad,' said Maguire.

'You know?'

'Carry on, Jenny.'

'Very well. If we take both a timeline and direction from the crash site to this compound... it's a long shot but Hamad has had French help over the years. What if any survivors thought they had an ally in him? Then let's assume the Wagner Group saw bodies at the crash site and thought them to be

French Foreign Legion? If the Russians are helping militant insurgents then Hamad's a target. If that's not their reason for attacking Hamad then...'

Maguire fussed the photographs and said, 'They know we have men on the ground. Which is it? To kill Hamad? Or eliminate any survivors?'

She shrugged. 'Look at the last two photographs, sir.'

At first glance there was nothing to see. And then at the extreme edge of one image Maguire saw the fish-tail wake of a boat that was out of the picture.

She said, 'An attack and a fast boat escape by somebody.'

'That we should be so lucky.' Maguire sighed and pulled out a communique from his desk drawer. 'Someone up there might be on our side, Jenny. I got this from Raglan via radio. He and six survivors were inside that compound.'

Jennifer Armstrong straightened. 'Well then,' she said quietly. Maguire thought there was a note of triumph in her voice. She smiled and slipped out another photograph from the second folder and placed it in front of her boss. 'Now it gets interesting.'

Maguire scanned the photograph. There was nothing to see. The usual flat landscape, oddly shaped perspectives from mountains and valleys as are all aerial reconnaissance photos, contours flattened by the one-dimensional image. 'Nothing,' he said.

She put another photo down on his desk. 'Same orbit, same location one hour and thirty minutes later.'

It was almost the same image but this time a tiny crucifix glistened in the sun. A small monoplane. 'It must have been camouflaged on that first pass.'

Jenny laid the next picture on Maguire's desk. 'Next

overflight. Same orbit. One hour and thirty-seven minutes later.'

There was no sign of the plane. 'You belong in the Magic Circle pulling rabbits out of a hat,' said Maguire.

She carefully gathered up the satellite images, tucking them back into their folders, then placed them neatly in front of Maguire. 'An attack. An escape. And someone flying out a previously hidden plane. God bless American satellites and owed favours.'

Maguire laid the palm of his hand on the folders. 'And Raglan. I hope.'

'The Americans did one final pass before putting their satellite on a different orbit further north where there's been increased fighting. Villages and towns burnt. Hundreds have been killed. And this one, sir, isn't such good news.' She put the glossy black-and-white image on his desk. Two vehicles. Dust behind them, moving at speed. He looked up at her grim countenance. 'Two Russian armoured vehicles moving fast away from the attack on the compound.' She handed Maguire a computer printout. A shaded view of the terrain. Two lines formed two sides of what would have been a triangle had there been a third connecting line. Maguire looked at the sharp angles converging on the eastern point. North to east to south. 'If we've read this correctly, sir – and it's a pretty big jump – let's say the point of the top line is the small plane and the line we've plotted takes it to the eastern point...' She let her sentence hang. Maguire was no fool.

'Then the line from the south takes the Russians in the direction of the downed aircraft we're searching for.' He let the sheet drop from his grasp. 'It's a question of who gets there first.'

33

Below ground, in the muted lights of the Electronic Intelligence Centre at Volokolamsk, General Verskiy stood before the tactical plotting screen. Major Lipetsk took a chinagraph pencil and looped a short line between two markers.

'You tracked the GPS signal I gave you?' said Verskiy.

'Yes, sir. The moment it left this location... here... at the lake. There was a brief loss of signal but we then picked it up again... closing on this location.'

'The target?'

The young major felt his throat constrict. It was not the location the general had originally given him. 'The target is as accurate as we can determine from the information you gave us, sir,' said Lipetsk, indicating a small triangular marker. 'But... no, sir. At least fifty kilometres off course.'

Verskiy gazed at Galina's projected line of travel. Not the target? Two things could have happened. Galina was so far astray there must be an issue he did not know about. Or, and the more he thought about it the more likely it became, the British agent had planted a false map when they had caught up with him on the London Underground. Galina was the only person who really knew what was happening and if her

GPS signal had shown her new location, then that was where the information lay buried.

'They're so damned close – they must reach it,' whispered Verskiy. It was not a question but a confirmation of belief.

Lipetsk's hand trembled as he pointed to a shellburst marker on the screen. 'There may be a problem.' A moment's silence followed his pronouncement. Like the messenger bringing bad news, the major stood back, awaiting the reaction.

Verskiy sat down and lit a cigarette. He gazed at the screen. 'The storm?'

Lipetsk referred to a computer printout and slid a dark line a few millimetres lower on the screen. Almost touching the target. 'Indications are, sir, that the storm centre is virtually on target. The winds are high and there is every likelihood that the target will be totally covered.'

Again the silence from Verskiy. Finally he nodded. 'Excellent.'

Bewildered, forgetting whom he was questioning, the young signals officer remonstrated, 'But, sir, the whole mission was generated by the target's location. If the storm covers it—'

'Not before our people reach it it won't,' Verskiy interrupted. 'I have armed units on the ground locked on to her GPS.'

Lipetsk glanced at the screen. 'It's too close to call, sir. If they do not get there before that storm hits then I can guarantee the target will be obliterated. It will be lost forever.'

'But you have pinpointed where my officer is now, which means it can be rediscovered.'

'With respect, general, even if they reach the objective, and the storm veers away, it is a storm of considerable strength – they could get bogged down.'

'They know the desert; once they find what we're looking

for they can sit it out. I have already ordered helicopters to be ready to retrieve my agent once she is brought out of there.' A country's border being violated was best left to the Russian mercenaries.

Verskiy stubbed out the cigarette, feeling a tantalizing sense of achievement. Everything depended on airlifting the document out before the British and French could muster a rescue mission. So far he had heard nothing that would suggest they had.

'It is almost over,' he said quietly.

'My congratulations, sir.'

'Not yet, the game is never won until you hold the trophy in your hands... We must win, Lipetsk. You too must pray that we win.'

The younger man looked uncertain. 'Sir?'

Verskiy stood and buttoned his coat. 'The price of playing the ultimate game, major. If we win we are rewarded more than any other; should we fail then the rewards will be... less favourable.' He looked at Lipetsk. 'Even an association with the project suggests complicity in failure.'

As Verskiy settled the fur-trimmed hat on his head, he smiled at the younger man, who looked decidedly less confident than his mentor. 'Fear is a harsh mistress, is she not? Who can deny her anything?'

34

Liisa cried out, Dragonović pushed himself back into his seat, Jordain cursed and Picot reverently crossed himself, clenching his eyes tightly as the overloaded aircraft plunged into the void.

Two hundred feet below the edge of the cliff the wind buffered against the face of the mountain and soared upwards: an invisible fist. When the air downwind of a range of hills is set in harmonic motion it creates fast-rising air known as a wave lift. Raglan had taken the biggest risk of all. Fly off the edge of the cliff and pray to God the wave lift would keep them airborne. The light aircraft responded like a feather on the wind and climbed, finding height and power.

They cheered, a shout of joy at being alive and the momentary thrill that the stomach-churning ride gave them. Only Dragonović remained silent, although he had enjoyed the risk, notching up another victory against mortality. The men were loud and swore like the soldiers they were. They joked with Dragonović and he allowed them a smile that created a moment of camaraderie.

Raglan broke the mood. 'Start looking,' he commanded. 'A plane, a broken plane, down there – somewhere.'

Dragonović glanced at Raglan. 'The sooner we find it the better.'

The object of desire waited, deaf to the insistent rattling of the sand against the Mustang's fuselage. The man and his machine that had scorched across the sky lay bound to the earth. The brief respite, the opportunity to see the beloved sky again, now lost. Impatient to rebury the mystery, sand swept along the desert surface like spray across an ocean. Soon the top winds would cut away the crests of the dunes and roll them down into the cockpit. Then the darkening storm would blot out the sun and crash down, dumping tons of sand across the imprisoned pilot, obliterating him from sight if not from memory.

Raglan scrutinized the map on his lap and tried to find some recognizable points on the ground. Dead reckoning had brought him most of the way out of one hell into another since they crash-landed in the C130. Now he knew they were almost there. From their height they saw what looked like a mountain range moving inexorably towards them. The visibility on the ground was shrouded by sand blown by the prevailing winds.

'We're close – it must be here,' he shouted, knowing it was the nerve-stretching anxiety that silenced his companions as they peered downwards.

Liisa felt the bite of gunmetal beneath the back of her shirt tucked firmly into her waistband. The killing was going to start again and the men who squeezed in the back of the aircraft with her and had seemed almost boyish when they laughed might well be the ones who would rape and murder her. If she had the chance, she would kill as many as she could and retrieve what lay hidden. She would have to keep Raglan alive to fly the plane. Beyond that she could not plan.

Dragonović's shout snapped her back. 'There! Something glinting, maybe reflection of a wing. Wind's blowing the sand away.'

Raglan banked the plane and dropped lower; he must've seen it too. Then the flickering light was gone, covered by sand and the lee of a dune.

They circled, looking for a landing place; the wind punched them and Raglan struggled at the controls. He knew Dragonović would not attempt anything until the wreck was located. It might not be what they were searching for and then Dragonović would still need him. Right now he needed to worry more about the small aircraft, which was struggling against the strengthening wind. First things first. Raglan lined up to land. The wings rocked in the cross wind. He crabbed the plane so that the aircraft's thrust could counteract the wind that was stopping him from aligning his approach to his landing zone.

'Jesus, we're going sideways!' barked Picot as the plane slewed and rocked.

'Shut it!' Jordain shouted, his fingers curled across the back of the front seats. He muttered. 'Bloody wing's going to hit the ground.'

Dragonović looked nervously at Raglan, who was

concentrating hard. 'Crab and slip, Raglan, for Christ's sake. Watch it!'

Raglan tore his eyes away from the landing zone and looked at Dragonović. His words revealed he also knew how to fly. So Raglan's life would be worthless once they found the document. Dragonović's hands hovered over the controls.

'You want to take it?' said Raglan. 'Go ahead. You get us down.'

Dragonović pulled his hands back; a trickle of sweat ran down from his temple. He shook his head. 'You do it,' he said, eyes fixed on the swaying ground below.

Raglan banked slightly, letting one wing's lift counteract the crosswind. They were thirty feet above the ground when he applied the opposite rudder, stopping the aircraft from turning. One wheel touched down; Raglan kept his speed constant, barely using his flaps; the rudder kept him on line. They bounced. The men swore. Landing in a crosswind needed a lot more practice than he'd had. They slewed to a halt, the hardpan giving out to soft drifting sand, but Raglan kept her nose up and jockeyed the plane into the wind.

The propellers stopped. They pulled their goggles on and escaped the confines of their frightening ride. Malik Bayo vomited. No one blamed him.

'A kilometre – east,' said Dragonović and led the way across the scrubland towards the dunes. Sweeping sand cut across them at knee height.

Raglan kept Liisa at his side, head down against the wind until they eventually crested a dune and saw the Mustang two hundred metres below. And they saw and heard the terrifying roar of the approaching monster now only a few miles away. Raglan gauged the storm's path. It was hurtling parallel to them. It hadn't turned. They would catch the edge of the swirling mass.

They careered down the dune, spilling and tumbling in the soft sliding sand. As they reached the bottom Dragonović held back, allowing Raglan and Liisa to go ahead. He pointed to the men, positioning them on to his flanks.

Then he walked towards Raglan and Liisa, who had already reached the grinning pilot in the cockpit.

Raglan moved his hands cautiously into the cockpit. Looking over his shoulder, he saw she was hanging back.

'I need you closer. He'll make his play soon,' he said, shouting against the wind. 'Watch them for me.'

She edged nearer. From the corner of her eye she could see the men were alert, ready for Dragonović's command.

Raglan clicked open the manacled briefcase. The dry leather cracked but held. The small medical pack came free. The writing was barely visible through the faded plastic but the operational designation – the mission heading – was clear enough. Raglan pressed the case closed again. The skeletal wrist moved, the fingers touching his own. He froze for a moment. The pilot's skull nodded in the wind.

He saw the look on her face. Was that fear or relief?

'Have you got it? He's coming,' she said.

Raglan's body blocked her. She couldn't see into the depths of the cockpit. 'Not yet,' he lied. Acid test. 'Move closer, I need the gun.'

She did the opposite and moved away, stepping quickly into the swirling sand. Raglan turned and faced Dragonović, judging the distance of the three men beyond the Serb. They would cut him down in the crossfire. The swirling dust made them turn their faces away every few seconds. There was less visibility now. They were on the sandstorm's flank, its edge sweeping across them, the roar from the storm's energy still frighteningly close. Dragonović slipped a commando knife from his webbing belt. As he moved towards Raglan, he turned and yelled into the increasing wind at the barely visible men behind him. 'Here! Come closer!' He gestured, peering into the yellow sand-filled light. The men bent towards him, pulling face cloths over nose and mouth as they staggered into the buffeting wind.

Raglan reached for the skeleton's pistol in his shoulder holster. The leather flaked; the gun came away easily. Had the dry desert air kept the mechanism in working order? If the hotshot pilot had been close to danger, then there would be a round in the breech. There was no time to check. Raglan turned, levelled the pistol and pressed the trigger. The .45 recoiled. Jordain was out on a flank; Raglan didn't know which of the other two men he had taken a snap shot at, but he ducked as the shot went wide. The others crouched. Dragonović faltered and rolled as a second bullet struck the place he had been standing. Raglan squeezed the trigger again but the weapon misfired. He had bought himself vital seconds.

Dragonović raised himself to confront Raglan but the Englishman was gone. The Serb cursed and staggered forward through the swirling sand to the aircraft as the men, too, closed in. Picot reached for his knife to cut away a length of his shirt to use as an additional layer across his mouth. The scabbard was empty. He hesitated. He'd had it on the plane. In his moment of uncertainty, a cowled figure stepped up behind him and rammed his knife into his neck.

He screamed. Jordain and Bayo turned towards the sound. The wraith disappeared as they levelled their weapons. Malik Bayo was the closest and went to the fallen man. Behind the goggles Picot's eyes stared blindly, the blood running from his neck into the sand.

'Fuck!' Bayo cried. He turned. 'Raglan's killed Picot!' he shouted to Dragonović and Jordain. He picked up Picot's weapon and stepped towards Dragonović.

'Stay close!' the Serb commanded. He waved in Jordain. The three of them close together was their best protection. Dragonović would let the desert take Raglan. Killing him was secondary now to retrieving the secret held in the plane. It was another ten metres to the downed Mustang. As he faced the target, Jordain and Bayo approached, fifteen paces between them. Jordain was ahead of Bayo by three metres when the ghostly figure loomed out of the storm. The knife plunged into the top of the black man's skull. No sooner had the attack been made than the phantom was gone. An animal cry soared above the wind's roar. Jordain turned and saw his friend stumble towards him, a combat knife protruding from his head. He fell to his knees and stayed there.

Jordain reached him, bent down and held him. Malik Bayo's mouth was slack. Spittle dribbled from his lips on to his sand-caked skin. He was already dead.

'Boss!' Jordain bellowed.

Dragonović turned as a shadowy figure ran through the storm. He fired rapidly. Not knowing if he had hit the target.

'Leave him!'

Visibility was down to nothing more than a few metres. Dragonović waited until Jordain was with him. He was alert for the shadow that had stepped from the storm.

'It wasn't Raglan. Too small.'

'Then who?'

'Who else? The woman.'

'Jesus. The medic?'

Dragonović's rifle butt was in his shoulder. He snatched a glance into the cockpit. 'There's a case. Grab it, Geordie. We need to get back to the plane. I'll cover you.'

Jordain glanced at the slack-jawed skull. 'You can wipe that stupid grin off your face, mate. The joke's on you,' he said to the skeleton. He bent double into the cockpit and snatched at the manacled briefcase. The skeleton's wrist bones snapped; the head dropped forward on to Jordain who jerked in panic, the briefcase slipping into the cockpit's footwell. He raised himself, laughed at his own stupidity, stretched down and grabbed the brittle leather. A sharp stab in his wrist. Twice. As he yanked the briefcase free another bite punctured the skin. Jordain saw the black colour inside the gaping jaws. He staggered back, dropping the case in the sand as the three-metre-long curled brown snake readied to strike again. Had he not thrown himself backwards the next bite would have been in his neck.

A startled Dragonović half turned. 'What?'

Jordain shook his head in disbelief. 'Snakebite. Black mamba.'

Dragonović took a step back as if the man had the plague.

'I need a tourniquet,' said Jordain, as reality bit as painfully as the snake's fangs. For a moment it looked as though the Serb would help; instead he snatched the briefcase and strode off into the storm.

'Boss! Help me!' Jordain staggered a few metres and fell to his knees, his arm bent to slow the poison. A shadow passed across him he looked up and saw Liisa's swathed face. There was blood on her hand and sleeve.

'I've been bitten,' he said lamely. 'Tie a tourniquet. Quick.'

She stood over him a moment longer and then turned to follow Dragonović into the swirling sand. 'Jesus,' he muttered. 'Bitch! Bloody bitch. For God's sake!' He got to his feet, found his rifle and grabbed it with his free hand. He wouldn't last long without medical help. If the gods were smiling he might reach the medical pack on board the woman's plane. He stared back at the Mustang, orientated himself towards the way they'd come and took a determined step into the storm.

Part of his brain told him he should not be moving. That exertion only increased the flow of the neurotoxin. Survival instinct forced his legs onwards. He stopped. A burning sensation crept along his arm from the bite wound. Painful pins and needles rendered his grip useless. His vision blurred, then cleared. He was on his knees again. He struggled to breathe. Someone was standing in front of him. Every instinct bred into the soldier he was made him reach for his rifle. It was pushed aside.

'No need, Geordie,' said Raglan, voice raised against the howling wind. He pulled out a field dressing from his pouches. 'Keep your arm bent.' Raglan applied a pressure bandage on the bites, which were still bleeding, then pulled free the canvas belt from the rifle and wrapped the strap above the wound and as high as he could up his arm. Jordain looked terrible.

'The bastard ran out on me.'

'It's the mission. It always comes first, Geordie, you know that.'

'Then why don't you do the same?' he gasped.

'I'm the good guy,' he said.

'And Liisa. She killed the others. Some bloody doctor.'

'I'm damned sure she's no doctor,' said Raglan. 'With any luck there'll be antivenom in the plane's medical kit.'

Jordain shook his head. 'Raglan, I know when I'm done. Can feel it. I'm dying, no two ways about it. Nature's way of telling me this is one mission I failed.'

'Shut up and save your breath.' He hauled Jordain to his feet, his shoulder burning with pain. He ignored it and bent a knee, draping the dying man across his shoulders, carrying him back towards the aircraft. 'Let your arm hang down, it'll slow the poison.'

The snake's neurotoxin and cardiotoxin venom was fatal. He knew Jordain would be unconscious in twenty minutes and dead in less than two hours if he didn't get antivenom. Raglan pushed through the soft sand. He felt the small plastic container press against his ribs. He had to reach the plane before Dragonović could take off.

'Geordie, you with me?' Raglan said, determined to keep the man conscious as long as possible.

A muffled groan was the only answer.

Raglan lengthened his stride despite the broken terrain and shifting sand, the weight of the stocky man bearing down on him. He gasped for breath beneath the cloth howli wrapped around his mouth. The goggles steamed up. Blue sky appeared through the sand haze. It was a stroke of luck. The rolling sandstorm had veered away, taking its misery elsewhere. He ripped away the cloth and pushed up the goggles. The storm's passing exposed the stark landscape before him. He saw two figures several hundred metres to one side. One ahead of the other. Dragonović had become disorientated and was wide of the plane's location. Liisa was two hundred metres behind him.

Raglan saw one side of the plane had sand banked against it. He changed direction, cutting across forty-five degrees from Dragonović, who had not yet seen the half-covered aircraft. From where he was, all he would see would be the sloping sand against the fuselage. A sand dune. Nothing more.

The four-kilo rifle was a strain on his arm. He almost discarded it to lessen his burden but ingrained discipline tightened his grip. Jordain was balanced precariously. He pulled the man's good arm across his chest and steadied him.

'Stay with me, Geordie. I'm not doing this for fun. Keep breathing. You hear me? Geordie! Say something! Come on!'

'You're... crushing my balls,' the man whimpered. 'I'm dying, Raglan.'

'If you can feel your balls you're still alive. Almost there, Geordie. The plane's right there. Hear me? Geordie?'

Jordain's breath came hard from Raglan's jolting gait. Raglan panted, urging himself on. 'Three hundred metres, that's all... he hasn't turned yet... hasn't seen us... push on, come on push... harder.'

He was two hundred metres from the plane when the first shot cracked through the air.

35

Raglan opened his stride, twisted left and right as best he could with his burden and the uneven terrain. A moving target zigzagging was difficult for a shooter. Dragonović had seen him and changed direction; he was running faster than Raglan but was still five hundred metres away. Automatic gunfire whip-cracked in the air. The assault rifle's range was three hundred. The bullets would travel beyond that but lose their effectiveness; the vortex of wind sucked behind the storm would throw off even well-aimed shots. The storm's abandoned offspring, dust devils, swirled and chased after it.

Raglan's lungs burnt. He stumbled, recovered and staggered to the plane. Fifty, thirty, ten metres. He fell heavily into the shade beneath the wing. Jordain's body rolled away. Raglan grabbed him, turned him on to his back, felt for a pulse. It was faint. How long before Dragonović reached them? He'd be wary, knowing Raglan had cover and was armed, and he wouldn't fire unless he had a clear shot for fear of striking the aircraft. Raglan reached into the baggage compartment, pulling free the green satchel medical kit, scrabbling through it. Hell, where was the antivenom?

His fingers found a separate plastic box tucked in the

compartment's corner. Antivenom. Ten vials. Raglan's memory scoured its archives from his time in Africa. Was it ten millilitres per minute or every ten minutes? His memory clicked into place. Raglan put ten millilitres into Jordain's vein, then snatched the rifle, peered around the edge of the aircraft, and saw Dragonović two hundred metres away, creeping slowly towards the plane using rocks and depressions in the ground as cover.

Raglan fired rapid shots to keep him at bay, then prepared another vial of antivenom and checked his watch. If Jordain was going to survive, he needed an injection every minute. Once again he eased the needle into the vein. Checked for a pulse. Weak but still there. He fired another three shots in Dragonović's direction. The Serb had gone to ground. Raglan was about to administer the third dose when a shadow loomed a hundred metres away. Raglan rolled, steadied and fired. The shadow was gone. Dragonović could circle the aircraft and choose his shot. He must know Raglan had retrieved the document because he had already abandoned the empty briefcase. Raglan went front to back along the aircraft's fuselage. There was no sign of Dragonović or of Liisa. The Serb was an experienced fighter. He would stalk and kill his prey.

Raglan injected the next shot of antivenom into Jordain's arm. Of the ten vials seven were left. There were three bites. Killing bites. Jordain would need all ten. Preferably more. He felt his pulse. He was still alive. The sound of a boot scraping on stones alerted him. He spun around. Dragonović levelled his weapon. Five metres. A killing shot.

The weapon clicked. The dust storm had jammed the mechanism. Raglan reached for his rifle but Dragonović hurled his useless weapon at him. It caught Raglan's arm and gave the Serb time to launch himself at him, his weight striking him like an ox. Raglan half rolled, but his attacker held on. They twisted, grappling for each other's face, bucking and kicking and rolling over the unconscious Jordain. Raglan's fingers gripped Dragonović's neck, forcing the heavier man to release one of his hands and attempt to ease Raglan's choking grip. Raglan brought his knee up, twisted his body and threw the Serb free.

Both men scrambled for Raglan's rifle but Dragonović kicked hard, his boot catching Raglan's shoulder.

'I'll kill you with my bare hands,' he spat.

Raglan recovered, crouched, squared his stance, waiting for the circling man to make his move. There was no need for Raglan to attack. Let him come. Let him commit. Now there was a combat knife in Dragonović's fist.

He lunged. Low strike, rammed up hard. A gutting blow.

Raglan half turned, forcing Dragonović's arm away into thin air, letting his momentum bring him close. Raglan struck him hard beneath his nose. His head snapped back. Blood spurted. The big man staggered. Raglan hit him twice more. Heel of his right hand beneath his chin, and a turning sharp jab aimed for his solar plexus. Dragonović's head snapped back, then his torso doubled. Air sucked hard, knees bent, eyes wide with pain and anger. Raglan took a step back and then drove his fist into the man's temple.

The Serb staggered, almost fell, but was too tough to put down. He backed away, caught his breath, spat blood and wiped away the phlegm from nose and mouth. He circled, fists curled, arms bent. He snapped a straight left, Raglan sidestepped, the grazing blow catching the side of his head.

Dragonović had momentum. He followed up with a blow to Raglan's kidneys.

Pain seared through Raglan. He blocked a flurry of blows; then he backed away, letting the big man come at him, the aggressor pursuing a weakened opponent. Raglan spun on his heel away from the next blow and kicked hard into the side of Dragonović's knee. Defying the numbing pain, the Serb made no sound. Then a guttural animal growl bellowed from his chest: impetus to hurl himself at Raglan. Wrapping his arms around the Englishman, he gripped his face with both claw-like hands and squeezed. Fingers in eyes and mouth, trying to blind and rip away Raglan's face. Raglan bit ferociously hard on one thumb, drew blood and felt the bone begin to give. Dragonović grimaced, and his grip loosened enough for Raglan to pull the crushing hands away. Raglan headbutted him twice in rapid succession. The Serb's arm swung wide and the lucky blow caught Raglan across the head. It spun him around and he tripped over Jordain's prostrate body.

Dragonović bent and picked up Raglan's rifle and levelled it. He clearly found it hard to balance but there was no doubt he could shoot and kill. 'It's over. Give me what you took from the cockpit.'

Raglan got to his feet. 'Why ask? You're going to kill me.'

'Because I don't know what you've done with it! Where is it? Inside here?' he said with a swift gesture of the rifle towards the plane.

'You'll never know,' said Raglan. He had no chance of escaping the burst of fire that would surely come.

'I'll take your legs out first, Raglan, damned if I won't.'

'Then I'll be in so much pain I'll pass out. I'll never tell you.'

'It's here somewhere!'

Raglan nodded. 'Somewhere, but even if you find it it'll take a lot for you to get this plane out of the sand. Why don't you let me dig it clear? We'll fly out together. I know what's wrong with it. You don't.'

Reality sank in. Dragonović saw it through the pain of his leg. The deep tissue would take time to return to full strength. A swirl of wind twisted sand around them but Dragonović kept the rifle aimed squarely at Raglan's chest. 'Get the shovel.'

Raglan reached into the storage compartment and pulled out the shovel. Dragonović gestured Raglan to move around to the other side of the plane where the sand had banked up. A long shadow appeared behind Dragonović. Liisa stepped into view. She levelled the pistol Raglan had given her.

'Drop your weapon. I'm armed. Turn slowly.'

Dragonović turned and faced her. He kept his rifle low. She was only five metres away. She couldn't miss. And it looked as though she knew how to handle a gun. There were bloodstains on her hands and arms.

'It was you who killed my men?'

'I'll take the information, Raglan.'

'No, I don't think so. You're no more a doctor than I am.'

'Who I am is unimportant. The document. Where is it?'

Raglan moved next to Dragonović. 'I've hidden it.' He nodded towards the Serb. 'He made the same threat. I gave the same answer. Kill me and you will never get it.'

'I'll kill him first.'

'Be my guest.'

'Drop your weapon,' she ordered Dragonović.

'I wouldn't do that,' said Raglan.

Dragonović looked at the Englishman.

Raglan looked at Liisa. 'You don't think I'd give you a loaded weapon, do you?'

A second of uncertainty. Another of disbelief. She squeezed the trigger. Dragonović flinched. The hammer fell on an empty chamber. She wasted no time checking the weapon, threw it aside and raised her arm to beckon someone Raglan couldn't see. A hundred metres behind her a man with a sniper's rifle stood from behind boulders. Rifle in the shoulder. A red dot appeared on Dragonović chest. The sniper's aim steady. A clean shot. Dragonović threw down Raglan's rifle and raised his hands.

'You Russian intelligence? GRU? One of Verskiy's people?' said Dragonović.

Raglan saw her look of startled acknowledgment.

'I'm an asset. Have been for years,' said the Serb.

Raglan slumped. The killer's link to the Russians was as damaging as any punch.

'Who else?' she demanded.

'Just me. We were confined to base before we left. I couldn't tell Verskiy what was happening. I doubt he even knows I'm here.'

Raglan heard engines start behind a rock-strewn hill. Liisa took a satellite phone from her satchel and gestured with it to Raglan. She smiled, stepped closer but kept enough space between her and Raglan as the sniper approached. Two Russian armoured vehicles hove into view.

'They're not GRU Spetsnaz. Mercenaries, then,' said Raglan. 'Wagner Group.'

'Friends,' she said.

'Let me help him,' Raglan said, indicating Jordain.

The sniper had almost reached them as the vehicles rolled across the uneven ground behind him. They pulled up and a dozen men climbed down. An armoured vehicle commander called out, 'Major Menshikova? You've got what you wanted?'

She sighed and looked at Raglan. 'Plenty of courage, these people, but bone-headed.'

'Not Liisa, then?'

She softened. 'Galina. Friends call me Gala.'

She gestured him to raise his hands and turn around. There were enough armed men for him to not have a choice. 'Search him,' she told the sniper. It was a thorough search. The sniper turned Raglan back to face her.

'Nothing.'

'He won't have it,' said Dragonović.

She studied Raglan. 'I could have these men break every bone in your body slowly. Dragonović wouldn't need any encouragement.'

'Then I'd choke on my own vomit.'

She nodded. Raglan was the sort of man who would die rather than reveal where he'd hidden the document. She casually checked inside the aircraft. She signalled a couple of men. 'Strip it. See if there's anything there that shouldn't be. A package. A sealed container.'

Raglan nodded towards Jordain again. 'He needs antivenom. There's enough to save him,' he said.

She shook her head. 'He's no use to me.'

'Like your partner back at Hamad's place? Major Golyev.' He allowed his recognition of the GRU operative sink in. 'Him I knew about. You not. Obviously.'

'But you doubted me.'

'My sixth sense. I usually manage to sniff out vermin. I was too slow this time. Did you sacrifice him to save your own skin?'

'He was badly hurt. I...' She faltered for a moment. 'I took his pain away.'

'So you kill your own people. You really are a piece of work.' He looked down at Jordain. 'He's one of mine. It costs you nothing. Give yourself a tick in the plus column.'

She thought for a moment and nodded.

Raglan was bending to administer the lifesaving dose when Dragonović's boot stamped down hard on the vials.

'It saves a bullet,' said Dragonović. 'Neither of you gets out of here alive and tells the world what went down here.'

Raglan's fist drove hard between Dragonović's legs. It put the big man on his knees. Raglan was on his feet. Rifles covered him.

'Enough!' she said.

Raglan looked with despair at Jordain. He felt for a pulse. Nothing. Raglan pressed his palm against the man's chest. He could feel no heartbeat. He smothered his hand with the other and began CPR. Dragonović had rolled clear, shook off the grinning mercenaries' helping hands and staggered to his feet.

Liisa watched the men strip out everything that might conceal a document. She studied the broken ground around the aircraft. Would Raglan have had time to hide it out there? She looked at Raglan working on Jordain, then kicked Raglan's neck, forcing him aside. She bent and searched the body. It didn't take long to find the plastic container.

'Nice try. You almost saved both him and what we're looking for.' There was no note of regret in her voice, just acknowledgement of the fact that Raglan had got close. She strode towards the vehicles.

'Kill him,' said Dragonović.

She studied Raglan for a moment. 'No. I owe him for getting me here. Let the desert take him. He has nowhere to go.'

'It needs to end here!' Dragonović insisted.

'This is my operation,' she said. She looked at Raglan. 'Let him take his chances out there. Destroy the plane.'

Unarmed, Dragonović had no choice but to follow her and the sniper as they moved away, leaving Raglan still at gunpoint with his arms raised. Two men ran forward, picked up his abandoned weapon and tossed it along with grenades into the doomed plane. Raglan turned and ran.

Half a dozen strides later he threw himself down. The grenades exploded; the plane boomed as Avgas ignited. The fuselage cracked, the wing broke, flames and smoke engulfed the carcass. Raglan got to his feet. He saw Liisa climb into the vehicle, cast a backward glance and disappear from view. Black diesel fumes coughed from the exhausts. They were soon out of sight.

The gods were laughing. There would be no success today. It was what it was. He drank from his water bottle, then took Jordain's half-filled canteen from the dead man's pouch. Raglan pulled out Ulrich Becker's old map. The retired legionnaire had marked a place that might just be close enough to the border for Raglan to seek help. If the Masalit's clan village was anywhere near the place marked on the creased map, then that and an old soldier's memory might be the only thing lying between life and death. Neighbouring Chad was his best bet. Legionnaires were stationed there.

He couldn't walk there in a straight line: the mountain range between him and the border would finish him. He squatted. Placed a finger on the map. Oriented his compass. It looked to be 150 kilometres. How far could he travel in a day in such heat and with little water? Forty kilometres would be good but unlikely. The heat haze shimmered on the horizon, turning rock outcrops into indistinct figures of men waiting to kill him. If he pushed it, he could get close in four or five days. If he reached a village with phone coverage, he could contact Maguire. If. He checked the map again and decided to take the flattest route he could find. If he avoided any roving bands of Janjaweed militants, he had a chance – a slim one, because his water wouldn't hold out and the heat of the day wouldn't drop much at night. It would take its toll.

The urge to bury Geordie pulled at him. But there was no time and the effort would put a strain on him. He needed every ounce of strength now. No good worrying. Time to crack on. Do it long. Do it hard. This was what his time in the Legion had been about. Marches of sixty kilometres and more across mountains in all weathers carrying a donkey load on his back. This was just a long walk. No weight to carry. Piece of cake. Wrapping the howli across his face, he struck out into the wilderness away from death and devastation.

36

He managed thirty-five kilometres on the first day. Rested for three hours as the sun went down, trying to find a patch of cooler sand that had been in shadow. The heat felt as fierce as it did during daylight. There were places in the desert where the temperature plummeted at night. Not here.

Moon and starlight guided him onwards. There had been nothing to salvage from the burnt-out plane. Even if he had a poncho or a ground sheet with which to make a still it would have been useless. There was no cold night to create condensation.

Thirst was going to be his biggest problem. He could go without food for days but not water. Without water he would last maybe three days in this heat. Being frugal with what he had might keep him going psychologically but he needed the water inside his body, not in the canteen, so that he could stay hydrated as long as possible, especially with the exertion that would be demanded of him. He drank most of it, kept a couple of mouthfuls for the following day and pushed on.

The horizon threatened another layer of approaching sand. He could see the small storm veering this way and that in the moonlight. He prayed it would continue on its intended path but when he felt the hot wind strike his face he knew he was out of luck. Raglan ran as fast as his legs and lungs would allow. The speed of these small desert storms was deceptive. He reached the biggest boulder he could find lying against an incline and pressed his back into it.

The roar came first. Then the splattering of grains of sand. Then the darkness as the storm overwhelmed him and the night sky. It dumped sand around him. He turned his covered face into the boulder, cupping his hands either side, desperately trying to avoid inhaling dust and sand. His legs were becoming heavy from the weight of the sand mounting higher. It was already at his waist and then his back. He focused his mind. It was hard not to panic because if the storm continued much longer he would be buried. Raglan stretched his arms above him, ignoring the one shoulder's complaint as he blindly sought a fingertip hold. He jammed the fingers of one hand into a fissure in the rockface, then found a ridge with the other. He pulled himself up. The sand funnelled down the sides of the boulder, adding more weight against him. He hung on desperately, the weight of the sand pulling him down. It was like being in a grain silo with tonnes of grain being poured around him.

He wasn't prepared to die like this but he was helpless. His strength would soon give out and the sand had reached his shoulders. Its weight was crushing his lungs. It was pure mental effort to take shallow breaths and not gulp air through the now damp cloth across his face. Spittle was holding the dust and blocking his airway. Disconnected images of his father appeared in his mind's eye. Father and young son hunched against a winter hailstorm. Where was that? He tried to recall, the mental journey taking him away from his predicament. Austria. It must have been when his father was stationed in Vienna. No, he told himself. That made no sense. His mind was playing tricks. He was starting to panic. He had to get a grip.

Raglan had worked alongside US Navy Seals and remembered a tactical breathing technique they used in high-stress situations. Before going into a hard action, men were keyed up, their breathing rapid. They needed to be focused. They needed to be calm. They settled their breathing by inhaling only through the nose, holding it for the count of four. Exhaling slowly through the mouth. Inhaling through the nostrils again. Hold for the count of four. Exhale to the count of four. He concentrated. He steadied his breathing.

Despite the prospect of drowning in sand, Raglan's heartbeat slowed. His mind dismissed any notion of panic. He did not know how long he clung to the rock but eventually the weight eased from his back and shoulders as sand slid away down the slope. His ears were no longer buffeted by the roar. It was receding. The storm had retreated. Gravity pulled more sand from his back. He pushed himself away from the boulder's protection, dragged off the goggles and unwrapped the howli from his mouth. Daylight. Blue sky tinged by the rising sun. He coughed and spat, then pressed a finger against each nostril and blew dirt from his airways.

He laboured through the deep sand and found firm ground again on the top of the low escarpment. The barren landscape had been altered by the ridges of sand but the horizon was clear. The Nile was too far to the east for him to be able to benefit from any of its tributaries but the lake they had travelled across lay to the west and he felt confident he would skirt its northernmost streams, which fed in from one of the many smaller rivers.

By day three his legs were protesting at every step. The savage landscape belted heat from the ground and the sky. He clambered along an uneven ridge to give clear sight of the way ahead. Whenever shade presented itself behind a rock or a dip in the ground, he took it and rested for a few minutes. His body was being punished but he kept his mind sharp, batting away any negative thoughts, staying focused on the point he had chosen to reach by the time the sun's arc had shifted. His spirits lifted when he reached patches of green vegetation. He cut free a small plant and crushed its bulbous roots, sucking the water through his parched lips. He spat out the pulp, did the same with another half-dozen and immediately felt the benefit of ingesting their moisture.

On the fourth day it was no longer the lack of water that concerned him but the dust trails from vehicles a few miles ahead. He squinted in the glare. They were turning towards him. Anyone in a vehicle would have the advantage of seeing further than he could. The ground rose to his left, foothills to the higher ground, rock-strewn: it would be hard going to put distance between him and the shimmering dust devils that headed towards him. He hunched, kept his eyes down and forward, eager not to take a fall, and ran as hard as his weakened body permitted – little more than a loping stagger. He used low boulders like a parkour runner, jumping from one to the other, making ground. Adrenaline feeding his exhaustion.

He saw what looked like a slender animal track winding its way upwards. The more height he gained the clearer the view of the distant vehicles, now free of the heat haze. Three 4x4 pickups, armed men huddled in the flatbeds. Still too far away to identify who they were. It made no difference. There were no friendlies out here.

His lungs burnt from the heat and his efforts. His throat and mouth were bone dry. He checked where the vehicles were. Seven hundred metres. Men spilling out. One 4x4 had a heavy machine gun mounted. Forty metres ahead of him the boulders splintered, shards flew everywhere. Rounds ricocheted. And then the sound-wave caught up. Heavy thudding staccato – fifty calibre. It could tear up the ground at two thousand metres. They were either bad shots or were cutting him off.

Raglan ducked and ran towards the fall of shot where gullies lay below the rock faces. The gunfire ceased. He heard indistinct shouts as men clambered uphill. Hardy fighters used to these extreme conditions, they were as nimble as mountain goats. They wore baggy pants and long loose shirts; their belts held ammunition and long knives. Raglan clambered higher. The machine-gunner saw him and laid suppressing fire three hundred feet above him. A small landslide tumbled down as the dry earth was loosened. Raglan kept going forward on all fours. Sucking hot air, ignoring the pain in his lungs and leg muscles. If the machine-gunner had wanted to kill him, he could have swept an arc of fire across his ascent and killed him outright. They wanted him alive. And falling into terrorist hands meant they would behead him.

Fear drove him to redouble his efforts. He skirted along a gradient; erosion had cut a path across a contour. It gave him hope. The men's voices were closer now, but he had a rhythm to his pace. He would outrun them. Massive rock formations shielded him from the machine-gunner. A dogged lope took him along the hillside where the path gave way to loose scree. He slid fifteen metres down, saw that he had flanked the 4x4s and the gunner. If he kept going and if luck was on his side he'd get away.

But what he couldn't see was the third vehicle that had driven along the hills to act as a cut-off. Now they were waiting, men of the mountains and desert, spread out. This was their hunting ground, and he had no way out.

Several men had aligned themselves across his escape route. He ducked and slithered between two large boulders, hoping that if snakes lurked there they would be more afraid of him than he of them. He squeezed through to the far side of the small gap, saw there was no one in sight and edged cautiously around the face of the boulder – coming face to face with a tribesman. The man was slower to react than Raglan, who struck him beneath his sternum. Had the man not stumbled backwards before the full force of the blow had landed he would have dropped silently. However, he cried out, Raglan's punch adding to his momentum but failing to cause sufficient injury. The man reached out and snatched Raglan's ankle: Raglan had no choice but to tuck himself in and tumble down the rocky slope. Sharp-edged stones lacerated his shirt and flesh. He broke his fall, used the momentum to roll on to his feet and scrambled on downhill. No shots followed him. For a moment he thought he had evaded them, but several more men appeared. He was boxed in. He crouched, hefting a rock in each hand, determined to kill as many as he could before dying on the barren hillside.

They advanced, weapons at the ready, confirming that they wanted him alive, otherwise he'd have been cut down by now. Three men rushed him and a fourth leapt down from behind him. He struck back hard, but his footing gave way. They kicked and he curled up, trying to protect himself, his ribs. A boot caught the side of his head. Then a voice cried out from somewhere. He half raised himself, spat blood, reached for his fallen knife and didn't see the rifle butt that cast him into darkness.

37

He awoke in a hut that stank of manure from the goats penned outside the half-moon entrance. Light filtered through the reed and wattle walls. He was chained to a stake in the ground, his back against the wall. Dried blood flecked his tattered shirt; he was badly bruised but there was nothing broken. Small mercies. One eye, struck by the rifle butt, was half shut. His boots, watch, map and compass had been removed, along with his webbing, which contained Maguire's hidden phone. There was a gourd of water next to him. He sniffed it and then slaked his thirst, feeling some measure of strength return to his limbs.

Daylight seared into the hut. He heard women's voices and children's shrill, excited shouts. A shadow blocked the entrance, then stooped and entered the hut. A man in his fifties or so. He wore a flowing white robe and a wrapped cloth turban around his head; his face showed refined Arabic features and white stubble. He squatted, unafraid, in front of Raglan, gazed at him and said something Raglan did not understand. Raglan replied in Arabic, asking if he was to be executed.

The man's expression changed; his eyebrows raised. He shuffled out of the hut. A moment later two men armed with AK-47 assault rifles came inside. One man covered him as the other released the chain; they tugged him outside. Squinting into the harsh light, he felt the heat from the sand beneath his feet. He was in a small village alongside a stream; most huts were of grass and reed with cone-shaped roofs, but some houses were more substantial, built with mud and grass. Rows of millet grew on the stream's banks, and the surrounding area was green and fertile. The hills around the village gave way in the distance to the mountains, but the boulders and rock formations on these foothills had eventually yielded to the fertile lowland. Women dressed in brightly coloured loose clothing covered their faces when he was brought outside. In the distance, near the trees, boys tended a herd of goats. A large grass and reed enclosure hid the four vehicles that had chased him. Raglan stopped and looked around. The stream was presumably a feed from the top of the lake. The waterways would swell in the rainy season and these nomadic farmers would move on. They were well armed, and in this part of the world, tribal conflicts meant no outsider could be sure who was friend or foe.

The man holding the chain waited, apparently patiently, while Raglan oriented himself. If there was a chance to run he needed a sense of direction. Then the gunman gestured with his rifle. They tugged him towards a grass-covered *masik*, a communal place where the men of the village gathered to talk, eat and pray. Raglan stood in front of thirty men, a mixture of seated elders and fighters with an eclectic assortment of assault rifles and spears. The man who had visited him in the hut stood and addressed the others. Once again Raglan did not understand the dialect. It was a rambling explanation; some of the men nodded, an occasional *hà* escaped their lips as if they had taken on board something the man had said.

Raglan wanted to explain himself but before he could speak the meeting became heated. Some of the other men stood and made threatening gestures. They spoke rapidly. The older man calmed them and then challenged Raglan.

He spoke Arabic. 'You are responsible for destroying three villages. Your men killed women and children.'

Raglan knew these tribesmen were not Janjaweed. They didn't wear the same clothing or have the armaments of the government-backed killers. It was time to fabricate a convincing story. 'I came here with men to rescue a woman doctor held by Faraj Hamad. Our plane was shot down. We escaped an attack by Janjaweed.'

Some of them men understood; others looked to the man doing the interrogating. Some shouted, pointing their weapons at Raglan.

'My people do not believe you. We have lost relatives in the attacks. We know of Faraj Hamad, but you Russian mercenaries show no pity, just like the Janjaweed.' He nodded to the men guarding Raglan – one tugged him out of the *masik*; the other cocked his weapon. It was to be a summary execution in revenge for killings the Russian mercenaries must have committed when they sought their GRU agent. Women gathered; children ran from their duties to watch the killing. The man pulling him along was not strong enough to resist Raglan yanking him off his feet, buying time to turn and face the angry men.

He shouted in Arabic that he wasn't Russian. That he was an Englishman. Asking if they were from the Masalit tribe. And for good measure repeated it again in French in the hope they might understand a common language often used in this part of Africa. '*Êtes-vous Masalit? Je suis anglais. Pas Russe.*'

The guard scrambled to his feet, dropping the chain, and the two men grabbed Raglan, kicking his legs from beneath him, forcing him to his knees, yanking back his head, a knife at his throat. There was no way out now. A soldier's mantra echoed in his mind. *Death is nature's way of telling you you've failed.* Raglan remembered the name of the old tribal chief that Ulrich Becker had mentioned from his time in the Sudan: 'Saleh!' he shouted. 'Saleh!' The older man raised a hand, stopping the blade being drawn across his throat.

He stepped closer. 'We are Masalit. Saleh was our clan leader. That was many years ago. How would you know of this?'

'I am with the Legion.'

The man studied Raglan and then saw the thin cord around his neck. He pulled out the cap badge medallion. 'Legion?'

As best he could from his constrained position, Raglan nodded. 'Foreign Legion. Yes,' he said, feeling a sense of gratitude to a small child and her gift.

Without another word the elder pushed the two men aside and helped Raglan to his feet, spitting out a command to the guards to unlock the chain. The gathered men rose too and huddled behind their spokesman.

The older man clasped his hands together and dipped his head. 'We are old friends of the Legion. We do not forget what is owed by our people. We ask forgiveness for the way we have treated you.'

Raglan looked at the gathered men and women. They'd had violence inflicted on their villages by Russian mercenaries. They had sought revenge. So had Raglan when it was necessary. What was there to forgive? In that moment he was grateful for having served in North Africa and being exposed to the local Muslim population. He searched his memory for snatches of the Qur'an to make as dignified an answer as he could. 'Whoever does not forgive others will not be forgiven,' he said, and then muttered quietly to himself, 'and I need all the forgiveness I can get.'

38

The tribal elders sat with Raglan in the *masik* as he finished the food and drink brought by the women. The man who spoke Arabic and some French explained they had tried to pursue the Russian mercenaries after they slaughtered villagers from their clan. The sandstorm had swallowed the killers, but they had been heading south towards the Central African Republic. The mercenaries were operating in the disputed zone, protecting their own people mining in the Kafia Kingi. What few weapons these farmers owned had been taken from Janjaweed militia they had fought in the past; as well as eking out an existence in the harsh landscape, they had been forced to become fighters when their villages were threatened.

The wounds Raglan had suffered during his escape attempt were at risk of infection if they weren't seen to soon. The elders instructed two boys to attend to the cuts. The men watched as the boys gently bathed the dirt from his back and arms and then applied a soothing paste. He made a point of not wincing in front of these men. He had seen north African tribesmen use the acacia tree for healing wounds. He asked the elder, who nodded and pointed beyond the village. By the time the boys finished and were dismissed Raglan had recounted his story, maintaining the lie that he was part of a rescue team whose transport plane had been destroyed. They returned everything they had taken. Maguire's mobile phone battery was dead.

The men had a rapid and incomprehensible conversation among themselves. The elders summoned the fighters; the hidden 4x4s were brought out. Raglan was embraced by his interrogator and urged to go with the men. As he walked across to the waiting vehicles, the village turned out to watch his departure. A child ran forward and held his hand silently, a simple gesture of goodwill towards a man whose brothers-in-arms had once saved the village. The fighting men in the vehicles didn't berate the boy, waiting patiently as Raglan slowed his pace to match that of the small child. Raglan touched the boy's head, looked into his face and for a passing moment saw the eyes of a child in another war, in a dark cave, many years before. A child who had tried to kill Raglan and instead lay dead by his hand. That was Raglan's burden. Among others.

The child turned and ran back to his mother. Engines started, wheels spun and like a desert wind swept Raglan away.

Hours later, shimmering heat became the reflection of water: a lake. A larger village, big enough for a dozen dirt streets, mud and reed houses, cattle, goats and sheep penned by a *boma* of cut branches of acacia tree thorns, sprawled next to the shore. The lake served as a defence across one flank, a slender rock-bound road allowed limited access to vehicles from the boulder-strewn foothills, and the main approach, the one they had taken to drive into the village, was a single dirt track worn into the flattest part of the landscape.

On the village's tree-edged perimeter, wooden watchtowers loomed beneath tree canopies. Any attack by the Janjaweed could be spotted quickly and the alarm raised.

The Masalit fighters wheeled the vehicles left and right, moving through the narrow maze until they pulled up next to a larger house with mud walls, tin roof and armed men at the gate. The clan's headman beckoned Raglan and the tribesmen inside. They squatted on rush-mat floors while the village elder sat in a chair. Raglan's escort began talking – about him, Raglan suspected, although once again their dialect was beyond his comprehension. The old man listened, nodded and made sounds of approval or understanding, Raglan didn't know which. Then the old man beckoned one of his men, who went to a battered chest, lifted the lid and pulled out a basket. The headman gestured him to take it to Raglan. The man bent low and offered it to the Englishman. The old man smiled, nodded and extended his palm as if to say *choose*. The basket held an assortment of mobile phones. Raglan picked the nearest. There was no point asking how it, and no doubt the others, showed a half-full charge: they obviously had solar chargers.

Raglan and two of his escort climbed three hundred metres up the nearest rock-strewn hill. The plain beyond showed fingers of streams feeding a green landscape. There was no sign of a telecommunications mast. Raglan checked the phone. He had a better signal here than in some places at home. He keyed in Maguire's number.

★

The conversation was brief. Raglan told him the bad news. He stayed on hold while Maguire contacted Delmar. They needed an extraction point. Once that had been arranged through the Foreign Legion's unit in Chad, Raglan was told where to go. This was no time for a debriefing – that would come when back in France. It was not all cold efficiency: Maguire expressed his relief that Raglan had survived. It was small comfort for Raglan, who had lost every man on this vital mission.

The 4x4s drove for five hours chasing the sun's arc, their worn tyres clinging to tracks barely wide enough for their vehicles. The drivers eventually wound their way down to a wadi and then squeezed through a gap in the overhanging rockface. Another dry river bed was on the other side. The men stopped and pointed across the scar in the landscape.

'Chad,' Raglan's driver said.

Raglan checked his map. The pickup had been arranged at a grid reference, and once he had shown the Masalit on this map, they had unerringly delivered him to the correct spot. The men insisted on walking with him to the riverbed where they embraced him.

'*Allah hafiz,*' they said in turn.

Raglan returned their blessing and made his way across. When he turned, the men raised a hand in farewell and drove away. In the vastness Raglan felt like the only man in the world. This mission had started years before when his father risked his life in a war zone to bring a prize so valuable it had served British intelligence for years.

Africa loses its daylight quickly and darkness swiftly suffocates the land as surely as death seizes a man's last breath. Raglan felt a similar sense of darkness creep over him. His father's legacy had been lost. As he gazed across the dusk-washed horizon he heard the distant sound of a low-flying Puma helicopter.

39

Far to the north, in a climate as severe in its own way as the desert, Alexei Verskiy slept alone in his bed. He didn't feel lonely – he had decided, long before his marriage, to wed himself to his work. It fulfilled him completely. Yet he had still experienced a tearing grief when the woman with whom he had shared so many married years had died. Expert medical care was not always available, even in the new Russia. Her illness could have been held in check elsewhere, but here even Verskiy's high rank could not help her.

There were moments when he had been tempted to accept the covert offer from a member of the British Embassy in Moscow to get him and his wife to the West where she would be looked after. It was the usual ploy. Find the weakness and exploit it. Such an offer would have to be repaid, and no matter what others in Russian intelligence thought of his ruthless, self-serving ambition, no one could deny his patriotism towards Mother Russia. How many times had he asked himself if it wasn't that patriotism which had killed his beloved Mila? But Verskiy would rather lose his wife than betray Russia. He buried her and grieved alone, haunted by her absence. To all who knew him, Verskiy appeared to be a man incapable of affection – that, like his grieving, was kept locked away.

The telephone rang. He answered before the fourth ring.

'It's me, Alexei.'

Andrei Golyev. His voice subdued. As if there were intelligence officers hiding beneath his bed.

'You have found the people I asked for?'

'Yes.'

'Not on the phone, Andrei.'

'Where?'

'There's a late-night bar around the corner from Prechistenka Street.'

'It'll be closed by the time I get there.'

'They know me. They'll open up.'

'Alexei, it's snowing.'

'Then it's unlikely you'll be followed. FSB officers don't enjoy getting wet.'

'I'm being followed?'

'Andrei, relax. It's a joke. Take a cab. Be there in an hour.' Verskiy replaced the receiver.

Verskiy walked two blocks beneath the street lights' glow. The only footprints were his. He turned at a side street and looked across the road. Left and right. Old habits. Alexei Verskiy was playing a dangerous game. If the traitor in the intelligence services had got wind of his mission, that he had sent a small team into Africa to retrieve an unsubstantiated document identifying the traitor, they would not hesitate to have him followed to see whom he met. Or worse. An apparently innocent passerby walking a dog might put a bullet in his head. Snow was a blessing. The satisfying crunch underfoot meant he would hear anyone approaching and could turn back once he saw fresh footprints.

Neither event impeded his journey. Once he reached the

small cluster of mostly closed takeaways he saw the pre-ordered cab waiting. He could easily have walked to the meeting place but the cab offered an extra safeguard against being followed.

Andrei Golyev shivered despite the bar's warmth. He shrugged out of his coat and dusted off his hat. Verskiy was already sitting in an alcove. The purple decor and low-lit wall lights created a sense of brothel-like intimacy. The bar was closed, the blinds pulled down. The owner, a pock-marked bruiser, had once been a well-known boxer, and had made enough money to buy the bar – with a little help from his old boss. Before turning professional all those years ago he had been GRU Spetsnaz, and was now one of the few men Verskiy actually trusted. He left a full bottle on the table, pulled on his coat and told Verskiy to drop the door latch when he left.

Golyev sighed with weariness. Fear had accompanied every step in his search of the old KGB archives. Agents from the past were careful to bury their backgrounds – he'd worked hard to uncover them. Those who committed atrocities and incited rebellions were the most scrupulous in hiding their traces – accounts of such exploits were held at the highest level of security. He twisted the paper napkin.

'My God, Alexei, you are playing with fire.'

'No, my old friend, we are not playing with fire, we are excavating the devil himself. If we get scorched along the way, it will be because we become careless.' Verskiy poured Golyev a stiff brandy to boost his confidence. 'Even so, Andrei, I bet this rekindled old flames.'

Golyev sipped, relaxed a little. Gave a nervous smile. 'Like old times, Alexei. I admit that. Any word on my son?'

'He's still on an active service operation,' Verskiy lied. Galina Menshikova and Verskiy knew better than to report her part in Yuri Golyev's death, which would not be declared until Verskiy saw fit.

The old intelligence officer nodded. Life for anyone working in the secret services had always been lonely. Particularly in Unit 29155, tasked with assassinations and destabilizing covert actions abroad. Secrets and half-truths. They dulled the embrace between families.

'Now, Andrei, do you have something for me?'

Golyev nodded. The brandy had warmed him and settled his nerves, but he kept his voice low. 'Six men stationed in east, west and central Africa in the time just before the Soviet Union was broken up. Leonid Dobrow: he was in KGB Second Main Directorate – foreign intelligence. He was old guard. A true believer. No sooner was he promoted than he criticized the quality of the new intakes and the decline in FSB professionalism. Said the young intakes were more interested in making money. He only lasted two years. No honours, a piss-poor pension and a lonely death from cancer eight years ago in a squalid room on the outskirts.' Golyev helped himself to another drink. 'Jesus, Alexei, the Party and the KGB of old would never have treated him like that.'

Verskiy remained silent. Scratch one name. Dead men don't betray their country's secrets. 'Who else?'

'Oleg Rybakov. Chief investigator of the interior ministry anti-corruption unit I commanded. They arrested him in 2014 for enticing FSB officers to take bribes so he could entrap them. He got out of prison after five years. I don't know where he is now.'

'No position within the security services?'

Golyev shook his head. 'Went to live with his sister out in the middle of nowhere. Then there's Viktor Molchalin. He had great success in Africa. Got arms shipments to anyone who needed them. Rose through the ranks quickly when he returned home.'

'I know him, Andrei. He was tasked with setting up the Sixth Service. They're the ones who shut down you and Rybakov for investigating and arresting corrupt FSB officers.'

Golyev nodded. 'Molchalin was the most corrupt of them all. Still is. Christ, I gave my life to my country. I ran the Internal Security Directorate, but I could have gone down with Rybakov simply by association. Now I'm little more than a clerk shuffling papers.'

Verskiy sipped his drink, eyes on the head-bowed man opposite him. 'You sold Rybakov out to save your own skin, Andrei. He was doing his job – entrapping *corrupt* FSB men to bring them down.'

Golyev's anguished look was genuine. 'I had no choice. I had more to lose.'

'So you saw to it that Rybakov carried the can. Made out that the entrapment was his idea alone. One brave investigator goes down and you don't.'

'Alexei, we did our job. These were high-ranking officials. We just didn't know who was close to the top and who was supposed to be removed.'

'You got your fingers burnt. Molchalin was never going to let you get to his door.'

Golyev shrugged. 'I know. Anyway, now his Sixth Service also controls witness protection.'

That struck a chord with Verskiy. Witness protection made it easy to keep gangsters, corrupt officials and those wanted by the police out of sight. The Sixth Service were the President's enforcers. What if these hidden men were used as a conduit to the British? Viktor Molchalin moved to the top of Verskiy's mental list.

'You see how dangerous this is getting?' said Golyev. His voice dropped again. Agitated. The powerful people whose backgrounds he had uncovered would be less than pleased to find he had delved into their past at the behest of military intelligence.

'Andrei, you have done exactly what I expected you to do. It was your diligence at the Security Directorate that was so impressive. Who else could I turn to? You were – you still are the best. And I can promise you, once I complete my investigation, you will once again be put in a position of authority.'

Golyev's eyes widened. Dared he hope for warmth and sunshine beyond the never-ending Russian winter of intelligence service exile?

'Yes, Andrei, we are doing a great service for Russia and you will have your reward. I give you my personal assurance. And once Yuri returns from his mission he will be honoured as befits the incredible work he has done for me. He is part of this. You see, old friend, we are all in this together.' Verskiy had always been an accomplished liar.

'Thank you, Alexei. I have not failed you. The two who ran the most effective operations back then were Deputy Chairman of the FSB, Mikhail Semenchyev, and General

Piotr Fedeyev, who as I don't need to tell you is now counter-intelligence in the Foreign Intelligence Service. They caused the West a great deal of trouble back then. Mozambique, Angola, the Congo, Zaire, Burundi. They were good, Alexei. My God, between them those two caused chaos. They tore Africa apart.'

The mention of two of the most powerful men in the Russian intelligence services caught Verskiy by surprise. He immediately dismissed Molchalin of the Sixth Service from his mind. Molchalin was powerful, had fingers in all the corrupt elements of Russian criminal and political society, but he did not have access to the hard intelligence that Semenchyev had at the FSB or Fedeyev had at the SVR. He felt excitement rise. To bring down either of them as a traitor would make him a legend in his own time. He had tightened the noose.

'Andrei, you have exceeded all expectations. But you said there were six men in Africa at the time. Who was the sixth?'

Golyev swallowed the last of his drink, stood and pulled on his coat. A mixture of uncertainty and fear crossed his face.

'Have you forgotten, Alexei? You were the sixth man.'

40

The hangar at Istres-Le Tubé was empty and cold, deserted apart from Maguire and Delmar, who sat opposite Raglan still wearing his desert combat clothing. Unshaven, unwashed, gaunt from fatigue, he went through the operation from the time they had stepped into the C130 in this very hangar.

'It was bad luck,' said Delmar.

'It was a stupid plan to start with,' said Raglan.

Delmar bristled. 'You took the Russian straight to the target. You handed her the secret.'

Maguire placed a restraining hand on Raglan before he could challenge Delmar further. 'Let me,' he said and pulled half a dozen black-and-white glossies from his briefcase. 'I had my people track the GRU woman back as far as we could.' He pointed out crowded photos in various parts of the world. 'These are covert pictures. This is the one that really interested us. Bucharest. Four years ago. See her there with that group? That's General Alexei Verskiy, deputy head of the GRU. Two days later she had returned to Russia and Verskiy was photographed with a group of envoys. See the man who's talking to them? Once a mercenary always a mercenary. That's the man in your Action Division unit. He was on leave when he travelled there. The man we know as Dragonović – who *you*, Claude, placed in the most sensitive of covert operations – was a sleeper. Not the best security checks. This mission was up against it from the start, but they had a man in your team. And if Major Galina Menshikova went down, then I dare say there was a means for Dragonović to take over. How doesn't matter – probably using the Wagner Group. But whatever way, they would have had him in play as well.'

Claude Delmar's stricken features appeared to age him even further. He would return to Paris and soon find himself demoted.

Raglan leant forward. 'You were after the glory at any cost. All you wanted was your people on this mission. If I'd had legionnaires as a backup we'd have dealt with the Russian mercenaries.' He glared at Maguire. 'Your lot aren't much better. Your damned politicians signed the men's death warrants.'

'I got you out!' said the head of the Action Division.

'Too little too late. The bloody horse had bolted.'

Maguire leant forward, a voice of calm between the two aggravated men. 'Raglan, are we certain that the document you initially retrieved was the one we wanted?'

'Definitely. It was my father's report given to MI6, concealed as he had explained.'

Claude Delmar looked from one to the other. 'What is this? A family business? Your father?'

Maguire said, 'Raglan's father was a defence attaché in Africa. It was he who brought us the Russian. He saved the Russian's life. Got his man out.'

'Then it's a pity his son was not as successful in avoiding getting my men killed,' said Delmar.

Maguire leapt to his feet and got between Raglan and the

Frenchman, saving him from Raglan's anger. Delmar kicked aside the chair and calmed his fight-or-flight response. Flight being the overriding instinct.

'This is your problem now, Maguire,' he said. 'We did what we could to help you out of a mess of your own making. We wash our hands of this operation. My report will not be generous when it comes to the man who led the mission. And it is not I who screens these men for security. I am Action Division, not a damned vetting agency – that's someone else's job.' He stormed off towards the open hangar doors. His jet was waiting on the tarmac to return him to Paris where Maguire and Raglan knew he would do whatever it took to blame the failure on them.

'Bird Sokol is waiting at the gate to take you home, Raglan,' said Maguire. 'I called him as soon as I knew you'd been picked up. I'm sorry. You were right about our end of the mission. The Foreign Secretary blocked us completely. We hung you out to dry and there was nothing I could do to send help. And by the time I had linked Dragonović to the GRU it was too late. You got there, remember that. You found what we wanted. The Russians had someone in place and they had Kremlin-backed mercenary forces. It was a close-run thing.'

'I'm not interested in being beaten, Maguire, or being kicked in the teeth by politicians. Can the Russians break the code? Can they identify him?'

'Sooner or later their cipher people will work it out. These things aren't rocket science. And now they'll have at least a week's start.'

'And what are you doing about it?'

'We're putting an exfiltration plan into operation. We have two teams in Moscow trying to plan a way out.'

'Your man knows this?'

'I told you he contacts us; getting word to him takes longer. Trouble is there's evidence that the GRU have increased their surveillance on embassy staff so we can't involve them at this stage.'

Raglan and Maguire stepped out into the cold night. 'The GRU don't have authority with internal security in Russia.'

Maguire nodded. By now they were in sight of the main gate where Raglan saw the tall figure of Bird Sokol waiting on the other side of the mesh wire, smoking. 'They're going for glory. They're playing a dangerous game.'

'This the Alexei Verskiy you know about?'

Maguire nodded. 'Their director in charge of operations and GRU deputy head. He has almost complete authority over their operations. His own boss is more interested in making business deals and money. Verskiy isn't crooked. That's his strong point. He's old school. Verskiy would definitely be behind the snatch and the killing in London. And if he thinks our mole is anywhere else other than GRU, he'll want a big scalp and he'll want it badly.'

'And is he? Somewhere other than the GRU?'

'Oh, yes, most definitely. If he were inside GRU and Verskiy discovered him, he would deal with it quietly. If he brings our man down it'll be world-breaking news.'

Raglan pulled Maguire up short before they reached the gate. 'I want in on this.'

'You want Dragonović.'

'He's the icing on the cake, Maguire. This is my father's legacy. It doesn't get any bigger than what he did. You need your people in Moscow to organize the exfiltration. Let them begin the operation. And then I get your man out quietly.'

'I can't back you on this. It has to be an official MI6 operation.'

'If you're putting people on the ground and the Russians are close to discovering who your man is, then they will be watching anyone they suspect like a hawk. If I go in I'm not part of any exfil operation. Not until you need me. I just need to know where you want him taken.'

Maguire considered Raglan's place in all of this. After all, he had involved Raglan by using his father's success in bringing the Russian into the MI6 fold. 'What we're planning is to smuggle him across the border to Latvia and then into Sweden.' Maguire sighed. 'First we have to convince him to defect. And right now he might not even know the GRU have run this operation.'

'No one's going to get him out if you can't make contact. Give me a name. I can't put a plan in place if I don't know who it is.'

'And I can't tell you in case you're captured. All the teams know is that they have to organize an escape route. In the meantime, we try and warn him and be in place.'

'Am I in?'

Maguire nodded.

'Then how do I get this thing done?'

'You still have that phone I gave you?'

'You never asked for it back.' He smiled. 'You've pissed off the French and got them off your back; you've got teams going to Moscow to lay a smokescreen. You're ignoring the Foreign Secretary. You knew I'd want in. The mission isn't over. Not yet.'

Maguire understood Raglan's imperative. 'All right. I'll give you what I can. That phone is scrambled, but even so, use burners in Moscow. Over the years we've worked on who was being used by our mole to get the information to us. Who knows how long the chain might be but our analysis points to no more than two, maybe three people, who are totally trusted. We have a go-between who sits between our Russian and the one who delivers his information.'

'You have a name of either of them?'

'No, but we have a place for the go-between where the information is delivered: it's a dead-letter drop. No physical contact. We want to reach out and set up a meet. If it's agreed, I'll tell you once you're there.'

He turned away towards the airfield and his waiting plane.

Raglan walked to the gate and nodded at the guard who slid it open. He clasped Sokol's outstretched hand.

'You always look like shit when you get back,' said Sokol.

'And your car still looks only fit for target practice.'

'Then you're made for each other,' said the hawk-nosed man as he strode towards the old Peugeot. 'Where to?'

'Home for a few hours.' Raglan slipped off the good luck cap badge medallion given to him by the schoolchild in his village. 'I need to return this to Dominique and tell her it did the trick.'

'That's tempting fate.'

'I gave fate a good kicking, Bird.'

Sokol grimaced. 'Fate's a tetchy bitch, Danny. She can bite back.'

Raglan heaved open the door and grinned. 'She lost most of her teeth back in the desert.' He teased the stainless-steel Archangel pendant from his shirt pocket. 'I took this off a dead Russian agent. It might help us identify his friends.'

'Us?' said Sokol.

Raglan wrenched open the door. 'You still have friends and relatives in Russia, don't you?'

41

The Russian mercenaries who had rescued Galina Menshikova were former GRU Spetsnaz men, loyal to their old service and to Verskiy who, when he had contacted them with an order to exfiltrate one of their own, had pushed hard across the Sudanese wasteland to fulfil their special mission. If they succeeded, they would cement favours back in Moscow. They had taken her back to their base in the Central African Republic, then flown her and Dragonović from the capital's airport to Moscow where Verskiy's car and the man himself waited.

Weary but satisfied, she had handed him the document, still in its original condition, still in the small medical pack. No matter how dedicated an officer she was, the demands made on her during the operation so soon after the London assassination had taken their toll. Verskiy complimented her on her success and insisted she rest but remain ready in case he needed her again and told her that Dragonović was now an asset he could deploy when the demand required it.

And so the most dangerous part of his hunt began. If there was indeed a high-ranking traitor, then he was in one of the two intelligence services that lay at the heart of the Russian Federation. The question now was whether he had got wind of the operation. Verskiy thought not. The other security services had too much to do controlling their own convoluted worlds to worry about the GRU. However, his power could still be challenged because he was now conducting what amounted to an illegal investigation. And he dare not step on the toes of the FSB. Mikhail Semenchyev, a contemporary of Verskiy's, was deputy head of the FSB, the true offspring of the KGB, a man known as the Ghost Hunter, whose job was to root out dissenting voices and traitors.

History defined the life of everyone who held office these days. After the seventy-two-hour attempted coup back in 1991, many of the Communist hierarchy were replaced. President Mikhail Gorbachev, who reformed the Soviet Union and its satellite states, was exhausted and resigned himself to the loss of his party. The chairman of the KGB, Vladimir Kryuchkov, misread the shift in power and arrested Gorbachev. Boris Yeltsin stood atop the barricades and turned the tide against the plotters. Kryuchkov was arrested and convicted and Gorbachev released.

Mikhail Semenchyev survived the purge that followed; he saw the opportunity for reward and power and seized it. It was Semenchyev who convinced the special KGB commando unit, the Alpha Group, not to storm the Russian parliament, which caused the failure of the coup and the downfall of his superior. The new Russian Federation was born. And the KGB gathered its strength and eventually manifested as the new Federal Security Service: the FSB. FSB power now lay in the palm of a handful of men. Semenchyev was one of the few.

Now Semenchyev had requested that Verskiy meet him in FSB headquarters at Lubyanka. Less of a request, more of a summons couched in the least offensive terms. Clearly his summary arrest of the indiscreet colonels at the ELINT signals complex had triggered interest. Verskiy had expected his actions to be questioned sooner or later. The signals intelligence complex was an area of shared responsibility between the agencies. He would have preferred to have kept the operation within the GRU family until the code embedded in the recovered letter was broken, but he comforted himself that he was under no obligation to say anything more than he wished. Still, he could not ignore the warning signs to be vigilant. Nor deny the tantalizing hints of fear that he felt.

On his desk sat the vital document recovered from the desert by Major Galina Menshikova, informing MI6 that a Russian KGB officer stationed in Africa was willing to betray his country. That information was written in plain language. Perhaps in haste. Perhaps because the time-consuming skill required to obscure the traitor's identity followed in a letter that made no sense to a casual reader other than proclaiming his codename was *Malaika*. It was, Verskiy learnt, a Swahili name for Angel. Why Swahili? Did that designate where the former KGB agent had served? Or was it just a random codename given by the Englishman who recruited him? The name *Malaika* offered no direct link to what Major Lipetsk had decoded from the message sent to London from the ground command in Chad before it was destroyed: that the mission was in danger of failure; that there was a chance everyone involved in the operation had been killed. That message had been in a straightforward code broken down by computer analysts. This document was damned archaic.

The faded paper of the coded document promised glory and death. Glory for Verskiy and death for the traitor. Once he had been identified. It was a matter of elimination. Only two men were likely. The first, Semenchyev, deputy director of FSB Counter-Intelligence; the second, an old adversary, Fedeyev of the SVR, the Foreign Intelligence Service, which handled all civilian intelligence while the GRU handled military intelligence. Fedeyev was the political man, Verskiy the military. They had often clashed in the past when they had both sent their people on the same mission abroad. Verskiy hoped the traitor would turn out to be Fedeyev. It would be sweet revenge for the times the SVR director had thwarted GRU operations in favour of his own.

Malaika. Angel. Verskiy imagined the scenario: exposure of the spy, plaudits from the President, retirement to a dacha in Petrovo-Dalneye. Honour and an increased pension. Checking his watch, he allowed himself a couple of hours' sleep before his meeting at Lubyanka. He would check with Lipetsk at ELINT to see if there was an increase in French or British radio traffic or coded information, anything indicating a sense of urgency. If they had any inkling that the GRU had now secured the document they would be putting plans in place to exfiltrate their traitor.

He lay on the old leather sofa beneath the wall map of the world and pulled his overcoat across him for warmth. This would be his last operation – perhaps even the most risky. He was tired and had spent too many years alone in a lonely profession. Before, he had found it hard to imagine life without suspicion and intrigue – the danger had always spurred him on. Now, except for the prospect of this being the highlight of his career, he was weary of the whole business. The Soviet Union had crumbled when he was still in his prime, when he could serve his country more vigorously. He had done his share of assassinations and would gladly do so again once he uncovered the traitor. Better, though, to let the man face public shame, condemnation and then the inevitable end of betrayal.

All in all, he was content it would soon end. Retirement, he grunted to himself. Maybe the peace of mind would kill him. He fell asleep quickly, daring to picture the hero's honours he would be awarded.

42

The two-room apartment in Moscow was on the sixth floor. The lifts were broken – Raglan assumed this was the normal state of affairs. The public areas were painted in the same faded pale blue so that when the overhead flickering fluorescent lights were on, which was most of the day and all night, the walls reflected a sickly green glow. Carpets had been ripped out; grime and bird droppings encrusted the window. The room was bare except for a rodent-ravaged armchair squatting in one corner, while in the next room a plastic-covered mattress sagged on a coiled spring base. A small bathroom led off the room. A toilet bowl and heavily stained enamelled bath with a cracked hand basin filled the space. Two ragged towels, likely to have been left by the previous occupiers, hung on hooks on the back of the door.

'A lick of paint and a wrecking crew will work wonders,' said Raglan.

Bird Sokol turned to the squat, overweight woman with cheese-grater skin wrapped in double cardigans and skirts. He thanked her and told her they would only be in the city for a few days. The woman muttered something, turned and shuffled back along the corridor.

Sokol shoved the door closed. 'No one asks questions around here. Plenty of people who want to stay below the radar. Stop complaining. They even left towels. She said the radiators come on for a couple of hours. I'll get a few home comforts later.'

'This your family home?' said Raglan.

'It was this or a cousin's village house two hours from Moscow. I used what contacts I had.'

'You must have really screwed them over in some past life, Bird. Or this one.'

Raglan dropped his small backpack and forced open the rusted metal window frame. Communist-era tower blocks bracketed the wasteland. Sokol swept his hand across what was little more than a shanty town.

'Garage Valley. They call it the Shanghai Slum,' he said. 'I grew up around here. There are still people down there I knew when I was a kid. They began demolishing the area for redevelopment about ten years ago. There used to be thousands of sheds, full of people with nowhere else to go. Now it's down to a few hundred. It's a hotbed of crime. Backstreet car-repair shops, hole-in-the wall cafes. Just the kind of people we need on our side.'

Raglan looked across the snow-covered roofs. The muted throb of techno music pulsed from a distant building.

'There're a lot of down-at-heel musicians rehearsing in those old places: they live rough like everyone else,' said Sokol. 'Cops don't come here; most of the place is run by biker gangs and they're a violent bunch. There are always fights with locals and illegals. Crazy place. That's the Moscow State University you can see over there. They have a bus and Metro station into the city. Takes about a half-hour.'

The roads into the estate – there were only a couple – were littered with abandoned or burnt-out cars.

'It's perfect, Bird. No one will trace us. No questions asked. Good access to the city.'

Sokol tipped his backpack out on to the bed. He spread out a map of Moscow and the surrounding countryside. 'You do your recce in the city. I need to work out the best route to make our way out. If Maguire's people are already being tracked, then we need to move fast when he gives us the go. Do we know where the target is yet?'

'No. Maguire is trying to contact him, but we don't know how or when.'

'Then we're still working blind.'

'Work backwards from the border crossing into the city. Once we firm up where he's at then we'll have an idea of what needs to be done.'

Sokol nodded. He pulled out a new mobile phone, checked the signal and was satisfied. 'Yours?'

Raglan did the same. Maguire's phone worked; so too did the new burner. Raglan threw his sleeping bag down on to the floor and fashioned his backpack as a pillow.

'You see any vermin climb in there let them know they're not welcome.'

Sokol grunted and nodded towards the window. 'It's the vermin out there we need to worry about if they sniff fresh meat.'

'OK, so what's your plan?' said Raglan. 'This is your neck of the woods.'

'I reached out,' said Sokol. 'Carefully.' He looked down into the squalid area below. 'I've tracked two ex-legionnaires I served with. One's Russian; the other's a German who married a Russian. They're connected.'

'The man and his wife? I should hope so.'

'Joke while you can, *mon ami*, we could soon be in deep shit. You might have escaped from a penal colony the last time you were here; this time they'll put a bullet in your head. You think the Russians won't find out who you are if they catch you?'

'Last time you got me out, Bird.'

'Yeah, well, I'm not your mother so I can't wet-nurse you all the time. These guys I've reached out to are connected to organized crime.'

'Oh, you mean the government.'

'Them as well. You don't survive here unless you can deal with someone who has the influence you need.'

Raglan saw where the conversation was going. All he had to do that was watch Sokol's gaze down into the Shanghai Slum. 'They're down there?'

'It's why I brought us here.'

'Connected with FSB or GRU?'

'Mostly internal stuff, so that's FSB. Dealing. Guns and drugs. Small-time compared to the national corruption, but they know people inside. They do business. If the FSB or the GRU want someone dead, you think they're always going to use their own people? It's a partnership between criminal and state. Same difference.'

'Bikers?'

Sokol squatted on the old chair, took two cans of energy

drink from a plastic carrier bag, tossed one to Raglan and popped his own. 'No. The Russian and the German have a good smuggling route in and out of Germany. Black-market stuff. They pay off the FSB Border Force.'

'And how do they help us? We're valuable merchandise to them. Just because they're ex-Legion doesn't mean they'll play ball.'

'It's a start. At least there was a time they were part of something meaningful. You can't wipe out what we all once shared, Danny. Leave them to me. I need time to think it through. See how best to use them. You're here to do a job. And more. If these people have the connections we need, then they might also know where Dragonović is.'

'Put him on the list of things to do.'

'But if he's still in play? Maybe still being used, then he could be on the streets with the GRU, and if he gets in our way we could have a small war on our hands. Better to know where he might be and take him out of the equation.'

'The mission comes first,' said Raglan.

'I know. But if we need to kill him, first we have to find him. Rats know where rats hide.'

Shanghai Slum's rough-looking characters gathered in doorways. Braziers burnt, destitute-looking men and women huddled, stamped their feet and cast suspicious glances at the two newcomers as they trudged across the wasteland. An angle grinder threw sparks as two men worked on a cannibalized car in a shed's dim interior. As Raglan and Sokol cut across a couple of the narrow streets, a group of men fanned out and blocked their way.

'Is this a welcoming committee?' said Raglan. 'I don't see anyone bearing gifts.'

'I should have mentioned they don't like strangers,' said Sokol. 'Stay here while I talk to them.' He walked forward and called out, telling them he and his friend were here to do business with two old friends, Gunther Meier and Semyon Mikoyan. That slowed their advance. One of them keyed in a phone number. Raglan and Sokol waited. The man making the phone call listened, nodded and then pointed Sokol towards a hut at the end of the street.

'Let's go,' said Sokol. 'My contacts are down here.'

The men muttered in less threatening tones now they knew the two strangers were connected.

Sokol banged on a metal door. It creaked open. A bead curtain was pushed aside. A swarthy bald man with heavy stubble laughed and greeted Sokol with a hug. Sokol introduced Raglan to Gunther Meier. They shook hands and like honoured guests Raglan and Sokol were ushered inside.

'Semyon, the Legion has arrived!' Meier called to someone in another room, a second hut attached at the back with a connecting door. Raglan glimpsed stacked boxes and crates. Contraband for the smuggling operation.

Semyon Mikoyan joined them, transferring a ledger from one hand and pushing a pencil behind his ear. The Russian looked more like a bookkeeper than a former legionnaire, belying the clichéd image of tattooed, muscle-bound hard-nosed men – although there were plenty of them in the Legion as well. Raglan and he shook hands, and the first thing he asked was Raglan's unit. Raglan told him. The Russian nodded, glanced at Sokol and broke into a grin.

'You are still the ugliest man who ever served,' he said.

'And you were the worst legionnaire I ever served with. How you lasted so long I'll never know.'

Semyon gestured with the ledger. 'I calculate the odds and act accordingly.' He looked to Raglan. 'You trust this Englishman?'

'With my life,' said Sokol. 'Many times.'

Raglan could tell that Mikoyan was the one who ran his and Meier's smuggling operation.

'All right,' said the smuggler. 'You tell us what you need, and we will put things in motion.'

'Two things,' said Raglan. 'We're looking for a Serb who's an asset for the GRU. If he sees me then it could jeopardize what we came here for. And we need to get someone out of the city. We don't know who and we don't know where. Not yet. But if it happens, then we need to have everything in place. Bird will stay and go over our options.'

The uncertainty of what he was asking for did not appear to trouble the two former legionnaires. Raglan knew why. There were times when uncertainty meant a legionnaire's life could be snatched away at any moment. Situations panned out or they didn't. You dealt with it.

'Then it's time for a drink,' said Gunther Meier.

43

Alexei Verskiy strode towards the guards flanking the doors of the FSB deputy's office, knowing that once his operation became more exposed, the creatures from the darkness of the political and military forests would form hunting packs. Verskiy, the old stag, the survivor of many an attack, welcomed the chase. At some point someone would try to stop his investigation and that might expose the traitor himself.

His Military Intelligence Directorate had had its share of disasters. They were almost disbanded after their failure in the Russian–Georgian conflict. They lost 40 per cent of their staff at foreign embassies. The power struggle within the intelligence community at that time had been intense. Other agencies had attempted to have the GRU signals intelligence units and satellite communications interception post near Andreyevka on the Chinese border reassigned to their arch-rival the SVR. Verskiy had clawed it back with the assassination attempt on former GRU agent Sergei Skripal on British soil – that operation was still considered a success by those in power despite the former spy surviving the poisoning. Attacking those who betrayed Russia pleased the President. No one escaped Verskiy's specialists. While the assassins in

Unit 29155 were sowing fear, a second group, Unit 21695, invaded other nations' computer networks across the world.

Verskiy's bold actions using his Spetsnaz men in the disputed territories of Ukraine and his advice on undermining the West had gone directly to the President. Nothing could stop him now. The mission in the desert had been a success. Alexei Verskiy's star was in the ascendency. His only nagging concern was that breaking the coded letter was taking too long.

The FSB adjutant, a colonel, offered no sign of recognition or respect to the GRU officer's status and rank. A cool approach intended to instil apprehension. Verskiy was ushered into the room whose high ceilings were richly decorated in the style of the old Tsarist palaces and whose floors sported elaborate carpets imported from the far-flung tribes of the old Soviet Union or perhaps even stripped from the government of Kabul during those mistaken days in Afghanistan. They did little to warm the room against the coldness of the deputy head of the FSB.

Verskiy was under no illusion. He might be speaking directly to the traitor himself. Only Semenchyev at the FSB and Fedeyev at the SVR were the key surviving men in power from those African days. Mikhail Semenchyev, Ghost Hunter, showed no sign of welcome. He nodded, then returned his attention to a file on his ornate desk, letting Verskiy stand while he read, tapping ash from his cigarette into the ashtray.

Verskiy waited. Large snowflakes wafted against the windowpanes like night moths against a car's headlamps.

Semenchyev glanced up. 'Alexei, forgive me. Colonel Yermolov, why is there no chair for the general?'

The adjutant knew the game well enough. Leave those who

had been summoned standing long enough to know who was in charge.

'My apologies, General Verskiy,' said the adjutant and placed a chair at Verskiy's disposal.

Verskiy settled himself. He had not been invited to remove his overcoat.

'May I get the general tea?'

Verskiy shook his head. When a prisoner being interrogated accepted that first gesture of kindness – a drink, a cigarette – he had already lowered his guard. The adjutant left the room. Verskiy suppressed a sigh. Old power plays never changed. He had used them often enough himself.

Mikhail Semenchyev raised his head from the file again. Closed it and smiled at Verskiy. Semenchyev was in his mid-sixties, clean-shaven, tall, still lean, with a good head of silver hair. A cultured man who spoke several languages and adored art and opera, he was also known for his love of the forests and hunting near his dacha in the prestigious Rublyovka area south-west of the city. He preferred being in nature to Moscow's 24/7 delights and distractions. A man of contradictions. And one who also sat on the Kremlin's security council, a confidant of the president, diligent in rooting out those who impeded the president's plans.

'It would be helpful to know why you had Colonels Tamarkin and Shevenko arrested,' he said.

'They spoke out of turn in front of a junior officer about my part in bringing down the Malaysian flight.'

Semenchyev nodded. 'Not unreasonable. A delicate issue. Still, a serious matter, Alexei. Removing two senior officers from a vital post without consultation.'

Verskiy remained silent.

'Can you expand more? We know there was something about the French sending an operation into the Sudan.'

'You do?'

'Of course. You arrest two top men, and we ask questions. It's natural. You have a mission in progress?'

'Yes.'

'Should we be concerned?'

'It's a GRU operation. It's well under way. I believe I will soon be able to draw it to its natural conclusion.'

If the FSB knew anything of Verskiy's operation Semenchyev was not letting on. Neither man would give away the information in their possession. That suited Verskiy – for a while longer at least. Providing Semenchyev did not interfere. Odds were he would not, because the GRU did not answer to him. If either of these men of power in the FSB or the SVR tried to stop his efforts now, they would expose themselves as the traitor. And Verskiy's reasoning at this stage of the game was that neither would impede him for that very reason. He was confident of success. And bringing down a traitor would polish the GRU's reputation and guarantee accolades greater than if he had single-handedly saved Stalingrad.

But now Semenchyev was waiting, expressionless. He would have to be given something.

'The operation was to seize information that might prove essential to Russian security interests. That's all I can really say.'

Semenchyev nodded. 'I understand. So, this has come about because of what? A hunch? An instinct?' He paused a moment. 'And some inconclusive radio transmissions from a mobile French tracking station in Chad?'

So, he knew that much. Then he'd know the aircraft had been destroyed. Did he know about the two officers Verskiy had sent?

'Information came to light, and I pursued it,' said Verskiy.

'Substantial evidence?'

'No, but certainly enough for me to give what we had some credence. Not enough to share and draw in more agencies. That would have been irresponsible.' Verskiy spoke with the calmness and skill that had served him so well over the years. Seemingly in absolute command, he defended his actions with the dexterity of a shadow boxer. 'It all fell squarely into my sphere of action. There are critical factors in the world arena – crucial new talks between Russians and Americans – and once I have concluded my investigation, it will give the President the upper hand.'

'How so?'

'Because if the British and French have not shared their incursion with their allies it drives a wedge between western intelligence agencies at a crucial time.'

Verskiy was juggling with fire to get the results he wanted. And fingers would get burnt if this meeting with Semenchyev was mishandled.

'Should we or the SVR be involved?'

'Not yet, Mikhail. I'll let this run and then bring you in. And I assure you there will be a role for you.'

Verskiy was putting himself between the President's favoured security service, the FSB, and the SVR, the Foreign Intelligence Service. The GRU had taken decisive action. Their military operations had always outplayed their rivals. Verskiy knew this suited the FSB, who were keen to play the GRU and SVR off against each other, letting those two agencies do the grunt work while the FSB sat on their hands. They'd step in soon enough to bask in the glory.

'You have used considerable resources and risked a lot. We must hope that the French don't believe we had anything to do with the shooting down of their troops.'

Verskiy was being told that the FSB knew more than previously admitted. Did they know about him directing the mercenaries? That a GRU officer was dead? That he had had a retired British MI6 officer assassinated?

'And with your operation still undisclosed, General Verskiy'—familiarity swiftly abandoned—'to lose is unthinkable.'

The final dismissal was a veiled threat.

Verskiy's cigarette case snapped closed as loudly as the huge, solid doors slamming behind him. He welcomed the coldness of the snow outside – despite the chill of the room, he was perspiring. He knew he was in danger. If his whole mission backfired and brought disrepute to an internationally beleaguered president with an increasingly vociferous opposition at home, then it might be more than his command that Verskiy would lose. He lit the cigarette. A snowflake settled and extinguished its glow.

44

Raglan begged off the drinking session, leaving Sokol to firm up what options might be open to them. As he made his way across the wasteland towards the university and the Metro station, small groups of men filtered out from the labyrinth of sheet-metal huts. But word had travelled quickly; they gave Raglan little more than a cursory glance.

An hour and a half later, with two changes and a twenty-minute walk, he was in the Tverskoy District outside Moscow Police Headquarters. He found a seat at a bus stop and watched the building. The last time he had been here he had been dragged out of a police car and thrown into an interrogation room, and from there sent to White Eagle Penal Colony No. 74, eighteen hundred kilometres east of Moscow. He keyed in a telephone number from memory. If Major Elena Sorokina was still in Moscow CID, then she could prove helpful. They had met in London a few years before. She had risked a great deal in helping him then; perhaps she would do so again. Briefly sharing a bed wasn't exactly a commitment.

She answered hesitantly, not recognizing the number that came up on her phone.

'Had your morning coffee yet? Do Russian cops eat doughnuts?' he said in English.

A hushed expletive in Russian in reply. He smiled. She still knew how to swear like a legionnaire.

'Where are you?'

'Outside.'

She swore again and then fell silent. Would she be prepared to meet him? She had every reason not to. It was dangerous to be seen with a convicted felon even though back then he had used a Russian version of his name. The Russian state had him listed as having died during an escape from the penal colony.

'There's a cafe a few blocks from here – in Tverskaya Street. You'll see it. High ceiling, lots of plants. An hour.' The phone went dead.

She was late.

By the time she walked into the vast coffee-shop-cum-restaurant Raglan had finished off a plate of five-cereal porridge with honey and had ordered an omelette with tomatoes and cheese. His third mug of coffee was being refilled when she arrived. She wore jeans and an unbuttoned thigh-length leather jacket allowing a glimpse of the service pistol on her hip. She tugged free her gloves and a thick woollen scarf. She showed no sign of welcome. She didn't want food, just coffee, she told the waitress, and then sat opposite Raglan, who paused halfway through the omelette, sat back and smiled.

'I was starving. I've come a long way, missed breakfast. How's Major Elena Sorokina these days?'

'Colonel Sorokina was well. Now she is not so sure.'

'Colonel? Putting me away into that camp did your career some good.'

'We played a good game, Raglan. We both got what we wanted. You found the killer who murdered my brother and your friend.'

Her coffee with whipped-cream topping arrived. He gestured to his food. 'May I finish?'

'Of course. You have come a long way. I can see that. You have a good colour to your skin. Your hands are still healing from scratches. The small cut on the hairline has broken the suntan. Things must be tough on the Mediterranean beaches even at this time of year.'

He swallowed the last mouthful. 'A warm early spring back in France and the beach volleyball can get rough.'

She sipped her coffee and dabbed the cream from her lips. They gazed at each other.

'So, Raglan, what are you doing in Moscow?'

'I'm a tourist. I'm on holiday.'

'Holiday?'

'Yes, you know, a vacation. Time out. I love Moscow. It's a great city. Clean. Roads are kept clear of snow. It's got the best Metro in the world; people in the street are friendly. It's a great tourist destination. The country's run by gangsters and killers but everything works.'

'Thanks for the coffee, Raglan.' She was about to leave when Raglan reached out and covered her hand with his own.

'I'm sorry, Elena, but I need help,' he said. 'It's very important.'

'Or you wouldn't ask,' she said.

'Exactly.'

'So, you are not on vacation and you did not come to see me, you came to see what I can do for you.'

'I came to see someone I trust.'

'Not desire?'

'That too.'

'I'm seeing someone.'

'Then he's a lucky man.' He raised his palms in surrender. 'I need to find a woman.'

He couldn't read her expression. Contempt or disappointment?

'Russian women are plentiful.'

'Not this one. I have unfinished business.'

'Dangerous business?'

'Yes.'

'Are you going to kill her?'

'That's not my intention, but she is more than capable of killing me. I want to find where she lives. She has information about a man I'm interested in. Better I find him before he finds me.'

Elena studied him a moment longer. 'What is her name?'

'Galina Menshikova.'

'And what do you know about her?'

Raglan hesitated. The moment he revealed she was a GRU officer, a serving police officer was likely to run a mile. He shrugged. There was no choice. 'She's GRU.'

Her reaction was not as extreme as he feared. Her eyes widened slightly, and the corner of her mouth turned down as if the coffee was too bitter. 'I know her address.'

It was Raglan's turn to look surprised.

She nodded. 'Number 3 Grizodubovoy Street.'

'You know her?'

'I know where she works. That's GRU headquarters. Every GRU officer has their registered address there.'

'I can hardly go and knock on their front door and ask for

her. Won't she have a driving licence application or some kind of utility bill on government or district databases?'

'The moment I start a search it will be flagged. I have no reason to try and locate her. You understand?' She dipped a spoon into the cream floating on top of her coffee.

Raglan guessed she was weighing up whether she could help him.

After a moment she looked unflinchingly at him. 'Raglan, I am Russian and I love my country. There are those of us who do what we can to apprehend criminals. You know that. Our system of government is rotten. It stinks. Those are criminals we cannot reach.'

'Sure. I don't want to compromise you.' Raglan winced. If she couldn't or wouldn't help him then he would have to risk having Dragonović loose on the streets – unless Sokol got any leads from his contacts. Raglan was going to have to abandon looking for the Serb and concentrate on the mission at hand. And it was drummed into every legionnaire that the mission was everything. He had always followed that edict, but he knew damned well the mission could be compromised if Dragonović was running loose in Moscow.

'What are you not telling me, Raglan?' said Elena, seeing the distant look in his eyes as something inside unravelled.

He shook his head.

'You said you trusted me.'

'I can't tell you, Elena. It's too dangerous.'

'My hands are tied but – well, I would always try and help you because of what you did for me the last time. When I first met you in London we helped each other – didn't we? – to find the man who killed my brother and hurt your family. We had a common cause, Raglan. We still do. Some of us hate what's happening to our country. But it's my job to protect the ordinary people, and I do it. So do my colleagues. I won't get involved in anything that might hurt anyone I work with or anyone we're trying to help.'

Raglan toyed with the coffee mug. Then told her what he could. 'The connection between Menshikova, the man I'm after and me being here is that a mission went wrong in Africa. And a very important man here in Moscow, a friend of the West, is close to being exposed and probably killed.'

'The two are separate things right now?'

'Yes.'

'You don't make life easy for yourself.'

He smiled. 'I have a low boredom threshold.'

She stood and wrapped the scarf around her neck. 'Raglan, I know what you do. It's not boredom. I think you have a death wish.'

Elena drove an unmarked police black BMW 5 Series. The most direct route towards the GRU headquarters was north along Leningradsky Avenue. Then ignoring signs for the hospital slip road, she continued until the road took them in a southerly direction past bland purpose-built supermarkets that served the surrounding brutalist blocks of flats. Raglan tried to orientate himself. The snow had eased, and even though the traffic was slow-moving, it wasn't heavy enough to cause traffic jams. He had lied and told her he was staying at one of the hotels near the university. Finally, she slid the car into the inside lane and told him to look at the curved modern building behind three-metre-high security walls as she drove past.

'GRU HQ,' she said, swinging around the corner on to a boulevard. 'It's not just that front facade and the building behind it,' she said. 'They have the whole block, all those buildings, right back to Khoroshevskoe Highway.'

She accelerated away. When they approached the Moskva River, she pulled over. They were on the more modern fringe of the city. Glass towers almost nudged each other, seemingly wedged into each other's space. Neon billboards promised nirvana shopping. 'I have to go. There's a Metro station over there. You'll be back in less than an hour.'

'Thanks, Elena. You didn't have to go out of your way. I appreciate it.'

'I wanted you to see where those people operate from. Raglan, for all I know she could be out at their training base north of the city. You won't find her hanging around the front door or the back gate. Let the matter go.' She looked at him as his hand reached for the door handle. He leant across to kiss her. She raised a finger stopping him. 'I'm on duty.'

He smiled. The door slammed. She checked her mirror for traffic then glanced back to where he would cross the road.

Raglan was already out of sight.

Her pang of regret irritated her.

45

Verskiy sat at his desk, studying the cipher. Major Lipetsk of ELINT, newly promoted, waited uneasily. His stance in the half-light of the general's desk lamp seemed a metaphor of his own position. Neither in darkness nor light, serving which master?

Verskiy looked up. 'How much longer before you uncover the name of the traitor? It's a letter, for God's sake. It's a promise to this Englishman's superior in London that a former KGB officer will work for the West. Why can't you give me the name? I put my faith in you, major. Are you going to disappoint me?'

'It is an unusual encryption, general. In the past, agents in the field and their handlers often used codes personal to themselves. Respectfully, sir, if the man you seek is still sending messages to the British, it is possible he will be using this same encryption. Old but... reliable.'

Verskiy kept his attention on the cipher and waved him away. Gratefully, Lipetsk left the room. No doubt, Verskiy thought, he was missing the comfort of his electronic world where human contact was at arm's length, and which did not challenge him in such a direct manner. And feeling the fear he had brought upon himself.

Time was short. Verskiy let his mind wander, seeking out anything that might point him towards the traitor and those who helped him deliver his information. Who would the traitor use to pass messages to the British? Nothing untoward had been noticed from Verskiy's increased surveillance on the British Embassy. Who would risk going between the traitor and whoever picked up the information? The code was old but reliable, Lipetsk had said. The written word. Would the traitor risk writing it out himself? Possibly, but if such a document was found and associated with the traitor, that heightened the risk of discovery. So perhaps the information would be passed verbally. Was that it? And then encoded by someone else? It would have to be someone with a like-minded desire to betray the State and have the skill to encrypt the message.

A devoted Communist mourning the past? No. Passing secrets made no contribution to the old Soviet way of life. A dissident then? Not a paid courier, but a person who believed in democracy. Yes. A dissident. Would that not pose too great a risk to the traitor though? Perhaps. It was also counter-intuitive. Hide the courier in plain sight. Verskiy's mind scurried through the labyrinth of possibilities like a rat seeking out a morsel.

There was a scrap to be had. Some information had come across his desk a few weeks ago. His officers made handwritten reports; nothing went into a computer until he had sanctioned it. He rummaged through a drawer in his desk, pulled out a sheaf of files, quickly dismissed most of them and then found the one he wanted.

If the operation was to be brought to a swift conclusion, then he knew he had to reach out. The next step was a risk, as much as the one he'd taken when discussing the operation with the FSB. He looked at the GRU officer's report in the file, thinking hard.

The report concerned an SVR surveillance operation being undertaken in Moscow. Mounting such an operation was beyond the Foreign Intelligence Service's remit, which meant they were sticking their noses into FSB internal security matters. If Verskiy threatened to leak that information back to the FSB, then the SVR might help him. Did the benefits of making such a threat outweigh making an enemy of the SVR?

Yes, they did, because Verskiy wanted the man mentioned in the report. He had a unique skill, which had pricked Verskiy's interest. He was a scholarly translator.

Verskiy dialled the number of his rival at the SVR: General Piotr Fedeyev. If the traitor still lived, then it would be one of these two men: Semenchyev at the FSB or Fedeyev at the SVR. Both men, like him, of the old guard. Unlike Semenchyev, Fedeyev drank heavily, perhaps to ease the burdens of conscience. Or perhaps to suppress his guilt at betraying his country. Verskiy knew he might be playing into the very hands of the traitor. He was balancing on a high wire that might be cut at any moment. But the risk was worth it.

Finally General Fedeyev answered his call.

'This is Verskiy. A complication has arisen in Africa.'

'That is not my area of responsibility.' Fedeyev's tone was sharp. He had no liking for Verskiy, and the fact Verskiy had called him meant his rival needed something from him, which immediately placed Fedeyev in a position of strength. 'However, if we can assist you, we will of course do so. We serve a common cause.'

'There is a rumour that you have someone being watched who might be useful to me.'

'A rumour?'

'More than. And I would rather deal with you than the FSB. They poke their noses into our business too often. I'm aware you've had a group of dissidents under surveillance, even though FSB have warned you off trespassing on their turf on more than one occasion.'

Verskiy heard the sharp intake of breath as the man on the other end of the telephone sucked in cigarette smoke. 'That is no concern of yours. You keep your nose out of foreign counter-intelligence.'

Verskiy remained silent. He had dangled the bait.

After a moment it was nibbled at. 'Military intelligence seems well informed. My question is: how do you come by this rumour? And why would you have an interest?'

Verskiy knew he had to give to receive but in this case giving was more than generosity. It could be turned to his advantage. 'For a couple of years we had an issue with some of our conscripts. Young men who were not happy being pushed around. I had my officers monitoring them. A couple of the conscripts fed information to a dissident group you were watching. My officers identified a couple of your men. Surveillance is a lonely boring business. My people talked to your people. There is one dissident of interest to me. One specific person. I have a coded document in my possession and he might be able to decrypt it. I need it done quickly. He's an old man. A priest. My officers tell me he translates old biblical texts when he is not saving souls.'

Fedeyev made a mental note to chastise his team for their

careless talk. 'I know this man. And the answer is no. We have been waiting for the moment when we can feed vital disinformation to him. No. He cannot be sacrificed.'

'The FSB might forgive you whoring in their backyard, but how would they feel if they discovered you are close to running a disinformation agent here? They won't take kindly to your stepping on their toes when it comes to internal security.' There, he thought, the threat was made. Would it have the desired effect on Fedeyev?

'Don't even attempt to blackmail me, Verskiy. You have no authority in this matter.'

'I have need.' Time to tell the half-truth. 'I have an overseas operation in place. Someone in British intelligence has written a coded letter and I need to break it. I believe the code might still be in use. I need to determine whether that is the case before I proceed further.'

There was a long pause: Verskiy knew this favour would have to be repaid handsomely. It gave Fedeyev the upper hand in any future negotiations with the GRU.

'I can't sacrifice him. He is too important to us. No, this is not the right time for me to lose him.'

Verskiy wondered if Fedeyev was playing a clever game. What if he were the traitor? He could either hide behind counter-intelligence protocols and keep his source hidden, or barter a pawn, as important as it might be. Verskiy's nagging doubt remained. He had shown his hand. The traitor could agree to sacrificing a link in the chain and have them killed before anything more came of it.

'There's no more important time than now,' he said. 'If you do as I ask you'll share in my success. If this man can help me then when the document is decoded you will be honoured by the President. This operation is critical, and the outcome will be glorious.'

'And failure might be catastrophic. I have no desire to lose my command if your plan goes wrong, or to lose a potential source to pass disinformation to the British. I'd also need to secure permission from my superiors or they'd think I was undermining their authority.'

'There will be no failure, Piotr,' Verskiy said, venturing into intimacy. It was time to throw caution to the wind. He played his final card. 'I will take full responsibility.'

Verskiy waited. If Fedeyev caught a whiff of success that might feed his own ambition without risk, then he would give him the dissident.

Finally, Fedeyev spoke. 'Commit that to paper, deliver it to my office by courier within the hour and I will identify the individual.' He hung up.

Verskiy saw the vortex before him. Now he was fully committed. The race was on. He dare not hesitate for a moment or the whirlpool would suck him down. Yet he could still back out. The seconds ticked by. He did not move, his mind juggling the possibilities.

A priest? Could fate be playing into his hands? A buried secret. Dead to the world. The most central belief in all Christianity is the doctrine of resurrection.

He reached for a sheet of headed notepaper.

46

Bird Sokol had bought a cooking pot and a two-ring gas camping stove, which now sat on a folding table alongside a bag of food from a supermarket. A small television set with an indoor aerial was wedged on a scavenged side table.

'Depending how long we have, I figured we'd need to eat in more than out,' said Sokol. 'And that,' he said, meaning the television set, 'is worth having for local news – which is just about the only channel it can get.'

He laid out three mobile handsets. New SIM cards partnered each.

'These should last a couple of days.'

Raglan and Sokol checked the phones worked. Sokol stripped and smashed his previous phone. Raglan was about to do the same when his rang. He answered.

'Raglan?' said Elena Sorokina.

'Yes, Elena.'

Sokol looked concerned. Raglan pulled a face, raised a hand to say it was all OK.

'You lied to me, Raglan,' she said.

Raglan stayed silent. Which lie had caught him out? There had been so many.

'There are ten hotels in the university area. You're not

registered at any of them. No one has passport details of any visitor checking in with your name or anything like your name. Are you using a false passport?'

'Elena, I'm staying in a rough area. With a friend.'

'A woman?'

'No, not a woman, a friend. We served together. An old friend.'

'Near the university?'

'Yes.'

'Where?'

'Are you interrogating me?'

'I'm asking.'

'I don't know the name of the building.'

'But you know the name of the street.'

'Elena, I'm staying with a friend. That's all,' he said firmly.

'I see.' There was a pause. 'I also lied, Raglan.' Another pause. 'I'm not seeing anyone.'

'Then we both lied because we wanted to protect ourselves and each other.'

'So it would seem. I don't think your friend's place is very nice. Not down there.'

'To be truthful, it's not.'

'Ah. The truth is good.' She paused again. 'I have a small flat. It's a half-hour drive to the city for me. It's close to a Metro station. It might be... more convenient for you.'

'I suppose it would.'

'There is only one problem.' She paused again. 'There is only one bed.'

'Do you think we could solve that problem?'

'We would have to see. Perhaps we should try. Tonight. At least the bed is warm.'

'That sounds a good idea, Elena.'

'Then you phone me later, after hours, and I tell you where.'

'All right. I'll be using a different phone.' Raglan said. 'This one is damaged,' he lied.

'Many cheap phones are. You call me on any phone.'

The line went dead. Raglan destroyed the phone.

'You have a date?' said Sokol.

'I have a bed.'

'Well, you weren't going to share mine. You trust her?

'I do.'

'That sounds like a marriage vow.'

'Bird, she has an apartment. It's a good idea if I can be off the radar somewhere else. Me there. You here. This thing's going to kick off sooner rather than later.'

Maguire's phone vibrated. Raglan answered.

Maguire said, 'We have the meet set up with the go-between.'

Raglan listened as Maguire gave him the location. He knew the name of the building; it lay south of the river. 'Does this individual know what's going on?'

'No, but it will take us a step closer to warning our man. If he discovers the GRU might be closing in on him then perhaps he will reach out to us. We have to be ready in case he does. The meet is this evening, fifteen minutes before closing. There's a ticket at the door in your name. You're a tourist, remember?'

'Who is it I'm meeting?'

'I don't know their name. Find a floor where there are fewer people. Sit and wait. They'll come to you.'

'Are your people in place?'

'It's a rush job but we have a couple of plans in mind. We're working on final details for a route out.'

'Bird has made contact here with people who might help us.'

'Keep the lid on them. If we have to use them, we will.'

Raglan felt there was more to be said. There was a hesitation in Maguire's voice. A nuance of uncertainty. He knew the feeling. Every dangerous operation was riddled with unanswered questions. 'What else? What about the GRU?'

'We would know if they had found a way of retrieving the information in that document. It would pinpoint the position our man once held in Africa and he would have been lifted. It would be big news. Believe me, we'd know about it. If they're still working on it then we think they'll dig out anyone they suspect of being used to help pass information to us. You need to get to the go-between, because we feel it won't be long before they do. Then it's game over. Ruthless efficiency has its advantages.'

Raglan left Sokol in the bare, unwelcome rooms for his friend to plan how to use the contacts he had. Raglan made his way towards the city, found a place to observe his destination's entrance for an hour before his scheduled meeting, watching for plain-clothes surveillance teams. Despite the cold and the snow underfoot, a handful of people were making their way inside the pagoda-like entrance of the State Tretyakov Gallery, even though it was to close soon. It was getting dark. Another hour and Moscow would be a sparkling city of lights. An illusionary fairy tale. If the GRU had people on the ground, they must have been lurking down a street drain because the open square and broad pavements in front of the building offered no space even for a stray cat to hide.

He picked up his ticket. Inside, the huge gallery could have absorbed a hundred times the few people who shuffled through the corridors. Raglan circled the foyer, took the stairs and then changed direction twice. The only eyes watching him were those that stared out of the paintings. Fifteen minutes later he found a painting that struck a chord with him. He stood gazing at the depiction of a pyramid of heaped skulls. The surrounding desert sky in the painting was flecked with crows, an ancient symbol of death. In the background were the adobe walls of a town, or perhaps of a desert fort. It had no link with the Legion's past, but he thought it evocative of wastelands where men fought and died, and it was a stark reminder of his own recent escape.

A soft female voice behind said, 'It was part of a series the artist called *The Barbarians*.'

Raglan turned to look at the diminutive figure. A snapshot judgement would place her as an elderly librarian. Her grey hair gathered in a bun, her figure slight, her eyes bright, no glasses, her skin with that unblemished healthy glow of someone who relished the brisk outdoors. Her woollen jacket and skirt could have belonged to a Scottish woman walking her dogs down a country lane in stout shoes. An academic, Raglan guessed. Someone blessed with knowledge of the rich Russian culture. She wasn't wearing an outdoor coat, which meant that perhaps she worked there.

'If my Russian is up to scratch the plaque says it's called *The Apotheosis of War*. It's striking,' said Raglan.

'I always find it frightening,' she answered, her eyes on the canvas. Then she faced him. 'Such images remind us of what awaits us if we do not restrain mankind's impulse to dominate and kill.'

'But there are times we have to deal with those who wish to do such things. To stand up to them.'

She nodded. 'It is why some of us do what we do.'

'And risk everything,' said Raglan. Was this his contact? He assumed so.

She shrugged. 'The next one along the chain bears the greater risk. I am a conduit. I pass on what I am asked to pass on. After I have done that I go back to my work here.'

'Until the next time.'

'Yes. Or until I am caught.'

'The man you help is in grave danger. I must get word to him.'

'Then you have to turn to God and pray.'

Raglan strode briskly from the State Gallery. The next link in the chain was in the Church of the Consolation of All Sorrows, a fast five-minute walk from the gallery. The evening service would have already started and it remained to be seen whether he could reach the contact if the church had a full congregation. Snow flurries threatened a heavier fall later that night. He passed an Italian restaurant, the warm ambience already enticing early diners to stop for a meal. Couples hunched intimately over their tables. It made him think of being with Elena again.

Turning left into Bol'shaya Ordynka Street, he saw the cross-hatched dome above the church's floodlit ochre walls. A handful of people shook the snow from their coats, stamping their feet outside the entrance, which had been cleared by a diligent workman. The women among them tied scarves over their heads. Raglan took in as much as he could of the surrounding area. A low wall with railings created a small courtyard; a door towards the rear of the wall led to the main street. It was a one-way traffic system. There was no time to explore further. He needed to identify the courier: the man who passed information from the highly placed Russian spy to the West. It was a priest. His church was an ideal place for secrets to be exchanged.

Candles and soft lighting illuminated the ornate interior. Columns soared to the high ceilings where the priest's incantation echoed softly, reaching the painted cupola above him where an image of Jesus and His angels gazed down benevolently on the priests and congregation. Raglan guessed there were sixty or more people in the confines of the nave attending the evening service. They huddled together, standing: the Orthodox Church did not have pews for the congregation. They faced the priest, murmuring personal prayers or a response to the liturgy. Raglan knew the Orthodox Church did not have the anonymity of the Roman Catholic confessional. Rather than being separated from the priest by a barrier or from the parishioners by a booth, the penitent was visible and audible not only to the priest, but to the others standing in line awaiting their turn. Sins and misdemeanours were recounted face to face. That would make it difficult for Raglan: a confessional booth would have made it easier to pass on the warning and information.

The latecomers had settled at the back of the congregation. Raglan remained with his back against the wall. His eyes scanned bowed heads. Artefacts glowed, caught in the soft light. A shadow from a flickering candle took his eye to where women were lighting more candles in a shrine to one side of the nave. There appeared to be three priests involved in the service, but the dim light subdued their features. Two were men in their thirties; the third was older. More senior. Thick grey beard and longer hair – none of the clean-cut, beard-trimmed appearance of the younger officiates. If the Russian had been passing secrets for all these years surely it would be to a man of similar age? Raglan watched the front door while edging along the wall, seeking a vantage point to look beyond the altar towards the sacristy or whatever it was called in Russian churches. He decided that once the service ended, he would follow the priest to where he changed from his officiating robes and then find a quiet place to approach him.

The service ended and the priest blessed the congregation; a few shuffled forward to bare their souls, but they were heard by the two younger priests. The older man disappeared out of sight into what appeared to be a side chapel. Hearing the details of endless sins could age a man, thought Raglan. He shouldered his way slowly through the crowd and saw the old man, still in his cassock, standing with a woman whose back was towards Raglan. The priest's head suddenly jerked up. Perhaps what she confessed had shocked even his hardened soul. He looked stricken. Took a step back. Looked around him as if wanting to escape. Too late. The woman placed a gentle guiding hand on his arm. She half turned. It was Galina Menshikova.

47

Two stout babushkas blocked Raglan's way and a man
uttered an irritated warning as Raglan pushed past them. He
kept his eyes on the old priest. Why didn't he step back into
the congregation? That would be his best chance. They might
shield him. And then Raglan saw the two men step from
behind a pillar. Leather jackets, jeans, roll-neck sweaters. It
was as good as a uniform for the security services. He saw a
flash of a holstered weapon. They bracketed the priest, each
taking an arm, and ushered him through a side door behind
the altar. Galina cast a quick glance behind her, checking that
no one had noticed, or if they had that they posed no threat.
Raglan got free of the crowd, followed the kidnappers but the
heavy oak door was bolted. They would spirit him away out
of a rear entrance.

He barged through the line of supplicants, ignored their
anger, and ran into the snow-flecked evening. Running down
the one-way street he found the small side road leading to the
back of the church. A black Mercedes G4 SUV was parked
behind an ambulance whose doors were open. The stretcher
was missing. They must be drugging the old man in case
he resisted. Raglan checked the 4x4's number plate. It bore
the letters AMP. That was used by one of four government

agencies, one of which was the Ministry of Defence. This was a blatant GRU operation on the streets of Moscow. Whoever was running the operation was not only stepping on the toes of the Moscow police but also the Federal Security Service, and the FSB was particularly jealous of its authority.

A Volvo estate was parked two cars before the 4x4. As Raglan got closer the Mercedes's doors swung open. Driver and passenger had seen him approach. They must have recognized the look of a man determined to cause trouble. The driver stood squarely in his way. The second man held off four metres to Raglan's left. Raglan glanced behind him. A second black 4x4 had swung into the end of the small side road and blocked traffic turning in. He slowed, pulled up his collar and hunched against the breeze. Light snow was still falling. He stopped. He was still a car's length from the black 4x4. The stocky man glared at him. Raglan gestured like any concerned citizen.

'*V chem problema?*' said Raglan.

'There is no problem This road is closed. An emergency.'

Raglan played it down. Look dumb, ask dumber questions. Take a step closer. 'In the church? I've just come from the service. No one said anything.'

'None of your business,' said the thickset man.

'I've got to get home. Can I get through?'

'No. Go back.'

Raglan scowled, rubber-necking towards the rear gate to the church. 'Anyone we know? Is it serious?' Another step closer. Close enough for the man to stride towards him with an outstretched hand. Now Raglan had the 4x4 blocking the line of sight from the second man who stayed in the empty street.

Raglan complained. 'Hey, take it easy, I just want to...' Raglan snatched the man's wrist, stepped inside, rammed his elbow into the man's face, twisted his arm, turning him downwards as he reacted in pain until he was face down in the gutter. Raglan slammed his boot into his neck. He reached down, pulled free the man's weapon, turned quickly around the front of the 4x4 and levelled the gun at the second stooge who was caught unawares. He had no choice but to raise his arms.

'Turn around,' Raglan said.

The man obeyed. Raglan struck him hard. He dropped. Raglan kept an eye on the broadsided 4x4 blocking the top of the street. There was only the driver, and he was outside the vehicle on the far side, explaining to the public why the road was closed. Snow flurries whirled on the breeze: a thin veil between him and the street guardian. Raglan dragged the unconscious man out of the road. He turned as the two men from inside the church wheeled out the unconscious priest strapped to the stretcher. They were no more than eight metres away when they saw Raglan. They drew their weapons as Galina stepped into view. The shock of seeing Raglan held her frozen for a moment. Her men fired almost simultaneously.

'No shooting, you fools!' she cried.

Raglan was no longer where he had been a moment before. He didn't have a clear shot at the two men. It was the third man who came through the gate on Galina's heels who shot instinctively at the fast-moving Raglan. It was Dragonović. The bullets punched through metal, shot out the front tyre and shattered the glass of the Volvo where Raglan had retreated.

He heard Galina order the men to get the priest inside the ambulance. She shouted again for them to stop shooting. A gunfight on the streets of Moscow would bring the cops. She was obviously still running the operation, but the men had overreacted. Raglan was about to be caught in a crossfire. Dragonović and the two men were in front of him; the driver blocking the end of the street had spun the SUV and headed towards his team as soon as shots were fired. A standoff. Dragonović could not step into view for a clear shot and Raglan could not put any distance between him and the kidnappers without making himself a target. The fast-approaching driver would not be able to open fire without risking the others. But once he drew closer, he would have Raglan boxed in against the other Merc. Like shooting fish in a barrel. And if there was a chance the Moscow PD would respond Raglan was happy to make a contribution. He stayed on one knee and levelled the 9-mm semi-automatic. This wasn't a standard military-issue weapon. The Gsh-18 and its armour-piercing rounds were designed for close-quarter combat and given to special forces. These were no ordinary military intelligence officers, they were GRU Spetsnaz. Tough men trained to go in for the kill.

Raglan fired repeatedly at the fast-approaching 4x4. The rapid gunfire would make the others think twice about trying to outflank him. The 4x4's windscreen shattered. Raglan edged half a metre to one side and shot again. The vehicle slowed, the driver, dead or severely wounded, lost control and the 4x4 careered into parked cars.

The sound of tearing metal and breaking glass muted the sound of the ambulance doors slamming closed, its engine starting and tyres skidding, trying to find grip in the snow. Raglan rolled, levelled the 9 mm and saw the ambulance leave, lights flashing and siren wailing. Galina had snatched the priest and was out of sight. She must be in the ambulance and Dragonović had followed in the second Mercedes, leaving behind three bodies and a crashed vehicle. Raglan saw a crowd choking the end of the road as they stared down at the carnage but were too fearful to venture further. Raglan ran after the disappearing ambulance, hit a speed-dial button and pressed the phone to his ear. Galina and her men would know the back streets. Elena answered.

'Elena! It's me!'

'I'm still at work. I said—'

'Listen! A priest has been kidnapped from the All Sorrows Church. They're in an ambulance. Going north in a side street. Gunshots fired. Three men down behind the church. You have to stop them, Elena. He has information. They'll torture him.' His breathing came hard but he kept the long, fast strides going. He tossed the empty 9 mm into a trash can.

'It needs to be official, Raglan, not on this phone. Get their direction. Emergency number is 102. I'll pick it up from despatch.' The line went dead.

Raglan stopped at the corner. He had lost sight of the ambulance and Dragonović's 4x4, though he could still hear its siren. His rubber-soled boots gripped the snow as he leapt, slithering, on to the bonnet and roof of a parked car and looked down the long street. He saw the ambulance turning into a side road. Instinct told him to run straight down the narrow alley opposite and try to cut off the ambulance when it hit heavier traffic. He pressed the three digits. The dispatcher answered. Raglan told her armed men had shot at people in the street and kidnapped a priest. He gave his location and told her the ambulance's direction as best as he could determine. And then hung up.

It would take another ten minutes of hard running to reach the Vodootvodny Canal south of the Moskva River. He sprinted back to the damaged Mercedes 4x4. One wing had been crumpled from the impact. The driver was dead. Raglan pushed him across to the passenger seat, pressed his foot on the brake and hoped the hefty vehicle would still start. The engine turned. The ambulance could be going anywhere. But if the GRU compound was a possibility, the ambulance had to be driving from this side of the canal along the one-way system and then cross the Chugunny Bridge.

He keyed in the satnav. Moscow's roads were always busy. There were choke points all across the city. The best he could hope for was to get across the river. Two routes came up on screen. It made sense that the kidnappers would know the busy one-way systems and avoid them. They would take the roads with the lighter traffic even if it meant taking longer to wherever it was they were heading. Raglan punched a bigger hole in the shattered windscreen, swung the steering wheel and floored the accelerator. Snowflakes stung his face but the Merc's speed pushed most of it upwards and across the roof.

He could see across the river that the traffic was flowing only in one direction. The wrong way. They were still south of the river. Sirens wailed somewhere in the distance. He hoped that would be Elena and other patrol cars. The ambulance's klaxon told him it had changed direction. He dialled 102 again and told the despatcher it was on a different route.

The wheels bit the compacted snow, made more dangerous from the fresh fall, as Elena's name came up on his mobile. Her voice was tense with concentration. He realized she must have her foot down and be hurtling through the traffic.

'We can't get a helicopter up in the snow. Despatch is

relaying everything. You tell them. They tell me. It's as good as we can hope for.'

'Elena, it's the GRU. Where would they take him?'

He heard the hesitation in her voice. It was the first time he had mentioned military intelligence.

She came back quickly. 'They wouldn't risk taking him openly to their HQ.'

'I think they're GRU Spetsnaz but they have contractors with them as well.'

She swore hard. 'They're based north of the city. Too far. They won't risk it. It's either a safe house, somewhere we don't know about, or... or if they're going east then they might go for a bridge across the river and north for Lefortovo Prison.'

'That's the best bet,' said Raglan.

'If they get him in there, we can't reach him.' The call ended.

Raglan forced cars aside as he sped past them. Keeping a hand on the horn, he flashed his headlights and pressed the hazard-lights button. Muscovites knew these vehicles were favoured by gangsters and security services. And seeing a couple of tonnes of black, bullet-riddled Mercedes G-Class SUV hurtling along the road meant only one thing. Trouble. They got out of the way.

The ambulance had its lights flashing and siren wailing. It too cleared traffic from its path with Dragonović on its tail. Raglan floored the accelerator. He lost sight of the ambulance. Dragonović and Galina Menshikova, a mercenary asset and a major in the GRU, were still working together and if the man responsible, Alexei Verskiy, had planned this operation, it looked as though he had used the GRU's own Spetsnaz unit as well as contractors. Had he excluded the other security services? Was this his own rogue operation? If it was, it was a gamble. A big one. Verskiy was going for the jackpot. Bringing down a Russian mole at the highest echelon of the Russian administration was one step away from being declared a saint. The priest was a go-between. He must know the code.

Erratic traffic slowed him. Raglan kept his eye on the ambulance as he approached a junction choked with wary drivers who had pulled over to let the ambulance pass. He saw Dragonović's 4x4 peel off but Raglan had nowhere to go. He slowed, wiped the wet flakes from his face, peered beyond the snarl-up, saw the flashing ambulance light turning in the distance. Something was wrong with the car in front. It was old, and its rear end twitched as snow slid away from its steep-sloping back window. Muscovites were once required by law to have a sticker displayed showing they had winter tyres fitted. The elderly driver had such a sticker but had either long forgotten to remove it or had always ignored the rule. He accelerated too hard. The car spun, caught a car alongside, it too then lost control. It was ten-pin bowling on ice. Cars nudged each other, spun, crashed and opened a gap across the intersection. Raglan eased the power on gently until the 4x4's fat winter tyres found purchase; then he increased speed, letting the surefooted vehicle do what it did best. The canal glistened alongside the road. Police cars were converging in the distance. Blue lights flashing. Sirens wailing. Trees soared in the distance. A park. A winter wonderland. The ambulance was stationary. The lights still flickered. Galina stepped out of the passenger side and stared in his direction. Just stood there. As if she was expecting him.

Raglan glanced at the cracked side mirror.

Another black Mercedes SUV had slewed out of a street two cars back. Raglan knew it had to be Galina's backup.

Was it Dragonović? Too late. The distraction and the stinging snow in his face made him miss another looming shadow hurtling across from another side street. He swung the wheel hard, trying to avoid the impact he knew was coming from the blind side. He saw the driver's face. Dragonović. Galina had baited Raglan with the stalled ambulance and the Serb had circled in the side streets waiting to pounce.

The heavy 4x4 slammed into the passenger side. The Mercedes lurched; Raglan was flung against the door frame. The impact threw the dead man against him, wedging his body between Raglan and the steering column. Raglan was trapped. The shunt rolled the 4x4. It tumbled across a safety barrier. Raglan tucked in his elbows to cover his face in a brace position. Seconds later it hit the river and icy cold water poured in. Most people drown by gasping for air when their body hits cold water; inhalation of even a small amount is enough to kill. Raglan gulped air moments before the cabin flooded. The 4x4 twisted and turned and plummeted downwards. The force of the water inside was too powerful to fight. The car hit the bottom nose first, teetered and fell forward on to its roof. The dead security officer's body remained jammed beneath the dashboard, trapping Raglan's legs. The man's hair undulated like sea grass in the current. Water pushed his lips apart, exposing a macabre smile of revenge. His blind gaze stared at Raglan.

Always the eyes of the dead.

48

The freezing water began its rapid assault on Raglan's body. Blood vessels in his skin constricted. Muscles tightened. His heart rate and blood pressure increased. Raglan knew it would take his body minutes to adjust to the cold-water shock from sudden immersion, but he might lose the use of his hands in seconds and then his arms. Holding your breath in cold water was always a problem. The colder the water the more difficult it became to survive. Raglan needed to get out of the river. Given the ice-cold temperature his physical and mental ability would be impaired in less than half an hour.

The murky water gave him no sense of what other obstructions might lie on the river bed. All he knew was that he was upside down. He grabbed the dead man's collar. Saturated clothes added to his already hefty weight but there was still some buoyancy from air trapped in his clothing. Raglan hauled. The man's body shifted, the swirling water lifted him slightly, and Raglan got his legs free and pulled himself through the glassless windscreen. The current tugged at him. He twisted, kicked hard, and caught a final glimpse of the dead man lying on his back, still wedged, facing Raglan, his smile and blind gaze now made more otherworldly by the current gently moving his arm up and down in a macabre farewell wave.

Raglan broke surface eighty metres downstream through blocks of swirling ice. He saw onlookers gazing over the broken rail; police cars bracketed the crash site. The cold water muted Raglan's hearing, but he heard the dull sound of sirens approaching. There was no river traffic. The busy roads above meant no one was likely to see him. Another hundred metres away there was a small jetty with a skiff tied alongside and an iron ladder leading to the quayside. The area above it appeared to be semi-industrial. Using the current, he swam closer to the far bank and the stone walls that would bring him to the boat. His lungs burnt from the cold. His numb hands grasped the side of the skiff. He pulled himself to the ladder and began his slow climb.

The road this side of the river carried less traffic. Raglan needed warmth. Despite his stiffness he jogged across the road and through a small park, the pathway leading to a narrow road and a sign telling him the small shop window in the grey stone building was a charity shop. Ignoring the women volunteers' querulous looks at his soaked and now frost- and snow-covered hair and clothing, he bought everything he needed, paid with wet notes and bagged his new clothing.

A narrow alley behind the charity shop had two commercial skips and the gap between them made an ideal changing room. He stripped off, ignoring his soaking feet. No charity shop in the world sold used socks. His phone rang.

'Raglan?' said Elena's voice, the sound of traffic in the background. 'Was it you who went into the river? Police dive teams are there now.'

He continued dressing. Hopefully anyone who glanced down the alley might think he was an itinerant by the bins.

'Cold-water swimming might be good for you but that was pushing it,' he said. His body was still cramping, his movements too sluggish for his liking.

'There's an alert, Raglan. A woman from a charity shop phoned the police. She was suspicious. We now have a bulletin out for you. They know the clothes you bought. They'll have a description. If that alert is picked up by the GRU they'll have their own people on the streets.'

Raglan kept the phone tucked between his ear and his uninjured shoulder as he relaced his boots. 'The man I was after drove me into the river. He won't stop now if he learns I made it.'

'I can't get to you, Raglan. I'm CID – this is out of my hands. Patrol cars will box you in once they track your route from that shop. Where are you now?'

Raglan finished dressing and tossed his wet clothing into the skip. 'No idea. Went through a park on the other side of the river. Wait.' He went to the end of the alley. 'Not too busy a road. Traffic one way. Domed church on my right. Rezinsky Street.'

He heard her sigh. 'They already have cars in that area. Head west and south. You'll have a better chance. I'll relay what I hear. Understand?'

Raglan was already moving across the street to a narrow passage between buildings on the other side. He was halfway when he heard the sound of a police siren. It was close, its insistent wail warning other cars to get out of the way. The police car slowed, one of the cops climbed out and ran towards him as the driver cut through the stalled traffic.

Raglan's body was still stiff from the cold-water immersion. He was slower than he should be and the rubber-booted police officer was gaining ground, his footfall pounding hard. The pursuing cop shouted a warning for Raglan to stop and then Raglan heard him telling his partner where they were heading on his personal radio. They intended to cut him off.

Raglan swerved down another back street, willing his muscles to move faster. As he turned a corner, he saw a stacked pile of black rubbish bags, half obscuring a high mesh fence and gate that blocked him. The gate was unlocked. He swung the gate open, pulling it towards him, pushing his back into the gap between the stinking rubbish bags and the wall. The Moscow cop rounded the corner and ran for the opening; as he stepped past, Raglan slammed the gate into him, sending him sprawling. Raglan kicked him once, a debilitating but not a deadly blow, then rammed closed the gate and heaved enough rubbish bags on to it to block it and slow any further pursuit.

He heard Elena's voice on the phone. 'Raglan, there's a car close to you. They radioed in that an officer is on foot in pursuit. You see him?'

Raglan ran along another back area that went off at a tangent. 'He's down.'

He heard the panic in her voice. 'Christ, Raglan, don't kill a cop.'

'I won't unless I have no other choice.'

He heard the background squawk of her car radio. She came back on the line. 'Patrol cars are moving towards the river. They'll cordon off streets and contain you. Can you see where you are now?'

'No. Back alleys. Staying off main roads.' He was running

hard but his legs felt like lead. It was all he could do to keep any kind of pace going. He knew she couldn't help him without knowing his location. 'Elena, soon as I break cover I'll tell you.' He switched off the phone.

He squeezed past a row of refuse bins filled with rubble from construction works on the upper floors of the buildings lining the alley. The scaffolding almost blocked the width of the street. Mesh netting hung down to protect anyone working below from falling debris. The work looked as though it had been abandoned. The area was too confined for a skip, even a small one, so builders would have had to manhandle the spoil away. The long alley between the tall buildings showed daylight at the end. Few cars had passed across the far entrance, so he reasoned it must be a side street. He was halfway along when a black 4x4 pulled up, blocking the entrance. A leather-coated man piled out. GRU. He had obviously picked up the voice traffic on the police net. Now he was moving towards him, gun in hand. Raglan had no way back in case the policeman had recovered – the cop wouldn't take any more chances pursuing a suspect, he'd be ready to shoot next time. The GRU man pushed aside a couple of wire cages full of discarded delivery boxes that blocked his way. Raglan was trapped.

He turned and ran back to where the builders' rubble chute clung to the side of the building. Large plastic bins, held together by chains, each narrow end fitting into the mouth of the one below, soared twenty metres to the top floor. He climbed on to a rubble-filled waste bin and gripped the rim of the barrel above his head. Each rim gave him a handhold and then a foothold as he climbed higher. He pulled himself up as fast as he could, cursing the pain in his shoulder but driven by adrenaline. The man below was fast approaching and wouldn't be interested in arresting him. The GRU had already made one failed attempt on his life.

Heaving himself inside the mesh netting, Raglan obscured himself sufficiently from the man below, who levelled his handgun and fired. Bullets thudded into the building; a couple struck the bins. Raglan was almost at the top; he climbed on to the scaffolding and then through an empty window frame, tumbling on to a vast open-plan floor. Builders' supplies, cement and bricks were stacked along one wall. He skirted the bags of cement. The place was deserted. There was no sign of any internal work being done. Maybe the owner hadn't paid the builder and work had been halted. The man below wouldn't try and clamber up the chute – he would make for the building's door and seek him out.

Raglan ran to the far end of the room. A staircase descended to similar empty floors below. The whole place looked as though they were offices being refurbished. He reasoned that if the building was not being worked on then the front doors would be locked and probably have some kind of security fencing across the entrance. That would slow the man pursuing him but would also block any escape.

He heard voices. Someone demanding entry. There must be a watchman on the ground floor. Raglan peered down. The gunman hadn't yet gained access. There was no way on to the roof and it wasn't worth risking going back down the rubble chute because odds were the cop would have brought in others to scour the back alleys. Ingrained training told him the best way to deal with an ambush was to attack. He ran down the stone stairway. The sound of heavy doors creaking open echoed upwards. An unseen man below was cursing the watchman. Raglan made it to the mezzanine floor where a dozen Portaloos stood side by side. Below, the broad expanse of what looked like a bank's vestibule was home to various pieces of equipment and machinery. He ducked back into an alcove as the GRU man stalked into the entrance area, gun in hand, and the elderly watchman, hands half raised in supplication, backed away. There was no time to confront him on the floor below. Raglan took out his phone. He had barely seconds to draw the man in.

He heard the man warn the watchman not to raise the alarm. Raglan squeezed himself behind one of the toilet cubicles as the sound of the man's boots came closer: he was climbing the stairs. He could hear the man's breathing as he stalked across the mezzanine. Raglan braced his back against the wall. He did a mental count. Seven steps more. The man's boots crunched on grit. Five. Almost there. Two. The phone's alarm beep sounded louder than he'd expected and it was enough for the gunman to turn and fire three shots into the cubicle next to where Raglan hid behind its neighbour. Raglan heaved. The cubicle fell forward. The gunman tried to avoid it; he turned on his heel to shoot again and his foot slithered on the gritty floor. By the time he had regained his balance Raglan had blocked his gun arm; a shot went wide and high. Raglan punched hard into the man's kidneys, then stepped in close, twisted the man's wrist into a swan neck. Bones broke. The man grunted in pain; the gun fell. Raglan kicked it away. It clattered down into the heaped mess of construction paraphernalia below. The injured man recovered, threw a punch that caught Raglan's injured shoulder. Raglan winced, dropped his shoulder, half twisting to let the man see he'd been hurt, giving him the confidence to step forward with a switchblade in his unbroken hand. Raglan bodychecked him unexpectedly, throwing up his injured arm to block the strike. The manoeuvre threw the man off balance. He stumbled. Raglan headbutted him. Unable to stay on his feet, the gunman's knees sagged and he teetered backwards, trying to regain his footing. His heels caught the top step and he tumbled down, falling heavily. He lay still.

Raglan retrieved his phone. By the time he reached the bottom step he saw the man was critically injured. He stared at the watchman, who appeared from his hiding place. Raglan nodded at the man, who in turn nodded back. No harm would come to him.

Raglan stepped out on to the street. There was no sign of any police vehicles. Perhaps they were blocking off the streets where Raglan was last seen while other cops searched the alleys. He pressed the speed dial for Elena. She answered quickly.

'Are you all right?' There was genuine concern in her voice.

'Bit of a rough day. I'm heading back. OK if I speak to you later?'

'Of course. Patrol cars have closed off half a dozen streets from where they last sighted you.'

'I'm nowhere near there.'

'I can try and find you. Take you back.'

He walked around the corner into a parallel street and put his hand out as if thumbing a lift. An old car pulled over.

'No, my lift's just arrived.' He hung up. It wasn't a taxi. Like many Muscovites pressed for money, ordinary drivers were happy to earn cash. The elderly driver asked where he was going. Raglan told him. They agreed a price: eight hundred roubles exchanged hands. The driver plastered the damp notes across the car heater's grill.

Raglan sat in the back seat, checked they were heading in the right direction. Told the driver to drop him outside the university. No point in telling him he needed to get into the area known as the Shanghai Slum. Even hard-up Muscovites would have turned down that drive. The bewhiskered elderly man kept up a running commentary about the ice-hockey playoffs. It had little effect on keeping Raglan awake. By the time the car had reached the first turn in the road he was fast asleep.

Back in the Shanghai Slum flat Raglan told Maguire what had happened. The call lasted thirty-eight seconds. Maguire's response was curt. 'Be ready. We're going to get him out whether he likes it or not.'

The brown-stained bath, with green tendrils from worn taps also marking the old enamel, was long enough to accommodate Raglan. While Raglan soaked in the hot water Sokol stirred a half-dozen ingredients into a pot on the two-ring stove. The small television screen showed news crews at the scene of the church, and then another report from the riverside crash.

'Turn it up, Bird,' Raglan called from the steam-laden bathroom.

Sokol bit on a hunk of bread he'd dipped into the pan as he cooked. 'Can't. It's on full. They're saying gangsters posing as security services kidnapped the priest. That he might have heard a crime boss's confession. They spin a good story here.' Sokol stirred the pot, chewing slowly. 'Now they say an off-duty security officer tried to stop the kidnapping, there was a gunfight, he gave chase and was rammed and killed. They've recovered his body and the vehicle from the river.' Sokol peered into the bathroom. 'Danny, if the priest is the link, then there's an old Russian saying: *Vot gde sobaka zaryta* – That's where the dog is buried. They'll find your man.'

Raglan climbed out of the bath. The water was as brown as the old enamel. He scrubbed the threadbare towel over himself and stood in the doorway watching the screen. Sokol looked at the palm-sized bruises on Raglan's back and arms from the crash. 'And Dragonović must be wondering if he scared you off.'

'He knows he didn't, Bird. There was another man across the river. The police won't get involved once they identify his car. They'll pass it along and go back to giving out traffic tickets. What's going on is above their pay grade.' He lifted his clothes off the hot steel-ribbed radiators. The window was open to ventilate the steam from the cooking and clothes.'

'I don't see how the GRU can talk their way out of this one,' said Sokol.

'I got lucky but me being there made a mess of their plans. And if they're using hard-core Spetsnaz men and a foreign asset as well, then they're off the reservation.'

Raglan took the pot of food to the window and spooned a mouthful as he looked down on the itinerants' township below. Lights glowed; generators hummed. Plumes of smoke from makeshift fires found their way through the falling snow. It was as welcoming as any fugitive could hope for.

'It's Dragonović's call, Bird. I don't give a damn about him one way or another. But if he finds me, then this is where it ends.'

49

Dragonović had stayed at the crash site and watched as police and rescue crews arrived. He had sent a GRU unit across the river when news of a man who might answer Raglan's description had been seen. He had not managed to raise the man since on his radio. Had it been Raglan? Could he have escaped the impact of the crash and then the freezing water? Police divers searched the river and the wreck was craned ashore. There was only one body inside. When he got to Lefortovo Prison, the ambulance had gone and Galina waited outside, smoking a cigarette. The sky was empty of snow but as grey as the stone wall she leant against.

'I waited while they dragged the river,' said Dragonović. 'Raglan's body wasn't found. I thought he might have been swept downstream. There was a sighting of someone on the other side of the river. It looks like he made it.'

She took a final draw on her cigarette. 'He got out of the desert, didn't he? A man like that doesn't die easily. Count on it,' she said.

'And we wouldn't have a problem if you'd finished him out there.'

She flicked the cigarette away. 'The general wants you. He's breaking the priest. You have skills he wants,' she said, her tone barely concealing her contempt for him.

Dragonović gazed up at the towering walls. 'That's why he uses me. I was a sleeper with the French for years: he trusts me and knows what I can do. So don't stand there and look as though you've just eaten some rancid smetana.'

'I kill when I have to. You do it for pleasure.'

'That's the difference between us. You're a cold-hearted bitch; I know what makes a man suffer.' He leant closer to her. 'Are you this frigid in bed?'

She turned away, but his arms caged her against the wall. 'C'mon, let's try it.'

'Listen, you stupid gorilla, Raglan crushed your balls once, I'll take a blade to them. Get out of my way.'

He bared his teeth. 'Turning me on now?'

'I won't tell you again.'

He looked down and saw the small, curved blade in her hand. 'Jesus, you'd do it, wouldn't you?'

'And hang them round your neck.'

He took a couple of paces back, hands raised in surrender. 'All right. But we'll be working together now. My balls and your cold heart could do wonders for the general's ambitions.'

'Not if I can help it.' She pushed past him, he snatched her arm, she twisted, releasing his grip, extending the blade in front of her. 'You don't touch me. Ever. Understand?'

Dragonović wasn't fazed by her rapid actions. 'You need to think this through, Galina. Raglan is here in Moscow. He was right on target at the church. He knew we were lifting the priest. He's here to finish the job and you should have finished him in the desert. Were you fucking him at Faraj Hamad's?'

She swept her knife hand for his throat, but Dragonović

batted it aside and an open-handed slap caught her head. She spun against the wall, knees buckling from the blow. He let her recover and made no further attempt to assert himself. He bent and picked up her knife. 'You'd better not have gone soft on Raglan. How the hell the bastard is still alive, I don't know, but I'll find him and this time he won't be going anywhere.'

'You'd better pray you don't find him. Or he you. He's formidable and he's smart.'

'I can take him,' said Dragonović.

'He has the edge.'

Dragonović's scowl told her he didn't understand.

'You did the unspeakable. You stopped him from saving a life. Someone who had served in the Legion. When you crushed those anti-venom phials you betrayed everything that matters to a man like Raglan.'

He tossed her knife towards the prison gate. He grinned. 'Fetch.'

Galina held his gaze. 'The Englishman. He will kill you. He's better at it.'

'This from a woman who killed her own partner when he was lying helpless after being tortured? You had better hope I find him, then there's only two of us who know that.'

'You're blackmailing me?'

He shrugged. 'Who would want to work with a woman who killed her fellow officer? I bet General Verskiy wouldn't be too pleased.'

'I did what I had to do.' She smiled. 'I followed his orders. We are all expendable, you dumb oaf.'

Galina walked towards the prison's main gate. Dragonović's brute force was a blunt instrument. She hoped he did find Raglan.

49

Interrogation cells in the notorious Lefortovo Prison were never lit or warmed by the sun. The cells, at different levels in the central Moscow building, never saw the sky. Many were below ground – burying the victims alive. A bare light bulb and its metal shade allowed a cone-shaped wedge of light into one such cell where the priest lay strapped to a wooden table. The broad leather restraints gave little when his body bucked under the electric shocks administered by the interrogators.

Verskiy had spent the better part of that day and into the night waiting for the man to break. He had gambled and he needed a result. The SVR believed the priest would be useful in spreading disinformation for those seeking change in Russia, which had hardened Verskiy's suspicion that he could be the courier. Why not? A priest who hears confession? A priest who keeps secrets? Verbal information passed on and then encoded by someone with the skill to translate ancient texts. It was a desperately long shot but one of just two options left open to Verskiy. Major Lipetsk was his only other chance of cracking the coded letter and he was taking too long.

The priest was naked; perspiration glistened on his skin, matting the dark hair of his body. His head was held in a vice-like grip by a strap, broader than those binding his wrists and legs. Another bound his chest tightly, denying him the comfort of cringing back from the pain.

A professional versed in the art of interrogation would spend days, weeks even, bringing the prisoner to the point where the required information was teased from him. It was a long process but it yielded results. Verskiy did not have the luxury of time. He had shown his hand to the two men in the other intelligence services. One might make his move and attempt to stop this torture. If he did, he would reveal himself as the man betraying Russia. So far, no such move had been made. Verskiy needed the key that would break the code, and this priest was his best bet to trace the identity of the traitor he sought. He had allowed Dragonović to use brute force. The Serb was an expert at inflicting pain without causing death, but the stubborn priest had retreated within himself and denied the bone-breaking agony. It was time to use other methods. Methods that risked breaking his mind and stopping his heart.

A suspended microphone hovered over his face, only three inches from his encrusted lips. They were careful that their victim did not bite through his tongue. Just before the electric shock thumped through his body, a GRU man would force a stained, cloth-bound length of dowel rod into his mouth. Another officer sat with headphones clamped over his ears, his eyes fixed on the dual needle points showing the level on the digital recorder in front of him. Dragonović stood close to the man's ear, droning the continuous question, over and over again. Just reveal the key to the code – then the man could die.

A white-coated doctor, coerced by Verskiy with threats

against his elderly parents, stood on the other side listening through a stethoscope to the irregular heartbeat of the victim. The cardiac monitor audibly and visibly reflected the erratic heartbeat from the adhesive pads on the man's chest. Every twenty minutes for the past few hours the doctor had released 2 cc of a 5 per cent solution of sodium thiopentone followed by a dose of amphetamine. Now they had increased it to 4 cc – pushing the man's weakened constitution to the limits. Neither the Americans nor the Russians had ever produced a so-called truth drug, but this system came the closest to manipulating a prisoner's mind. Sodium thiopentone or sodium amytal: both served the same purpose. The risk was in the fine control it took to keep a victim hovering between consciousness and unconsciousness, particularly after sustained torture, when the balance became one of life and death. Intravenous tubes, one for the thiopentone, the other amphetamine, slid deep into the central vein of each arm. The room stank from the man's retching and loss of control over his bladder. Cigarette smoke sat like marsh gas in the fetid air.

Verskiy needed this man kept alive. How long before his victim's heart gave out – shock or drugs rupturing a coronary artery or wall? The indicators on the digital recording barely moved, their quivering reflecting the man's laboured breathing. The doctor turned towards Verskiy, who stood at the door. Shaking his head, he indicated how close the man was to death.

The SVR believed the priest could have been used to sow disinformation into foreign governments, notably the British. If Verskiy lost the man without getting the key to the code, he would certainly face punitive measures if his own people could not then break it. His enemies would have an iron-clad case against him. He had signed a declaration assuming full responsibility.

None of these fears showed on Verskiy's face. He nodded for the doctor to push the man further.

The doctor checked the litre bag of saline that dripped continuously into the priest's vein. He had piggybacked the two other bags, the sodium thiopentone and amphetamine. He opened the valve on the intravenous drip, allowing another mixed dose of 5 cc into the man's vein. The victim shuddered as the drugs began their destructive journey.

Dragonović and the GRU men had stripped to shirtsleeves hours before; the doctor sweated not only from the airless conditions but the fear of what might happen if he failed to keep his so-called patient alive. Verskiy had not moved from the room since the interrogation began. But now the man was dying. Dragonović leant close to the semi-conscious man on the table. The same question. The same demand. And this time, instead of the usual laboured breathing the level indicators on the recorder leapt slightly. The operator clamped a hand over the headset and scribbled the words down. He could barely hear but they could always boost the recording later... no, there they were... the same words again.

Verskiy watched, willing the man to hang on to life – the next few seconds were vital. *The key to the code. Just give us the key.*

The doctor took the stethoscope from his ears and wiped his face. The heart monitor bleeped in a monotone. The doctor removed the intravenous drips and the cardiac monitoring pads from the corpse. He had violated the Hippocratic Oath he had taken twenty years before. There was only the perverse compensation that he had done his duty: by using his skills he had kept his patient alive as long as possible.

Dragonović and the GRU officers relaxed. It was over. They lit cigarettes and began to chat amicably as the operator pulled off his headphones, tore a sheet from his message pad and handed it to Verskiy.

Verskiy read the text, crumpled the sheet and left the death cell.

Dragonović retrieved the paper, unfolded it and read the priest's dying words.

I forgive. God will not.

50

Beyond the fairy-tale Kremlin lights and traffic snaking slowly around and beyond the river, the glittering city faded into the low-lit Shanghai Slum. Raglan stared down at what was little more than a shanty town. Sokol had gone to meet his contacts while Raglan stayed in the room. He was expecting two calls. The one from Elena came first, as he thought it would.

'Are you all right?' she asked.

'Sure. A few bruises is all.'

'You should have come to me afterwards, Raglan. I told you, my bed is warm.'

'I wish, but that would have been too big a risk for you. Better we keep our distance now. The GRU's Serbian asset was backing up their operation. He got to me and rammed me into the river. That's twice he's tried to kill me and if he finds me again he'll have another go, now they know I'm in Moscow and was involved in trying to save the priest. I couldn't risk getting close to you. I wish I could have.'

'Thank you for thinking of my safety.'

'I couldn't stop them, Elena. They got the old man.'

She sighed. 'I know. He's dead. Like you said, they tortured him at the prison.'

'You're sure about that?' Raglan knew the priest's death

would help accelerate the exfiltration of the Russian spy. He unconsciously glanced at Maguire's phone on the table next to him.

'I have contacts at the prison and the coroner's office. The official line is still that he was kidnapped by an organized crime boss. His body was dumped.'

'Are you involved in the investigation?'

'Yes. It's a sham of course. If the intelligence services are involved, then we will close the file quickly.'

'Even though there were government licence numbers on those vehicles? Can't you challenge them?'

'They can be bought on the black market. We are CID, not security, and they can do what they want. It would not be the first time gangsters have used stolen plates. Nothing can be proved.'

'Elena, it was GRU. I saw them,' Raglan insisted.

'And how do we bring you forward as a witness? Your real reason for being here, whatever that is, will end.'

They fell silent. Time was against them now. Raglan projected a half-dozen scenarios that might soon become reality. 'Elena, I don't want to drag you any further into this.'

'Isn't that my choice? Besides, I don't share my bed with just anyone, you know.'

He smiled, imagining her on the other end of the phone. 'I don't know when I'm going to have to move again. It will be soon. '

Her voice softened. 'You call me and I will do what I can. I would be happy if you stayed alive.'

She hung up. Raglan guessed that had they talked much longer they would have yielded to their mutual desire and thrown caution to the wind. One thing Raglan was certain of: whatever was going to happen would happen in hours not days. He heard the roar of motorbikes. Mostly Harleys by the sound of their growling engines. He looked down and saw twenty or more bikers weaving their way out of the Shanghai Slum, their headlights piercing the gently drifting snowflakes. A momentary distraction broken by the ringing of Maguire's phone.

'The courier was a priest. And he's dead,' he told Maguire.

'You're certain?'

'Yes, got it from a contact here,' said Raglan, hearing the edge in Maguire's voice, knowing the operation's pace had just shifted up a gear. 'What happened to the go-between at the gallery? If they were lifted, then chances are the priest talked.'

'They're still in place,' Maguire said. 'They raised the alarm as soon as they heard he was taken.'

'Then it's doubtful the GRU got anything.'

'Too late for everyone, Raglan. You have to get the subject out tonight. We think there's every chance their analysts must be close to unravelling your father's encrypted document.'

Raglan looked down on the sprawling shacks below. 'I don't know if the people we have here can move that quickly.'

'Forget them. There's an Audi A6 hire car in your name. It's parked outside the Frunzenkeya Metro. We have people on the ground. One of them will meet you there. There are others in play.'

'Where am I going?'

'The Khamovniki District. You'll be given the address when you get the car.'

'Are you still planning on Latvia?'

'Yes. You'll be given the route.'

'Maguire, innocent people are dead because of this man. I'm not taking another step until you tell me who it is I'm getting out.'

'It's a long game, Raglan. There are others involved. People you don't need to know about. If you get stopped, I can't help you. Remember, you're a tourist. The car's satnav will show you've been to St Petersburg. You're on an art gallery tour. Make sure you have your passport and visa with you to back up the tourist gambit. The other side is closing in.'

'A name, Maguire.'

'It's need to know. All you have to do is get him across the Latvian border.'

'No,' said Raglan. 'First the name, then the game. Who is it I'm transporting?'

51

Major Lipetsk studied the document. His hands were trembling. He was in a soundproof room a hundred metres below the concrete bunker complex. Several landline telephones stood side by side, each colour-coded for the connection to those senior members of the intelligence and security services essential to the safety of the Russian Federation. Beyond the large window, in the main room, the tracking screens and rows of computers held their operators' attention. Links from the furthermost parts of Russia fed information constantly.

Lipetsk had aligned himself with the most powerful man in military intelligence and had been tasked with decoding the contents of an age-old message revealing that a Russian intelligence officer, a former KGB man stationed in Africa, was prepared to serve MI6. Had Lipetsk been informed by anyone other than General Alexei Verskiy that such a traitor might still exist from so long ago he would not have believed them. But now he was standing in that secure room, deliberately half lit so as not to reflect the two men who stood with him behind the window glass.

The men had been polite. They offered no threat. Sent to ensure that only he would see the vital information that would now bring about the downfall of a highly placed figure in the Russian intelligence community. Major Lipetsk's throat constricted. He must not lose his nerve now.

My God. The name he saw on the sheet of paper played tricks with his mind. This was no straightforward exposure of a traitor. It did not compute. That is what his mind told him. Analysis was his bread and butter. Informed and intelligent projections had been what propelled him through the academy and placed him in the nerve centre of everything vital to the Federation. He turned to face the two men, his hand hovering over one of the phones. One smiled benignly. He must have understood the confusion Lipetsk felt. The second man remained expressionless.

The first man held his folded coat, hands crossed in front of him. For a second he exposed the face of his wristwatch and checked its time against the nuclear-regulated clock on the wall. A small gesture, a raised palm of his hand. Not yet. Do not make the call *until told*. Lipetsk looked up at the clock. Everything being equal he would be given permission to make the call when the slow ticking hand reached the top of the hour.

Three agonizing minutes away.

The snow fell steadily, lying unblemished, the urgent haste of a biting wind now gone. Drink and cigarette in hand, Alexei Verskiy gazed out from his apartment into the silent night. He had read the Russian poets, but dismissed their metaphorical nonsense, the momentary imagining that these descending snowflakes were the souls of the dead, piling up, smothering the living. True, he had caused the death and imprisonment of the guilty – and of many who were not – but this was nothing more than wet snow blanketing the city.

These were final desperate hours. It was good that Lipetsk was fearful of failing. It drove a man to strive harder. Lipetsk and his analysts had assured him they were close to breaking the coded message. After the priest had died Verskiy knew he had thrown caution to the wind. Which of the two men he suspected would come for him? Mikhail Semenchyev or Piotr Fedeyev? FSB or SVR? The old beasts would not restrain themselves for much longer.

The phone rang.

'General Verskiy. It is Major Lipetsk. I have what you need. The code is broken. I have a name for you.' Lipetsk's voice sounded shaky. His discovery had obviously unnerved him.

Verskiy's heart raced. He stopped himself from asking the name. 'Who has seen the decoded message?'

'Only my best analyst and myself. Shall I bring the information to you, general?'

'No. I'm on my way. Stay where you are.'

He rang off, gulped down the last of his drink, tugged a scarf from the coat rack and shrugged into his overcoat. Settling his fur hat firmly on his head, he was about to open his front door when he heard voices in the stairwell below. He eased open the door. A woman's voice, her laboured breathing telling him it was Mrs Barinovna from the floor below. She was complaining. Nothing new there. Satisfied there was no immediate threat, he closed his front door behind him. There was an 'Out of Order' sign on the lift. He glanced down and saw the overweight woman ascending step by laborious step, her wheeled shopping bag clunking at every pace, carried not by her but by a lift-maintenance man in grey overalls emblazoned with the name of the lift company.

Verskiy glanced down the stairs, waited as Mrs Barinovna thanked the engineer and then berated him for the unreliability of his machinery. How was she supposed to do her shopping? The engineer apologized and assured her it would be repaired that very night. Verskiy held back, waiting until his neighbour's door was closed and the Good Samaritan engineer turned to descend the steps. Verskiy stayed a dozen paces behind him and called out.

'Your people were here a month ago. Is it an ongoing problem?'

The engineer stopped, held the banister and half turned to face him. 'I'm sorry, sir, but this lift has been working without any problems for several months. We had a crew here back then if you remember?'

It was the correct answer – Verskiy's question had been bait to flush out an imposter. Verskiy took no chances when anything unusual presented itself. Keeping far enough behind the engineer, he followed him down the several flights of stairs until he reached the entrance hall. Protective mats and tools lay across the floor; the lift door was open exposing the inner working of the shaft; a second man lay on his back half under the stalled car. The Good Samaritan got down on his hands and knees and leant in close to his partner.

'Anything?'

The second man sighed. 'Damned if I can see what's stopping it. Cables are fine.'

His partner slid down next to him on his back. 'It's the electrics again. They never upgraded these older places. It's the valve box at the back like last time. I'll have to get inside.'

Verskiy kept his distance, wanting assurance that everything he heard was authentic. That there was no threat to him from strangers in his building. He reached the apartment building's door, pressed the release button but the door did not open. The Good Samaritan pulled himself up from where he was working.

'Sir, I'm sorry, it's the same electrical connection from the lift. I had to bring the old lady through the service entrance.' He went back to his inspection. Again, Verskiy felt no threat. But the back door? He pulled out his phone, pressed a speed dial. It was answered almost immediately by his driver.

'Sir?'

'Bring the car around the back. Hoot when you're here.' He ended the call, watched the two men a moment longer and then went around the lift shaft to where deliveries and tradesmen usually entered once they had been buzzed in. He waited in the stairwell, lit a cigarette and thought of the ambitious Major Lipetsk. He would be further rewarded for his efforts. Breaking an arcane code that identified the traitor was worth anything the man wanted. By the time the cigarette had burnt halfway down as he listened to the engineers' muttered curses, the car horn hooted. It was safe.

He pulled open the door and stepped out past the refuse-collection area. His car waited, the yellow signal indicator tinting the falling snow. He peered at the driver who turned to face him behind the wheel as if checking his passenger was safely through the rear entrance. He didn't recognize the night-shift driver. Verskiy heard the click of the doors being electronically unlocked. The rear passenger door was level with his approach. He reached for the door handle. His footfall crunching the snow muffled the sound of another behind him.

Too late he turned, felt the sting behind his ear and then the immediate giddiness as he pitched forward against the car, his gloved hands unable to find purchase on its wet roof. His legs sagged. Strong hands held him. He stared up. Spiralling white flakes descended from a distant dark place. And then his cheek was pressed into the snow.

Raglan eased the Audi out of its parking area as the two engineers came out of the building. They stooped to help Verskiy's replacement driver and the man who had injected the GRU deputy lift his body and place him into the boot of Raglan's car. They were gentle, laying his head carefully on a pillow and then pulling a down-filled sleeping bag over him, wedging him in carefully so he wouldn't roll and be harmed. The boot's interior had been made as comfortable as possible. Raglan closed the boot lid. The two bogus engineers retreated to clear away any sign of their presence in the building. The driver got into Verskiy's car and parked it fifty metres away, tucking it into the building's parking bays. The fourth man faced Raglan. Someone he had never seen before. He was English.

'We have a tracker on the car. Eight hours to the Latvian border post. Stay on the main M9 route. It's a busy highway. The border post is at App Burachki. There's a lorry park there near an Aris petrol station. Turn off and take the forest road. It's used by loggers and after another forty minutes will take you across the border. The fence will be cut in between border-guard patrols. You'll be met at Zilupe just inside Latvia. He'll be coming out of it by then. The drugs might keep him quiet an hour longer. Hard to tell beyond that.' He handed Raglan a map. 'You've got a full tank. Petrol stations are marked along the way. If for any reason you're stopped by highway police and they check, the map'll make you look like a nervous tourist. There's enough cash in the glove compartment to grease a few palms. Spot fines are easy money for them. Last thing: the boot can't be opened without this.' He pressed a small push-button device into Raglan's hand. 'That means no one can get in to check it out if you are stopped. Tell anyone who asks that the boot mechanism is faulty. They can try if they're that keen. They won't succeed. OK. That's it. Good luck.' The stranger turned away, pulled up his collar and trudged off into the night as Verskiy's driver strode across the parking area to join him. They were soon out of sight.

Raglan looked at the few street lamps along the narrow service road behind the blocks of flats. Subdued spheres of light in the night's silence. No one had called out, raised an alarm or peered from their windows. Just another late, quiet winter night. Even the car's tyre tracks were being covered. The only explanation Raglan could think of when Maguire had told him Verskiy's name was that the GRU man had been out to protect his own skin. That he'd needed to ensure no one but himself retrieved the information that could expose him. The very man who had led the operation to retrieve his father's letter to British intelligence was the Russian spy.

It didn't make any sense. The subterfuge of being spirited away had to be window dressing in case anyone saw him being taken. A twisted world of men resurrecting the past in order to protect the present. It was perverse.

He climbed in behind the wheel. Maguire was waiting in Latvia six hundred kilometres away.

All Raglan had to do was get there and deliver the most important man British intelligence had ever recruited.

52

Raglan checked his mirrors constantly in that first hour of driving. The roads had been kept clear by snow ploughs and gritters. He had allowed cars and lorries to overtake him, then sped up and took up a defensive driving position to ensure the Russians didn't have a surveillance team on his tail. Given the urgency of the operation Raglan had told Bird Sokol to stay in the Shanghai apartment. If anything went wrong and they needed a Plan B, then he would use the smugglers.

It had stopped snowing when another hour later he pulled into a service station, its neon lights crisp in the clear night sky. He backed into the parking area well away from the main building and checked on his passenger. Verskiy remained unconscious. Raglan felt his neck pulse. It was slow and steady. There was no sign of any discomfort. Verskiy's overcoat and the sleeping bag kept him snug. Satisfied that his passenger was safe, and that they were not being followed, he rolled back on to the highway. All being well he would hand the spy over within the next seven hours.

The Audi purred. The road ahead was clear. There were noticeably fewer cars on the motorway. The towns along the route absorbed late-night journeys. Fewer lorries were travelling. Some had pulled over for the night. Raglan found a jazz station on the car's radio. A Kenny Burrell guitar number eased into the cab. Raglan settled down for the long drive.

The further west he drove the clearer the sky became. The Audi's high-beam headlights picked out the unlit road ahead. Shadows from the forests loomed either side. Five hours further on, the illuminated sign for App Burachki's border control came into view. The road surface became rougher, single-lane traffic both ways. A service station's lights glowed beyond the forest, their glimmer dusting the treetops. He slowed. The slip road for the lorry park was a kilometre ahead. He glanced at the satnav and then flicked on the reading light to double-check against the map. Returning the cab to its soft light from the instrument panel he peered through the windscreen. The forest workers' entrance was little more than a wooden-built post and gate. He checked his mirrors; there was no traffic behind him.

Once he had driven on the forest track for a hundred metres, he switched off his headlights, stopped the car and got out into the refreshingly cold night air. Raglan peered into the forest. The immediate treeline had been cut back by twenty metres or so either side of the track, making a road wide enough for a log-hauling lorry and felling machines to travel unhindered. Moon- and starlight picked out the route until it disappeared from view, swallowed by the forest.

He drove on without lights until the darkness engulfed him again. Raglan relied on old special forces skills. At first he edged forward slowly, and then instinct took over once he had a feel for the road. It narrowed. With the cab in darkness his eyes could pick out the darker pattern in the ground in front of him. The road ahead turned and as Raglan drove into the bend, he saw that it became wider, and swept into a broad turning circle. The border should be close now. The scraped track ahead allowed a sprinkling of night sky to glint on metal. Dark shapes. He braked. Stared hard into the night. And was then blinded by a dozen vehicles' headlights. A loudhailer squealed, followed by a command.

'Bring the vehicle forward. No tricks. We are armed.' The voice spoke in English. The accent was Russian.

Raglan dragged the gear lever into reverse. He would run for it. But two more headlights appeared thirty metres behind him. He was trapped.

'Come forward. Slowly,' the voice instructed him again.

There was no choice. The forest was a perfect place for an execution. Raglan broke open his burner phone, stripped out the battery and snapped the SIM card. He drove the car forward slowly. Given a chance he would run for the trees across the felled landscape. The closer he got the more he saw the impossibility of escaping the crescent of armed FSB border guards training their weapons on him. Raglan stopped the car ten metres from the officer with the loudhailer. He opened the door and dropped the broken SIM card into the snow.

It was the end of the road.

Ghostly figures, backlit by their vehicles' headlamps, made no attempt to approach him. Raglan peered through the stark light past the fur-hatted Federal Border Guard Service officer with the loudhailer. A car was parked between the guards' 4x4s. Its driver got out and opened the rear passenger door. A tall man emerged, his gloved hands putting on a fur hat, like those worn by his men, except it did not bear an FSB Border Guard badge. He pulled up the collar of his overcoat. He stepped closer but stayed behind the officer who gestured two men from one of the off-roaders. They came forward carrying a medical pack, went past Raglan and opened the boot with a similar device given to Raglan for that purpose. Raglan realized the operation must have been compromised even before he had left Moscow and that this man was a high-ranking intelligence official. A cigarette lighter flared; the man dipped his head to the flame. The brief illumination gave Raglan no chance of seeing his features. The man seemed unconcerned about the drama unfolding.

One thing Raglan knew for certain. If they shot him his body would never been found. The civilian took a folded sheet of paper from his breast pocket. Raglan glanced behind him. Verskiy had obviously been injected with something that revived him. He was groggy though, and had to be held upright by the two men who frogmarched him to stand before the Border Guard officer. Verskiy had balls, Raglan gave him that. He shook free the two men holding him and stood unsteadily facing the armed men. A breeze fluttered snowflakes down from the branches. Verskiy was bareheaded; a wisp of hair lifted: he smoothed it. If there was to be a firing squad moment, this is how it would look.

Raglan remained where he stood. No one had made any immediate threat against him. He stared at the civilian, whose face was still in shadow. He was taller than Verskiy, slighter in build, his leather-gloved hands held the cigarette between two fingers while he read from the document.

'Colonel General Alexei Verskiy, Deputy Director Main Intelligence Directorate of the General Staff of the Armed

Forces of the Russian Federation, you are charged with treason. You have undertaken a covert mission to retrieve evidence that you spy for British intelligence. You have removed senior officers from their posts at the Volokolamsk Electronic Intelligence Centre in order for you to have a recovered document decoded, intending to expunge your name identifying you as that person known to the British as codename *Malaika*. Once that information was proven to exist by your replacement officer, Major Pavel Lipetsk, you dismissed Colonels Tamarkin and Shevenko from their posts to avoid detection. You then arranged for your British paymasters to smuggle you into Latvia and then on to the United Kingdom. You will be tried and sentenced based on this and further evidence going back to your time in Africa as an active KGB agent.' He folded the document and put it away. 'That's enough. I don't want to stand out here in the cold. You know the rest.'

'So it is you,' Verskiy rasped, barely audible, throat dry from the drugs.

'It is I who caught you, Alexei.'

'I will bring you down,' said Verskiy. 'Major Lipetsk telephoned me before I was kidnapped and drugged. Made to look as though I was defecting. He broke the code. He has the traitor's name. Your name.'

'It was my people who made him phone you. And it appears that the young Major Lipetsk did not wish to remain associated with you. We can only assume the reason he killed himself was his discovery that you were the traitor.'

Raglan heard Verskiy gasp. All hope lost. A faked suicide. Lipetsk had met his end at this man's hands. Verskiy made no protest as two plainclothes officers took hold of him again.

The smoking man stepped closer to Raglan but remained far enough back not to be recognized. His face in shadow, the fur hat foreshortening his features. Raglan smelt the rich toasted tobacco smoke.

'You will hand me your phone.'

'I destroyed it.'

'Of course you did. A man like you would have done so as soon as he sensed danger. It was to be expected. You would not wish us to trace who you had been in contact with in Moscow. No, I meant the phone that Maguire gave you. It's to be expected that he would make sure you had a Service phone. That is MI6 Standard Operating Procedure.'

Whoever this man was, Raglan realized he knew everything. He handed over the phone. 'Verskiy wasn't the spy,' said Raglan. 'And if you had been alerted to what was going on, you could have stopped me anywhere on the road. The main highway would have just as easily boxed me in as here. This was an operation to be rid of a man who could have blown thirty years of secrets.'

The man's cigarette glowed; he exhaled, and dropped what was left of it into the snow. 'A powerful man responsible for many deaths.'

Raglan still couldn't see the man's features. 'But you chose here. Away from the public gaze. Close to the border. As if an authentic attempt was being made to cross a border illegally. How close am I?'

'Three hundred metres through the trees behind me.'

'So he'll be shot trying to cross,' said Raglan. 'It's an execution.'

'It's expedient,' said the tall man.

'It's murder,' said Raglan. 'My father saved your life all

those years ago. You think he would feel any different about this?'

'Your father was a pragmatist, Raglan.'

Raglan saw the two plainclothes men turn Verskiy to face the border, tantalizingly close. They stepped away. A third man appeared from the darkness behind them. He fired three shots from a semi-automatic pistol in Verskiy's back. The silent night reverberated from the heavy-calibre gunshots. Somewhere in the forest, crows cawed in panic and broke free into the night sky. Verskiy pitched forward. His leg trembled, a death-throe response. The three men waited. There would be no coup de grâce to the back of the head. The official report needed to be seen as a genuine escape attempt. One of the men bent and placed fingers on Verskiy's neck. The second man stepped back a dozen paces, produced a camera, photographed the body and then helped the others drag his corpse to a waiting black panel van.

'So I won't get out of here either,' said Raglan.

The man turned his back on Raglan and lit another cigarette as two of the border guards walked forward. Then he stopped and looked back. 'You will be returned to Moscow and interrogated. I expect we will find that you are a hapless tourist duped into carrying an unknown cargo. Payment for your efforts is in the glove box. But your involvement must be seen to be questioned. Your father and I were good friends, Raglan. As you say, he saved my life. I save yours.'

Raglan was handcuffed. 'You and my father. What was it? The connection? You shared something before Africa.'

The Russian didn't answer for a moment. 'We each had a son we loved. A son we felt we had neglected because of our work.'

Raglan was bundled into the back of a Federal Border Guard 4x4. Headlights behind him were switched off. Darkness enfolded the execution site. All that remained was the dull glow of the master spy's cigarette.

53

The security guard at the State Tretyakov Gallery watched the gallery's director get out of a taxi and walk towards the main doors. He was surprised to see her. It was still dark. He liked the elderly woman. She always had a kind word for him, unlike others who saw him only as a lowly night-watchman. The street lights cast their eerie glow on her as she stepped through the snow. He stepped smartly to the heavy door and swung it open for the diminutive figure.

'Director Zaitseva, coming to work at this time? It's so early.'

She stamped her feet on the mat. 'Ah, Borislav, good morning. Thank you. You know how it is. Every once in a while I have an important call coming through from Australia. They sit in the sunshine while we freeze. Time zones mean nothing when you are enjoying the warmth, eh?'

He closed the door behind her. 'Summer can't come soon enough for me, that's for sure. Shall I make you tea?'

She waved a hand and walked past him. 'No, no, thank you, I'm fine.'

Lights flickered ahead of her as she climbed the stairs and then made her way through the galleries. Eyes followed her.

She glanced at them. Only the painted figures knew why she came to the office so early on these days. They were silent witness to her involvement in the business of spying. Her boots clattered across the floor. Echoing. More lights flickered on. Shadows banished. But not the fear. Since she'd learnt that they had murdered the priest her muscles had ached with the tension of waiting for the knock on her door. It would have come by now had he given them her name and what Verskiy wanted. She had not told the Englishman how she and the priest shared the secrets, and had done for so many years. If one was taken the other would be the main source of passing information. What had to be encrypted would be done laboriously by hand as it had always been these many years past. Safer that way.

She reached her office door, turned and looked back at the length of the gallery floor behind her. It was quiet. No following footsteps. Not that there would be. Looking over her shoulder was an old habit. She closed the door, hung up her coat and hat, straightened her skirt and put on her desk lamp. She reached for the telephone, pulled it closer and then settled back, hands folded in her lap, eyes closed. Heart beating a little faster than usual.

Ten minutes later, five to the hour, as always, the phone rang, jarring the silence. She let it ring four times and then answered, watching the length of the gallery in case the kind-hearted Borislav had decided to make tea for her after all and left his post. The voice on the end of the line was one she had known since childhood. Both families had suffered under Stalin. Hers first, his only much later, which had turned his face to the West.

'Margarita, I am sorry for what happened.'

'He was a good man of the Church and the people. God embraces him now.'

'Verskiy is dead.'

The vein in her neck pulsed, heartbeat thudding. She clasped the phone with both hands to stop them from trembling. There was no point asking the how and the where of Verskiy's death. She sighed, her whisper barely audible. 'Thank God.'

'We had a plan, the British and me. That is why we used the Englishman. He could have been sacrificed if necessary.'

'Is he alive?'

'Yes. The British want him kept that way. He is an asset to them. He's at Lubyanka. His whereabouts during his time in Moscow cannot be established. No hotel will have him registered. He's out on a limb and he will soon be questioned. He must be made to appear innocent. My people and others must be convinced.'

'How can I help?'

'When his car was searched, they found a brochure for a Russian arts tour that included private accommodation. It was something we put there before he took Verskiy.'

'I understand. He was here at the gallery for a private viewing. That can be verified.'

'How is your nephew these days?'

She smiled to herself. He knew everything. 'Yes, his apartment is vacant. He's studying in Berlin.'

'Well?'

'Yes, of course. But the Englishman will not know that when he is questioned.'

'Then he'll need to have his wits about him. Give it a few hours. We'll leak information to the news channels. And then our people will question him. Can I leave it to you, old friend?'

She nodded. 'I will do whatever I can.'

The call ended. She replaced the receiver. She switched off the desk lamp. Her audience waited expectantly. Watching her next move. Reading her thoughts. She flicked a switch on her desk and plunged them into darkness. Her shoulders slumped as tension drained away. She eased back into the chair and closed her eyes. It would be only a few short hours before being questioned – until then she would enjoy the most untroubled sleep she'd had in years.

54

Maguire had stayed at the office on the night of the operation. Raglan had not known what lay in store. That Maguire was not waiting across the Latvian border. Assurances had been given that Raglan would not be harmed, but if the operation had been compromised then assurances were worthless. Russian inter-agency rivalry and political power plays could still bring the whole business tumbling down. Everything would be lost, including Raglan.

It was 3 a.m. in London when Maguire's phone rang.

'Raglan?' said Maguire.

The Russian voice that answered was one Maguire had never heard before. 'Maguire, I have your man's phone.'

'Is he alive?'

'He is being driven to Moscow as we speak. I gave you my word through our contact at the gallery that he would not be harmed, and I have kept my word.'

'What happens to him now?'

'He will be questioned. Not by one of my top people, but by someone who is slow in his thinking and who will be briefed.'

'Are you going to deport him?'

'No. That could imply a degree of collusion between the British embassy here that we wish to avoid. Your embassy people set up the exfiltration; Raglan delivered. That is all we needed. I will of course be questioned by my own higher authority but my reputation is that I dig out traitors. The irony is not lost on me.'

'Then what happens to him?'

He heard the older man sigh. Perhaps, thought Maguire, he had been doing this for so many years that even he grew tired of the challenge to stay alive, mired in intrigue.

'Once the interrogation is over, I'll make my recommendation that he is released. A stupid tourist who took money. He has no connection to British intelligence, he is not even resident in the UK, he lives somewhere in France. It won't be a problem. He will walk out and make his own way home.'

'There are others who wish him dead.'

'That is out of my hands. He must take his chances. I suggest you do not have anyone in the embassy approach him. He should be ignored. And I will destroy this phone now that you have been given the facts.'

'Thank you.'

'Tell your people at the embassy I will use the gallery contact for any future communication. As usual, do not try to contact me.'

'That policy nearly caused your downfall. Natural enough for you to use a priest to reach out to us, but now we know the woman at the gallery was your link to him. The priest is dead so she's all we have. Dead-letter drops are dangerous. You must know that? You told her, she tells the priest, he leaves a message for my people. The risk is greater now.'

'I cannot allow it to be any other way. I will come to you when necessary. My people know their tradecraft. All your people have to do is watch for the sign we give them.'

Maguire knew he had no bargaining chip. This man was vital. 'Are we ever to meet?'

'I doubt it. I like it where I am.'

'I can only offer you my government's immense gratitude for what you have done for us.'

'Belief is a personal matter between a man and his conscience, is it not?'

'Yes, it is, but you have never been closer to being exposed than in these past few days. When did you realize General Verskiy was tracking you down?'

'He gave an ambitious young signals officer a chance to prove himself. He replaced men loyal to me. It was a red flag. It was a risk he took to keep his cards close to his chest. It turns out he was a poor card player.'

'I regret that the priest died.'

'It is the great risk we all take. His abduction was a GRU-led operation.'

'Then Verskiy had broken into your circuit.'

'I do not think so. He was an old priest with outspoken views, so yes, the SVR might have had him under surveillance. If that was the case then he was traded by them to Verskiy. We use the people we trust. There is always a risk and there is still a risk for your man, Raglan.'

'They couldn't know about him,' said Maguire, thoughts racing through how Raglan's cover might be blown.

'The GRU do know about him. Raglan tried to save my priest. He was nearly killed doing it. If any of those GRU officers recognized him then they will know of his likely involvement in Verskiy's abduction and death. They are not stupid people, Mr Maguire. They will hunt him down. He will be released after questioning. I cannot protect him. He is on his own. I hope he gets out in time. And now, I think it is time we all went to bed. It has been a testing time. Goodbye, Mr Maguire.'

The call ended. Maguire felt the tension seep from him. So much had been out of his control. Verskiy had been murdered and made to look the traitor. He had been a good servant to his country during his career. His methods may have been distasteful, but he had remained loyal and now everything he had fought for had been snatched from him and his name besmirched. The professional in Maguire felt a tinge of regret for the man. All he hoped for now was that Raglan would make it out.

55

Andrei Golyev was always the first at his desk. Despite his demotion, the former investigator of corrupt state officials continued to lead his small team by example. His organizational skills served him well as he collated years of government bureaucracy, readying the paper mountains for digitalization. The people under him were thankful their boss was not an ambitious younger man who would find fault with them, so that he would not be blamed for anything going awry. Golyev simply wanted to work out his time without drawing attention from the wrong people. Never again would he risk doing that.

He had been at his desk since seven that morning. He had walked from the Metro station, taking a longer route to his office than going directly to the main entrance. The snow was hardening on the footpaths, but he had his shoe grips fitted and relished the cold bite of the fresh air before the descent into the Lubyanka basement. A tantalizing hint of blue sky appeared briefly, but with a forecast of more snow he knew the promise of sunshine was still only that.

Younger members of staff began arriving with their takeaway coffee from the cafe on the opposite side of the square. The canteen coffee was an acquired taste, one he had learnt to live with over the years. They greeted him and each other, then sat, switched on their computers, gazed at their screens, shuffled the documents piled on their desks and sucked on the plastic lids of their paper cups like babies on a nipple. Golyev had his own chipped mug. They teased him that when he retired the FSB would copper-plate it as a parting gift. He usually replied he would prefer it to be gold-plated. That was about as much levity as anyone enjoyed in their grinding day-to-day existence.

Irina Kameneva was always later than the others by ten minutes. It was a fact of life. You live so far out in one of the old Soviet blocks it takes an age for the bus to get through, especially if the gritters never reached the side streets. The round-faced young woman pulled off her scarf, balanced her coffee, shrugged out of her coat and hung her ear muffs on the coat hook.

'At least it's not snowing this morning,' she said.

'Good morning, Irina,' said Golyev.

The old man was benign but protocol and good manners were not to be ignored.

'Oh, good morning, sir.'

He raised his eyes over his reading glasses perched halfway down his nose. Waiting.

'Sorry I'm late.'

'The bus?'

'Yes, sir.'

'The gritters again?'

'Yes, sir.'

Always the same conversation when it snowed; there were other excuses when it did not. 'Very well, Irina. There's work to be done.' And always the same gentle rebuke.

She sat at her desk and fussed, watching the screen as she logged on. 'Not just the gritters though, sir. Did you hear about General Verskiy?'

Golyev flinched, nervous at the mention of the name.

'I have not.' He looked at her, waiting, as did everyone else.

Irina enjoyed being the bearer of important news, but she did so carefully, showing no sense of celebration. 'He's dead.'

The staff gasped. Golyev felt his chest tighten.

'How do you know this, Irina?' said Golyev. It was his prerogative to question her before any gossip took hold among his staff on their lunch break.

'My brother. He told me when he arrived home this morning from his nightshift. It's all anyone is talking about.'

Golyev knew her brother worked for the FSB's Border Guard Service in the building adjoining their own. 'What happened?' he asked.

Irina drew in a slow, deep breath. Her features creased as she thought about the news. 'He was accused of being a traitor. That he spied for the British. They caught him at the Latvian border last night.'

'Who caught him?' said Golyev, forcing back acid bile from his gullet.

'The FSB and a border patrol. They say an Englishman drove him there.'

'How did he die?' Golyev asked, his voice fading. He already knew the answer.

The shocking news seemed finally to have penetrated Irina's psyche. She hesitated. Her voice barely above a whisper. 'Shot while trying to escape.'

Golyev's hand trembled. He replaced his pen carefully on his desk. It was important to remain calm. He had helped

Verskiy discover the names of former KGB agents who had served in Africa, and of those who were still involved in today's intelligence services, one was second in command at foreign intelligence, the other deputy chairman of the FSB. Had Golyev slipped up? Had his research been something more than a straightforward enquiry for the GRU general? Alexei Verskiy had been the sixth man on the list who had served in Africa. What in God's name had Golyev got himself into?

One of the men muttered, 'Death to all traitors. He got what he deserved.'

Golyev tapped a fingernail on the desk. 'Illya, we do not know the facts.'

'We do now,' said the young man. 'The FSB don't fuck about with people like that.'

The room was hushed except for the gentle swish of air from a computer's fan.

'Irina,' said Golyev. 'Are they holding the Englishman for questioning next door?'

She nodded. Then, as if remembering: 'Your son works for GRU, doesn't he?'

Golyev's staff turned their gaze on him, making, he felt, an immediate association between him and a traitor. He pushed back his chair.

'You all have work to do,' he said evenly. He shrugged into his overcoat and reached for the door.

The young man, Illya, sensing with animal instinct a vulnerability in the old investigator, said, 'Are you coming back, sir?'

Golyev stared him down. He was too old a hand to be threatened by a kid who had never risked his life for his country. The younger man averted his gaze. He had gone too far.

'There is more to this I want to find out. I will return, Illya, be assured of that, but the question is: will you remain here when I do?'

There was nothing better than putting a wet-behind-the-ears younger man on notice. Golyev could still wield a threat. He closed the door behind him, took a deep breath and walked down the long corridor towards the connecting door to the Border Service. Verskiy, a traitor. Golyev did not believe it. But that of course did not matter. There were others in power in this very building who apparently thought differently. What mattered now was to try and find out if his son had been too close to Verskiy. If he would be dragged down with him. Guilt by association. The old game never changed. Perhaps this Englishman might know.

56

The night Verskiy was killed Raglan had made an informed choice. The man waiting in the forest said he knew his father. That his father had saved the Russian's life. Raglan decided he was genuine. If they were going to kill him they would have done it deep in the forest. Despite his hands being handcuffed behind him, he could have escaped, but instead he hunkered down on the back seat of the 4x4 and slept. The two border guards paid no attention to him. They had several hours of night driving ahead of them. One thing Raglan learnt before he fell asleep was that they were taking him to Lubyanka.

It was soon after dawn when the 4x4 swung around the traffic lanes in front of the Lubyanka building. They took Raglan in through the rear entrance of the main building, HQ for the Border Guard Service. The two guards strode through the tiled corridor, each gripping an arm. Again Raglan did not try to resist. He had seen the inside of prisons and police stations before and first impressions were usually the same, wherever they were. The same dour servants of the state shuffling paper, drinking coffee, scratching their arses, and here, nine hundred metres from the Kremlin, no doubt quietly hoping their President hadn't used their pensions to build his palace.

As he expected, he was strip-searched, possessions bagged, his clothes returned to him. Then he was seated in a windowless interview room and left alone, handcuffed to a chain in the floor beneath the table. Raglan guessed he had been there for a couple of hours by the time he heard voices in the corridor outside.

Andrei Golyev checked who was on duty at the Border Service custody desk. So many of those who served had done so for the better part of their lives, clinging to their jobs; the stout, bearded man behind the glass window staring at his computer screen was one such limpet – like Golyev himself.

'Misha, how are you, my friend?' said Golyev.

The man's beard parted, showing tobacco-stained teeth. He gripped Golyev's hand warmly. 'Andrei, you crawled out of the pit to come and say hello to an old friend?'

Golyev kept his voice low but met the man's eyes directly. 'This is business,' he said. 'Verskiy.'

The custody officer shared Golyev's discretion. 'Mother of God, who would have thought it? So, word's out, then?'

'One of my girls. Her brother.'

The big man's eyebrows scrunched together. 'Oh, yes, it's, er...' He grinned. 'Whatsisname.'

'Kamenev.'

'That's him.'

Golyev nodded. 'This Englishman they brought in. Anyone spoken to him yet?'

'Too early for the fat-arsed bastards upstairs.' Misha glanced left and right. 'Andrei, you want to speak to him?'

He grinned again. 'Like the old days eh? Dig out the worms under the logs.'

It was exactly what Golyev wanted. 'I don't wish to get you into trouble, Misha.'

He took Golyev's elbow with one hand and guided him to a door beyond his counter. 'Andrei, you know how it works. They shit on me; I shrug my shoulders and tell them who am I to argue with an FSB investigator. How would I know they buried you in the basement?'

'Has an arrest sheet been done?'

'Would they dare bring him in without one? Paperwork is the lifeblood of us all, Andrei. Even these pig-thick border guards know how to fill in the blanks on a report sheet.'

'Can I look at his possessions first?'

'Sure. In here. He didn't have much. And the question I asked myself was this: if he was a tourist, why didn't he have any luggage? And for another thing, I bet no one has checked any of the hotel's registers, eh? I bet that's what you're thinking.'

'Of course,' said Golyev, although the thought had not yet crossed his mind.

'These pricks who do the interrogating these days won't ask those questions until it dawns on them. It's the old guard like us who get straight to the heart of the matter.' He opened a door into a small room with compact shelf compartments. He pulled out a paper bag, its top folded and banded with a security strip. 'Put it back when you're finished and then I'll take you into him. I'll get you his arrest sheet.'

'Misha, what about security cameras and microphones?'

'Not switched on until official interviews start.' He nodded towards the paper bag. 'Don't worry about the security tag.

I'll rebag it. Nothing's been logged yet. Not until they formally charge him.'

He patted his friend's shoulder and closed the door behind him.

Golyev waited until he heard his old friend walk away. He spilled out the contents. Misha was right. There was little to look at. There were few things to identify the man: his passport; his wallet which yielded a couple of credit cards. There were some roubles and American dollars, always good when you needed something in a hurry. A wristwatch but no rings, so this Daniel Raglan was probably not married. Passport stamps showed Paris as his main international airport. His visa was genuine. So what could connect him to Verskiy? There was nothing here.

He was pushing the contents back into the paper bag when he felt something hard caught in the corner of the stiff brown paper. He shook it free. A thumbnail-sized stainless-steel pendant on a thin cord clattered on to the table. Golyev's mouth dried. His fingers trembled as he turned it and saw the engraved image of the Archangel Michael.

57

Raglan waited stoically for an investigating officer to arrive. He had been denied food and drink, his association with a traitor enough to make him presumed guilty. For all anyone knew he was a British agent sent to smuggle out a top Russian spy. The bare room was a small part of the game. Nothing to distract the person sitting chained to the floor. A hard chair, a plastic top table. No natural light. Complete isolation to make prisoners reflect on the seriousness of their situation. For many it gave them time to crack. The fissures of uncertainty slowly breaking into the deep crevasse of a confession.

But Raglan was not one of those who would yield to these basic techniques. He knew he would either be charged or released. The time to worry was when they took you into a courtyard or dank cellar and put a hood over your head. And by then it was too late.

Raglan looked up as the door opened and a stooped older man came in with an overcoat over his arm. He wore a dark green pullover under a jacket with elbow patches. His tie knotted snugly into a collar a size too big. Raglan guessed he spent most of his working day hunched over a desk reading documents: no one doing that wanted a tight-fitting collar or to wear out their jacket sleeves. At first glance he might be taken for an academic, a teacher of history or philosophy. He had an almost timid demeanour, as if he didn't want to be noticed when walking into a room. But Raglan sensed he was more formidable than he looked: Raglan never took anything for granted or at face value. Raglan tagged him as the 'professor', a memory technique to make interrogators identifiable. Time became chaotic when you were captured. Remembering who asked what, or behaved in a certain way, when different people were sent to question him to find cracks in his story, was a way of keeping a sense of order for himself.

Golyev pulled out the chair opposite Raglan. There was no self-conscious smile from the investigator. No downward shift of the eyes indicating what might be a dreadful fate for the prisoner. He stared benignly.

'I would like to ask you some questions,' said Golyev.

Raglan glanced past him to the camera tucked up in the room's corner. There was no small pinprick of light to indicate the interview was being recorded. If that was the case it meant there would be no evidence should they decide to get rid of him. Any information logged at the custody desk could also be erased. Nothing was impossible inside Russian intelligence.

'You're welcome,' said Raglan.

The softly spoken interrogator had already established his non-threatening technique. Raglan had been trained to endure physical interrogation and sustained questioning. Professionals like the man sitting opposite would draw out the information they wanted through subtle questioning. He would engage in something akin to conversation and through that lower his suspect's guard. Then he would double back and challenge previous statements, slowly but unequivocally unpicking the narrative.

'You appear to be very calm, given where you are,' said Golyev.

'I haven't done anything wrong,' said Raglan. He shrugged. 'Well, I took some money for helping someone. I didn't know he was an important man.'

'More than important, Mr Raglan. He was a high-ranking intelligence officer. You can see that this places you in far more jeopardy than you imagine.' He stared at Raglan. 'But I think you know that already.'

'That I'm in more serious trouble or that I knew his identity?'

'Either you are a professional or you are an innocent tourist. I believe you are a professional.'

Raglan did not respond. The roadblock in the forest was pre-planned. Did the 'professor' know that or was he the official voice of whatever department dealt with these matters?

'The officers who brought you here: their report tells me little enough. Why don't you explain what happened.'

Raglan shrugged. 'All right. I was approached by this man in a bar. He seemed upset. Said he could see I was a tourist. And would I drive him to the border if he paid me?'

'And you asked no questions?'

'He didn't look dangerous and I did nothing more than what Muscovites do to earn a bit of extra cash. Besides, I always wanted to see Latvia.'

Golyev checked his watch. He knew he had little time

before Raglan was officially questioned. 'In what hotel were you staying?'

'I stayed with a friend.'

'His name?'

'I don't think I should tell you that because you say I am in serious trouble. I don't want to drag another innocent person into this mess.'

Golyev knew it was a waste of time to pursue the trivial details. 'You are tanned. You're an Englishman. Europe has little sunshine this time of year and your passport has no recent stamp showing you were anywhere hot.'

Raglan did not answer.

'The man who was in your car was Alexei Verskiy. He was deputy head of military intelligence. Mr Raglan, he was not a man to try and escape from anyone. He was hunting a spy. I believe he was close. You are part of a group who organized his kidnapping, are you not?'

Raglan remained silent. Any soldier captured by an enemy would answer only three questions. Name, rank and serial number. Raglan was no longer a soldier but defensive training was deeply ingrained. He would give what he had to when the time came. When it became more brutal. Eventually everyone cracks. It was a matter of how long he could hold out when they got serious.

Golyev did not appear to be fazed by Raglan's reluctance. He nodded. 'General Verskiy came to me for information about an operation in Africa that took place many years ago. And now I face a well-tanned man who is obviously physically fit, who looks as though he can deal with hazardous situations and who I believe was involved in his kidnapping. Because that is what it was. A planned kidnapping. Did General Verskiy have an operational team of GRU agents in Africa? Is that why he was taken, because he had discovered something of vital importance?'

Raglan gazed past him. He found a spot on the wall, a small crack in the shape of a stick insect. Better not to make or keep eye contact with the interrogator. The eyes can expose half-truths and lies. His gaze was interrupted by Golyev dangling the stainless-steel pendant in front of him.

'The Archangel Michael. Defender of the Faith. The Supreme Angel renowned for his courage. He commands the Heavenly Host. It is an important icon, especially to those of the Orthodox Church. Now the important question is: why did you kill the man it belonged to?'

Raglan needed to divert this man's attention away from Raglan's own immediate predicament. It was clear his interrogator knew about the GRU agents in Africa and he did not need to be branded a killer of one of their men. 'I didn't kill him. One of your people did.'

'The FSB had no operational unit involved.'

'Not FSB. Verskiy's people. Yes, I was in Africa, and we were captured by a warlord. Your man had been tortured. I found him dead. There was a second GRU officer involved. She told me she had killed him before he was broken and revealed details of their operation. She had a cover as a medical doctor. He was her pilot. I reckon he saved her life and endured what they did to him, otherwise she would have been tortured as well. For what it's worth, he was a brave man.'

Golyev showed no sign of emotion on hearing that his son had been tortured and then murdered, apparently by a colleague. 'You expect me to believe that?'

'Her name is Galina Menshikova.'

The man's fingers slowly curled the pendant into his fist. He nodded, pushed back the chair and gathered his overcoat.

'Thank you,' said Golyev. 'Good luck, Mr Raglan.'

He closed the door gently behind him.

58

Prostitution is illegal in Russia but it's still big business. There were GRU men who spent their off-duty time in one particular noisy club. The arrangement suited both the women and the officers. Sometimes the women needed favours and the security men were happy to oblige.

Dragonović didn't frequent the club but he used the place to put the word out among the GRU men that he was looking for the Englishman who'd witnessed the abduction of the priest and who could identify him, Galina Menshikova and the men who were on the operation that day. And then the news broke. Losing the general made the GRU men nervous. They were all vulnerable now. The director himself would be under investigation, given that his deputy had run two operations under his nose without him, it seemed, being aware of them. That showed he was not in control. More questions would follow, and if the Ministry of Defence dug deep enough, the GRU might be buried in its own shallow grave. Being independent of the politically controlled FSB and SVR now made the GRU a wounded beast in the world of Russian intelligence.

Dragonović wasn't too concerned: he had saleable skills. He had achieved more than most covert operatives by staying undercover in French intelligence for all those years. If an investigation into Verskiy's operation went wrong, the Wagner Group would embrace him and he would make good money with the mercenary army. But first he wanted Raglan dead. If the Englishman was not taken care of, Dragonović would be looking over his shoulder now that British and French intelligence knew he had played both sides. Raglan would have enough contacts to root Dragonović out wherever he worked, be it Russia or any other country. The person he needed onside was the woman. Dragonović was an outsider, but she could search. Cut corners. Find Raglan.

Major Galina Menshikova jogged along the riverside on her morning run, ignoring the biting wind searing her lungs. It had stopped snowing and the crust of soft snow crunched under her steady, rhythmic stride. The tracksuit hood slightly obscured her peripheral vision, and she did not notice the figure on the far side of the road angling their run towards her. She wore ear buds, a steady hypnotic rap beat carrying her along. She spun around at the sound of someone behind her. She slipped; strong hands grabbed her, and she was about to fight when she saw it was Dragonović. He released her and pulled back his own tracksuit hood.

'Your phone's off.'

'I'm on leave.'

'Verskiy is dead. Shot. The morning news flagged it. Details are sketchy. But someone's brought him down.'

He could almost hear Galina's mind race.

Dragonović looked around and took her elbow. 'Come on, we need to talk this through.'

She snatched free her arm.

'Don't be stupid,' he insisted. 'If his death is connected with what we did, then we might be next. Who knows what the hell he was up to? We don't even know if the mission was official. We lifted that priest and I was there when his heart gave out. Whatever Verskiy wanted from him he didn't get it. Maybe he panicked and bolted and now his death has dropped us in the shit pit.'

Galina was no fool – she knew any association with an unauthorized mission could have repercussions. 'What happened?'

Dragonović shook his head. 'Sometime last night, or early hours this morning. He made a run for the border. The FSB were waiting. Is there anyone you can ask about it?'

Galina pulled out her phone and dialled a number. She swore and ended the unanswered call. 'Voicemail.'

'Whoever you're phoning, can you trust them?'

'Yes.'

'You're sure? Would they usually answer?'

'Yes.' Her face creased with doubt. Was this the start of being blocked? Of being on the wrong side? Then her phone rang. 'Evgeni, I was worried when you didn't pick up.' She listened, glancing at Dragonović, nodding. 'You're sure?' she said. She got the answer she needed and ended the call. 'The FSB will question us about Verskiy. We've done nothing wrong, remember that. We filed our operational reports; that's all anyone will be interested in. We have no knowledge, none of us, no one involved on this mission, of what was in that document Verskiy wanted so badly. We carry on as normal.'

'To hell with that. I'm not waiting for a knock on the door.' She grabbed his arm. 'It's the Englishman.'

Dragonović scowled in disbelief. 'Where is he?'

'He was arrested at the border. He's being questioned in Lubyanka but then he's going to be released. In two hours he'll be out. Someone's pulling strings.'

'He's involved with Verskiy?'

'My contact said Raglan was paid by him.'

'To get across the border? Bullshit. Verskiy was being lifted, guaranteed.'

'There's no evidence of that.'

'He saw us take the priest. What if he uses that as a bargaining chip? That puts everything on us. Verskiy's bullshit story about the priest being taken by gangsters was never going to hold up, not after Lefortovo. Someone always talks and the one thing the President likes is the PR he's done with the Orthodox Church.'

Galina considered what Verskiy might have done to get to the priest. 'He didn't just drop into our laps. Verskiy must have done a deal with someone. One of the other agencies who might have been using the priest. Who knows? It doesn't matter now. Raglan can't use that information to bargain for his release because then he'd have to reveal his own part in the whole operation. The FSB won't know Raglan was involved in our mission to recover Verskiy's document. No, he'll be playing dumb and the FSB have nothing to pin on him other than what they've got.'

'It's enough they've got Raglan. It's enough he has information that could hurt us. And if he doesn't use it now, he can use it when he needs to play his get-out-of-jail-free card.'

She knew Dragonović had a point. 'Raglan knows I killed Yuri Golyev, but that's not enough to cause us problems – it was an operational necessity.' She faced the Serb. 'For once you're right. It's the death of the priest that could bring us down.'

Dragonović felt a stab of anxiety as he saw a black 4x4 SUV approaching in the distance. Moving slowly. Too slowly. Kerb-crawling. 'If he's being released, then we should take him. He's loose on the street. We know enough people to track him. We rid ourselves of him once and for all.'

Galina looked past him as the vehicle got closer.

The 4x4 stopped next to them. The kerbside window wound down. 'Major?' said the plainclothes man.

'Jesus,' said Dragonović. 'They're on to us already.'

Galina shook her head. 'Raglan isn't my problem. He's yours. I was there to arrest the priest. That was my job. Me and the GRU officers were official. You and the others were freelance assets. They'll cut you free. You're expendable.' She glanced towards the waiting vehicle. 'These're my people. They're not here to hurt us. They're here to protect me.'

She climbed into the rear of the 4x4, which sped away into the traffic, leaving Dragonović alone on the windswept pavement. He cursed her for the bitch she was, leaving him in the lurch. Making him a target. He pulled free his phone, pressed a speed-dial button and spoke to the gruff voice belonging to one of the men involved with him on the priest's kidnapping and torture.

'There's a problem. We need to stop the Englishman. He knows too much. Get the others. Two cars by the rear gates at Lubyanka.'

59

Raglan's interrogator was on edge. A senior official had been caught trying to escape, and only those in government and intelligence circles knew how far his influence reached. Over the years his name had been in the public arena like every other head and deputy head of the various agencies. And already the news channels had the story. Leaked, of course, then denied and finally confirmed. Nothing new there. But the Englishman had a simple story and was sticking to it: he had met Verskiy in a bar near to where Verskiy lived, and been bribed by him to drive to Latvia.

'You, a complete stranger. This man approached you and offered you this money?' The interrogator had touched the plastic-wrapped bundle of US dollars on the table in front of him.

Raglan played innocent. A dumb tourist who got himself into trouble. 'No, not at first, come on. Give a man some credit. He saw me; we started talking. But I could see he was nervous.'

'Did you think he was trying to pick you up?'

'The thought crossed my mind.'

'And he came right out and said he wanted to be smuggled out of the country?'

'Not in so many words.'

'What *few* words did he use?'

'Look, he was well dressed, he looked like a businessman. We drank a lot. I'm not used to your Russian vodka, and I was happy to listen to him. Then he said he was in trouble with the tax authorities. Said that Russian tax inspectors were going to take everything, that he had money in Latvia in a subsidiary company but needed to get there in a hurry. I said I didn't want to get involved in anything illegal.'

'But you knew this story meant it *was* something illegal.'

Raglan shrugged. He pulled a face. 'Tax inspectors. Who's to say what those bastards won't do to a man. C'mon, I bet you claim expenses you shouldn't? Don't you? Y'know, a meal here and there. Take the wife or the girlfriend out for a bite. Or both. Not at the same time of course.' He smiled knowingly, man-to-man stuff. His interrogator did not smile back. Raglan reckoned he was in his forties. The wedding ring had narrowed the flesh on his finger over the years. A long marriage then. A grinding job. A crappy flat. Probably a couple of kids. Of course he fiddled his expenses. If the top men were corrupt why shouldn't the foot soldiers do the same?

The interrogator placed a finger on a brochure in a plastic evidence bag. 'This was found in your car.'

Raglan had already noticed what lay in the plastic folders. Somewhere in there was his alibi.

'That's right. Art tours.'

'So, you came to look at paintings in our galleries.'

'That's the best place to see them, yes.'

The sarcasm was lost on his interrogator. 'Where did you go for this vacation in Russia?'

'Oh, first stop was St Petersburg.'

'You took a plane?'

'No, I drove. The art gallery there is amazing. Do you like art? Russian art, I mean.'

'I have more important things to do than stand looking at pictures hanging on a wall.' The grim-faced interrogator pulled another sheet of paper forward, also in a plastic folder. 'And you stayed here in Moscow in the Filyovsky Park District.'

Raglan concentrated. Maybe this man wasn't such a slow-thinker? Raglan didn't know if this was a trap. Say yes and be contradicted; say no and look a fool if someone had laid the ground work for him.

'Probably, yes.'

'Probably?'

Raglan leant back as much as the chained handcuffs would allow. He gazed at the ceiling, pondering. 'I can't remember the name. Your streets in Moscow are difficult. It sounds right to me.'

'You remember the building then? The number.'

Raglan knew he had no hope of guessing correctly. 'Your street addresses are very confusing.'

'Come now, you are on an art and accommodation tour, and you don't know where you stayed?'

'No, sorry.'

'The director of the state gallery was interviewed and said she arranged your accommodation. She said you stayed at her nephew's empty apartment. That this was not uncommon for visiting tourists. Are you denying this?'

Raglan glanced away in thought. Had the question been laid as a trap or given as an alibi? Given, or rather instructed to be given by this man's superior. A way out provided by the man in the forest who worked on the upper floors of the Lubyanka building and who was probably watching the interrogation. The pinprick light on the camera showed it was recording.

'No, of course not. Why would I deny it? I just didn't know whose room I was using. I remember it belonged to a younger man. I was very grateful because your hotels in Moscow are eye-wateringly expensive, so I was glad the trip had a room thrown in. I came to Moscow to look at art. The rest was unimportant. It was a small apartment for a couple of days. I'd have slept on a park bench if I had to. Not in this weather of course. You understand? I'm an art teacher in a small school in France. A village school.'

'But you are English.'

'The French forgive me for that. Work is hard to find. I don't earn much.'

'And yet you drive an expensive car here. An Audi A6.'

'I was lucky. I'd ordered one of those small town cars and they had all gone when I got to the desk. They gave me an upgrade.'

The interrogator checked his watch. He had been told by his superiors not to waste time on the tourist. It was routine. No one from the British Embassy had been alerted. His instructions were that this man was not an agent for British intelligence, that he lived in France, and it was feasible he was telling the truth. The politicians did not want any of the problems that would arise if they arrested and interrogated a tourist. He didn't know why he had been told by those upstairs not to press too hard with this man. Question and confirm. That was all. Then write the report. Bad enough the deputy head of the GRU had tried to defect. That was enough leverage for the politicians to do some hard-nosed bargaining with the British. The Englishman's story matched the evidence found in the car. The woman who ran the state art gallery had seen a newsflash about Verskiy's attempt to escape and recognized the car. She had contacted the police expressing concern about the driver, and her enquiry had finally reached the FSB in Lubyanka.

The interrogator gathered the evidence together and pushed back the chair. He gestured for Raglan to present his handcuffed hands; then he unlocked the restraints.

Raglan rubbed his wrists. 'That's it? I'm free to go?'

'I don't know. Perhaps you will be deported or charged with currency smuggling. Those decisions are not mine to make.'

'Who will know?'

'Someone else.'

'Who?'

'I don't know.'

Raglan smiled. 'You're taking the piss, aren't you?'

The interrogator was at the door. 'Mr Raglan, you are lucky you were not shot. In fact, I do not know how you survived. You were involved in a serious crime. And your story?' He shrugged. 'I think *you* are taking the piss.'

60

Raglan was left alone for another thirty minutes. The door remained open. The custody officer passed by once or twice, glanced at the man sitting in the interview room and continued about his duties. A phone rang, echoing loudly down the passage against the harsh surfaces of walls and floor. He heard the receiver replaced, the shuffle of boots, a door opening and closing and then the same custody officer came into the room and placed a sealed evidence bag in front of Raglan.

'You're free to go.'

Raglan spilled out his belongings. The archangel pendant was missing. So too the American dollars. He looked at the stony-faced jailer.

'Everything there?' said the officer.

Raglan nodded. 'Everything is there,' he said dutifully.

'That's what I thought. That's why we use a security tag.'

'Can I make a phone call?' Raglan asked.

'We don't run a taxi service here,' said Golyev's old friend without softening the curt reply with a smile.

Raglan pocketed his belongings and followed the man out of the door; he beckoned one of the uniformed border guards. 'Show him the way.'

'I can find my own way out,' said Raglan. 'Straight down there and—'

'Shut up. You do as you're told in here.' He nodded to the man. 'Get him on the street.'

Raglan didn't argue. The executioner spy from the woods had obviously pulled enough strings to cover the box-ticking exercise. The guard led him across the yard toward the street gate. Moscow city traffic roared in the distance in a shocking contrast to the deathly quiet of the interview room deep inside the notorious building. He'd been lucky – he only had to think of the Russian penal colony to know that. He was thankful not to have been taken to Lefortovo Prison – a much harsher environment. Maguire's Russian spy had done as much as he could to protect the son of the man who had once saved his life. Now the debt had been repaid. And Raglan was on his own.

The rear gate led to a narrow street past the guard posts and wire mesh fence. There was construction work on the perimeter. Unlikely someone was trying to dig their way in. Stacked containers provided temporary offices and storage. The restricted area had a sentry box with a uniformed attendant wearing a high-vis jacket to stop anyone parking at the rear of the building. Not that any member of the public would get that close to the rear of Lubyanka, but Raglan could see that in the distance there was traffic moving freely. He oriented himself. If he walked that way he would come out at the major traffic roundabout in front of the building.

He had to get into a public space as soon as possible. If there were GRU officers who now had an axe to grind, they could trap him in an area like this. He needed a phone box and there wasn't one in sight. He turned to head for the distant traffic, but then saw a black E-Class Mercedes with two men inside, parked several cars along. He could see from the way the driver sat, head bent, that he was watching the Lubyanka gate in his wing mirrors. Raglan knew there would likely be a second car nearby. The intention would be to herd him into a dead end.

He kept close to the building's wall in the driver's blind spot and turned away to a narrow one-way street that cut between the backs of faceless government-style buildings, six storeys tall. No cars were parked this end of the street. He strode along the ungritted pavement. Tyre tracks rutted the frozen road surface. Raglan looked ahead to the gentle bend two hundred metres ahead. The street widened sufficiently to allow one-side street parking. Most cars were parked nose in. One car had straddled two inward-looking bays and parallel parked. The driver was sitting with his foot resting on the brake pedal. A BMW 5 Series. For a moment he thought Elena might have got wind of his detention and come to pick him up, using the lights to draw his attention, but there was no attractive Moscow police colonel behind the wheel.

He angled across the street, using a building as cover, and saw two men inside. Even at this distance the features of the big man in the front passenger seat were unmistakable. The Serb was waiting. Raglan had no choice but to carry on. A crumbling eight-foot-wall supported a sheet-metal gate, its height obscuring what lay beyond. It looked the best bet to escape the street, but once on the other side he might find himself boxed in. If he made a run for the gate Dragonović would see him and Raglan would be trapped between the two cars.

A young man, wrapped up well against the cold, courier-style shoulder bag slung across him, woollen hat pulled low over his ears, emerged from one of the government buildings. He was saying goodbye to someone on his phone. Raglan stepped two metres in front of him. It brought the man up short. In the moment before he could decide what to do, Raglan raised a hand, a gesture meaning no harm.

'Can you help me? I've had my phone stolen and I have to phone my wife.' He flourished what cash he had. 'Just a quick call. Nothing more. Please.'

The man's eyes stared at the fistful of roubles, but he pressed the phone against his chest as if it were his only child.

'What?' was all he could say, eyes darting around.

Raglan had moved no closer. 'My wife. The debt collectors are going to get to my house and if I don't warn her, then she'll be frightened. You see that black Beemer up there? That's two of them. They're going to repossess everything. I've just sorted my debt payments out – but not in time.'

The man licked his lips. The money was a temptation. He nodded. Raglan reached forward and gave him the money, which he stuffed into his pocket. Raglan held out his hand for the phone.

The man shook his head. 'Give me the number.'

The man was no fool. It was the sensible thing to do. Raglan gave him Elena's number; the man keyed it in. He listened.

'Tell her it's Raglan.'

'Raglan?'

'I'm English.'

'You speak good Russian. Your wife's Russian?'

'Yeah, absolutely. Russian women are the most beautiful in the world. Everyone knows that.'

It raised a smile on the man's face as he concentrated, and

then he was connected. He told her he was phoning for her husband, Raglan, pressed the speaker button and extended it forward.

'Raglan?' she said.

'Elena, the debt collectors are following me. My phone's gone; this young man's helping me out.'

'Where are you?'

'Rear streets of Lubyanka,' he said.

The young man piped up, 'Malaya Lubyanka Street.' He even smiled as he made his contribution.

'I'll come to you,' said Elena. 'Ask whoever's holding the phone to show you where the French school is. It should be very near to you. There's a side passage next to it. There's a road on the other side.'

The man was engrossed in the conversation. 'You mean Milyutinskiy Pereulok?' he called.

'Yes! There!'

'OK,' said the young man. 'I'll show him.'

'Ten minutes,' she said. The call ended.

The young man pocketed his phone and pointed beyond the parked cars. 'There. That green metal fence. You can just see the tops of the trees. That's the school playground. The street you want is on the other side once you go down the side passage.'

'Thank you,' said Raglan.

The young man was relaxed now. 'Good luck.' He walked past Raglan, who looked to where the BMW stood between him and the gate. Two hundred metres to the car and another 150 to the school. He checked the street. Counted twenty-eight parked cars. Dragonović was eighteen cars along. Beyond the other ten the road widened slightly, fifty metres before the school. Raglan couldn't see what lay in the wider part of the street but there was a blue, moveable barrier across that side of the road – the same barriers that had been placed by the authorities between the car parking bays and the pavement.

He checked his watch. He had to give Elena enough time to negotiate traffic. Raglan could make the run past Dragonović and then have time to reach the other side of the school but he needed to slow the Serb down. Once Dragonović and the man with him started the car and gave chase they'd have to drive along the street and find a side street to take them to the other road where Elena waited. With luck he and Elena would be able to put some distance between him and the BMW. If Dragonović wanted Raglan he would have to work for it. Raglan would decide where to take the fight.

He ran at a crouch, hugging the wall. The driver's seat was kerbside, Dragonović was watching his wing mirror, looking back down the street, and Raglan realized their slightly off-angle parking had created blind spots. The driver's window was down a couple of inches and cigarette smoke curled out, the glass steamed up from body heat. Dragonović leant forward and wiped a cloth against the windscreen. Their arrogance at commandeering two parking bays played into Raglan's hands. He snatched the barrier, upended it and rammed it under the driver's door, the base of the barrier locking it into the raised kerb.

The men's startled reactions bought him time. Raglan ran hard. The engine started, but the wedged barrier held them fast. The driver couldn't turn or move forward, the car dragging the metal barrier and catching the parked car in front. Raglan looked over his shoulder. Dragonović was out of the car, manhandling the barrier. Brute strength cleared it as Raglan passed the empty school yard and turned into the side passage. He saw traffic on the road at the end of the block. Cold, sharp air bit into him as he kept a steady flat-footed rhythm, giving himself the best chance of staying upright on the slippery surface. An engine strained and tyres skidded on the street behind him. He zigzagged. As he lost his footing, a double shot rang out, the bullets ripped through the air where a second before he had been standing.

He rolled, hit the wall, heard the zing of ricochets as two more shots were fired and saw two women turn into the passage from the other road. They hesitated. Raglan knew that Dragonović wouldn't care less about innocent civilians being hurt. He grabbed the railings and vaulted into the school yard. The Serb would have to move position to shoot again. Raglan landed and then vaulted back into the passage. He'd bought valuable seconds. Running hard, he waved the women away. They needed no second warning.

At the end of the passage an older model Ford Focus pulled into the kerb. It wasn't the high speed and robust BMW police car Raglan expected. Elena leant across and pushed open the passenger door.

'Hurry!'

Raglan pulled closed the door; she turned into the following traffic. It was a two-way street. There were major roads five hundred metres away. That gave Dragonović and his backup team time to find a side road and give pursuit. The last thing Raglan saw of Dragonović was him slamming closed his car door and talking into a two-way radio as Elena pulled out quickly, moving the manual box up a gear and then back down to gain more revs as she accelerated, cutting across traffic. Horns blared.

Raglan hung on. 'You been demoted?'

She dared a glance. A smile. 'It's mine. I'm off duty.'

'I'm sorry, Elena. I've dragged you into this. There's a black 5 Series and a second car. E-Class Merc. Back of Lubyanka,' he said. 'They'll come hard and fast.'

They reached the busy thoroughfare in front of Lubyanka, Elena wrestling the wheel with sufficient expertise to weave into the traffic. She cast a worried glance at him. 'I'm not trained for evasive driving, Raglan.'

'Then let me drive,' he said.

61

Elena pulled in beneath an underpass. As she ran from driver to passenger side, she had her semi-automatic pistol in her hand. Raglan was behind the wheel.

'A fast-moving BMW weaving through traffic, half a kilometre back,' she said.

Raglan pressed the accelerator as she strapped in. Her car was already moving faster than she realized possible.

Raglan checked the gauges. All were good. The old Ford Focus was smooth, soft on corners, but ran well. She had obviously looked after it.

'Get us out of here, Elena, you know these streets.'

'Anywhere?'

'The university.'

'Studying won't help us here, Raglan.'

'A different kind of education: the Shanghai Slum.'

She fell silent. He glanced at her. She shook her head. 'I can't go in there. I've put some of those people away. They'll shoot me on sight.'

He'd been stupid to suggest it. A colonel in the Moscow CID would be a prime target even if she hadn't been responsible for sending gangsters and their friends away for long stretches. It was a no-go zone for the authorities.

'I'm calling this in,' she said, taking out her mobile phone.

Raglan overtook a car. Watched for the weaving BMW demanding his attention. 'I don't know how many men they can call to back them up. I'm guessing what we see is what we get, and I don't know if these are official GRU officers or contractors. A lot of people could get hurt – that's why I want to draw them to the Shanghai.' He moved into a fast-moving lane. 'I didn't expect you to end up there with me,' he said. 'You're getting out at the Metro station this side of the river. They'll follow me into the slums. I'm taking them to where no one else can get hurt. Except them.'

She was about to answer when an overbearing black shape pressed against her door. Its weight forced the lighter car into the inside lane. Car horns blared. The Merc had come from nowhere to sideswipe the smaller car while Raglan had been watching the BMW. Raglan fought the wheel. The heavier car was pushing them ever closer to the barrier. The fast-moving one-way traffic hurtled past them. Raglan glanced across Elena to the Merc; he saw the driver's window slide down and the passenger lean forward levelling his pistol. Raglan slammed on the brakes. Metal ground against metal as the Merc scraped alongside. Elena ducked from the impact.

'Shoot!' Raglan shouted.

He angled the car, but the rear window on the Mercedes shattered as the gunman fired at the target on his rear wheel, not caring if he smashed his own windows to do it. Shards of glass splashed against the Ford. Elena threw an arm over her eyes; Raglan swerved, dropped a gear, forced the engine into high revs, nudging its offside nose into the Merc's bodywork behind the rear wheel. The gunmen's car was travelling at speed and the sudden, sharp impact into the heavy beast's nearside rear wheel arch meant the driver had to apply opposite lock to stop his car from spinning. Elena's weapon was a standard-issue Makarov. Same age as the old Soviet Union. The all-steel 9 mm wasn't much good beyond twenty metres. Her target was less than five.

She fired the semi-automatic repeatedly into the windows. Blood splattered glass on the passenger side, the shooter's head slamming against his door frame. He slumped. The sudden burst of gunfire from what was supposed to be an ageing car owned by a civilian made the driver swerve, but experience immediately kicked in and he accelerated. Raglan saw the BMW was three cars closer, coming up fast. Dragonović would find a gap, come in hard on Raglan's side and box them in.

'Next exit,' Elena shouted. 'There!' She pointed to the approaching slip road thirty metres away.

Raglan swerved and accelerated as the Merc tried to block them, but Raglan squeezed between the bruising car and the barrier. Sparks flew. Tortured metal screeched. Elena swore. The BMW was almost on them. In the rearview mirror Raglan saw two cars pushed aside as the heavy four-track forced its way through. Cars spun, others swerved, tyres burnt rubber. People were getting hurt.

'Call it in!' said Raglan.

She raised the phone, but a sudden shunt from the BMW hurtled their car sideways down the turning. Elena was flung back, her head whipped sideways, phone and weapon thrown from her hand. Raglan hauled the handbrake, slammed it down a gear, accelerated and spun them back around. Elena reached down for her phone but it had gone under the seat. Her finger teased the semi-automatic back into her hand. She was half bent, the world spinning as Raglan pulled off his manoeuvre. They had reached the end of the turnoff. A narrow entrance offered itself. 'Sharp left. Now! Then right.'

Raglan braked and in a half-slide got the old car into the alleyway. It was a built-up area. The BMW overshot. Reversed and followed. Raglan swung into a service road.

'One hundred metres left again.' Elena gripped her service pistol with both hands.

The one-way system served them until they turned and then a parked delivery van blocked their way. Raglan swerved, forcing an oncoming car off the road. The black shape appeared in the rearview mirror but Raglan was through and the irate driver he had forced off the road had driven on and stopped the BMW from getting any closer.

'Another right, and then straight.' She tried to reach her phone, but it had been flung too far back under her seat. She heard Raglan curse. Looking up they could see the Mercedes was shadowing them on a parallel road.

'I can't outrun them, Elena. How far to the Metro?'

'Twenty minutes.'

'We have to take one of them out. Yes?'

She nodded. She had no flak jacket and the men after them were hardened professionals. They would shoot to kill.

'Elena, I need a road to get ahead of the Merc. Then ambush them before the Beemer gets to us. There's only one man left in the Merc. Better odds.'

She nodded and assured herself. 'Better odds.'

'Which way?'

She focused. Pictured the myriad streets ahead of them. Moscow was a high-density city. They were south of the city centre and north-east of the lower bend in the river where tree-lined suburbs merged into low-rise apartment blocks.

'Elena!'

She nodded. Mentally mapping the route ahead. 'Three streets ahead. A two-way road. Take it. Go left. Two hundred metres past a small park there are three blocks of flats. It's a dead end. There's a cycle path closed down because the parks department vehicles are working on it. It cuts right across between the buildings. There are access bollards either side of the path. This car will fit. You'll get ahead of him.'

Frozen windswept snow clung to north-facing tree trunks. The roads were not yet gritted. The car's winter tyres fought the compacted ruts. Raglan floored the accelerator, blasted his horn at a slow-moving car reversing from a parking bay and swerved, nearly losing control as they skidded.

She pointed. 'There!'

Raglan slowed the car, turned into a dead-end square that served three apartment blocks, saw the narrow track she indicated and two small vehicles being used to haul away the tree surgeon's work in the distant treeline. He kept his foot down, mounted the access ramp across the pavement. His wing mirror shattered as it clipped the metal bollard. Elena looked behind her. For several seconds there was no sign of the BMW. Then it appeared. It stopped. Reversed and sped off. It was too wide to fit through. She had bought them vital minutes.

'They were close.'

'I saw them,' said Raglan. He was forced to slow the car to nudge past the half-on, half-off trucks that nearly blocked his route. Three of the four workers shouted. Elena pressed her badge against the windscreen. They quickly backed off.

'The scenic route,' said Raglan as he increased speed. 'How far?'

'See that small bridge? Go beneath that and then the cycle path joins the road. They have no choice but to be on it.'

The car wallowed in slush-filled ruts. He slowed, making sure they had traction, and as soon as the tyres found purchase gently increased his speed. There was no sense in getting bogged down and only idiots threw a car around an icy, muddy track. He kept the gears low, nursed the revs, his foot light on the accelerator. He saw the road ahead. It threaded into another tree-filled suburb.

'If we stop on that blind corner he'll have to turn into us and I can get a clear shot.'

Raglan nudged the car between identical bollards at the end of the path. A cluster of gloomy apartment blocks dulled the street. Raglan went down the pavement, reversed on to the blind bend, giving Elena a clean shot. It suddenly felt quiet. The stillness was tangible after their adrenaline-fuelled escape.

'We should think this through,' said Raglan. 'You're going to have a lot of explaining to do.'

She kept her eyes on the blind bend, her weapon on her lap in her right hand. Left arm already across her body on the door release. 'I'll worry about that later. '

'There must be a better way out of this,' he said.

She faced him. Raglan had smothered her gun hand with his own.

'You were minding your own business when a stranger hijacked your car,' he said. 'He was being pursued. It looked like a gangland feud. I do the shooting. Any witnesses in these apartments will see a lone gunman. You were a hostage.' He gave her a knowing look.

'And when we get to the Metro?' she asked.

'You struggled. Managed to escape. You call it in. There'll be enough reports to verify the car chase and the shooting. End of story. And the insurance will replace the car.'

'I need a new one anyway,' she said. She sighed, shaking her head slowly. 'Raglan, you are a dangerous man. How long do you think you can survive doing what you do?'

'We're not talking about me. This is about the world of trouble I'm bringing down on you. Give me the gun.'

Everything Raglan said made sense. She resisted the gentle pressure of his hand. 'I can do this.'

'I know,' he said, gently leaning across so that their lips touched, at the same time exerting more pressure for her to release the weapon.

'You cause me much trouble, Englishman. I ask myself why I let you. The answer is unclear to me.'

Raglan reached behind her seat, recovered her phone, keyed in a number and placed it on the dashboard. 'Once we're at the Metro station tell the man who answers to be ready.' He eased the gun from her hand and before she could raise even a half-hearted objection he got out of the car and walked to the opposite pavement from where the car was parked. The Merc would have to swing around the corner: the driver would see Elena's car. There would be a moment of uncertainty. That was all Raglan needed.

He waited. Listening for the sound of a big engine. He didn't have to wait long. At first he heard the unmistakable tinkling of a damaged wheel rim. The sound faded as the car slowed for the corner. The driver did as expected. He stopped when he saw the car and the woman inside. Too late he twisted to look across his dead companion to the man at the passenger window levelling a semi-automatic. The split second it took for him to take his foot off the brake and accelerate was a split second too long. Raglan shot him twice. His head jerked back; his leg spasmed in death. The car lunged into a parked car. The passenger door fell open, the dead man slumping half out. Raglan recognized them as two of the men who'd been with Galina Menshikova when they kidnapped the priest. A car alarm echoed around the buildings. Raglan leant in and took the two-way radio. He pressed the send button.

'Your men are dead, Dragonović. You come for me and you'll join them. Final warning.'

He cleaned his prints off the radio and threw it back on to the driver's corpse. Faces appeared at windows. He looked up; they quickly turned away. No one wants to be a witness to a daylight shooting. Not in Russia. He climbed behind the wheel. She remained silent as Raglan drove away. They were nine minutes from the Metro station. If they could survive that long.

62

Raglan slowed the battered Ford Focus as Elena navigated him towards the Vorobyovy Gory Metro station. Once there, the two-kilometre-long Metro bridge would take him to the other side of the river. They kept checking behind them as he weaved in and out of the traffic. It didn't take long.

'They're behind us,' said Elena. 'Eight, nine cars back.'

'All right, let's get you out of here.'

'I'm a Moscow detective. I don't run from fights. Let's take them here, rather the slums. Together.'

Raglan accelerated. They would soon see him. 'This isn't running, Elena, this is staying alive to fight another day. You saved me today and I owe you. I didn't expect them to come for me so quickly. I've dragged you into this and for that I'm sorry.'

'I'm not.'

'Another time and maybe another place we'll find each other, but this is an intelligence nightmare and you need to turn away now. Powerful people are involved. People we can never challenge. These killers I can deal with. You understand that?'

'I do. And once this is finished, you will have to get out.'

'That's right.'

'If they don't kill you.'

'They'll have to work hard at that.'

She fell silent: sullen acceptance. Then, a small gesture. 'Over there. I'll get out.'

Raglan kept the black BMW in sight, swung out of traffic and into a tangle of smaller streets.

'Don't stop. Slowing down will be enough. Then go.' She opened the door; Raglan slowed. The BMW was out of sight. 'Find me again, Raglan. I would like that.' Elena Sorokina rolled out of the car, recovered and ran into the protective corner of a building.

Raglan accelerated. There'd be time to think of being with her later. Not now. Now looked to be the final reckoning for what his father started all those years before.

Dense suburban high-rise buildings hunched below dark, snow-laden clouds as they tumbled downriver. On the far side of the river a forest stretched along its length. Bare branches shivered in the escalating wind. The Luzhniki Bridge, three lanes in each direction, known locally as the Metro Bridge, carried traffic on the top level and the Metro trains below. Raglan stormed on to the long concrete span, forcing cars to swerve in a deliberate attempt to show his pursuers where he was. They were soon on him. A sudden glare lit his rearview mirror. He looked over his shoulder. A stadium's floodlights had come on: had they not drawn his attention he would not have seen the BMW carving its way to the outside lane. Raglan was on the inside closest to the safety railings and the river below. He felt a muted vibration beneath him as a Metro train rumbled across. He hoped Elena was on it. If

Dragonović got alongside the more powerful car would shunt him through the railings. He let them draw closer. Four well-spaced cars in the middle lane were between him and the BMW. Raglan didn't need to second guess their next move. They moved into the fast lane. The moment a gap presented itself they would cut in and ram him off the bridge.

Raglan's eyes darted to his side and rearview mirrors. A car on his left in the middle lane moved rapidly ahead. It gave Dragonović's driver the perfect attack line. The BMW sped up, its nose angled towards him in the vacated space. Raglan braked hard, swung the steering wheel sharply and came in behind a slower-moving car. The Serb's driver could not dip back into the faster-moving traffic in the outer lane again. Raglan had the upper hand. They were nearing the end of the bridge. The Shanghai Slum was twenty minutes away. Raglan waited for a gap in the traffic. Dropping two gears he accelerated into a space pushing the revs higher as he cut into the outside lane and sped past the BMW. He was approaching the riverside parkland when the BMW finally followed.

Dragonović cursed in his native tongue when Raglan bettered them. His driver, a former GRU Spetsnaz operative trained in high-speed pursuit was good, but even he couldn't magic the traffic away.

Dragonović bent and lifted a submachine gun from the footwell. He checked the thirty-round box magazine from the weapon. The driver glanced down.

'Get me close and I'll kill him in the damned car,' said Dragonović.

The driver concentrated on his quarry. 'You'll bring the cops down on us. Killing him here isn't the place.'

'The park. We take him there.'

The driver nodded, slewed the car into a tight racing skid as he cut off other drivers. 'No need. I don't think he knows where he's heading. The Englishman has no chance now,' he said.

'What's ahead?'

'Garage Valley. We call it the Shanghai Slum. It's a no-go area.' He grinned at the Serb. 'Bad people, really bad people doing very bad things. The dumb bastard is driving right into our hands. He's a dead man.'

'If it's that bad they could turn on us,' said Dragonović.

The driver shook his head as he accelerated. 'We've done drug deals with them. No one raises a hand against us – if they did they'd be buried. No, he's ours.' He pressed a dial button on his dashboard. 'I have someone on the inside.'

63

Raglan nudged the car slowly through the sheet-metal gates
that were usually closed, part of the slum's fortress-like
defence that kept unwelcome visitors at bay. He manoeuvred
into a narrow access road between sheds. The wind pushed
away the smoke from the stovepipe chimneys. Some doors
were open, but most were closed against the cold. Chained
dogs sought to escape the freezing temperature in their rough
shelters built out of pallets. Hundreds of corrugated roofs
were covered in snow, but the rutted track had been kept open
by those who had business in the Shanghai. An assortment of
people stared as he drove by. The bearded, tattooed men he
saw inside the open sheds could have been lifted from any
biker gang in any part of the world. As he passed, open doors
clanged shut. No witnesses.

If Elena had dialled the number he gave her, then Bird
Sokol would be waiting. That would even up the odds.
Raglan glanced left and right as he entered the labyrinth. The
dispossessed, the desperate and the downright dangerous
lived here. As Raglan drove, he saw the end of each alley
he passed had a track parallel to his, both left and right,
and the steady throb of powerful motorbikes increased as
outriders shadowed him on those roads. The biker gang was

blocking any chance Raglan had of changing direction. Or escape.

He turned the car to where Sokol waited with the two former legionnaires, Gunther Meier and Semyon Mikoyan. All three were bloodied. There were also a dozen other men with them. A bear-size bearded man, presumably their leader, his height and bulk enhanced by the black sheepskin coat he wore, waited with Sokol and the others. He smoked, and even from where Raglan sat behind the wheel of the car, the gangland tattoos on the back of his hands and face were visible. Raglan flashed back to the White Eagle Penal Colony No. 74. That desolate place of punishment would always be embedded in his memory, as was the *torpedo* he'd fought when he was incarcerated there: a killer for the *vory-v-zakone* – 'thieves with honour', or murderers, pimps, drug dealers, racketeers. But they had a code within their gangs and right now it looked as though Raglan had to deal with them. He hoped this gangster wasn't related to the man in the penal colony because Raglan had left him in a bad way. He pulled up short, climbed out of the car and extended his arms. One of the men patted him down and found Elena's weapon.

'You are Raglan,' said the bearded man, accepting the gun.

Raglan glanced at Sokol, whose shrug told him the situation was no longer under control.

'I am,' said Raglan.

'I am Mikhail.'

Bird Sokol said, 'My friends and I did not invite him. He gate-crashed the party.'

The man called Mikhail ignored Sokol. He smiled. A gold tooth shone. 'These three hurt some of my best men.' He thumbed behind him vaguely. 'Hurt them bad. They will be no use to me for a few days. It was a good fight.' He stepped closer to Raglan. 'I have business interests here. And you have fallen into that sphere of interest.' He looked up into the threatening sky. 'Soon it will be dark and soon it will snow, and then the snow will cover those who die here tonight.'

Men like him ruled by their physical presence. They didn't need to threaten anyone needlessly. When the time came any warning given would be backed up by decisive action. One thing Raglan was certain of, bodies *would* be lying beneath the snow before first light. Tyres wallowed through the slush road behind them, and the BMW hove into view. It was quickly surrounded by the bear's armed men. Raglan watched as Dragonović came out, hands raised.

The driver was more casual. 'It's all right, these are my contacts,' he assured the Serb.

Dragonović stayed at the car, blocked by two of Mikhail's men, as the driver strode towards the big man. They embraced.

'Mikhail, you have him. Good. There's a deal to be done.'

'Gregor, there's always a deal to be struck with your people. Though the last one did not go so well, nyet?'

The driver splayed his hands in a small gesture of helplessness. 'I sent my condolences. Your brother went too far. We helped you take down the competition but he...' The driver shrugged. 'He got greedy and they killed him. There's always a risk.'

'That's true,' said the gangster affably. His eyes had barely moved, but it was signal enough for two muscled men to seize the former GRU man and strip him of his weapons.

'Mikhail! You don't fuck with us!'

The gangster's voice lowered; he spoke slowly. With intent. 'You said you would protect him. We had a deal.'

'This is a big mistake. This is stupid. My people know I'm here!'

Mikhail ignored his protestations and offered Raglan Elena's weapon. Raglan kept his hands down. 'No, you take it,' Mikhail insisted. 'You are going to need it, aren't you? That big man next to the car. He is the one who wants you dead. That's what your friend told us.'

Raglan glanced at Bird. Neither showed any sign of fear. Both knew their lives depended on what the big man wanted.

'Take it,' said Mikhail again, still calm, still without threat. Matter-of-factly.

Raglan curled his fist around the pistol.

'Good, good. Now, you see this GRU piece of shit. You shoot him. Please. You do this now.'

The driver struggled but they kicked his legs away, forcing him down, the men standing at arm's length as they each twisted his wrists in an agonizing lock.

Mikhail extended his hand. 'A simple thing to do, Mr Raglan.'

'No.'

Cold air exhaled as Mikhail sighed. 'Gregor is correct. We would cause great trouble if we kill someone who was once a GRU officer. He would have friends in high places. Shoot him, Mr Raglan, by the time I count to three, or we shoot your friend here.'

Raglan looked at Sokol. He remained stoic. Gazing expressionless at his friend as one of Mikhail's men pressed a pistol into his neck. Execution style.

Mikhail's eyes were on Raglan. The doomed man swore, begged and threatened.

'One... two...'

Raglan shot the driver dead.

'Three. Good timing, Mr Raglan. Have no regrets. He was a pig. He was a man without honour.'

One of Mikhail's men placed a plastic bag over Raglan's hand and took the weapon from him. 'Now, you see we have violated no agreement between us and those who do work for a government agency. It is your fingerprints on the weapon. We will offer it in evidence to prove our innocence in this matter.'

And Raglan knew ballistics would also show two other men were shot dead with the same weapon. He glanced at a gaunt-looking Dragonović, who remained at the car, covered by armed men.

'You have done us good service, Mr Raglan. Now to your business. Some sport, I think.' He looked at Dragonović. 'We take him to one end of the street, and send you to the other. We cordon off several streets. Each man will have a pistol and three bullets.' He gave an expansive gesture to the gathered men. 'And we will have a wager who survives. If it is him, he goes free. He will lay blame for this man's death at your door. And if you kill him then Gunther and Semyon will use their smuggling operation to take you and your friend anywhere you wish. On this matter I give you my word.'

64

What sunlight there was slipped away as the day shortened and the sky darkened. The wind gusted, whipping snow from rooftops and furling it neatly into small snowdrifts between the shanties. The toxic smell of diesel generators clung to the narrow passageways; their throbbing reverberated among the dwellings of those that were not served by electricity. Here and there warm light spilled out from sheet-metal shacks. Beyond the shacks motorcycle lights formed a barrier, beams cutting through the narrow passageways here and there as the bikers formed an arena on the edge of the killing zone.

Raglan moved on the diagonal. Crouching by darkened walls, cold-stiffened hands gripping the semi-automatic. As he skirted buildings, he heard various sounds from inside the sheds. Music, television, voices – some raised, but still muted by the snow's insulating weight. The sounds covered the noise of his approach as his boots crunched on frozen patches. He edged around one building, stepping carefully into the deeper snow. It erupted. A snow-covered dog lunged, its chain long enough to allow it to attack. Raglan fell under its weight, his back thudding against the shack's walls. The animal was silent except for a low growl as it clamped its jaws on his outstretched arm. One bullet would kill it. One bullet was expensive.

The dog's strength forced Raglan down into the snow. It was essential he stay on his feet. He rolled, taking the dog with him until he had his body half on the determined beast. He struck it behind its neck but its jaws tightened. The dog had the advantage: four legs and muscled, twisting strength. Raglan got to his feet and dragged it up. If shooting the dog was the only option he dare not risk a head shot. A bullet might glance off its curved thick skull. And its head was thrashing from side to side. Raglan's muscles in his shoulder and back felt as though they were tearing free. Damn the risk. He pressed the pistol's muzzle into the dog's chest and shot it. The impact and shock from the 9-mm bullet immediately released its jaws. It whimpered and fell. Blood coughed from its jaws. It lay, tongue lolling, eyes balefully locked on the man who had killed it. Then it died. It was only a dog, but the eyes of the dead still accused him. Despite the ache in his arm, Raglan laid a hand briefly on the dog's head. It had only been doing its job.

The gunshot's boom had given away his location. He ran across the narrow road, ducked between buildings, crouched, settled his breathing and listened. Then he moved off again, slowly, trying to find softer ground. Every time his foot pressed down, the compacted ground beneath the snow crunched.

He peered around a shed. Warm light seeped out from a half-open door further along the narrow access track. He had no cover, and the soft but intrusive sounds coming from the various living quarters made any approaching footfall impossible to detect. He oriented himself. The wind was now at his back. The gate he had entered through was a long way to his right, his start point a few hundred metres to his left. That meant Dragonović was probably to his front.

He saw the slum's cross-hatch layout in his mind's eye. The Serb had had the advantage of being downwind when he started, and if he were Dragonović, he'd have stayed downwind to reduce any chance of being heard despite throbbing generators and the sound of televisions. Raglan stepped across the narrow space. It was not a footfall that alerted him but the sudden silence as music being played in a shed shut off mid-song. As if someone inside was aware of an intruder close by.

A glimmer of movement thirty metres away showed Dragonović behind him. Raglan threw himself down. Two shots zipped through the air. Dragonović had instinctively fired twice. Ingrained training – years of killing. A double tap. One bullet scorched Raglan's thigh. A flesh wound, no more, but enough to leave a blood trail if Dragonović found enough light to follow it. The second pinged into a metal shed and ricocheted off into the night. Raglan rolled out of the open space into the gap between the buildings.

A reed-thin man, tattoos snaking up arms and neck, wearing jeans and singlet, stepped into the cold night, wielding a pump-action shotgun. The pungent smell of confined marijuana smoke came with him. A second man staggered out, similarly dressed, grasping a near-empty vodka bottle. He was drunk and high enough to bellow a warning at no one in particular, cursing whoever was shooting. Obviously neither man was aware of Mikhail's lethal contest. Raglan limped further into the shadows but Shotgun Man heard him. He fired intuitively towards the sound and the pellets thumped into the side of his neighbour's house. Shouts of alarm came from within. The distraction helped Raglan make good his escape. The drunk slipped; Shotgun Man jacked another shell into the chamber. Raglan was saved by the roar of a motorbike barrelling down the passage towards the gunman. Harsh warnings were given. Shanghai Slum's security bikers worked for Mikhail. By the time the two had been admonished Raglan had pushed on to the next narrow roadway.

The rumble of motorcycle engines increased. Their headlights were now much closer, their spotlight beams throwing shadows closer to where Raglan limped on. They were herding the two contestants into a more confined area, which as good as told Raglan that Dragonović was close by.

Butchered cars lay alongside a large shed that took up a corner plot. No light or sound seeped out from the ill-fitting doors. No smoke came from the chimney to be whisked away by the wind. Raglan's leg muscle cramped. He tugged free his belt and tightened it above the torn flesh. The wind had shifted to the north-east, its knife-edge cutting through clothes, burning cheeks, eye-wateringly cold. Raglan pressed a handful of frozen snow against his leg wound. It was time to use the weather against Dragonović. Let him spend more time in the bitter wind. Muscles would stiffen. Reactions would slow.

Raglan edged around the large oil drums and a tarpaulin-covered generator, past engine parts in varying degrees of disrepair. The empty building was a working garage. He skirted the metal walls and then forced a side window, tucked the handgun into his waistband, turned his back on the window and reached up, grabbing a handhold and hauling himself up and in.

The trailing leg seeped blood. His jeans were already

encrusted with it. Raglan let his eyes adjust. The metal sides of the shed were pockmarked from years of cold weather; pinprick holes appeared here and there in a scattered pattern. A couple of windows on the far wall were covered in hessian sacking. Motorcycle headlights sent their beams through the holes in the wall as if they were laser-beam gunsights. As his eyes grew accustomed to the dark interior he made out four cars, an old pickup over an inspection pit, chain pulleys for lifting engines, and a large, unlit cast-iron stove in the middle of the floor. Reaching out to steady himself, he grabbed a bottle of vodka from the work counter. He spilled some on his thigh wound but denied himself a pull on the bottle's neck.

A shadow passed the backlit window. He heard the press of weight against the door as someone tested it. Raglan moved further inside the workshop, slipping behind a car for protection as he levelled the pistol, aiming at the door. Dragonović had one shot remaining and if he was foolish enough to push through, he would die. He wasn't. Raglan failed to see the rear blacked-out window between the garage and the next building. The passage between the two was wide enough for a man to get through but was too narrow for the bikers to backlight him. A shotgun blast splattered the interior. The pellets tore into metal. The boom was deafening inside the metal building.

Raglan hunched into cover as Dragonović came through the rear window, landed, rolled and fired indiscriminately again. There was no need for Raglan to guess where he got the shotgun. A dope-smoking drunk would be lying dead in one of the alleyways. The pinhole beams were broken as Dragonović ran crouching across the far side. Raglan fired one shot, heard it strike metal and knew he had missed. Big men don't move quietly in cluttered spaces and the Serb was no exception. He pushed a mechanic's trolley across the floor to cover his own movements. It rattled, struck a workbench, clattered over on to its side. The racket gave him time to move in the opposite direction.

Raglan tracked him with the pistol but couldn't see the target. Both men were vulnerable with the biker's headlights piercing the back wall, but the shotgun weighted the odds against him, especially as his leg was slowing him down. Raglan lay flat, listening for the attack he knew was coming. A man with a shotgun could blast his way forward. The Serb did exactly that. He fired two spread shots from the pump-action. Lethal pellets tore into metal. Raglan slithered beneath the pickup and dropped into the inspection pit. He saw Dragonović's legs and fired his remaining round. It hit Dragonović's calf. The Serb cursed, lost his balance, tumbled forward, the shotgun thrown clear from his grasp. He slammed against the truck where moments before Raglan had been sheltering. Raglan reached up, grabbed his neck and hauled him into the pit. The Serb's weight helped him as he was torn from Raglan's hands. He landed heavily. Raglan kicked him hard. Dragonović curled, rolled, got his back against the wall, pushed himself up and struck at the dark shape assaulting him from the blackness. In the confined space they were close enough to smell each other's sweat.

Both were wounded, but still they connected time and again with vicious blood-letting strikes. Fighting in a grave-deep hole in the ground. Two pit bulls going in for the kill. Dragonović hit Raglan's injured shoulder repeatedly, forcing him on to the defensive. Raglan half turned, brought up his arm to protect his shoulder and to halt the searing pain being inflicted. He got inside Dragonović's defence, repeatedly hammering his elbow into the Serb's face. Dragonović hunched, ducked and weaved, trading more blows in a flurry of hits that sent each man back against the walls. Then Raglan hit him twice more. Short, sharp, fast, with the heel of his hand aiming at the bridge of the Serb's nose. It cracked.

Dragonović stumbled backwards, arms flailing to stop himself from falling. If he went down he'd be finished. His hands swept across the top of the pit wall. Cold hard metal touched his hand. A long-handled adjustable spanner. He swept it into the pit and swung. Metal clanged. Raglan stepped back to avoid the crushing blow but the spanner had caught the underside of the pickup, snaring a cable, an inspection lamp that flared into life. The cable dropped, swinging low, throwing up grotesque shadows on the men's faces. Now they could see one other and the damage each had inflicted. More importantly, they saw the look in the other's eyes.

The Serb couldn't get enough room to swing the spanner. He hurled it at Raglan, who twisted, knocking it aside, and then kicked Dragonović's wounded leg, forcing the big man to gasp with pain. But then he recovered and grappled with Raglan, punching low into kidneys and ribs. Raglan elbowed the side of the Serb's jaw, forcing him back.

Heaving for breath, sweat-soaked despite the cold. A few seconds' respite.

'Fuck's sake, Raglan,' Dragonović gasped. 'Don't you ever get tired of this shit? We should work together. Not do this.'

'You made it personal. It needs to be settled,' said Raglan, seeing the glint from reflected light on the killer's face: haunting and stark. Focused. Trying to lower Raglan's guard with his offer. Dragonović lunged, kicked the fallen lamp, extinguishing its light. Ducking low, he rammed Raglan's midriff, slamming him back against the pit wall, then whipped up his head to smash Raglan's jaw and teeth. Raglan knew it was coming, turned his head away and brought up his knee. It connected on the tip of the Serb's chin. It snapped his head back with such force that Raglan heard the bones crack in his neck. The surge of power from the attack vanished. The weight of the Serb's body pulled Raglan down. He slumped with Dragonović smothering him.

Time slowed. Raglan let the exhaustion and pain take him. Like a child in the dark of his room the memories flooded back. The starkly bright colours of Africa. The deaths of others. Then he heaved aside the dead man and climbed painfully out of the pit. He found the door and banged his fist against it.

Voices called outside. A crunch of snow, the sound of a bolt cutter releasing a padlocked chain. A biker pulled aside the door. Raglan stepped into the glare of motorcycle headlights and took a deep breath. The cold air never felt so good. It was snowing. He raised his head and let the snowflakes settle on his face.

Figures approached from beyond the headlamps. Raglan squinted. Mikhail, Sokol, Gunther Meier and the smuggler's bookkeeper, accompanied by Mikhail's gangsters, emerged into the light.

The tattooed man studied the bloodied Raglan standing unsteadily in front of him. He grunted. 'The Serb was bigger and looked to have the advantage. You cost me money, Englishman.'

'That's the second-best thing that's happened tonight,' said Raglan.

For a moment it looked as though the scowl on the *vor-v-zakone*'s bearded face foreshadowed imminent violence. Then his features broke into a grin. 'You Foreign Legion people, you are mad dogs. Raglan, you are not welcome here. You are trouble. Go home while there is still time.' He turned to the two smugglers. 'Take him wherever he wants.'

Mikhail turned away and walked into the night, followed by his men. The bikers disappeared too. Raglan limped forward. Sokol grabbed him and took some of his weight.

'Thanks, Bird.'

'You had me worried. For a while I thought I'd lost my bet.'

'There were moments you nearly did.'

The German ex-legionnaire cleared aside an abandoned wheel from Raglan's path. 'Once Mikhail uses your fingerprints on that gun to clear himself you won't get out of Russia. Where shall we take you?' he said.

Raglan felt the night air freezing his sweat-soaked clothes. 'Somewhere warm,' he said.

EPILOGUE

Major Galina Menshikova parked her car and trudged through the snow towards her apartment on the eighth floor of the Soviet-era tower block. The huddled buildings, lights blazing, beckoned their residents home as she, like others, returned from work. It was five in the afternoon, already dark, winter clinging as steadfast as the icicles now that the east wind had picked up. It found its way through coat and scarf as she pushed against the building's worn entrance doors.

The rusting metal frame groaned, reminding her that she was destined to remain in the old building for the foreseeable future. She had been on the brink of promotion but that wasn't likely now her boss had been executed. Verskiy was no more a traitor than the Pope was a Russian Orthodox priest. He had misplayed his hand. It had been high stakes and he had lost. It was that simple.

The lift doors closed, the cables creaked, the car shuddered upwards. Graffiti festooned the walls. She would be interviewed by her own people before the FSB questioned her, but she was in no danger. Her career to date had been exemplary. As the lift creaked past the sixth floor, she wondered if she might actually still get that promotion. It was possible. She had pulled off the London part of the operation and succeeded in the desert. The motives behind the operation were sound. Neither she nor the other GRU officers were privy to the inner workings of the general's mind. He had been trophy-hunting and then fell into the bear trap himself. She raised her eyebrows at her own analogy. She would make it clear when she was interviewed that Verskiy had been the driving force behind both ends of the operation; beyond that she and the other officers were doing their duty.

The door cranked open. She stepped into the corridor. Sounds of people living in cramped apartments seeped under their doors; the smell of cooking permeated the corridor. The fluorescent corridor bulbs cast a sickly green light. She opened her apartment door and stepped into the interior's freezing air. She placed her hand on the radiator. Stone cold. The boiler in the building's basement must have gone out again.

She switched on the light in the narrow passage at the front door, walked past the galley kitchen to her right and stepped into the dog-legged sitting room. One of the metal-framed windows groaned, half open ahead of her, swaying in the wind. She leant forward to pull it closed. The sudden pressure on her ankles startled her. She pitched forward into the night. Stricken, her mind unable to grasp what had happened as the blurred snow-covered ground raced towards her. She gulped air, flailing her arms.

There was no time to scream.

Blood seeped from her shattered body, staining the dirty snow. Those who'd seen her fall ran on to the street, others abandoned their cars and sprinted over to where she lay. The faint-hearted turned away while those of a stronger disposition stood over her and gazed up at the open window. Another suicide, someone muttered; others grunted agreement and muttered prayers. No one noticed the stooped figure of the elderly man who came out of her building, who did not even glance at the broken body, who had no need to do so.

Andrei Golyev touched the pendant at his throat. The Archangel Michael. Defender of the Faith.

AUTHOR'S NOTES

Russian Intelligence Services
& The Wagner Group

The GRU (*Glavnoje Razvedyvatel'noye Upravlenije*), the Main Intelligence Directorate, changed its name in 2010 to G.U., Main Directorate, but it is still referred to as GRU and is responsible for all of Russia's military intelligence. It outlasted the KGB when the Soviet Union collapsed in 1991. It is subordinate to the Russian military command led by the Defence Minister, and thought to be the biggest spy agency in Russia. GRU Spetsnaz (special forces) units and GRU officers are tasked with acts of intelligence-gathering, sabotage, cyber disinformation and assassination. They were responsible for the nerve-agent attack in the UK city of Salisbury in 2018, and key players in the Russian attack and annexation of Crimea and supporting rebels in 2014 in the Donetsk and Luhansk provinces in eastern Ukraine. More recently they are the agency believed to have infiltrated saboteurs into strategic areas in the full Russian invasion of Ukraine.

The FSB (*Feraedl'naya Sluzhba Bezopasnosti*), Federal Security Service, is a successor to the former KGB that was disbanded in 1991. They are tasked with Russia's internal security and gathering intelligence on possible terrorist activity, and with uncovering foreign spies. The FSB also has clandestine units which have been known to operate outside of Russia in various assassinations. The US State Department believes it was FSB agents who poisoned opposition leader Alexei Navalny. The FSB reports directly to the Russian President.

The SVR (*Sluzhba Vneshney Razvedki*) is the Russian Foreign Intelligence Service and a key component of Russia's Security Council. The SVR works in parallel to the GRU. It is responsible for the collection and dissemination of intelligence gathered about the Kremlin's external adversaries. They undertake a broad range of activities from disinformation to assassinations and have deep-cover agents in place in foreign countries.

The Wagner Group officially has no direct links to the Russian government but it is often tagged as Putin's Private Army, and their covert operations are critical in shaping the Kremlin's risk-assessment for conflict escalation. They are a fully equipped fighting force, believed to be funded by Yevgeny Prigozhin, a Russian businessman. Their strength is thought to be in the region of six thousand men. The Group is active in the Ukraine, Middle East, Syria, Libya, Sudan, the Central African Republic and the Sahel region. The European Union imposed sanctions on them and anyone known to be associated with them when their mercenaries were accused of committing human-rights violations in various areas of conflict, including the Central African Republic.

ACKNOWLEDGEMENTS

I'm grateful to the following who were generous with their time and advice as I researched elements of this novel. Dr Grenville Major, who once again kindly advised me on medical matters. Retired commercial pilot Keith Chiazzari, with more patience than I could have hoped for, tirelessly considered all my aircraft issues. LTC Steven H. Bullock (Retired), Army of the United States, generously spent time helping me understand satellite overflights and how electronic surveillance might be avoided for the benefit of this novel. Igor Troitskiy in Moscow once again extended a helping hand in advising about that city's locations.

When it came to a jet fighter plane trying to bring down a Hercules transport I needed help from someone who had experience of fighter tactics and air-to-air combat manoeuvring. David R. Lawrence, ex-RAF, explained how a slow-moving plane could try and evade a high-performance aircraft.

I hope all my contributors will forgive any errors, or changes I have made to the advice provided.

My thanks to Ian McLean for his breadth of knowledge regarding various intelligence matters and his overview and comments on the manuscript. My appreciation to my editor

Richenda Todd for her razor-sharp insight. My thanks to my publisher Nic Cheetham for his continuing support and enthusiasm for the Englishman – Dan Raglan. And also to his wonderful team at Head of Zeus. Very special thanks to Isobel Dixon and everyone at Blake Friedmann Literary Agency for their hard work behind the scenes in bringing Raglan to a wider audience.

David Gilman
Devonshire
2022